BLOODROSE

BY ANDREA CREMER

Nightshade
Wolfsbane
Bloodrose

BLOODROSE

ANDREA CREMER

www.atombooks.net

ATOM

First published in the United States in 2012 by Philomel Books, an imprint of
the Penguin Group (USA) Inc.
First published in Great Britain in 2012 by Atom

Printed and bound in Great Britain by
Clays Ltd, St Ives plc

Papers used by Atom are from well-managed forests
and other responsible sources.

MIX
Paper from
responsible sources
FSC
www.fsc.org
FSC® C104740

Atom
An imprint of
Little, Brown Book Group
100 Victoria Embankment
London EC4Y ODY

An Hachette UK Company
www.hachette.co.uk

www.atombooks.net

For my parents

I am about to take my last voyage, a great leap in the dark.

—*Thomas Hobbes*

AIR

PART 1

ONE

I COULD HEAR each heavy beat of my heart. The sound seemed to ebb from my veins out of my body, traveling across the empty space between the shimmering portal and the dark house.

He was there. I had no doubt. Though I couldn't see him or even catch the slightest hint of his warm, smoky scent, I knew he was there. Waiting for me. But why? Why would Ren come to this lonely place?

My gaze traveled over the shadows that twisted as clouds slid over the moon, reminding me too much of wraiths. I stared at the sky so I didn't have to look at the houses, or the skeletal frames of those left unfinished. Time had been frozen here. The mountain slope, cleared of trees to make way for a cul-de-sac and ring of houses, whispered of a past unreachable. The sprawling Haldis Compound—or what would have become the Haldis Compound—lay before me, composed of luxury homes built exclusively for the pack Ren and I would have led together. Our pack's den. Our home.

I turned to face Adne, trying to hide my shivering. "Stay out of sight. You'll hear me if there's a problem, and if I come running, you'd better open a door fast. No matter what, don't come looking for me."

"Deal," she said, already backing toward the forest. "Thank you, Calla."

I nodded before I shifted into wolf form. Adne melted into

shadows. When I was satisfied that no one would be able to detect her, I began to stalk toward the house. Its windows were dark, the structure silent. For all appearances it looked empty, but I knew it wasn't.

I kept my muzzle low, testing the air. We'd arrived upwind from the compound, which left me feeling vulnerable. I wouldn't be able to pick up the scent of anyone hidden by night's veil until I was almost on top of them. My ears flicked back and forth, alert, listening for any sign of life. There was nothing. No rabbits dashing for cover under brush, nor did nocturnal birds flit through the sky. This place wasn't just abandoned; it felt cursed, as if nothing dared tread within the boundaries of the clearing.

I picked up my pace, covering the distance to the house, leaping over snowdrifts, my nails scraping on rivers of ice that had frozen on the pavement. When I reached the front steps, I stopped to sniff the ground. My eyes followed fresh paw prints that became boot tracks, climbing the steps. Ren's scent was sharp, new. He'd arrived only slightly before we had. I slowly moved up to the porch, shifting forms to open the screen door. I carefully turned the doorknob. The house wasn't locked. I let the door swing open. It made a slight creak but nothing else. I slipped inside, closing the door and turning the dead bolt. If someone did come after me, I wanted warning of their arrival.

I shifted back into wolf form, moving through the front hall, tracing Ren's scent to the main staircase. I tried not to cringe as I passed the entrance to the dining room. A beautiful oak table, probably antique, was surrounded by chairs. Four on each side, one at the head and one at the foot. Ten. It was too easy to imagine meals there. Our pack together, laughing, teasing, belonging.

I climbed the stairs slowly, wishing my nails weren't clicking on the hardwood. When I reached the second floor, I paused, listening. The house only answered with silence. Still trailing Ren's path through the house, I passed three bedrooms and a bathroom, until I reached the door at the end of the hallway. My heart slammed against my rib cage as I entered the master suite.

Only a few steps in, I stopped. Wisps of moonlight curled through the room, illuminating the stately bed, piled with satin pillows, draped in jacquard linens, boasting tall ebony posts at each corner. Matching armoires sat against one wall. On the adjoining wall, a mirrored vanity and settee faced the bed.

Ren's scent was everywhere. The smoke of aged wood lingering beneath a chilled autumn sky, the smooth burn of well-worn leather, the seductive ribbon of sandalwood. I closed my eyes, letting his scent pour over me, filling me with memories. It was a moment before I could shake my ruff, sending the past scurrying as I tried to focus on the present.

The light from outside filtered in through tall bay windows with a seat nestled beneath them. Curled beneath the windows, partly cloaked by shadow, was Ren. He was lying very still, head resting on his paws. And he was staring at me.

We stayed like that, frozen, watching each other, for what felt like an eternity. Finally I forced myself to take a step forward. His head snapped up, hackles rising. I heard his low, threatening growl. I paused, fighting off my instinct to snarl at him.

He stood up, still growling, and began to pace back and forth below the window. I took another step forward. His fangs flashed as he barked a warning. I dipped my head, not wanting to give any sign of aggression. It didn't matter.

Ren's muscles bunched and he lunged at me, knocking me onto my side. I yelped as we slid across the wood floor. His jaws snapped just above my shoulder as I rolled away. I scrambled to my feet, dodging when he lunged again. I felt the heat of his breath and his fangs brushing against my flank. I whirled, snarling, and faced him, bracing myself for his next attack. When he struck for the third time, but his teeth didn't cut my flesh, I realized what was happening. Ren didn't want to attack me. He was only trying to scare me off.

Squaring my shoulders, I barked at him. *Stop!*

I met his dark eyes, which were on fire.

Why won't you fight me? He bared his teeth.

I tracked him, turning in a slow circle as he stalked around me. *I didn't come here to fight.*

This time when he lunged, I didn't move. His muzzle was inches from mine, and he snarled, but I didn't flinch.

You shouldn't be here if you aren't ready to fight.

I'm always ready to fight. I showed him my own teeth. *But that doesn't mean I want to.*

His rumbling growl slowly faded. He lowered his head, turning away from me and walking back to the window, where he stared up at the sky.

You shouldn't be here.

I know. I padded toward him. *Neither should you.*

When he turned to face me, I shifted into human form.

The charcoal wolf blinked and then Ren was standing in front of me, gazing down at my face.

"Why are you here?"

"I could ask you the same thing," I said, biting my lip. The fact that he whiled away the hours in an empty house built for us was not the reason I'd come here. But it was hard to push those thoughts away. Standing in this room, on this mountain, in this house, everything felt like it was about us. I could barely remember the outside world. The Searchers. The war.

His eyes flashed, but then went hollow.

"It's a good place to be alone."

"I'm sorry," I said. The words felt like ice in my throat.

"For what, exactly?" His smile was razor sharp, and I cringed.

"Everything." I couldn't look at him, so I walked through the room, staring at nothing in particular, moving past furniture with empty drawers. A bed no one would sleep in.

"Everything," he repeated.

I was across the room, standing on the other side of the bed, when I turned around, staring at him.

"Ren, I came to help you. It doesn't have to be like this."

"Doesn't it?"

"You don't have to stay here."

"Why would I leave?" he said. "This is my home." His fingers grazed the satin surface of the bed linens. "Our home."

"No, it's not." I gripped one of the bedposts. "We didn't choose this; it was chosen for us."

"You didn't choose this." He walked to the other side of the bed. "I thought we would have had a good life here."

"Maybe." My nails dug into the wood varnish. "But it wasn't really a choice. Even if it might have been good."

"You never wanted it. Did you?" His fists were clenched at his sides.

"I don't know," I said. My heart was beating too fast. "I never asked myself what I wanted."

"Then why did you run?"

"You know why," I said softly.

"For him," he snarled, grabbing a pillow and hurling it across the room. I stepped back, forcing my voice to remain calm.

"It's not that simple," I said. The moment he mentioned Shay, something inside me stirred. I still felt sad, but stronger. Shay hadn't just changed the path of my life. He'd changed me. No, not changed. He'd helped me fight for my true self. Now it was my turn to help Ren do the same.

"Isn't it?" He glared at me.

"Would you have been able to kill him?" I asked, holding Ren's gaze. "Is that how you wanted to start a life with me?"

Part of me didn't want to know the answer. Could he really want Shay dead? If I was wrong about Ren, coming here was a terrible mistake. We would fight and I would have to kill him. Or he would kill me.

He bared sharp canines at me, but then he sighed. "Of course not."

I slowly moved around the bed. "That's the only life they would have offered us. Killing the people who need to be helped."

He watched me approach, remaining stone still.

"The Keepers are the enemy, Ren," I said. "We've been fighting on the wrong side of this war."

"How can you be sure?"

"I know the Searchers now," I said. "I trust them. They helped me rescue our pack."

His smile was harsh. "Some of it."

"The others made their choice."

"And I didn't?" His eyes were obsidian dark, angry. But I didn't think his rage was directed at me.

When I closed my eyes briefly, unable to take in the torrent of regret that flooded Ren's stare, I was back in Vail, in a cell deep beneath Eden. I remembered the desperation in Ren's voice, the fear in my own.

"They said I have to."

"Have to what?"

"Break you."

I shuddered as the memory of slamming into the wall and tasting blood in my mouth rushed over me. Forcing myself back into the room, I caught Ren's slightly sick expression and I knew his mind had been in the same place.

I swallowed, clasping my hands so they wouldn't shake. "I hope you didn't."

He didn't answer, but gazed at me.

"I don't believe you wanted to hurt me," I said. "And I don't think you would have, even if Monroe hadn't—"

My words dried up in my throat. It was true, but that didn't take away the memory. The horror of those moments had been etched on my bones.

"I wouldn't have," Ren whispered.

I nodded, though I wasn't sure I believed it. What mattered now was getting him out of here and away from the world that twisted him into someone who could hurt me. He started to lift his hand, as if to touch my cheek, but then let it drop back to his side.

"Did the Searchers send you to find me?"

"Sort of."

His brow shot up.

"Monroe wanted to find you," I said.

Ren's jaw tightened. "The man my—the man Emile killed."

I noticed the way he'd stopped himself. He didn't want to call Emile his father.

"Ren." I reached out, taking his hand. "Do you know?"

His fingers gripped mine. "Is it true? Did Emile kill my mother?"

I nodded, feeling tears slip from my eyes.

He pulled his hand away, fisting his fingers in his dark hair, pressing his temples. His shoulders began to shake.

"I'm so sorry."

"That man." Ren's voice cracked. "That man, Monroe. He's my real father, isn't he?"

I watched him, wondering how he'd put it all together. "How did you know?"

Not much time had passed between the fight in Eden's depths and this strained moment where I stood looking at Ren. I'd known him since we were both pups, but I felt like in the last twenty-four hours, we'd aged decades.

Emile began to laugh. Ren still crouched between his father and the Searcher, his charcoal eyes blazing as he watched Monroe lower his swords.

"I won't hurt the boy," Monroe said. "You know that."

"I guessed it," Emile said, eyes flicking to the snarling young wolves. "Make sure he doesn't escape. It's time for Ren to avenge his mother."

"Ren, don't! He's lying. It's all lies!" I shrieked. "Come with us!"

"She's not one of us any longer," Emile hissed. "Think of how she's treated you, how she turned her back on all of us. Taste the air, boy. She stinks of the Searchers. She's a traitor and a whore."

He glared at me and I stumbled back at the livid fire in his eyes. "Don't worry, pretty girl. Your day is coming. Sooner than you think."

I jerked sideways when Connor grabbed my arm and tugged hard. He pulled me toward the unguarded door.

"We can't leave him!" I shouted.

"We have to." Connor stumbled into me as I fought to free myself but quickly regained his balance, locking his arms around me.

"Let me fight!" I struggled, desperate to go back but not wanting to hurt the Searcher who was dragging me away.

"No!" Connor's face was like stone. "You heard him. We're gone. And if you go wolf on me, I swear I'll knock you out!"

"Please." My eyes burned when I saw Ren's fangs gleam and my breath stopped when Monroe dropped his swords.

"What is he doing?" I cried, dodging when Connor tried to grab me again.

"This is his fight now," he said through clenched teeth. "Not ours."

Ren jumped back as the swords clanged on the ground in front of him. Though his hackles were still raised, his growl died.

"Listen to me, Ren," Monroe said, crouching to meet Ren at eye level, not looking at the other two wolves bearing down on him with cruel slowness. "You still have a choice. Come with me and know who you really are. Leave all this behind."

Ren's short, sharp bark ended in a confused whimper. The other three wolves continued stalking toward the Searcher, undeterred by their enemy *having abruptly laid down his arms.*

Connor's arm swung around my neck, catching me in a painful headlock. "We can't watch this," he snapped, slowly wrestling me out of the room.

"Ren, please!" I shouted. "Don't choose them! Choose me!"

Ren turned at the desperation in my voice, watching Connor pull me through the doorway. He shifted forms, staring bewildered at Monroe's outstretched hands, and took a step toward him.

"Who are you?"

Monroe's voice shook. "I'm—"

"Enough! You're a fool, boy," Emile snarled at Ren before smiling at Monroe. "Just like your father."

And then he was leaping through the air, shifting into wolf form— a thick bundle of fur, fangs, and claws. I saw him slam into Monroe, jaws locking around the unarmed man's throat, a moment before I was whipped around.

Ren didn't look at me when he spoke, ripping me free from the blur of memories. "When he laid down his swords, I thought he was crazy. Maybe suicidal. But there was something about his scent. It was familiar, like I knew it."

I watched as he struggled to speak. "But what Emile said. I didn't understand at first. Until he ... until Monroe was bleeding. The scent of his blood. I knew there was a connection."

"He loved your mother." My tears ran so hot I could have sworn they were scoring my cheeks. "He tried to help her escape. A group of the Banes wanted to rebel."

"When I was one," he said.

"Yes."

Ren sat on the bed, his face buried in his hands.

"Monroe left a letter." I knelt in front of him. "He wanted us to bring you back."

"It doesn't matter now," Ren said.

"How can you say that?"

He lifted his face. The ragged expression on his face felt like claws in my chest.

"Where would I belong, Calla?" he asked. "I don't have a place in that world. Even if my mother tried to go there and my father used to be there. Both of them are gone. Dead. Dead because of the life I do belong to. There isn't anything that links me to the Searchers. I'd only be an enemy to them."

I understood his feelings too well. We'd both lost so much. Our pack had been torn apart. Our families broken. But there was still hope. The Searchers proved themselves to me when I fought beside them. They weren't so different from Guardians. We were all warriors, and we'd shed blood for each other. Our enemies had become friends, and the wolves could find a new home among the Searchers. I believed that, but I needed to make Ren believe it too.

I grabbed his hands, squeezing his fingers tight. "You do have a link to the Searchers."

"What?" He was startled by my fierce words.

"Monroe has a daughter," I said. "Her name is Ariadne."

"He has a daughter?" Ren asked.

"You have a sister. A half sister."

"Who's her mother?" He stood transfixed, a flurry of emotions racing through his eyes.

"A woman who helped him when he was mourning Corrine," I said. "But Adne's mother is dead too."

I bowed my head, thinking of how many people this war had destroyed. I pushed the grief away, trying to focus on Ren. "She's two years younger than us. And she's the reason I'm here."

"She's the reason," he said.

"Yes," I said, frowning as he scowled. "We should go."

"You should go," he murmured. "They want Shay and you. Even with a sister, I don't fit into that equation."

His words were like a slap in the face.

"It's not enough." He looked at me sadly. "She's a Searcher. I'm a Guardian. What am I without a pack?"

My stomach lurched. How often had I asked that very question of myself? The pack was the essence of an alpha. We were meant to lead, to bond with our packmates. Take that away, and life lost its meaning.

His eyes were on me. "What do you want?"

"What?" I stared at him.

"Can you give me a reason to go with you?"

"I already have," I said, quivering as his words sank in.

"No," he said, leaning toward me. "You've given me reasons, but not your reason."

"But—" My words were hushed, shaky.

His fingers traced the lines where my tears had fallen. It was a light touch, barely brushing my cheek. But it felt like flames chased each other across my skin.

"Give me a reason, Calla," he whispered.

I gazed at him. Blood roared in my ears. My veins were on fire.

There wasn't any doubt in my mind as to what he was asking. But I couldn't give him what he wanted.

Ren's dark eyes were full of pain, a pain for which he thought I was the only salve.

"Ren," I whispered. "I want—"

And then I was leaning over him, my cropped hair brushing against his cheeks as I bent to kiss him. Our lips met and I felt like I was diving into oblivion. The kiss grew deep, immediate and hungry. He lifted me up and I wrapped my legs around his waist, molding my body against his. Our kisses were so full of need, so long, so fierce that I could hardly gasp for breath. He laid me on the bed. Our bed.

His hands slipped beneath my shirt, stroking my stomach, sliding up, pushing aside my bra. I moaned and bit his lip, reveling in the full press of his weight against me as our bodies began to move together.

With each touch of his fingers my skin came alive, crackling like tinder under a lit match. Burning away fear. Burning away sorrow. Burning away loss.

I heard my own cry of pleasure as his mouth followed the path of his hands, and I struggled for thought in the face of torrid sensation.

I shouldn't be doing this. I can't be doing this.

My mind reeled as I called up the image of Shay. He'd been the one to open this world to me. His hands, his body had set my soul on fire for the first time. I'd wanted him so much, and at that moment I was sure Ren was lost, that he'd chosen the Keepers' path, I'd drowned my grief by giving in to the flood of desire for Shay.

But what if Ren hadn't chosen? What if we'd left him behind too soon? What if Monroe had been right?

When I'd been faced with encounters like these with Ren in the past, I'd been restrained by the Keepers' Laws, always afraid to give myself over to the passion he stirred inside me.

I loved Shay. I had no doubts about that. But I couldn't deny the powerful reaction I had to Ren, to how much he wanted me. I wondered if there was a bond between us that couldn't be broken, forged from our shared pasts, born out of the pain of our life as Guardians. Was that bond stronger than the new love that had sprung up between Shay and me?

Ren's hand slipped between my thighs and I shivered. My body knew what was coming and it screamed for more. If I'd had any notion that being with Shay would have smothered the allure of Ren's caress, it was swept away in that moment. Through my night in the garden with Shay, I'd had my first taste of lovers' secrets, and I was intoxicated with wanting to know the ways Ren would bring my body to life. And I wondered if giving him that pleasure would somehow take away the horrors he'd been dealt because of me. His touch pulled me back in time, into a past where we were together as it was always meant to be. Where my mother was alive and my brother wasn't broken.

His lips were on mine again. I twined my fingers in his dark hair.

"I love you," he murmured, briefly breaking the kiss. "I've always loved you."

My heart skipped a beat. "I—"

It was like Shay was there, whispering in my ear.

You loved him.

Yes.

But not the way you love me.

I love you.

Shay. I'd only ever said those words to Shay. I didn't want that to change.

What the hell am I doing? I loved Ren. I still loved him. But this place, these intimate ghosts that held me in this room, on this bed, murmuring of past promises and stolen dreams, none of it was my life now. Lingering here, no matter what my feelings, only kept us from escaping a fate we hadn't chosen for ourselves.

My pulse was racing. Ren kissed me again, but I felt like I was in the arms of a restless spirit that haunted me and not the lover I wanted.

"Wait," I whispered. "Please wait."

"Don't," he said, moving his mouth over my neck. "Don't do that, Calla. Don't try to leave. Just be here. Be with me."

Couldn't he see it? There was no here. This place was empty, full of nothing but sadness and—if we lingered—death.

"Ren," I said, pushing at him gently but firmly. I was beginning to panic but didn't want to show it. Every word, every move had to be chosen with the utmost care. If I said the wrong thing, I might send Ren running back to the Keepers. While I couldn't be with him the way he wanted, not here, not now—maybe not ever—I wasn't going to lose him either. "It's not safe."

"What?" He straightened, blinking at me. "Oh. Oh, of course.

Look, Calla, I'm sorry about the other girls. I know that must be strange for you, and it wasn't fair, but I swear I was always careful. I'm completely healthy. It's safe."

I stared at him and then burst into laughter.

"I'm not lying," he said, looking slightly injured by my outburst.

"No," I said, trying to catch my breath. "I believe you."

"Good." He smiled and leaned in for another kiss. But I squirmed away; the passion that had caught me off guard when I'd first found Ren wouldn't snare me again. This place was dangerous for both of us.

"No," I said again. "I meant it's not safe because the people who built this house want me dead. We're using time we don't have. We need to go."

"Not yet." He reached for me. "We aren't in danger. No one comes here. Not ever."

His words made me shiver as I wondered how many times Ren had come here. How often was he forced to be a lone wolf rather than the pack's alpha?

"Yes, yet." I sidestepped to dodge his hands. "Adne's waiting out there. Your sister."

Ren's expression transformed, desire and frustration giving way to amazement.

"My sister," he murmured. I made a mental note of his reaction, which I might need again. Ren's alpha instincts—his need to claim me—could be diverted by Adne. She was the family he *truly* needed. His sister was the only link to a past that offered him salvation from the brutality of Emile. From the pain of knowing his mother had been killed by the Keepers and that he'd never known his real father.

"We can talk about this when we're back at the Academy." I hurried to fix my clothes, trying to ignore the guilt that tore through me. It was hurtling at me from both sides—I didn't know what I'd say to Ren once we got out of Vail and I didn't know what I'd tell

Shay about what had transpired here. My own feelings were a jumbled chaos that seemed impossible to untangle.

"You're not getting out of this," he growled, pulling me against him. "I'm not letting you go. Not again."

"I know," I said, not resisting when he kissed me, wondering just how deep a hole I was digging myself into. But I was afraid that saying anything to counter Ren's hopes would make him change his mind about coming with me. I couldn't let that happen.

"Good."

I felt him smile through the kiss.

We left the bedroom, hurrying down the stairs. When we reached the front door, he paused, turning to look at his surroundings.

"It's a shame," he said. "It really is a nice house."

"There are more important things in life than houses," I said, reaching for the doorknob.

He put his hand over mine.

"There's one more thing I need to tell you before we go," he said.

"What?" I asked in a clipped voice, wanting to get back to a safe place and away from the seductive spirits that lingered here.

He leaned down, lips brushing my cheek as I opened the door. "I like your hair."

TWO

BACK IN WOLF FORM, I quickly led Ren away from the graveyard of homes. As we neared the tall pines ringing the site, I skidded to a halt. Lifting my muzzle, I tested the air, wanting to be sure we hadn't been watched or followed.

I already told you no one comes here. Ren nipped at my shoulder. *Ever.*

I looked at him, my skin crawling beneath my fur as I again wondered how often Ren had been to this place. Ren's life had more loneliness than I'd ever imagined. I hoped I was about to fix that.

She's just ahead.

I trotted toward the forest.

Adne came out to meet us, approaching cautiously. Her eyes were wide as they settled on Ren.

"All good?" she asked in a light tone, but her voice cracked a little.

I shifted forms. "Yeah."

Ren tilted his head, looking at Adne. He padded toward her, sniffing the back of her hand when she extended it. I wasn't sure what he'd recognized, but his tail wagged. He shifted into human form.

"Ariadne, this is Renier Laroche." I sidestepped so they were facing each other without me in between.

She smiled and said, "Adne."

At the same moment he said, "Ren."

They blinked at each other, then laughed. I looked back and forth between them. Ren's tall, muscled form was not anything like Adne's. She was a wisp of a girl whose stature belied her ferocity. But they shared something. My chest burned when I realized they both looked like Monroe. In the short time I'd spent with the Haldis Guide, he'd proven himself the best leader I'd ever known. We would all miss him in the fight to come.

"I'm glad Calla convinced you we're the good guys," Adne said, her voice more confident now.

Ren nodded. "I'm sorry about your father."

"Our father." She hesitated and then took a step forward, reaching her hands toward Ren.

He wrapped her small, slender fingers in his. They stood like that for a moment. Then Adne leaned into him, resting her head against his chest.

Ren looked startled, but he quickly wrapped his arms around her.

He had to clear his throat before he could say, "You know, I always thought it would be cool to have a kid sister."

"Be careful what you wish for." Adne looked up at him and grinned. "I'm kind of a brat."

Ren laughed.

I couldn't help myself. "She's not kidding."

"Thanks, Lily." Adne glared at me, but she was laughing too. "What do you say we continue trading insults where we're less likely to be in mortal peril?"

"She calls you Lily?" Ren was gazing at her, astonished.

I groaned. "She does."

"Great minds." He flashed a wicked smile at me before winking at her.

Maybe this reunion wasn't such a good idea after all. But something inside me that had felt hollow since the attack on Vail was giving way to a comforting warmth. Hope.

"So how are we getting out of here?" Ren asked. "Do you have a car? Or a snowmobile?"

Adne pulled the skeans from her belt, flipping them high in the air and catching them again. "Just wait till you see your sister's mad skills."

When Adne first started to weave, Ren shifted back into wolf form, ears flattened, snarling at the lights that sparked through the air. She paused, glancing over her shoulder.

"This is a lot harder if you interrupt me. I don't want to have us landing in Greece instead of Italy."

Ren's bark was full of surprise. I smiled at him and he changed forms.

"Italy?" He stared at me. "That's a joke, right?"

"No joke," I said. "I haven't seen much yet, but what I have seen is beautiful. It's on the Mediterranean coast."

"I've never seen the ocean," he murmured.

I threaded my fingers through his. "I know."

Adne turned from admiring the finished portal and looked at us. Her eyes flitted to our clasped hands and she threw me a questioning glance. I averted my gaze. Her question was one I couldn't afford to answer.

"You ready?"

That question I could answer. "Let's go."

"Are you sure it's safe?" Ren asked as I pulled him forward. I didn't know if he was dragging his feet to give me a hard time or if the portal actually made him nervous.

"We only lose one out of every five travelers," Adne quipped, stepping behind us and shoving us into the light.

On the other side of the portal Ren was gripping my hand so tightly it hurt. I shook my fingers free, flexing them.

"Sorry." A blush slid over his cheeks. "Where are we?"

"My room," Adne said, closing the portal.

"This is the Academy," I said. "It's where the Searchers live and train."

"The Searchers live in Italy?" Ren frowned.

"Sometimes." Adne looped her arm through his.

"Where are you going?" I asked, hurrying to chase her through the door.

She called over her shoulder, "We need to tell Anika about this right away."

"Really?" I was already nervous about introducing Ren to the Searchers. Working our way up to Anika struck me as a more appealing idea.

"Trust me," Adne said, sensing my anxiety. "The sooner we tell Anika about this, the less trouble we'll be in. Hopefully."

"Great," I muttered.

Ren was staring at the walls of the Academy just as I had when we'd first arrived. His body was tense; I could see the tightness of his shoulders and back. I couldn't blame him. This place reeked of Searchers—and theirs was a scent we'd been trained to recognize as a threat.

When we reached the doors of Haldis Tactical, Adne squared her shoulders, took a deep breath, and knocked.

I heard muffled voices on the other side of the doors; a moment later one door opened, revealing a Searcher I didn't know. She eyed us suspiciously.

"We need to speak with Anika," Adne said before the woman could question us.

"We're in the middle of Council," the woman said stiffly.

"I'm aware of that." Adne straightened to her full height, which wasn't very tall, but she managed to appear menacing. "This is an emergency. I wouldn't be here otherwise."

The woman pursed her lips. "I'll inquire as to whether she'll see you."

"She'll see us." Adne pushed past the now-sputtering woman. I threw her an apologetic glance and darted after Adne, taking Ren's hand and pulling him into the room with me.

Anika and about a dozen other Searchers were gathered around the table. I didn't recognize most of them. Connor was there, as were Ethan and Silas. They were all watching Logan. The Keeper leaned against the table, looking far too much at ease for my liking.

"Like I said." Logan took a drag from his cigarette. "I don't know that I can reveal the location of Shay's parents without further reassurance about my own safety."

Anika was rubbing her temples. "Would you please put that out? I don't want to ask again."

"I'm simply acting according to my current circumstance." Logan blew a smoke ring, scenting the air with tobacco and cloves. "I thought prisoners were always granted a cigarette before their execution. And since you all keep threatening to kill me, I believe I should always have this small luxury afforded to me as long as my life is at risk. Don't you?"

Ren and I growled in unison when Logan gazed at us, a slow smile curving one corner of his mouth. He began to laugh, shaking his head as he took another drag off his cigarette. Silas stared at us openmouthed. Connor stood up as Adne approached the table. He frowned at her, but then his eyes found Ren and me.

"Holy shit," he breathed before turning to Adne, his voice quickly becoming a shout. "What the hell did you do?!"

Adne balked but gave him a steely look. "What I had to."

"Ariadne, what's the meaning of this?" Anika had risen.

Adne opened her mouth to respond, but before she could speak, a snarl ripped from the room. I heard a crash as a chair was thrown back, smashing into the bookshelves behind the table.

"What is he doing here?" Shay's face was like a thundercloud. He didn't bother to come around the table. He was over it in a single leap, leaving me no time to launch into an explanation.

The air around Shay rippled, tinged with the rusty hue of his rage. I caught the scent of Ren's own fury, sudden and violent, as he stepped in front of me, blocking Shay's approach. It was an act of possession, as unmistakable as if he'd thrown a gauntlet at Shay's feet. Ren was an alpha, and he was reclaiming his place.

He dropped to the ground, a massive charcoal wolf snarling at the golden wolf, who bared his own fangs, bristling, muscles bunching as he prepared to strike.

I tried to speak, but it was as if an invisible hand was strangling me, my words choked off by own rising horror.

What have I done?

The Searchers were drawing their weapons. Swords slid from sheaths; daggers flashed in the sunlight. Crossbows took aim. At Ren.

Shay launched himself forward, slamming into Ren. They tumbled across the floor, a mass of teeth and claws slashing out from golden and dark bodies. The furious struggle moved with such speed as the rival alphas tore at each other that their figures blurred, becoming a play of light and shadow. Fortunately for Ren's sake, the lock of their limbs around each other made it impossible for any of the warriors to take a clear shot.

I smelled the blood before I saw it. Metallic and rich, its scent filled the air. Shay twisted, sinking his teeth into Ren's shoulder. Ren snarled, his own jaws clamping down on Shay's foreleg. They slid along the floor, a crimson trail staining the marble beneath them. And then they broke apart, struggling to catch their breath, bracing for the next attack. Ren howled as Shay hunched down, ready to leap back into the fray. The ring of Searchers took aim at Ren once more.

"No!" Adne's cry broke through their growls. She threw herself between the two wolves, shielding Ren with her body. Startled, he yelped, but stopped himself from snapping at her.

Shay was equally thrown by Adne's appearance. He scrambled back, still growling, but staring at her. He stalked sideways, angling for a new line of attack. Adne draped herself over Ren like a cloak. The dark wolf snarled in aggravation, trying to shake her off.

"Calla!" Adne stared at me, eyes wide. "You have to stop this!"

Connor strode across the room to Adne's side. I expected him to drag her off Ren, but instead he turned around, adding his body as another buffer between her and the Searchers. He drew his swords.

"I suggest everyone else put their weapons away. Now."

Logan was grinning, taking slow pulls off his cigarette.

Anika's eyes narrowed. "I trust there is a reasonable explanation for this chaos?" She was looking at me.

I nodded, walking forward until I stood between the two wolves. "Shay, Ren." I gave an icy glare to each of them. "Shift. Back. Now."

They both hesitated, hackles raised, gazes moving from me to each other.

"Now," I said, flashing my fangs.

Ren shifted first. Adne toppled over when the tall boy bumped into her. Connor grabbed her arms, looking like he was about to shake her in frustration. Instead he just held her, eyes alight with anxiety.

Shay was still glaring at Ren when he shifted.

They were both breathing hard. Stains darkened the shredded fabric at Ren's shoulder, while Shay clamped his hand around his bloodied forearm.

The room was full of the scent of their blood and the sharp tang of the Searchers' fear. The warriors had lowered their weapons, but I knew it would take only the slightest provocation to spur them into attack. Shay was their only hope at winning this war. If Ren posed a threat to the Scion, the Searchers would kill him without hesitation. I had to convince them we needed Ren's help.

I took a deep breath, putting as much strength into my words as I could muster. "Anika, I apologize for the intrusion. Adne and I had to take care of something. A vital rescue if this alliance is to succeed."

I was grateful Adne managed not to gape at me.

Anika arched her eyebrow. "You ran your own clandestine operation?"

A slow smile pulled at my lips. "I apologize for the surprise. I didn't trust that I could share my plan with such an untrustworthy creature in our midst." I glanced at Logan, whose grin vanished. My confidence bloomed.

"A rescue, you said?" The suspicion in Anika's gaze was less pronounced, but still there.

Adne cleared her throat. "Yes, Anika. A rescue warranted by my father's sacrifice."

At the mention of Monroe's death, murmurs passed among the Searchers. Worried glances, uneasy shifting of weight stirring their bodies.

"Your father was killed in combat," Anika said. "A terrible loss, but casualties are a way of life here."

"It was more than that." Adne took Ren's hand. He looked surprised but smiled at her. Shay's brow knit together as he watched Adne draw Ren toward Anika.

"Anika, I'd like you to meet Renier Laroche. My brother."

Gasps filled the room. Shay stiffened, glancing at me with wide eyes. I nodded. The fury in his eyes swirled with newborn curiosity, giving me a breath of hope. Shay had liked Monroe, respected him. And he'd quickly befriended Adne, who was desperate to keep her brother safe. Maybe playing on those sympathies could lessen his hatred of Ren. I had to reassure him. It was ripping me up inside that Shay might think I'd betrayed him by going to rescue Ren. When I thought about the way I'd coaxed Ren away from Vail, I felt even worse.

"Ren, this is Anika." Adne ignored the flurry of whispers and disbelieving stares. "Anika is the Arrow. She leads the Searchers."

"Sorry to crash your party," Ren said, eyeing the gathered Searchers warily.

Anika frowned and looked at Connor. "The letter." Her hand rested on her coat pocket.

Connor's face was grim. "Yes."

Anika stared at Ren, then glanced at Adne with a sigh. "It was a fool's errand."

I bristled. "No, it wasn't."

The Arrow turned to me. "The son of the Bane alpha is here. His presence risks everything. His first move was to attack the Scion and—"

I snarled, cutting her off. "He is not Emile's son. He is nothing like Emile."

This time the weapons drawn were aimed at me. Shay and Ren both growled, moving beside me. Thankfully they ignored each other, focusing their attention on the Searchers.

Anika held up her hand. "Speak your mind, Calla."

My heart slammed around my chest. This was it. This was the moment that would make or break everything, pulling Guardians from our past and hurling us into the future. And it all rested on my shoulders. Could I bear this weight? Was I truly the alpha I'd always wanted to be?

"He is Monroe's son." I pointed at Ren. "And he's your best hope to win this war."

"He's what?" Shay's voice was deadly quiet.

"I'm what?" Ren kept his own voice to a whisper, but the look he'd thrown me was a bit alarmed.

Damn. That was the problem with impromptu plans. You didn't have any time to weigh their consequences.

Ignoring them, but knowing I'd have to deal with Shay's jealousy later and that I still had a lot to explain to Ren, I kept my focus on Anika.

"The Scion is your weapon," I said, touching Shay's uninjured arm. His skin was hot under my fingers and I could feel his pulse jumping. I wanted to pull him close to me, but I didn't dare. Not yet. "But you still need an army."

"Your turncoat pack is hardly an army," Logan said. "And Emile's bastard certainly hasn't shown himself to be a leader."

I was forced to let go of Shay so I could grab Ren's hand, holding him back when he snarled at Logan.

"And why are you here, Logan?" I glared at him. "Because you lived up to your father's expectations?"

He pulled his gaze from mine and I smiled, knowing I had him. "You lost your inheritance, didn't you? Failed in your duty? That's why you had to run. Your little kingdom has crumbled, hasn't it?"

Logan didn't look at me. He lit another cigarette.

"He has a point, Calla," Anika said, though her expression showed that she had no love lost for the Keeper either. "Your pack isn't an army."

"But we can bring you one," I said.

"How?" One of the Searchers I didn't know stepped forward. His shaved head and hooked nose gave him a hawk-like appearance. When he spoke, I heard traces of a French accent. "Monroe is dead. The potential for an alliance died with him."

I gave the sour-faced Searcher a hard look as I walked up to Logan, taking the Keeper's shirt in my fist. "Tell me, Logan. How many Banes did your father kill when Corrine's betrayal was discovered?"

Logan's eyes bulged. "How can you expect me to know about that? I was a child!" He gaped at me, disbelieving that one of his former servants would now threaten him.

My blood was singing as the peppery scent of his fear filled the air. "I can hardly imagine that Efron Bane would leave his only son so poorly prepared as to not know his future pack's true history."

Logan's face was growing paler by the second. "But . . . I . . . ."

"Answer her." Ethan had come to my side. I heard his dagger hiss out of its sheath.

"Twenty-five," Logan said. "Twenty-five traitors were killed."

"That wasn't so hard, now, was it?" Ethan smiled.

I snarled and Logan backed against the table.

"How many wolves knew that Emile wasn't Ren's father?" I asked.

"None." Logan ground his teeth. I slammed him against the tabletop.

"None that we knew of," he whimpered. "But there have been rumors since the revolt. It was no secret that Corrine despised her mate. My father kept the truth quiet, but Emile's temper gets the best of him at times. He wanted to kill the child. He was ordered not to."

I glanced at Ren, whose face was drawn. I wished I could spare him the pain of this knowledge, but I had to get answers out of Logan.

"Would you say that the Bane pack lives contentedly under Emile's leadership?"

Logan swallowed hard. "Perhaps not."

I let him go, turning to Anika. "What's happened in Vail will have thrown the packs into chaos. The Nightshades aren't loyal to Emile Laroche. They're loyal to my father. My family."

Connor was nodding. "Good girl."

"What are you proposing?" Anika asked.

"Guardians need alpha leaders. The bonds of the pack are what make us fight so well. The Keepers made a serious mistake by killing my mother and deposing my father. We'll exploit that mistake."

"Don't they know their packs well enough to avoid such an error?" the hawk-faced man asked.

It was Ren who answered. "Their pride makes them believe their rule is absolute."

Anika turned to Logan, who had scrambled to his feet. He glared at me, but gave a reluctant nod.

"And you believe that you and this boy can be the new alphas?" Anika's steely gaze was on me. "Both packs will follow you?"

"We are the alphas. One Bane, one Nightshade. The packs

will follow us. We can unite them and lead them against the Keepers." In truth I wasn't at all sure they would, but it was the only thing I could think of that might convince the Searchers to welcome Ren.

"There are those still loyal to Emile," Logan said, rubbing his throat where my tight grip had left bruises. "You won't sway them all."

I kept my focus on the Arrow. "We can sway enough. Enough to make a difference."

"It's Monroe's plan, Anika," Connor said. "This is the revolt he wanted to stage from the beginning."

"I know," she said. "Very well."

She crossed the room to stand before Ren. "Welcome, Renier. Your father was a good man."

"No." Shay's eyes were wild. His knuckles were white as he clenched his fists.

"Shay, please," Adne said. "This was always the plan Monroe hoped for."

"I can't go along with this," he said. "It's not what Monroe wanted. It's what the Keepers wanted, forcing them to be together. Calla doesn't belong with Ren."

Ren bared his teeth at Shay. "She does. She always has."

"I will kill you before I let you touch her." The air around Shay was rippling again. "You aren't the only alpha and you know it."

My breath caught in my throat. Shay understood. His wolf instincts were teaching him faster than I ever could have anticipated. He was the interloper, and he was ready to challenge Ren for rule of the pack.

"Give it your best shot." Ren smiled, just as ready to accept that challenge.

Shay stepped forward, only hesitating when Anika drew her sword, barring his path.

"Someone throw a bucket of ice water on these two," Connor said.

"Calla," Adne said. "Make them stop."

The truth of her words was like a slap in the face. I could stop them.

Pushing past Anika, who sheathed her sword, I stood between Shay and Ren.

"Listen to me, both of you." I placed a hand in the middle of each boy's chest; their heartbeats thrummed against my fingertips. "This ends now."

"Of course it does," Shay said. "You have to choose."

"He's right," Ren said, looking past me to glare at Shay. "Choose, Calla."

"I won't choose," I said. "Not yet."

Their hearts both skipped a beat in sync, revealing their shared uncertainty. A wave of giddiness washed over me. I was the alpha, and I didn't have to submit to anyone. I finally was able to follow my own path, a destiny I could discover for myself.

"I don't need a mate," I said, measuring my words. "I need soldiers. You two are the best I know. I need you. Both of you. Will you fight for me?"

Neither boy answered. They glared at each other, both waiting for the other to make the first move.

I let my words drop into their silence like stones into a deep well. "Will you fight for me?"

Shay frowned. "Always, but—"

"No buts," I said, turning to Ren. "Will you?"

"You know I will." His eyes were wary.

"Ren leads the pack. He's the key to cementing this alliance with the wolves still in Vail," I said. "Shay gets his hands on the Elemental Cross and leads the Searchers into battle."

I glanced at Anika, who nodded.

"What about you?" Shay asked.

I smiled. "I'm the one who makes sure we all get along."

"Good luck with that," Ren growled.

With a quiet laugh, I moved my hands from each of their chests to grasp their wrists.

"I don't need luck," I said. "You're going to swear to me that you'll help and not hurt each other. You're about to make a blood oath."

"Uh . . . what?" Shay stared at me.

"Until this war is over, winning it is all that matters." I pulled on them until they were standing face-to-face, inches apart. I could feel the tension pouring off each alpha. The scent of sunlight and thunderstorms swirled with the smoke of autumn bonfires and sandalwood.

"Heal each other," I said.

"No," Ren said.

"I need my warriors whole. You made each other bleed." I ignored Ren's bewildered expression. "Now undo the damage."

"You've got to be kidding me." Shay grimaced.

"I can't begin to tell you how much I'm not kidding." I stepped back, folding my arms over my chest. "Until I choose a mate, I'm the only alpha here; I've made it clear that I'm not making a choice right now. You two answer to me. Prove your loyalty. Heal each other."

"I don't believe this." Ren groaned, but he bit his arm and held it out to Shay.

"No way." Shay started to back off, but I snarled.

"Do it."

"Damn it, Cal. You're heartless," he said, biting his own wrist.

"I know."

Shay and Ren glared at each other, eyes locked as they drank each other's blood, bonding them as packmates even though they still despised each other.

"Nicely played, alpha," Logan murmured.

As much as I wanted to level a stony gaze on the Keeper, I couldn't stop my own smile. Something inside me was running free, wild and howling its joy.

THREE

"SINCE THAT'S SETTLED, can we talk about winning this war?" Connor sheathed his swords.

From the way Ren and Shay continued to glare at each other, I knew their rivalry was far from settled. But this uneasy partnership was the best I could hope for at the moment. At least they weren't shredding each other's flesh anymore.

I turned to face Anika. "No more secret meetings where I'm not invited. If you want wolf warriors, you include us at every turn. Strategy and execution."

The hawk-faced man snorted but kept silent when Anika shook her head at him.

"That's fine, Calla," she said. "Shay had already insisted on that point before you arrived."

I smiled at Shay, but he was still glowering at Ren. I wished he would look at me. If he could just meet my eyes, maybe he'd see how hard this was for me. How much I wanted to pull him aside, to be alone with him and explain all of this.

Anika turned back to the table. Large maps covered its surface.

"Logan's informed us that the Keepers are going on the offensive," she said. "Purgatory was just the beginning. We're running out of time."

"In what way?" I asked.

"Time to collect the pieces," Logan said. "We'll be expecting you, of course."

He'd lit another cigarette and recomposed his nonchalant attitude.

"If they're waiting for us at the sites, we don't stand a chance," Anika said. "Any element of surprise we can still hold is vital. We need to move on each of the sites quickly, one strike following immediately after the other. No waiting. No delays."

"You need someone to run interference." I turned in surprise at the sound of Ren's voice.

Anika raised her eyebrows.

Ren shrugged. "Like Calla said. Shay's leading the Searchers. I lead the wolves. Let us do what we do best: fight."

Connor whistled. "You want to open another front?"

"Not another front," Ren said. "Two teams. A decoy and the real team sent in after."

"It would pull attention off the sites." Adne grinned at her brother. "The stealth team would go in for retrieval while the strike team did the fighting."

Ethan nodded. "That could work."

"Any team drawing that kind of attack would suffer heavy casualties," the hawk-faced man objected.

"Who are you?" I barked, frustrated by his constant sniping.

"Pascal is the Tordis Guide," Anika said. "His team would be joining the attack that Ren's proposed."

She gestured around the room. "The group gathered here are the strike teams from each of the outposts. You already know the Haldis team, but Tordis, Eydis, and Pyralis have gathered at my request to plot our course. For this effort to succeed, we must work in concert."

I gazed at the Searchers. Assembled in Haldis Tactical, the core team members looked weary but alert. It made sense: they were staring death in the face. We all were. I met Pascal's scornful gaze and my heart ached for Monroe. The Tordis Guide clearly didn't share the same empathy for Guardians that Monroe had encouraged.

"Pascal's right," Ethan said. "The decoy team would suffer heavy losses. But the way I see it, we're not getting out of this war without heavy losses no matter what."

"We need those pieces," Anika said. "We can't finish this without them."

Pascal's lips thinned, but he inclined his head.

Shay cleared his throat. "Ren's right. I think two teams is the way to go here."

"Agreed," Anika said.

"But I have a request," Shay continued, throwing a cold glare at Ren.

"And what is that, Scion?" The Arrow watched him, her eyes narrowing.

"The stealth team will be backing me, right?" he asked.

"Of course," Silas piped in. "We know now that you're the only one who can remove the pieces from their resting places."

The Scribe winced when Connor fixed a stony gaze on him.

Shay nodded. "Then I want to pick my team."

"Excuse me?" Anika frowned.

"I need to fight beside people I trust," he said. "I'm not going into the sites with strangers."

"We've been fighting this war much longer than you have, child." Pascal's face was mottled by rage. "How dare you presume—"

"Oh, put a lid on it, Pascal," Ethan said. "I've seen this kid fight. You don't want to mess with him. Let him pick his own team."

"It's not unreasonable for you to select your teammates, Shay," Anika said. "But would you object to the Guides for each outpost weighing in on your choice? They'll be taking heavy casualties in order to protect your team."

"If they want," Shay said quickly. "But I'm only talking about the retrieval team. And my companions are coming from Haldis . . . which no longer has a Guide." He glanced at Adne, sadness shadowing his face.

I was a little surprised to see Ren put his arm around Adne when Shay spoke. She looked up at him with a weak but grateful smile.

"Do you really think you have the skill to make these decisions?" Pascal glared at Shay.

"Calla and I found Haldis on our own." Shay bared his teeth at the Guide. "So yeah, I think I have the skill."

Pascal spluttered at Shay's words. Shay and I shared a quick, conspiratorial smile. It was amazing how almost dying from a giant mutant spider attack could end up being a good memory. But it was. And not only because we'd killed the beast and retrieved Haldis. That was the day Shay had become a wolf to save my life. I realized I held that knowledge close, treasuring its intimacy along with the joys of our first days running together through the wilderness near Vail. Before our world had fallen apart, and running for joy had been displaced by fleeing for our lives. After all that had happened, it seemed strange to think of him as once having been just human—though as the Scion he'd never been ordinary.

Shay caught me watching him and arched his eyebrow. A blush surprised me as its heat bit into my cheeks, but I answered his quizzical gaze with a smile before I looked away from him. I'd never been much of a daydreamer, but thoughts of Shay—particularly of the moments we'd shared alone—captured my mind a little too easily.

Connor laughed. "Nice job, kid. I've never seen Pascal speechless before."

"I believe this issue is settled," Anika said. "Pascal will assemble the decoy team for deployment tomorrow morning. What are you envisioning for the stealth team, Shay?"

"Small," Shay said, running a hand through his hair. "Adne

weaves the door, putting us at the entrance to the cave. I'm assuming it's another cave?"

Silas nodded.

"Connor and Ethan as Strikers. Calla, Nev, and Mason backing them up."

"We're integrating the Guardians this soon?" Pascal asked. "We don't know that we can trust them."

"You can trust them," Ethan said. I stared at him, hardly believing what I'd just heard.

"You're going to trust us too," Ren said, offering Pascal a cold smile.

Pascal grimaced, but didn't bother to argue with Ren.

"The decoy team was my idea," Ren continued. "I'm not missing its trial run."

Fear needled my skin. Ren's plan was a good one, but the Searchers were right. The decoy team would be hit hard. They wouldn't get out of the fight without losses. I didn't want Ren to be one of them.

"And Sabine, one of my packmates who's here," Ren said. "I'm guessing she'll want in too."

"She's only just recovered from her injuries," Ethan said. "I think she should stay behind."

Ren laughed. "Have you seen how we recover? I don't know what happened to her, but if she's had pack blood, she's fine. She'll be more than ready for a fight." He glanced at Logan. "Besides, if we're going up against the Keepers, I'd like to see you try and leave her behind."

Logan shuddered.

Ethan didn't respond, but his mouth set into a hard line.

I was surprised by how quickly Ren had settled into his role here. We were surrounded by lifelong enemies, but he'd taken command without hesitation. He was a natural leader, confident and strong. I could see it burrow into Shay. Each time Ren spoke, Shay bristled.

Shay was a leader too, taking control of this war in which he'd play such a vital part. And he wasn't ceding pack rule to Ren. By taking some of our packmates, including me, with him to retrieve Tordis, Shay had made it clear he'd be leading wolves, not just Searchers.

How would the pack respond to Ren's return? Would any new allegiance they felt for Shay dissolve? Nev and Sabine had loved Ren. Ansel and Bryn had thought he was a good alpha. But I also remembered what Sabine had said. *Ren made a mistake. If he wanted you so much, he should have come here. He should have been here to fight for you.* He was here now, but was it too late? I wondered if she'd still feel loyalty to her former alpha.

Thoughts of my pack, of our bonds, brought me back to the wolf I was the most worried about.

"What about my brother?" I asked Anika. "What have you decided about him?"

"Nothing's been decided yet," Anika replied carefully.

"It wasn't his fault."

"According to Logan, your brother betrayed our location to the Keepers of his own volition. He wasn't forced to do so."

"You don't understand what they did to him. They destroyed his wolf. They broke him. They promised they would make him whole again. He had no choice!"

As much as I didn't want to think about it, I wondered if I wouldn't have done the same thing had I been in Ansel's place. I couldn't imagine life without the ability to shift. The wolf was who I was. Without that part of me I would feel like I was nothing. Just like Ansel did.

"We're taking that into consideration," Anika said.

"How could Ansel have told the Keepers about the Denver hideout?" I protested, growing more desperate. I couldn't make my brother a wolf again, but at least I could try to set him free. I turned pleading eyes on Connor. "You saw what he was like. He didn't have any strength left."

Connor looked at Logan, who smiled cruelly at me.

"He didn't need strength," Logan said. "All he needed was a simple invocation. A spell that revealed the location of the supplicant. The only thing your brother had to do was read the words aloud."

My throat closed as I remembered two nights before, when I'd tried to turn Ansel. Tried and failed.

He reached into his pocket, pulling out the crumpled paper.

"Ansel, what is that?" I asked, trying to get a better look.

"Leave me alone." His eyes rested on the dirty scrap for a moment before he gripped it in a tight fist, pressing it against his chest. "It's from Bryn, okay? I managed to hang on to it while the Keepers had us separated."

He'd lied to me. There had been no poem. No last words of love from Bryn. Only betrayal scribbled on a slip of paper. Logan watched me, still smiling while the truth twisted like a knife in my belly.

Shay's hand was on my shoulder. I let myself lean into him, the reassurance of his touch easing my fear about Ansel's fate. "They won't hurt Ansel. I made them promise."

A growl rumbled behind us. "Could you not touch her?" Ren didn't make it sound like a question.

"Bite me," Shay snarled.

"Stop it. Both of you." I rubbed my throbbing temples, pulling away from Shay even though I wanted him to wrap his arms around me and find comfort. If I was going to referee this game, I had to stay neutral. I could see now while it might make me powerful, at times it would leave me miserable.

"We did give our word, Calla," Anika said. "No harm will come to your brother. But we also can't risk freeing him."

"But you'll let him come and go at will?" I pointed at Logan.

"If you haven't noticed, everyone in this room is armed," Anika replied coolly. "Logan was escorted here from his cell. He'll be escorted back. Make no mistake. He's a prisoner, not a guest."

"Thanks, that's lovely," Logan said, blowing smoke rings into the air.

I glared at Logan, wishing I could bite off those fingers and let him try to hold a cigarette without them. As much as I wanted to convince the Searchers they shouldn't trust him, I knew I was right about Logan. He was here because he'd lost his place among the Keepers. Logan was just like his father: he'd only ever been interested in power. Somehow he thought the Searchers were his way of getting it back. I just couldn't figure out what angle he was playing.

Anika surveyed the map on the table. I knew the conversation about Ansel was over. Fury bubbled up inside me. If I couldn't fight for him, at least I could fight. Edging forward to peek at the map, I saw mountainous terrain.

"That's where we're going?"

She nodded. "Mürren, Switzerland. At dawn. We'll send in the decoys first. The cave is here. We'll draw the Guardians away from the entrance and then send in the stealth team."

"You up for early morning bear baiting, Pascal?" Connor laughed.

For the first time Pascal cracked a smile. "Of course, *mon frère*. It's what we do best."

"Huh?" I frowned at Connor.

Connor cocked his head at me, then his eyes went wide. "You don't know?"

"Know what?"

"Oh, man." Shay glanced from me to Ren. "The other Guardians are bears?"

"What?!" Ren and I exclaimed in unison. I looked at him. The other alpha's face mirrored the shock I felt.

"Just the Guardians of Tordis," Silas replied. "You really didn't know about the other Guardian forms?"

My skin felt too tight. I wanted to shift and bolt from the room.

Ren managed an answer. "No. We didn't."

"Was that bear that attacked me when we met a Guardian?" Shay asked me.

"No," I said, still shaken. "That was just a grizzly."

Not once in my life had I considered the idea that other forms of Guardians might exist. Our wolf packs were closely knit. We were proud of our ferocity and of our skill as warriors. The Keepers made us feel like we'd been chosen. That we alone could serve them in the war. More lies.

Ren threw me a puzzled glance. "You saved him from a bear?"

"I don't want to talk about it." I folded my arms across my chest. "I want to know more about these other Guardians."

Silas puffed up. "It's quite genius, actually. Keepers created Guardians naturally suited to each environment they would protect. Wolves in Colorado. Bears in Switzerland."

A stocky, dark-haired Searcher from a team I hadn't been introduced to smiled grimly. *"Y las yaguares en Tulúm."*

"Sí. Las yaguares." Silas shuddered. *"La muerte en las sombras."*

I didn't speak Spanish, but I knew he was describing another type of Guardian. My stomach twisted. I'd always felt that we were special somehow. Even if we were servants, I'd felt a sense of privilege of lives marked by exception. Now it turned out that we were just convenient.

The shock of learning wolves weren't the only Guardians created by Keepers wasn't the only thing gnawing at me. Everything about this scenario—the strategizing, the strike teams. Haldis Tactical was the place where Searchers planned their attacks. Where they'd planned their attacks on Vail. I didn't have any doubts about whose side we should be on, but I wondered if I would ever feel at ease here.

Silas was still talking. "It would be the perfect system, except for the—"

"If you call them a sin against nature again, I will end you." Ethan's hand was on his dagger's hilt.

"Look who's a born-again Guardian evangelist now." Connor laughed. "What's up with that?"

A blush slid up Ethan's neck. "Nothing. They're our allies. That's all."

"Sure it is," Connor said.

Ethan swore and turned his back on Connor.

FOUR

BRYN HAD BEEN RIGHT about Ansel's quarters. They weren't so much a cell as a sparsely furnished bedroom. Though from looking at Ansel, you'd have thought he was back in the Keepers' dungeon. He was curled up in the window seat, head pressing against the glass.

In the distance you could see the sea lapping at the shore, but the idyllic setting had no effect on Ansel's blank stare. I could see now why the Searchers posted outside the door were so relaxed. Their ward seemed to have no interest in escaping, and even if he did escape, he had the strength of a wet noodle. My bones ached as I watched him. Why did it have to be Ansel who suffered?

Bryn sat next to him, stroking his hair. I was surprised to see Tess sitting on the opposite side of Ansel, a plate of oatmeal cookies in her lap. As they sat opposite each other, Tess looked almost like Bryn's older sister. Tightly curled ringlets crowned each of their heads; Bryn's bronze locks glinted in the sun while Tess's blue-black curls took on an almost violet hue. The former Haldis Reaper turned mother-like caretaker of my little brother watched Ansel with a kind but worried expression. Mason stood near her, munching on a cookie. Nev and Sabine were a short distance apart, speaking to each other in soft tones.

Nev saw us first. His mouth opened and closed, but rather than speak, he jerked his chin at Sabine. She turned. And hissed when she saw Ren.

"You."

Ren didn't move when she flew at him. Her fists pounded his chest. "How could you?! How could you let that happen to us?!"

With considerable effort Nev pried Sabine off Ren. She struggled before turning to bury her head in Nev's shoulder, sobbing.

"Sorry, man," Nev said, stroking Sabine's ebony hair.

Ren shook his head. "I deserve it."

I couldn't decide if I agreed with him or not. When Nev and Sabine had left the Bane pack, Ren stayed behind. He was their alpha. His duty was to lead and protect them, but he'd thrown his lot in with Dax, Cosette, and my old packmate, Fey. Their betrayal stung. Did Sabine blame Ren for how she'd suffered? Did she think it was his fault Dax and Cosette were still with the Keepers?

Bryn didn't leave Ansel's side, but she gaped at us. "Oh my God. Ren."

Mason hesitated before coming to Ren and catching him in a quick hug. "Good to see you, man. In one piece and such."

"You too, Mason."

"How?" Sabine sniffled, still clinging to Nev. "How is it that you're here? I thought you left us."

Ren looked at the floor. I had to help him. Even if I still felt uneasy about why Ren had briefly chosen the Keepers over us, he was here now and we needed him. A broken, grieving alpha was no good to our cause.

"He was manipulated," I said, and he smiled weakly, keeping his eyes downcast. "Ren is here because he has a sister who wanted to save him."

"Okay," Bryn said. "Now you're not making any sense at all."

"Adne," Nev murmured, peering at Ren. "Right? I knew there was something about that girl."

I nodded. "Her father was Monroe—the Searcher who led our rescue mission. He was also Ren's father, not Emile."

"Heavy," Mason said.

"Tell me about it," Ren said.

The sound of ceramic shattering brought all our eyes to the window. Tess was standing. Shards of the broken plate lay at her feet. She crossed the room, taking Ren's face in her hands.

"You're Monroe's son?" Her eyes were brimming. "Corrine and Monroe's son?"

Ren nodded.

"Thank goodness Adne isn't alone." Tess laughed despite her tears, wrapping her arms around Ren, who looked startled but not upset by the gesture. "Monroe would be so, so grateful that you're here."

"Thanks," Ren said, his own voice getting rough. "I'm sorry I didn't know him."

"Me too, sweetie," she said, wiping away her tears.

Bryn was still frowning. "Monroe and Corrine? I don't understand. How would that even be possible?"

"It's kind of involved, but it's possible. We're gonna have to leave it at that," I said. "We've got other things to do now that Ren's here."

"What other things?" Mason asked. "Please tell me they're things that involve kicking some Keeper ass."

I grinned. "That's exactly the kind of things they are."

"Hold on," Bryn said. "I'm all for fighting the Keepers, but do the Searchers want our help?"

"They rescued us, didn't they?" Mason rocked back on his heels.

"I suppose." Bryn's eyes wandered to Ansel, who was still staring off into the distance. I was already counting her out of this fight. She was only concerned with helping my brother. And that was fine with me.

Tess spoke up. "Monroe and Corrine first met because a group of

Banes planned to rebel against their masters. We were going to help them. Unfortunately the plan was discovered."

"The Keepers killed my mother," Ren finished. His eyes had gone flat.

"Shit." Nev kicked the edge of the rug. "They are just total shit."

"No kidding," Mason said.

I didn't want us to get lost in our own rage against the Keepers. "There have been other, older alliances between Guardians and Searchers, but none of them could last."

"Because no one can defeat the Keepers." Sabine glared at Tess.

"Until now." Tess didn't falter under Sabine's cold eyes.

"Shay can stop them," I said quietly. "That's why they wanted to kill him."

"Says who?" Sabine snapped. "That stupid prophecy Connor and that punk-rock brain trust, Silas, were talking about? What if it's all lies? Nothing we've heard up to this point about our past has been true."

"Let it go, Sabine," Nev said, squeezing her shoulder. "These are the good guys. They saved us, remember?"

Sabine's lip trembled. "Go to hell." She shoved Nev away and ran from the room.

Mason shook his head. "She's not seeing the silver lining, is she?"

"She'll be okay," Nev said, watching the door close again. "It's a lot to take in."

Ren nodded, though the tight set of his jaw told me he was worried about her.

"We may need to rethink our teams," I said.

"Yeah," he said. "Looks that way."

Mason tugged on the collar of his shirt. I glanced around at my packmates, realizing they were all dressed in Searcher garb. I suddenly wanted to laugh.

Mason gave me a quizzical look and I shook my head.

"Where's Shay?"

"Still with the Searchers in Haldis Tactical," I said. "They keep him pretty busy."

He fidgeted, coughing before he spoke again. "So, uh, Ren's here . . . and Shay's here?"

"Yes," I said.

Bryn glanced nervously at Ren and then me. "Who's our alpha?"

"I am." I waited for Ren to object, but he didn't.

She chewed on her lower lip. "And Shay and Ren?"

"Are backing me up."

Ren sighed, but he nodded. "We're backing her up."

Mason grinned. "She is woman, hear her roar."

Bryn giggled. "Awesome."

My answering smile was so broad it hurt a little.

The door opened and Anika entered, followed by Adne. A moment later Shay walked in. As soon as he joined us, the air crackled as if it were filled with ozone. Ren moved to the other side of the room, putting as much distance between himself and Shay as possible. I appreciated the safeguard, forcing myself to stay in place rather than going to Shay like I wanted to. Nev and Mason exchanged a glance and didn't hide their grins fast enough.

"If you two make any bets, I *will* find out about it," I said. "And you'll be sorry."

Mason managed to look abashed. Nev shifted his gaze from my pointed stare with a sly smile.

Adne followed Ren, looping her arm through his in a casual gesture, but I saw her fingers lock around his arm, steadying him as he glared at Shay.

Anika's face was stern as she surveyed our small Guardian pack. "I trust you're aware of our shifting circumstances."

We all nodded. Anika smiled, turning to Tess.

"I'm told you have a proposal for me?"

Tess straightened. "It's about us orphans."

"Us orphans?" Anika's brow furrowed.

My chest tightened as I looked from Tess to Ansel. She was right. Tess and Isaac had been posted in Denver, at the Searchers' hideout. Now that Purgatory had burned, Tess couldn't do the Reapers' work of smuggling goods under the Keepers' noses. She'd lost her home; her job; her partner, Isaac; and her lover, Lydia. All because we'd shown up and turned her world upside down. If anyone should hate us, it was Tess, but all she'd done was treat us with kindness, my brother especially.

"Me and him." Tess gestured to Ansel. "We've both lost our place in the world."

"His status is still being considered, Tess," Anika said. "You know that."

"Of course," Tess said. "But I think it would benefit everyone for him to prove himself useful."

I watched her, suspicion nestling against my spine. Ansel wouldn't be exploited in any way while I had a say in it.

"What did you have in mind?" Anika asked.

"My outpost is gone," Tess said. "But I still have training for basic Academy tasks. I can help in the garden and in Eydis Sanctuary. I'd like to take the boy with me. Teach him some of our ways."

"Do you really think that's wise?" Anika paced across the room.

"I think it would be unwise to leave him unoccupied." Tess's eyes slid over Ansel's arms. His skin was crisscrossed with bright red hatch marks. Older cuts were healing; newer scratches were just beginning to scab over.

"He'll never be unsupervised," Tess said. "I'll take full responsibility for his whereabouts."

"I'd want to send a Striker to accompany you as well," Anika said.

Tess nodded. "If you think that's necessary." She looked at Ansel again, her face making it clear that she didn't think he was a threat to anyone. As I gazed at my brother, or rather at the shell of a person that he now seemed to be, I wondered how anyone could see him as dangerous. Then again, he had been swayed by the Keepers to betray us. Brute strength wasn't the only threat to worry about.

"I'll consider it," Anika said.

"Don't bother," Ansel said without turning his face from the window.

Tess didn't react to his dead voice, but Bryn twined her fingers in his. "Come on, An. You should go with Tess. Doing stuff will take your mind off . . ." Her words trailed away.

"I should just stay in here," Ansel said, pulling his hand out of Bryn's grasp.

Her lip trembled. I wanted to grab my brother and shake him for treating her with such carelessness.

Anika frowned, peering at my brother. "You'd prefer to stay confined?"

"I'm where I belong," he said.

Anika beckoned to Tess. "Let's discuss this elsewhere."

The two of them left the room. Bryn was still trying to coax Ansel into conversation. When he finally pushed her away after several attempts, she got up and went to Mason's open arms. He hugged her while she quietly cried.

Ren came to my side, which made Shay growl. He quieted when I cast a warning glance in his direction. I wished I could do more. I hadn't had a chance to speak to Shay alone since Ren had returned, and the longer I had to wait to steal away with him, the more I worried that Shay would misinterpret all of this.

"I think I might be able to do something here," Ren murmured in a low voice so only I could hear him.

"Like what?" I asked.

"He needs to know you can make the wrong choice and still deserve a second chance." A painful lump formed in my throat at Ren's words. The alpha was the only one who could relate to Ansel's betrayal. Maybe he could make a difference.

I nodded, raising my voice to address the others. "Let's give Ansel some time to think about it."

"Actually, that would be great," Adne said, smiling at me. "'Cause I'm here to give you an official tour of our digs. You haven't seen how awesome it is here. You've pretty much just seen the dining room and your quarters, right?"

"I went to the healers' place with Ethan and Sabine," Nev said. "The Sanctuary?"

Adne nodded. "So Nev knows where to find Band-Aids, but not much else. How about it? You guys wanna see the place so you don't get lost?"

"I'd say yes," Shay said, meeting my eyes. "Considering the fight we're going to provoke tomorrow morning, this might be your last chance."

FIVE

HAVING SEEN PARTS OF IT from the inside, as well as approaching it from the outside, I'd known the Academy was huge. Still, its enormity was overwhelming as we followed Adne through the sparkling halls. She started at the top, the floor where we'd spent most of our time since arriving. The third level of the Academy held most of the residences plus the areas unique to each wing: Haldis Tactical, Tordis Archives, Eydis Sanctuary, and Pyralis Apothecary. Fortunately, Adne had remembered that it was better to describe the Apothecary to my packmates than subject them to its discomforts. The second floor housed the Academy's training rooms: scholarly, mystical, and combat, plus a few more residences. The first floor offered plenty of storage for weapons and gear. It also featured the dining hall, kitchens, and baths for each wing of the Academy.

"Why are they so far away from our rooms?" Bryn had asked. She'd always been concerned about access to bathrooms. It made sense as she spent more time in bathrooms than any person I knew "putting on her face," as she'd say. I wondered if Bryn was already experiencing separation anxiety from her extensive makeup collection.

Adne was still explaining about how the kitchens and baths were on the lowest level because it offered the easiest links to water and geothermal energy as we returned to the dining hall for the evening meal. The large room was already buzzing with activity. I spotted Tess, Connor, and Sabine gathered at a table. Ren was also with them, though I noticed he'd left a couple chairs empty between himself and Sabine. Apparently they hadn't cleared the air about Vail yet. I stopped in my tracks when I saw that Ansel was sitting beside him.

"Oh!" Bryn's hand flew to her mouth when she followed my gaze. Her eyes brimmed.

Tears pricked the corners of my eyes. Ren had been right. Ansel was fidgeting, but there was more color in his face now than I'd seen since he first showed up in Denver.

Tess saw us and waved. My stomach was growling when we settled around the table. Within minutes tureens of spicy fish soup and heaping bowls of pasta were being passed around the table, as well as a bottle of lemon liquor Connor produced with a flourish. One sip of the bright yellow concoction had enough fresh lemon to bite into your tongue, followed by a kick that almost knocked me out of my chair.

"What is this?" Mason's face was scrunched up.

"*Limoncello.*" Connor laughed. "Local specialty."

"Wow." Sabine licked her lips with a shiver. "That's ... something else."

"Something good," Nev said, dishing up another plate of pasta.

"Corrupting the kids already?" Ethan had approached the table. I looked up at him in surprise. I'd been so busy scarfing down food that I hadn't noticed he was missing from our group.

"What I do best," Connor said, passing the bottle around again. "Wanna pull up a chair? Really good eats tonight. We should advocate for a longer stay in Italy."

The addition of Guardians to the Haldis team made for a crowded table, even with the number of Searchers we'd lost in the past several days.

"Taking into account what's about to go down, I'd hope the food is good," Ethan said. "Every meal could be our last."

"Thanks for ruining my appetite." Bryn stuck out her tongue at him and then smiled at Ansel.

Seeing him briefly smile back at her had more of an effect on me than the *limoncello*. I crossed my fingers, wishing with every ounce of my being that Ansel really was coming back to us.

Sabine scooted her chair over, making space for Ethan beside her. "Here you go."

Ethan looked at her and then away. "Actually, I'm not hungry. Just saying hello."

Without another word, he turned around and left the dining hall.

"Is he always so grumpy?" Mason asked with noodles dangling from the side of his mouth.

Nev elbowed him with a chuckle. "You have no manners whatsoever, huh?"

"I'm a fierce beast, man," Mason said, wiping tomato sauce from his chin. "What can I say?"

"Ethan's still a little uneasy around Guardians," Adne said. "Don't take it personally." She was slurping her soup with abandon. It looked like everyone had been getting tired of whatever the Iowan menu had been. What she'd said about Ethan wasn't clicking in my mind. Ethan had certainly been open with his hatred when I'd first shown up, but lots had changed since then—including his attitude. Even this morning he'd defended us to Silas. So why would he say that and then refuse to eat with us? It didn't make any sense. My questions vanished when Bryn passed a bowl of luscious fresh fruit.

While the rest of us continued to stuff ourselves, Sabine was picking at her food. She spent about ten minutes making patterns with her pasta before she stood up, mumbling something about being tired, and hurried out of the room.

Watching her go, Connor laughed and shook his head.

"What is it?" Adne frowned.

"Nothing," Connor said, but he was grinning like a fool.

Suspicion buzzed in my ear like a gnat. Unable to quell my

curiosity, I excused myself from the table. I wasn't sure why I was following her, but something irresistible pulled me after Sabine's jasmine trail. Plus if I'd tried to eat another bite, I probably would have passed out.

Sabine had followed the curving corridor to the first level's entrance to the garden. I had an eerie sense of déjà vu, having taken this very path myself last night. I peered through the glass doors, but the garden had bloomed into its full, lush glory in the two days since the Weavers had moved the Academy to Italy. Hanging vines, fruit trees, and thick hedges blocked my view.

I slipped into the garden, shifting into wolf form so I could prowl the paths on silent paws. Guilt nipped at my heels, but I couldn't fight off the suspicion that something important was about to happen in this garden—something that affected my pack. As an alpha, I had to know.

Moving along the path, close to the hedges so I wouldn't be spotted, I followed what I thought was the sound of voices. Quiet, but persistent, like the bubbling sound of a distant stream. I'd almost reached the heart of the garden when I caught sight of two figures. Their bodies gleamed ghostly silver in the bright veil cast by the near-full moon. I tucked myself against the trunk of the nearest tree, letting the shadows cloak me.

Sabine paused in front of the stone bench where Ethan was sitting. Ethan continued to sharpen his dagger; he didn't look up.

"You can't do it forever, you know," she said.

"Do what?" He kept his eyes down; the dagger's blade seemed to glow in the moonlight.

"Ignore me."

"It's nothing personal."

"Of course it is."

His shoulders hunched slightly at her words, but he didn't speak. A rustling of the bushes on the other side of the tree caught my attention. I had to bite down on my tongue so I wouldn't yelp when a brown wolf slunk from the undergrowth.

Calla?

I bared my teeth at Shay. *What are you doing out here?* As much as I wanted time alone with Shay, this wasn't how I'd envisioned it.

I was going to ask you the same thing. When you left dinner, I thought you might be sick and I wanted to make sure you were okay. Then when I saw you go into wolf form outside the garden, I wondered what was up.

My ears flattened. *Nothing. Get out of here.*

He tilted his brown-furred head at me, green eyes curious and intent.

"I just want to talk with you." Sabine's words cut through the night air.

Ethan didn't move; she stood silently. Waiting.

Shay's ears flicked as her voice reached us. *Is that Sabine?* He took a step forward. *And Ethan?*

Get down! I nipped at his shoulder.

Hey! He bared his teeth, but a moment later his tongue lolled out. *You're spying on them.*

I flashed my own canines. *Don't be ridiculous.*

That's a pretty pathetic attempt at denial, Cal. He turned and bellied back into the brush. *Besides, there's a much better hiding place over here. You'll get spotted for sure where you're standing.*

I stared as his brown body disappeared into the dark foliage. A moment later I scuttled over the ground after him.

Our bodies pressed together amid the thick branches. I let myself snuggle into his fur, enjoying the way our scents blended in the night air. It reminded me of our first adventures together as wolves. Long night hunts after which we'd eat our fill and then curl up together for a nap beneath the shelter of a pine tree or tucked under the huge trunk of a fallen tree. Watching the golden brown wolf beside me, my heart twinged with longing for that freedom. The uninterrupted hours where the wilderness and the world belonged only to us.

Inch over a little more; I can't see. I pushed my muzzle against his shoulder, making the excuse to wriggle even closer to him.

I knew you were spying. He edged farther into the hollow, nipping my jaw affectionately.

Be quiet; I want to know what's going on. But as I peered at the pale silhouettes of Ethan and Sabine, I rested my head on Shay's forepaws. He laid his chin on the back of my neck, giving my ear a playful lick.

Why do you care what they're doing anyway?

Because it's Sabine and Ethan.

Good point.

Ethan had finally lifted his chin to look at Sabine, whose hands rested on her hips as she watched him.

He sheathed the dagger and sighed. "Fine. What do you want to talk to me about?"

"I'd like you to stop avoiding me."

"I'm not avoiding you." He sat up a little straighter.

"Really?" Sabine smiled thinly. "You could have fooled me."

Ethan stood up and walked along the path away from her.

Sabine's bell-like laughter rang through the night air. "See, you're doing it right now."

He turned, shaking his head. "I'm not much for company. Particularly the company of wolves."

"I see." She followed his retreat toward the rosebushes, heavy with red blooms turned black by the shadows. "So that's why you're working so hard at it."

He stopped and frowned at her. "I'm sorry?"

"You're doing everything you can to stay away from me, even though it's not what you want."

His own laugh was harsh, but his words had an edge of fear. "Since when do you know what I want?"

"I know every time you look at me."

Whoa. Shay scooted closer to the edge of the bushes.

Shhh! I nipped at his shoulder, but a heartbeat later I moved up beside him.

Ethan stood frozen in place. Sabine took another step toward him.

"Spending time with me isn't a betrayal of your brother," she said.

He jerked back. "How did you—"

"Tess told me," she interrupted. "I think she's concerned about you."

"That's none of her business," he said, voice shaking. "She shouldn't get involved."

"I don't think she wants to get involved." Sabine's voice curled like smoke in the night air. "That's where I come in."

He stared at her, wild-eyed, looking like a rabbit caught in a snare. She reached out and rested her palm in the center of his chest.

"I'm not so different from you, Ethan. No matter what you might think. Feel how your heart is racing?"

He stared at her slender fingers and nodded.

Her other hand grasped his and pressed it against her breastbone. She didn't take her eyes off his face. "So is mine."

A sound emerged from his throat, a sharp cry somewhere between pleasure and pain. Their two silhouetted bodies became a single, dark tangle of limbs when he reached out and pulled Sabine against him, kissing her.

A low chuckle filled my mind. *That's our cue. Let's go.*

But . . . I was staring at the entwined pair, entranced by the scene while knowing it wasn't my place to watch any more.

Come on, Cal. Shay's teeth gently grasped the ruff of my neck. *Your questions are answered. Would you have been happy if anyone saw our night in the garden?*

I fought the urge to snarl at him. *I'm coming, okay, stop pulling me. I'm not a puppy.*

Behind us, I heard Ethan's low groan and I flushed beneath my fur.

See. Shay crawled from the brush in the direction of the garden's entrance.

We stole from the garden on silent paws. When we were safely in the shadowed doorway, we both shifted forms and slipped inside the Academy.

"War makes strange bedfellows." Shay grinned. "Good for them."

"I guess."

"You don't approve?"

"It's just a little weird." I frowned. "A Searcher and a Guardian?"

"It's not the first time," he countered. "Monroe and Corrine—"

"Are both dead," I interjected, still troubled by what I'd seen. I wanted to be happy for them, but the loves I'd seen here had all ended in horrible loss. And the battle of our lives was ahead. I was afraid for Sabine and Ethan. I was afraid for all of us.

"This is different," he said. "Sabine isn't stuck with the Keepers. She's here, she's safe, and she's free to do what she wants. Probably for the first time in her life."

I nodded slowly.

"Still worried?" His mouth crinkled as he watched my furrowed brow.

"I can't help it." I remembered Tess sobbing when Lydia had died.

His arms slipped around my waist. My hands came up against his chest, but just to rest near his heart, not to push him away. I curled my fingers in his shirt, pulling him closer.

"What are you doing?" I asked, noticing the sly expression on his face.

"Easing your mind," he murmured, and bent to kiss me.

"Wait." This time I did push him back. "We should go—"

What I'd intended to be an invitation to my room died on my lips when he became very still. His arms still encircled me, but I could have sworn he'd stopped breathing.

A sound like the blending of a cough and a growl bounced off the walls in the hallway behind me. Shay's fingers dug into my hips and I knew who was there, watching us.

"Don't let me interrupt." Ren moved toward us slowly, stalking. "Never mind. I'd like to interrupt."

Shay's answering growl vibrated through my limbs. Still heady from our covert encounter in the garden, my instinct was to wrap my arms around Shay and warn Ren off with my own snarl. But those were instincts I had to ignore. I twisted out of his grasp, positioning myself between them.

"Truce, remember?" I bared my teeth at them.

"It doesn't look like he's playing fair," Ren said.

"I'm not playing at all." Shay laughed. "It's not a game to me."

Ren bristled. "You know that isn't what I meant."

"Stop it." I put my hands up, making sure neither alpha took a step closer to the other. "Don't do this."

"I'd just like to understand what you were doing alone with him." Ren didn't take his eyes off Shay.

"Nothing," I said. This was exactly why I'd wanted to get out of the hall and into my room, where we wouldn't be seen. "We were talking, Ren. I can still talk to Shay alone."

"It didn't look like he was after conversation to me," Ren said.

"He's right." Shay smiled wickedly.

"Let's see what I can do about that pretty smile." Ren lunged at him.

I swung around, slamming my fist into Ren's chest. He faltered, glancing at me in surprise.

The wolf inside me howled in frustration. How was I supposed to keep these two from killing each other?

"I'm serious. You will not hurt each other," I snarled. "Do not cross me."

Shay laughed. "Nice jab, Cal."

I whirled and kicked Shay in the stomach, sending him stumbling back against the wall.

"What the hell?!" he shouted, rubbing his abs.

"I'm talking to both of you!" My head was throbbing. "How do I make it more clear? Stop trying to gain an upper hand. You're both being total jackasses. I can't stand it."

Shay winced and I regretted my words. My frustration arose from my inability to pursue my own desires as much as the chore of regulating their abundance of testosterone.

"She's right," Ren said.

Shay glared at him before turning his eyes on me. When I met his gaze, I stepped back, reeling from the pain I saw there.

"So what, then?" he asked. "Nothing that happened between us matters now? He's here and all that is just over?"

"No, Shay . . ." The words were hard to push out as my heart rebelled against my mind. I saw flashes of the garden, was once again swimming in passion guided by moonlight. I felt the warmth of Shay's skin against mine. I remembered waking wrapped in his arms only to be full of desire again at the simple sight of him sleeping beside me. Blood roared in my ears. "That's not what I meant."

"What happened?" Ren's question was like a dam against the flood of memories.

Shay opened his mouth to respond, but my hard stare silenced him. He held my gaze for a long moment. My blood ran cold when I saw how much this exchange cut into him.

"Nothing," Shay said, turning away. "Good night."

I watched his retreat, the knot in my belly tightening until the pain was almost unbearable.

"What was he talking about, Calla?"

I forced myself to face Ren. When I met his dark, worried eyes, I shook my head.

"Leave it," I said softly. "Please just leave it."

His mouth set in a hard line, but he nodded. "Can I at least walk you to your room?"

"No," I said, my voice trembling. "I think it would be better if you didn't."

I felt empty, and Ren was too good at reading my emotions. A part of me still couldn't believe that he was here. That despite all we'd lost, he'd been saved. I wished I could tell him how much it meant to have him near me, how much strength I gained by knowing another alpha would be in this fight. But following that trail of thoughts would get me in serious trouble. If I let him play the role of comforter when I felt this vulnerable, I'd end up doing something foolish.

"Fine." I saw the flash of anger in his eyes before he headed in the opposite direction from the path Shay had taken. "Sweet dreams, Lily."

When they were both out of sight, I wandered, slightly dazed, back to the stairs, climbing slowly toward the third floor and my room. I wondered if sleep would come. Despite how weary my limbs felt after the chaos of battles and clandestine rescue missions, my mind was in a frenzy.

By not choosing a mate, I was forced to lead alone. Was I strong enough to do that? The freedom of solitude swirled through my veins, equal parts joy and terror. When I reached my room, I paused, staring at the door for several minutes, pretending I wasn't glancing every few seconds at the next door along the hall. Shay's door.

Swearing under my breath, I gave up trying to ignore the pull toward his room. I hesitated outside. The episode with Ren had been the worst kind of blunder. I'd alienated both of them, but I was more worried about how I might have hurt Shay. Would he still be angry?

Did he know that I'd wanted to be alone with him ever since Adne and I came back from Vail? Would he still want me, knowing that I had to try to keep a balance between the two alpha males?

I knocked on the door, cursing my own lack of conviction.

"Who is it?"

"It's Calla."

He made me stand in the dark hall for at least two minutes before he opened the door. He was wearing a plain white V-neck T-shirt that offered a teasing glimpse of his chest muscles and light cotton navy pajama pants. I had a similar but slightly more feminine set of sleepwear in my drawer. Apparently they were Searcher standard issue.

"What?" His unfriendly tone told me I wasn't forgiven for what had happened downstairs.

"Can I come in?"

He walked away, leaving the door open. I followed him into the room, closing the door behind me. My pulse began to jump, knowing that I was alone with him in his bedroom. I'd been waiting for this moment all day, but now that I was here, I felt unsteady. Nerves rattled my bones. If Shay thought he couldn't trust me, everything I'd fought for could fall apart.

Shay stretched out on his bed. He had a very old book propped on his chest.

"What's that?" I asked.

"Scion lore," he said. "Apparently, being the Chosen One means you get homework."

"Homework from Silas?"

"Yep."

I stayed a few feet away from the bed, watching him. His lean form, lounging against the pillows, made my skin feel electric. I wished he would look up and stretch his arms out to me. He kept his focus on the book.

"So how long are you going to be mad?" I asked.

He didn't answer.

I sighed. "Shay, I'm not trying to hurt you. I just think it would be a bad idea to rub Ren's face in what's going on with us. It could ruin everything."

Shay laughed. "Way to use a dog metaphor."

"You know what I mean."

I also knew it was more than just keeping Ren's temper in check, but I wasn't sure Shay could handle that information. Saving Ren had been necessary. I didn't want to admit how good it felt to have him back, to be near him again. But the constant buzz of hope that accompanied Ren's return only made me feel worse about what I knew it must be doing to Shay. The malice roiling in both their eyes whenever the alphas looked at each other verged on explosive. As much as I wanted Ren beside me, Shay needed to know that I hadn't abandoned him. I had no idea how I could balance the power between the two males without making Shay feel rejected. I'd made a terrible mess. Shay was angry with me and my instinct was to be defensive, but that wouldn't solve anything.

He tossed the book aside, looking at me. "Look, I realize I'm being a jerk. I'm sorry. He brings out the worst in me. He always has."

"The first step in recovery is admitting you have a problem." I smiled.

He laughed, but a moment later his somber expression returned.

"I can't stop the spinning top that's my brain right now," he said. "I'm trying to figure out what it means to be the Scion, but all I want to do is find out where my parents are."

"Logan hasn't said anything?" I watched Shay's chest rise and fall with a heavy sigh.

"He's playing hard to get . . . or something," he said. "I don't even know if I believe they're alive. I can't stop thinking about them . . . and I know it's not what I have to focus on right now."

"No one would blame you for that, Shay," I said. "Of course you want to find your parents."

"As long as I save the world first," he said.

"I guess there are strings attached," I said, smiling.

"Strings tied to anvils," he said. "Speaking of which, we have our own baggage and I think yours is ready to drag you back to the altar."

"Shay—" A small growl came out when I spoke.

"You know I'm right," he said. "Ren thinks you belong to him; he always has."

"He's an alpha," I said, not wanting to defend Ren so much as try to explain the situation to Shay. "He still sees me as his mate."

"And do you see yourself that way?"

"It's complicated." I looked at the ground. *Lame, Calla. Lame.*

"Maybe that's why, with him around again, I feel like you don't need me anymore."

"How can you even think about that?" I asked, avoiding a direct answer. "You're the Scion. You're the only reason that the Searchers might be able to defeat the Keepers."

"I thought Ren was the best hope for winning this war."

"We do need Ren," I said, ignoring his angry glance. "He could make or break a Guardian alliance. But all the Guardians in the world can't do anything about wraiths. You can."

"And yet that doesn't seem to get me anywhere with you," he said. "The wolves are what matter to you. More than anything."

"Of course they do," I said. "I'm an alpha."

"So am I," he said. "As much as Ren is. I'm newer to the pack— that's all."

"I know that, Shay." I frowned. "But I think you're missing the point."

"You're the one missing the point, Calla." His smile was bleak. "Do you think being the Scion matters to me if I lose you? Because it doesn't. None of this matters. You're the reason I need to win this war. I'm fighting for you. Not for the Searchers. Not for anyone else. It's all for you."

My pulse thudded in my veins, heavy as a bass drum.

He lay back on the bed, gazing at the twinkling starlight above us. I watched him, wondering what to do. I didn't need him. I didn't want to need him. In order to lead, to fight this battle, I couldn't afford to need anyone. But that didn't mean I . . .

When I realized what had to happen, what I *wanted* to happen, my mouth went dry. Then my heart sped up, matching the flare of heat in my blood.

"I don't need you, Shay." I couldn't hide the hoarse edge of my words.

Shay grunted without looking at me. He didn't see it when I pulled my shirt off.

"But I want you," I said. My heart felt like it was in my throat. A raw vulnerability like nothing I'd ever felt churned within me, and I knew this was what real love was like. And it was terrifying.

He finally turned toward me, pushing his hair back out of his eyes. "You wa—whoa." He sat up, swinging his legs over the edge of the bed, but he didn't stand.

I walked slowly toward him. "If I needed you, I wouldn't be me."

He didn't reply, but I watched his Adam's apple move up and down when he swallowed.

"Do you understand?" I asked. My hands were shaking.

Seduction was new ground for me. I'd been worried about Shay feeling rejected, but now I was the one whose nerves spiked at the thought that Shay might still be too angry to welcome me into his arms. What if he threw me out of his room? The restrictions put on alpha females hadn't allowed me to be the pursuer; I could only be pursued. The mysterious workings of romantic relationships were still unfamiliar territory for me. It didn't help that my pulse was racing at a pace that I thought might break the sound barrier.

"Yeah." Shay had to clear his throat to get the word out. He rolled his shoulders back, recovering, leaning back on his elbows in a careful, but superficially casual pose. "I think so."

"You think so?" I was only a foot away from him.

A slow smile slid across his mouth. "It would help if you showed me."

I stopped in my tracks. *Show him? I am so out of my league here.*

"Unless . . ." He was still smiling. "You don't want to."

There was no hint of fear or doubt in his voice, only a gleam in his eyes that made them vibrant. I could see the challenge there. The wolf inside me snarled at the provocation from another alpha.

It wasn't a matter of making a choice. Pure instinct drove me forward. I was standing over him, pressing my palms down on either side of him, forcing him to lie back. My lips curled, bearing sharpening canines. I drew a deep breath, wondering if he was afraid of me. But fear's sharp tang didn't linger in the air. Only Shay's scent, thunderclouds crackling with lightning, swirled around me, mixing with the smoky amber of our mutual desire.

"This isn't choosing," I said, my words husky. *Balance. I'm supposed to keep balance. Damn.* It was going to be much, much harder than I'd realized. I wanted him so much.

Even as I battled against my passion, struggling to remember that I wasn't allowed to be here—in Shay's room, on his bed—my resolve evaporated. He was simply too close, his skin too warm and inviting. And I loved him. The wolf within me howled for a mate. The pull of his body was magnetic; I couldn't turn away.

"Isn't it?" Shay smiled. "What is it, then?"

"A lapse in judgment," I said, though it didn't sound convincing.

"Works for me." Shay's canines were sharp. His arms wrapped around me, pulling me down onto the bed. He rolled over, pinning me beneath him.

"I love you," he murmured before he kissed me. I returned his kiss, aching to be closer to him.

"I know you don't need me, Cal," he said, moving his lips along my throat. "That's why I love you. But I want you to know I belong beside you, with you. I may not have been the one chosen for you, but I want to be your mate. Your alpha."

His words jolted through me, an electric current of desire. He understood so much about who I was. What I wanted. How I lived and loved. Heat swirled through my limbs. I slid my hands beneath his shirt, running my fingers over the muscles of his back. He pulled his shirt over his head. My heart stuttered at the sight of his carved torso giving way to the cut of his hips, the rest of his body only covered by drawstring pajama pants. In the next moment I was pushing those down too.

As the rest of my clothes peeled away, I buried lingering doubts. One night of bending my self-imposed rules to reassure Shay couldn't hurt. Could it?

Whatever the consequences, as Shay's hands and lips moved over my body, I knew how foolish my question was. I hadn't slipped into Shay's room late at night to rid him of doubts about my feelings. I was here for myself.

I twined my fingers in his hair, bringing his face close to mine. "I love you, Shay," I said. "Always."

SIX

THERE'S A REASON they call it the morning after. I woke up before dawn with my heart slamming against my ribs. Gray light filtered through the room. Clouds had rolled in overnight, leaving the sky above flat, the color of slate.

As I hurried to pull on my clothes and get myself out of Shay's room before he woke up, I silently berated myself. Not only did I feel like a total bitch for leaving Shay alone not once, but twice, I also felt the potential consequences of my decision to stay with him last night piling up on my shoulders like heavy stones.

Questions darted in and out of my mind as I grabbed clean clothes from my room and rushed to shower. Would Ren know? Would Shay gloat and provoke a fight? Innumerable worst-case scenarios played out as I headed straight to the bath, all of them ending with Shay, Ren, or me bleeding and the alliance destroyed. Right now facing bear-shaped Guardians or even a wraith had more appeal than dealing with fallout from my love life. As I scrubbed my skin well past exfoliation, regret lingered, following me like a shadow. I didn't want to pretend that last night with Shay hadn't happened. Every kiss, every caress I shared with him felt right, made me want him even more, but revealing myself to the group could put our mission at risk. Close memories of spending the night wrapped in Shay's arms sent a hot shiver over my skin, but I knew I had to push them away. Like so many times before, I was caught between duty and passion. Too much was at stake to let my heart rule; it had to be my head calling the shots from now on. If I chose my mate now, our shaky alliance would crumble.

When I arrived at Haldis Tactical, Anika and Pascal were already there. Flanking the Tordis Guide was a group of Searchers I didn't know. Much to my surprise, Ren stood in their midst, and it looked like he was giving instructions. I assumed they were Pascal's decoy team and I shivered. Ren's plan was a good one, but he was risking himself so soon.

Ren lifted his head, almost as if he'd read my thoughts. He gave a curt nod, turning his attention back to the team. I pushed back the desire to join their group, leading beside my fellow alpha. But that wasn't my fight. Not today.

Ethan and Sabine entered the room together. I tried not to stare. They weren't speaking or even touching, but one glance told me it would take a force of nature to pry them even an inch farther apart. Seeing them offered a rush of relief. At least I wasn't the only one dealing with romantic complications.

Trying my best to be casual, I approached them. "Morning."

"Hey, Calla." Sabine eyed me suspiciously. Apparently casual was not my forte.

Ethan just nodded.

"Did we miss the boat?" Connor asked. He sauntered in with Adne just behind him.

"You're actually just in time," Anika said.

"Damn."

Adne gave me a brief wave while Connor continued his conversation with Anika.

"Hey." I jumped at the touch of a hand on my shoulder.

"Sleep okay?" Ren asked.

"Uh . . . yeah." *So far, so good.*

Never mind. Shay walked in with Mason and Nev. They were all chomping on rolls and fruit. The scent of freshly baked bread made my stomach growl.

"Hungry?" Ren grinned.

"I skipped breakfast."

"Plenty to share." Mason tossed me a roll. I tore into it, pretending it was hunger and not anxiety that kept me from looking at Shay. He was standing right next to Ren. I kept waiting for something to happen. A smirk, a smug glance—any movement that would signal to Ren where I'd spent the night. Despite how delicious the roll tasted and smelled, when I swallowed, it felt like a rock landed in my gut.

Considering I'd scrubbed my skin hard enough in the showers to leave it red and stinging for several minutes, I hoped I'd gotten every trace of Shay's scent off me, but I didn't dare meet his gaze. Now that he was close, I could smell thunder and rain-drenched leaves, which made my toes curl. Heat climbed into my cheeks.

Desperate to distract myself, I focused on Ren. "How about you? Good night's sleep?"

"Not so much." He grimaced.

I tried to keep my voice casual as I imagined Ren passing by Shay's door and hearing what we'd been up to all night. "Your room not comfortable enough?"

He laughed. "That wasn't the problem."

My pulse had become a frenetic staccato. He must have found out somehow.

Ren rubbed his temples. "I had company."

"Excuse me?" My voice took on a high pitch that I didn't like at all.

Silas stumbled in, gasping. If it hadn't been for his cobalt and black hair, I might not have recognized him. He'd traded in his wannabe rocker wardrobe for classic Searcher garb. There was even a sword in scabbard hanging from his waist.

"Did I miss it? Am I late?!"

Anika frowned. "Considering I granted you a special dispensation for this mission, you certainly could have been more timely."

"Sorry, Anika." Silas shoved his mad hair out of his face. "I couldn't decide which writing tools would travel best. I settled on pencil and pen—one each, and a Moleskine." He held them up proudly. "Plus I was up most of the night tutoring our new recruit."

Ren sighed loudly enough to catch Silas's attention.

The Scribe made a sour face. "He was a rather difficult student."

"Silas?" I glanced from Ren to the mad-haired scholar. "He was your company?"

"Still jealous?" Ren winked at me.

"I was not jealous," I said.

"Really?" Ren said. "So that harpy-ish tone was your normal speaking voice?"

My cheeks flamed again, but this time had nothing to do with my clandestine sleepover with Shay.

"Dude, if you want to change teams, welcome aboard." Mason grinned. "But you could do way better than that punk-a-doodle-do."

Silas went beet red, sputtering, "I was giving him vital information about our mission."

Mason shrugged. "Everything that happens in the bedroom is vital."

"He's not wrong." Nev slung his arm around Mason's shoulders.

Silas was opening and closing his mouth, but no sound came out. Ren took pity on him.

"He told me about how special you are," he said, flashing Shay an unfriendly smile. "Because of your great-great-times-a-hundred-grandmother Eira who got us into this mess when she became a demon's mistress."

"Thanks for reminding me," Shay said. "So now you know why you and Calla were supposed to cut my throat instead of a cake at your wedding. Too bad that didn't happen."

Ren stiffened. "I'm not sorry you made it out of Vail alive. As for the rest of it . . . we'll just see how that turns out, won't we?"

Shay smiled slowly. "We certainly will." I held my breath, waiting for him to strike back with a hint about my visit to his room. But he only glared at the other alpha. Luckily for all of us, Shay's brain did not seem to have been completely overrun by his male ego.

"I didn't give all the background you needed." Silas had recovered a bit as his lessons were rehashed. "You kept growling at me."

"You called me an abomination." Ren's teeth were sharp. "What did you expect? A kiss?"

Mason coughed. "You could do better."

Silas ignored him. "I'm merely stating the facts. Guardians were created in violation of natural laws. You *are* an—"

Ren's hand was around Silas's throat, lifting him to his tiptoes and choking off his words. "Say it again and you'll be very sorry."

Adne grabbed Ren's arm and jerked him away from the Scribe. "He doesn't mean any harm."

Ren smiled at her as he dropped Silas. "Just making sure."

Adne returned his smile, laughing. "We all know you're not to be trifled with, big brother, you don't have to prove it."

"He's lucky you came to his rescue." Ren slid his arm around her shoulders. "That's twice now."

"Twice?" I asked.

"Last night and just now," Ren said.

"I was up late," Adne said. "I heard Silas's lecturing when I walked by Ren's room and figured I should get in there before things got ugly."

"We were past ugly," Ren said. "But we hadn't reached violent yet. Your timing was impeccable."

"I'm awesome like that." Adne grinned. "Besides, you and I have a lot to catch up on."

Ren turned a smile on Adne more tender than I'd ever seen from him. Connor was also watching the pair. A twisted smile, bittersweet, flickered across his mouth and I knew he wished Monroe was here to see his children together.

"What's the bookworm doing here anyway?" Connor pulled his gaze off Ren and Adne to glance at Anika.

"I'm going with you." Silas shoved his notebook and writing tools back into the satchel slung over his shoulder.

"The hell you are!"

Silas puffed up his chest. "These are the final days. The events about to transpire must be recorded."

Connor cast a pleading glance at Anika. "Please tell me this is a joke."

"He's right, Connor." Anika smiled thinly. "And there's precedent. Scribes make up the core teams for missions we designate as 'historic.'"

"The professor could mess with our game," Ethan jumped in.

Anika shook her head. "Despite your personal feelings, Silas is fully trained in operations and combat as all Searchers are required to be. He's going."

"Can't you just give us a dictaphone and we'll record the play-by-play for posterity instead?" Connor asked.

"Don't be ridiculous," Silas said. "You couldn't string a sentence together, much less observe the nuances of what will mark the Scion's epoch."

"Epoch?" Shay laughed. "I'm epochal now?"

Silas glared at him.

"Fine." Connor turned away from Anika, heading back to Adne's side. "Just don't get in our way."

"Are the teams set?" Anika asked.

"Almost," Ren answered. "Sabine, I was hoping you'd come on the decoy run."

Her eyebrow shot up. "You're leading it?"

He nodded.

She glanced at Ethan, who shook his head. "I'm heading into Tordis with the Scion."

Sabine folded her arms over her chest, jerking her chin toward Ethan. "Where he goes, I go."

"The Searcher?" Ren cocked his head, regarding her curiously. "Really?"

"Ask another question and I'll take a bite out of your ear, Ren." Sabine smiled, her fangs bright.

Ethan remained silent, but I saw the corner of his mouth trying to twitch into a smile. Beside Ren, Adne jabbed her elbow into his side when he tried to object again. The alpha glanced at his sister. When she shook her head, he shrugged.

"If it's what you really want," he said.

"I'll take her place on the decoy team," Nev said, throwing a wink at Sabine. "Sabine can go to Tordis and stand by her man."

"Bite me," Sabine snarled, moving an inch closer to Ethan. Ethan looked like he couldn't decide whether he should laugh or bolt.

"Where's Bryn?" I asked, though I thought I already knew the answer.

"She's staying with Ansel," Mason said. "Tess got permission to do some work in the garden with him today. Bryn won't leave his side."

I nodded, having expected something like that. Knowing Bryn would be with Ansel was a relief. As much as having my beta fighting by my side would be helpful, it was better still hoping that her unwavering devotion might pull my brother out of his cycle of self-hatred.

"It's for the best," I said. "She's where she belongs."

My eyes met Shay's for a brief moment and my heart skipped a beat. Other than a subtle gleam in his moss green eyes, he gave nothing away. No matter how deeply love, lust, and jealousy ran between the three of us, this morning we had another battle to face.

"Okay, Nev," Ren said. "Why don't you come meet the team? We're heading out in a minute or so. You don't happen to speak French, do you?"

"There's a language requirement now?" Nev laughed as they walked away. "Man, you should have mentioned that before I volunteered."

Our smaller team approached Anika and the other Searchers, waiting for orders.

"When you're ready, Pascal." Anika gestured to the Tordis Guide.

Pascal nodded at one of his team members, who drew skeans from his belt and began to weave a door.

"How will we know when the Guardians have taken the bait?" I asked.

"Pascal only needs five minutes," Anika replied.

Connor laughed. "He's good at making a scene."

"*Merci.*" Pascal grinned at him.

Anika lifted her hand in salute as Pascal, Ren, and their team passed into the shimmering portal.

From where I stood, I couldn't make out much other than glistening white and stark blue. Snow and sky. A hard lump caught in my throat when Nev shifted, trotting through the door. Ren, still in human form, turned toward us. He caught my eye and smiled, and then a charcoal gray wolf rushed after the team.

A moment later the door winked out.

"What now?" I asked. My fists balled up. There was about to be a fight and I wasn't there. My skin felt too tight. I wanted to be a wolf in battle. That's who I was. Who I'd always been.

"We wait," Anika said, giving me a sympathetic smile. I met her eyes, realizing that as the Arrow, she gave orders but rarely joined the fight. A steely flash in her irises told me she hated missing out as much as I did. There was no clock in the room, but it felt as though my pulse ticked off each minute they were gone. Anika, who'd been pacing back and forth in the room, suddenly stopped. "Now, Adne."

Adne had already begun to move, immediately lost in the intricate dance of her weaving. Multicolored, glimmering threads of light streamed from her skeans, twisting, braiding, slowly forming into the pattern that would be our door.

A door to what?

Tordis lay ahead. If we succeeded, Shay would have the first sword of the Elemental Cross. Remembering Logan's hideous creation that had waited for us in the bowels of Haldis, I shuddered. What was hiding in Tordis?

"Okay." Adne was breathing hard. When Connor put his arm around her, she leaned into him.

"You all right?" he asked.

She nodded. "Just making sure we're right on top of it."

Ethan strode toward the door. Sabine, in wolf form, stayed close on his heels. He nodded once to Anika before passing through the portal.

I peered into the doorway. Through the shimmering passage I could see the almost-blinding whiteness of snow occasionally cut by jagged black rock.

A soft touch on the small of my back made me jump.

"Sorry." Shay was smiling at me. "You ready?"

"Yeah," I said, throwing a teasing grin back at him. "You nervous?"

"Nah." He rolled his shoulders back. "I'm the Chosen One, remember?"

I laughed when he twisted to show me the ice axes he had strapped on.

"For luck," he said. "And 'cause we're headed for another mountain."

"Let's hope we have more than luck working for us." Connor

laughed, brushing past us and into the portal. He threw a disgusted look back at Silas, who had pulled out his Moleskine and was already scribbling notes. "Don't say anything embarrassing, kiddos, 'cause apparently it's all on the record from here on out."

Adne tapped her foot. "Could you guys get a move on, please? The other team would probably appreciate us getting this done as quickly as possible."

"Sir, yes sir!" Shay grinned. He took my hand, squeezing my fingers before turning to follow Connor. Instead of letting go, I pulled him toward me, raising up on my tiptoes to brush a soft kiss across his mouth.

"You don't need luck," I said. "But I'm still glad you brought the axes."

He drew me into a longer kiss until Connor whistled. Shay shook his head as he let me go and followed the Searcher through the portal.

The warmth of Shay's grasp was replaced by a cold touch. I glanced down to see Mason, a wolf, gazing up at me. I shifted forms and was greeted by his voice in my mind.

Follow the leader. Ladies first.

I'm no lady and don't you forget it. I nipped his shoulder.

Good point. Mason's tongue lolled out. *I don't think proper ladies let themselves be kissed like that.*

Shut up, Mason.

Just tell me. He yipped, wagging his tail. *Would you have let lover boy get that close if Ren was still in the room?*

I said shut up.

I just need to know what kind of odds I should be getting from Nev. He barked when I bit his flank, chasing him into the glittering doorway.

When I hit the ground on the other side of the portal, two thoughts screeched inside my head. That the air pouring into my lungs was the coldest, freshest I'd ever breathed.

I gulped the frigid air. How high up were we?

Glancing around, I got my answer. The ground sloped away from my feet at an angle that seemed impossible. If I took one step down, I was sure I wouldn't be able to stop until I reached the bottom of the mountain. If I turned the other way, I could see blue sky in the distance, partially blocked by a cloud drifting past. A cloud at eye level.

Shay was turning in a slow circle, careful to keep his footing. "Where are we?"

"Altitude fourteen thousand, seven hundred fifty feet," Silas rattled off. "Latitude seven degrees, longitude forty-six."

"In the Swiss Alps," Adne interpreted as she closed the portal. "Not too far from Mürren."

She pointed one of her skeans at the sheer obsidian rock face a few feet in front of us. "That's the passage to Tordis."

Shay stared at the black wall and voiced the thought that lodged in my own mind. "But there's no entrance."

"There's an entrance," Adne said, sliding the sharp spikes back into her belt loops. "It's just tough to see."

Ethan was already moving toward the dark surface. When he reached it, he put his hands out, walking sideways, all the while sliding his palms along the rock. He stopped, gave a small cry, and disappeared.

Sabine whined, rushing to the wall. She sniffed the edge, pawing at the rough black stone. Suddenly a hand appeared, reaching for her. She yelped, tumbling backward. I jumped forward, terrified she'd begin the long, unending fall down the mountainside. My jaws clamped into the ruff of her neck as I leaned back on my haunches while digging my paws into the snow.

Let go, Calla. She snarled.

Not until the law of gravity isn't working against us. I growled back.

Mason's voice reached both of us. *Stop fighting her, Sabine. You don't want to fall off this cliff. You wouldn't be an attractive pancake.*

She growled but stopped struggling.

Thanks, Mason. I held on to her, probably digging my teeth in a little harder than I needed to, but she'd almost taken us both for an unwanted skydive. I was pissed.

When I felt sure that we were both upright, I released her. She threw me one spiteful look before turning back to the rock wall.

Ethan's head, which looked like it was detached and floating against the black surface, appeared just as the hand had. "Sorry! I was just trying to show you the way."

Sabine and I moved toward Ethan's bodiless head. Scanning the rock wall, I still couldn't see where the rest of him was hidden. It wasn't until we were practically on top of him that I saw it. A crooked opening like a gash in the mountain's hide. Beyond Ethan lay only darkness. I wanted to whimper but covered it with a snarl.

Shay was right behind me. "How inviting."

Ethan turned away, beckoning to us. "Let's go."

A bellow, full of pain and rage, pulled me around. Barreling up the steep slope, churning snow and ice in its wake, was a bear. But it was larger than any bear I'd ever seen. Its girth was double that of the grizzly that had attacked Shay near Haldis. This creature looked like something left over from the ice age.

"Ethan!" Connor shouted. "Looks like one got past the other team."

Ethan's crossbow appeared from the slit in the rock before the rest of his body. By the time he fully emerged, he was already firing. Sabine, Mason, and I chased after the flying bolts.

Our downward charge, aided by gravity, was almost too fast. We'd have no control when we hit the bear, which meant the first strike had to count. When we got close, I smelled copper and salt. The bear had already been wounded.

It's running from the other strike team. I threw the thought to my packmates. *Try to find the wound.*

Got it, boss. Mason sprang into the air. He came down on the bear's back, digging his teeth into its shoulder to keep himself from tumbling past it. Just as Mason went high, Sabine ducked low. She squeezed her limbs tight to her body, flattening herself to the slope so she slid under the bear. When it was directly over her, she struck. Her muzzle clamped onto the bear's underbelly.

The bear roared, slowing. It turned in circles, trying to shake the wolves loose. As it moved, I saw the gash in its side. I leapt, striking as hard as I could into the bleeding wound. I bit down until my teeth met bone. The bear rose onto its hind legs, roaring its fury. Mason and I went flying, our bodies crashing into the snow-covered slope. But the bear's desperation to rid itself of our ripping teeth threw the beast off balance. It tipped over backward. Sabine, still clinging to its belly, landed on top of the bear, which now lay on its back. Not wasting a moment, Sabine tore into the bear, shredding its abdomen. The bear swung at her, but she leapt out of the way.

The bear struggled to roll over, but Sabine's attack had been fatal. Blood and gore spilled onto the ice, creating a river of crimson that flowed over the edge of the cliff. The bear groaned once before going still.

Any more? Mason lifted his muzzle to the wind.

Not that I can tell. I turned to Sabine. *Nice work.*

She sniffed. *Whatever.*

We trotted back up the slope.

"We clear?" Ethan asked.

I shifted forms. "That was the only one."

"Good." He slung his crossbow over his shoulder. "Though I'm not surprised. Pascal's team isn't sloppy. He'll be furious even one got away from them."

"They might have thought he wouldn't get far," I said. "The bear was already injured. Sabine just finished the job."

"She sure did," Connor said, leaning over and whispering loudly to Ethan, "Hey, man, your girlfriend is kind of scary."

Ethan glared at him and Sabine snarled.

Connor pointed at her bared teeth. "See. Look at that."

"You're asking to get bitten," Adne said, grabbing the back of his duster and pulling him out of range of Sabine's muzzle. "Let's get on with this."

Ethan laughed and slid back into the cavern.

Sabine followed the Searcher, while Mason took up a position at her flank. I kept a few feet back from her and could feel Shay following close beside me. I glanced over my shoulder to see Connor, Silas, and Adne at the rear of our group.

The darkness glowed red as Ethan set off a flare, basking the walls in crimson light so that it looked like the rock had begun to bleed. The tunnel was narrow. We squeezed our way through a passage barely wide enough for Ethan to fit through. I held my breath as he grunted and pushed his way forward. We had to shift into human form to wriggle sideways between the rough walls of the cave.

A constant sighing of wind moved through the cavern, mournful and unsettling. Ethan's flare sputtered out, but instead of that plunging us back into darkness, the passage remained illuminated. No longer red, the walls took on a soft, opalescent hue. I heard Ethan's breath catch.

He looked at us over his shoulder. "We're not alone."

"Guardians?" Connor asked.

Ethan nodded. "Three of them. Still human."

I crept up beside him, peering into the light. The tunnel opened up to a snow-covered hollow, nearly a perfect circle cut out of the mountain. The space was hidden from the outside world, accessible only through the narrow passage we'd scuttled through. On the other side of the open space an immense glacial wall covered the mountainside. Sunlight struck its surface, making the innumerable shades of blue sparkle like gemstones. The bright reflection made it almost impossible to see the outline of an opening in the ice, but I knew that Tordis lay within that glacier.

But between Tordis and our party, smoke was rising toward the sky. Three people huddled around a small campfire. They were outfitted in full winter gear, enough to withstand sudden, harsh weather shifts on the mountain.

"We'd better attack while we still have the advantage of surprise," Connor said.

"I don't think we do," Ethan said. "I'd bet they're just waiting for us to show. We've scouted this area in the past and haven't encountered Guardians beyond the first passage in. This group is new."

"The Keepers are tightening their watch on the sites," Shay said. "They know we're going for the pieces."

"Not much we can do about that now, is there?" Connor said, drawing his swords.

"Wait." I put my hand on his arm.

"Wait for what?" Connor said.

"They're Guardians," I said. "Like us."

"Sort of." Ethan was frowning.

"Let me talk to them."

"Are you insane?" Ethan said. He'd unshouldered his crossbow.

"She's not," Shay said. "The more allies the better. Maybe the bears are disgruntled employees too."

Ethan shot him a withering glance.

"You'll be right behind me," I said. "Anything goes wrong and you attack. I'll be okay."

Connor looked at Ethan, who shrugged. "She's the alpha."

"Okay, Calla," Connor said. "If you think it's worth a try, go ahead. Just keep in mind bears are grumpy, stubborn animals."

"And they smell bad," Ethan said.

"You want me to go with you?" Mason asked.

"No," I said. "I'll be less threatening on my own."

"Good luck," Shay said as I slid out of the narrow passage into the sunlight.

The moment I stepped into the open, the three Guardians were on their feet, watching me approach. I lifted my hand, waving, walking steadily forward. They didn't shift, which I clung to as a hopeful sign. The unmistakable fragrance of bear musk hit me and I wrinkled my nose. Ethan wasn't wrong about their scent. Not pleasant.

One of the Guardians stepped forward, pushing back the hood of its parka. A woman with dark eyes and braided copper hair stared at me.

"Pourquoi vous êtes ici, le loup?"

Why are you here, wolf?

My three-and-a-half years of French class got me that much. Wolf. She knew what I was. But there was no way I'd be able to answer her in French.

"My friends and I are searching for something," I said, hoping she spoke English.

She smiled. "You have friends who search." Even her heavy French accent didn't mask the spiteful emphasis she placed on the word *search*.

"The Searchers are friends to our kind." I kept walking forward. The other two Guardians had taken flanking positions close to the first woman. "Our masters made us believe otherwise, to our detriment."

"These are broad claims for one who is but a child," she said. "Perhaps you have been misled because of your youth."

"I learned the truth about the war," I said. "And we've been fighting on the wrong side."

She laughed, tossing a glance at her companions, who grinned. "No, *petite loup,* your friends are only more desperate to trick you because they know they will lose this battle."

I didn't know if I shuddered because of the blast of icy wind that hit me or from the harshness of her tone.

"The wolves may be fools." She lifted her hand, and I watched her nails lengthen into claws. *"Mais nous ne craignons pas la guerre."* In the next moment the shadow of a giant beast blocked the sun from view. I staggered back.

"Calla!" I heard Shay shout as the immense she-bear swiped at me, but I was already rolling along the snow, shifting into wolf form as I tumbled.

When I scrambled to my feet, she roared, clawing at the crossbow bolts that protruded from her dark fur. The bear's fury filled her deafening bellows.

Crossbow bolts buzzed through the air. The she-bear ignored them, charging me instead. I braced myself for her attack, catching a glimpse of Mason and Sabine flashing past to meet the onslaught of the other Guardians.

A flash of golden brown fur caught my eye and I knew I wasn't alone in the fight. Shay struck at the bear's flank just before she reached me. The blow caught her off guard. She turned her head and I lunged, locking my jaws around her neck. My teeth tore through thick tendons, but I couldn't get a strong enough grip to crush her windpipe.

She rose onto her hind legs. Still clinging to her, I swung from her neck like a rag doll. I heard Shay barking below me; the bear grunted in pain and I knew he'd attacked again. Kicking up with my back legs, I propelled myself away from her, releasing my grip and flipping through the air. While it wasn't graceful, I managed to twist around and land on my feet.

The bear was bleeding profusely from the wound I'd left on her neck and bites Shay had inflicted on her flank. Connor was beside him now, wielding a sword in one hand and the short, wide blade of a katara in the other. While Shay kept the bear's attention, Connor stalked close. With incredible speed he slashed the wound at her neck, widening it, and then plunged the katara into her chest. The bear shuddered. Connor had just enough time to spin away, pulling his blade free, before she collapsed.

"Let's go," Connor said, bolting toward the others.

We reached Sabine just as she leapt aside while two bears, one black and one ash brown, lumbered after her. The shaggy black bear roared, dropping lifeless to the ground. Ethan's bolt protruded from its left eye.

The brown bear gave what appeared to be a casual bat of its paw, but the blow sent Sabine sprawling. Ethan shouted, running to her side. The bear roared, charging at the shaken wolf. Mason stood his ground between the bear and Sabine.

A blade whirled past Shay and me. The sharp steel of Connor's sword sank into the bear's side. It roared but didn't falter. Connor swore. I threw myself at the bear's hind legs, snapping at its hamstring, but I missed, crashing to the ground. Shay caught the bear's left heel in his jaws. It kicked hard, shaking him loose, leaving Shay on the ground beside me.

The bear suddenly stumbled, its right front leg jerking out at an awkward angle. A silver rope stretched from the bear's shoulder, pulling it off balance. It took me a minute to recognize Adne's spiked chain whip. Silas had his arms around her waist. The two of them hauled on the whip, dragging the bear onto its side. It roared in pain, swatting at the whip's length.

"Connor!" Adne's knuckles were white as she clung to the other end of the whip, and Silas's face was as pale as her bloodless hands.

Connor dove forward, his left arm pulled back. While the bear fixed its gaze on Adne and Silas, Connor punched the katara's blade into the wound at its neck, driving the steel deep into the bear's throat. The beast's roar became a gurgle and it slumped into stillness.

Connor grunted as he pulled the blade from the bear's throat, wiping it clean on the snow. "Some fight."

"So much for alliances," Ethan said. Sabine had shifted to human form. He helped her to her feet and was studying her face.

"I'm fine," she said. "Not my first fight."

"That bear hit you hard." He touched her cheek.

"I can take it."

He smiled. "I'd rather you didn't."

Shay's nose pressed against my jaw. *You okay?*

Yeah. I shouldered into him as we stood up. *Thanks for the help.*

My pleasure. His green eyes sparkled with mischief. *I've been looking for some bear-type payback for a while now.*

I wagged my tail, sending my laughter into his mind.

"Time for the main feature." Connor was standing beside us. He looked at Shay. "I think you'll need your hands for this."

Guess the fun's over. Shay licked my jaw and I laughed again.

Fun?

Of course. You didn't have fun?

He was still watching me when he shifted into human form. I rested my chin against his palm, licking his fingers. Fighting with Shay at my side was more than fun. It was everything.

SEVEN

"SO THIS IS TORDIS," Shay murmured as if we'd entered a holy place.

Haldis had always been imposing. Its maw-like opening acted as a warning, never inviting exploration. Tordis couldn't have been more different. The claustrophobia-inducing, dark passageway into the mountain kept a secret carved into the silver-blue glacial wall before us. A secret that might have been the most exquisite place I'd ever seen. The ice-filled cavern wasn't just beautiful, it was breathtaking. Each frost-covered surface captured light, reflecting it back into the space. The tunnel was bright, covered by a glimmering net of sunbeams, delicate as lace but far more captivating to the eye. The dancing web of light was broken only by a small, dark opening on the far side of the cavern.

Shay pointed at the crawl space. "Looks like that's where we're headed."

"How do you know?" Ethan asked.

"Haldis was in an antechamber off the main cavern," Shay said. "I'm guessing Tordis is the same."

"Fair enough," Connor said, despite Ethan's deepening frown. "Let's go."

I lifted my muzzle, opening my jaws to let the frigid air slide over my tongue. Nothing. No alarming scents. No off-putting tastes that might alert me to danger.

Shay was watching me. "Any sign of mutant spiders, Cal?"

I barked and wagged my tail.

He frowned. "Really? Are you sure?"

It does seem awfully appealing for a Keeper lair. Sabine's voice carried an edge.

I know. I glanced at her, then back at the cave. *But I can't pick up anything.*

So what now? Mason asked, pawing at the ice.

We keep going. I trotted forward.

"I don't like it," I heard Ethan grumbling. "Something's in here. It has to be."

"Yeah..." Connor drew a long breath. "But if there's no creature feature waiting..."

I twisted my neck around, impatient with their hesitation. I wanted to get Tordis and get the hell out of here. If the Keepers hadn't left something hideous to guard this place, it was my best guess that our arrival had triggered some sort of alarm and soon this place would be swarming with nasties. Just like when we'd rescued my packmates from the dungeon below Eden. But in Tordis, I couldn't see or smell anything that signaled we weren't alone. Other than the bear, I hadn't spotted any sentinels or stone gargoyles hidden in the clefts of rock, waiting to alert their masters to our intrusion upon the sacred site. Even so, I didn't want to linger here—the best strategy was for Shay to grab the piece of the Elemental Cross that was hidden here and for us to get back to the Academy as quickly as possible.

I was about to growl at my lagging companions when Connor's eyes, which had been flicking around the tunnel, suddenly went wide.

"Calla, stop!"

My growl became a whimper as his warning came a second too late. My front right paw came down and met—nothing. There was no longer an ice-covered floor beneath me. Gravity and my own forward momentum propelled me into the empty space. A hole that I still couldn't see, even as I was falling into it.

Even my hind legs desperately scrabbling against the ice proved useless. My body tumbled over the invisible ledge.

I howled, but my cry of terror became a squeal when pain jolted through my limbs, traveling from my tail and rocketing up my spine. I hung in the air, kicking and snarling.

"Damn it, girl!" Ethan shouted. "Hold still."

It finally registered that I wasn't falling. The pain had resulted from Ethan catching me . . . by the tail.

My heart was pounding, my pulse deafening as it roared through my veins. Even as Ethan pulled me back up, each moment agony when he tugged on fur and tendons, I still couldn't see where the floor had ended and the hole began.

And then I was back over the ledge. My weight collapsed against the frosted stone of the cavern floor. Ethan released my tail and dropped down, resting on his heels as he let out a huge breath.

I scrambled up, snapping my teeth at him.

"What the hell?" He glared at me.

Shifting forms, I returned his ferocious stare. "That was *my tail.*"

"Well, sorry," Ethan said. "I guess I should have let you fall."

I stared at him; an abashed smile finally won out over my humiliation.

Ethan shook his head, laughing. "Some thanks."

"Yeah," I said, knowing I should offer him a real apology, but my butt still hurt. "I guess I owe you."

Connor scanned the cavern, eyes narrowed. " 'Twas beauty killed the beast."

"What?" I frowned.

"The cave." Shay followed his gaze, shaking his head in frustration. "It's the death trap. That's why there's no mutant spider."

"Fascinating." The scratch of Silas's pencil on paper echoed in the cavern.

Connor glared at him. "You know, this would go a lot better if you didn't talk."

Silas ignored him, lost in his furious note taking. He inched up near the invisible lip of the pit, trying to peer into its depths. "Impressive."

Ethan set off another flare, tossing it into the space where I'd fallen. For the briefest moment I could just barely make out the shape of the abyss. A perfect circle, probably four feet in diameter. The flare fell and fell and fell. Its red gleam finally disappeared, but there was no sound of it hitting any surface. Just silence that settled into my bones, making me shudder.

"Oh God," I whispered, trying to press back the vision of myself falling. I glanced at Ethan, swallowing hard.

He just nodded. He lit another flare, chucking it ten feet ahead of us. It bounced once on the ground and then it too disappeared into another invisible chasm.

"Damn it."

He did it again. This time hurling the flare twenty feet beyond our group. It didn't hit anything, vanishing from sight almost instantly.

Mason whined. He and Sabine circled me nervously, their fur brushing up against my skin.

"Fantastic," Connor said, crouching down. He turned his head back and forth. "How are we supposed to get through?"

"How many crevasses do you think there are?" Shay asked.

"No way to know," Ethan said. "The flares hardly make out the holes. This cavern was built to trick the eye. Even with the change in light it's tough to know how well we can mark them."

"Let's throw Silas in another one," Connor said. "Maybe they aren't all that deep."

"Hey!" Silas moved away from the edge.

Shay took a knee next to Connor. "You guys brought ropes, carabiners, and pitons, right?"

"In case we had a climb in store," Connor said. "You got a plan?"

Shay was already pulling the axes off his back. "I'll have to climb, all right, but on my belly."

"What do you mean *you?*" Ethan asked as Shay handed him an ax.

"How often do you guys climb?" Shay asked. He'd taken a rope from Connor and was looping it around his body.

"When we have to . . . ," Connor answered, his brow furrowing.

Shay grimaced. "That's what I thought. That means I'm the most experienced. I'll set the line."

"No way," Ethan said. "You may have the most experience, but you're also precious cargo. We can't risk you."

Shay smiled. His canines were sharp. "How many of your friends, and mine, do you want lose because we got stuck here? You or Connor will take forever to get across. I know how to do this. I'll be fast."

I'd begun trembling at the thought of Shay crawling between crevasses none of us could see. I also wondered if he realized he'd just numbered Ren among his friends.

Connor ran a hand through his hair, agitated. "How can you be sure about that? We don't know how far this trap goes."

"See how the cavern narrows about fifty feet out, leading right to that crawl space?" Shay pointed to the far end of the glittering space. "I'd put good money down that the trap ends there. Tordis is on the other side of that next passage."

"You don't know that," Connor said.

"Yes, I do." Shay lowered his gaze, suddenly quiet. "I can feel it."

Connor snorted. "Well, at least the Force is with you."

"Shut up," Shay growled. "Let's get started. Give me the pitons."

Adne tossed him a backpack.

"We shouldn't endanger the Scion," Silas said, turning to Adne. "What about opening a door?"

"A door where?" Adne said, gesturing toward the invisible death traps. "Even if we found a ledge out there, who knows how wide it would be? Someone could step through the door and fall right in a hole."

"Which is why I'm going out there," Shay said. "I need to get to the gap on the other side of the chamber. If this setup is like Haldis, this is the trap; the other side should be clear sailing."

"If you fall before you get there—" Ethan began.

"The piton will catch me and you guys can haul me back up," Shay cut him off, hammering one of the pitons into the floor with the blunt edge of his ax and knotting the rope around it. "I'll make my way across, set the rest of the pitons, and secure the line at the other side. Then you guys hook safety lines on and get across quickly. No one will fall. Or if they do, they'll only drop a few inches before the line catches them."

"I don't know . . ." Connor looked uneasy.

Adne sighed, kneeling down to help Shay locate the remaining cams and carabiners. "It's a good plan, Shay." She met Connor's warning glare. "You know it's a good plan. And the only plan. Pascal is counting on us and we're already well over time. We didn't plan for that second group of Guardians."

"Fine." Connor handed Shay another rope. "Attach this one too. We'll hang on to it in case the piton gives."

Shay gave him a hard look. "My piton won't give. I'm not a moron."

"Just take the second rope," he said.

Managing not to take a swing at Connor, Shay secured the second line to his body and moved a foot from the spot where I'd slid over the edge. He dropped to his hands and knees. I wanted to call out for him to be careful, but I worried that I'd only undermine his confidence.

Fifty feet doesn't sound like much of a distance, but watching Shay making steady progress through the cavern verged on painful. He had an ice ax in one hand, at times swinging it down and burying it in the ground in front of him as he inched forward. He placed the cams at regular intervals, threading the rope through. A zigzagging path began to emerge as he crossed the cavern. Even with the rope outlining our route, the crevasses remained impossible to see. To the naked eye it looked as though a deranged, or very drunk, climber had charted his nonsense course along a flat surface. Only the memory of the floor dropping out from under my paws reminded me that I couldn't believe what I was seeing.

Shay suddenly swore, the sound echoing through the ice-coated chamber.

I screamed. Shay was falling. And then he wasn't. He'd swung his ice ax up, burying it in the side of a crevasse he hadn't found soon enough. He hung from one arm, but the safety line he'd placed had already pulled taut. Just as he'd predicted, he only dropped a few inches. But that didn't stop my heart from trying to break free of my rib cage.

"You okay?" Connor's call was strangled.

"Yeah," Shay yelled. He also sounded a bit breathless. "This part is going to be a problem. These two holes are only separated by about three inches."

"Damn," Adne said. "That's narrower than a balance beam."

"And I'm no gymnast." Mason's laugh was tight. He and Sabine had both switched back to human form when Shay began his crossing. Wolves might have good reflexes, but if we were strapping into climbing gear to make the passage, we'd need to be human.

Shay placed a piton, securing himself to the side of the crevasse.

"I'm going to carve out some holds here," he shouted. "We'll have to climb across the side at this point."

"Climb?" It felt like cotton had been shoved down my throat. Scurrying along the edges of the pits was one thing, voluntarily dropping down into one was another.

Mason leaned over, elbowing me. "That was pretty damn sexy— did you see what he can do with his shoulders? Shay's the wolf to beat, I think. I may need to give Nev better odds."

I growled at my packmate, but Mason just laughed.

True to his word, Shay was chopping at the wall with his ax, creating small fissures in the rock where a foot or a hand could be placed. He moved forward, placing another piton, making more holds. He'd almost reached the dark gap in the shimmering ice wall. Finally he found the other side of the crevasse and climbed up, setting a piton and hauling his body over the lip of the pit, the force of his push propelling him straight into the crawl space. Then he tumbled out of sight.

"Shay!" Connor yelled. "You all right?"

I held my breath until Shay's head poked out of the darkness.

"I'm good!" He was on all fours, unable to even kneel without hitting his head on the roof of the tunnel. "The ceiling's low, but we'll all be able to squeeze in. And there's light on the other side. I'm pretty sure we'll find the hilt where that glow is coming from."

"Nice work!" Connor called. He was already threading a line through Adne's belt. "You cross first," he said to her. "If something jumps out at the Scion in that little cave while most of us are still crossing, you get him out of here."

She nodded, biting her lip.

"The line's secure over here," Shay yelled, waving and pointing at the final cam he'd fixed into the far wall. "Get started!"

Adne moved stiffly, as if she had to force herself toward the edge of the first crevasse. I didn't blame her. I didn't want to go anywhere near them either. Silas picked up the rope and was about to hook himself in when Connor snatched it away.

"You're last," he said.

"What?" Silas's eyes bulged.

Connor grinned, handing the rope to Sabine, who started after Adne. "This seems like a thrill-a-minute episode in your marvelous history, doesn't it? I think our crossing deserves your best writing endeavors."

Silas stared at him before slinking backward. To his credit he did begin to write again immediately, though I couldn't have guessed whether he was describing the cavern or lodging another complaint against Connor.

I hung back with Silas, not because I craved his company but because I wanted to wait until I absolutely had to make the crossing. Adne was already on the other side, squirming past Shay into the narrow tunnel. My stomach clenched as I watched Sabine swing down into the crevasse. Her lithe form seemed to take naturally to climbing as she easily found Shay's holds. Ethan was behind her, followed by Mason.

"You're up." Connor was clipping a carabiner onto my belt and sliding the safety line through it.

I managed a nod. Words, even thoughts, wouldn't surface as I moved to follow Shay's rope. I'd never really thought I was afraid of heights, considering I'd spent my life in mountains. Somehow this was different. The slopes around Haldis were soil and rock. Even when it was snow-covered, it was familiar. This cavern, hidden in the heights of the Alps, full of ice and light that wove a wickedly beautiful web in which to snare its prey, made my blood as cold as the mountain air I breathed. The cave's deception unnerved me in ways I'd never experienced. I didn't want to go farther into its depths. I wanted out.

I gripped the rope, willing myself to start across. Looking at the far side of the cavern, I met Shay's eyes. He was waiting for me, hovering on the lip of the crawl space. He lifted his hand.

Get to Shay. Get to Shay.

I forced all other thoughts out of my mind. The only thing I wanted more than to escape this death trap was to be with him. If I could make reaching Shay my goal, I could do this. An ice-edged wind swirled through the cave, its sounds bouncing off the walls in millions of whispers, murmuring in my ears about slipping, falling. I pulled myself along the rope, trying to shut out the wind's voice, knowing it was more Keeper magic trying to seize on my fears and manipulate me into making a fatal error.

"It's all right, Calla." Shay's voice broke through the whispers. "You're almost there."

But almost there meant I'd reached the final crevasse. I stared at what appeared to be a solid, sparkling ice surface. I only knew it wasn't because of the way Shay's rope line suddenly dipped well below it.

"Get a move on!" Sabine squeezed beside Shay at the entrance of the crawl space. From her vantage point on the other side of the pit she stared down at me, flashing a challenging smile.

Anger flared and I seized on it, swinging down into the crevasse. My feet scrambled against the sheer face and for a moment I panicked. But then my foot slipped into one of Shay's holds and I could breathe again.

"You've got it!" Shay's voice was both warm and relieved. "Just a few more feet."

I pushed myself from hold to hold. My arms were burning. It felt as though the crevasse was trying to pull me off the wall, sucking me down into oblivion.

And then Shay's hands were locked around my forearms. He hauled me over the edge of the crevasse and into his arms. I scrambled into the crawl space, knocking him backward. His face was buried in the crown of my hair.

"Hey. You did great."

I almost pushed him away, not wanting to show any weakness and embarrassed that he so easily sensed my fear. Instead I let that impulse go and turned my face up to kiss him. When his arms went around my waist, all my anxiety from the climb faded.

"Thanks." I smiled, deciding it was okay that I felt better leaning against him. After all, navigating death pits with climbing gear did not fall under an alpha wolf's job description.

Silas coughed; he clung to the edge of the tunnel, waiting for Shay and me to make room for him to crawl inside—I guessed Connor had given him a reprieve. Shay pulled me farther into the narrow cavern toward where Sabine, Nev, and Mason were huddled. The Scribe was peering at Shay and me. "I just wondered if you might offer a comment as to where you think a relationship between a Guardian and Scion could lead? If we survive, that is." He held his pen poised. I didn't know what startled me more: the question or that he had his notebook out not five seconds after that crossing.

Shay shook his head, letting me go and turning to move farther down the crawl space. I smiled slowly at Silas, letting my fangs catch the dim light that slid into the tunnel from the ice cavern.

"Silas! I didn't know you were writing gossip columns now." Adne scuttled past us to the end of the rope, offering her hand to Connor as he climbed out of the crevasse. "I thought you were recording history."

Silas turned beet red but didn't answer.

"You good?" Adne asked Connor.

"Yeah."

Shay, who was already heading for the silver gleam at the end of the tunnel, turned and called, "Let's finish this."

Sabine, Mason, and I exchanged a look, and in the next moment three wolves were at Shay's heels. The second tunnel was dark like the first, though it was much narrower. I kept testing the air, but just like when we'd first entered the cavern, I could smell nothing. No monster lay in wait for us. We were alone.

The subtle flame bloomed into bright light at the far end of the passage. I closed my eyes, making a silent wish that we weren't about to encounter another room full of deadly traps. Shay stepped into the light. And smiled.

We followed him into a room that was familiar and unfamiliar. The space was open and well lit. Unlike Haldis, which had been filled with warm hues, this room sparkled with cool silver and misty blue. I felt like I'd seen the colors before and realized that I had. The walls of this cavern mirrored those of the Tordis wing of the Roving Academy.

"Oh," I heard Silas breathe behind me. I knew what he was looking at, what we were all looking at.

She was here, just like she had been at Haldis. A woman, ethereal, floating at the center of the room. But now I knew her name: Cian. Shay's long-dead ancestor. The warrior who'd given her life, her act of sacrifice transforming her into the only weapon that could save us now.

Her hands were extended toward Shay. Once again I found myself locked in place, unable to move a muscle as Shay reached for her, swiftly crossing the space between them. When his fingers touched hers, the light vanished and darkness engulfed us. All was silent.

I waited, listening to the sound of my heartbeat.

"Are we dead?" Mason whispered, and I knew the spell had released us.

I couldn't help it. Shifting forms, I laughed. "No."

"Oh, good." Mason began to laugh too.

Light slowly returned to the room. Cian had vanished, leaving Shay standing alone at the center of the space. A slender blade lay flat on Shay's palms.

Silas stumbled forward like a man caught up in a religious vision.

"Tordis." He reached toward the blade, remembering himself at the last second and snatching his fingers back.

"Nice work, kid." Ethan kept his distance but was eyeing the blade admiringly. Sabine stood beside him in human form, and I noticed that her fingers were interlaced with his.

"It's so light," Shay murmured.

Connor snorted. "As air?"

He grunted when Adne kicked him in the shin.

I took a cautious step closer and peered at the gleaming metal, though I didn't know if metal was what I was looking at. The blade's surface shimmered with movement, the roiling of swift storm clouds, the endless swirl of winds.

Shay's jaw twitched. "Here goes nothing."

He grasped the flat of Tordis's blade between his thumb and index finger, carefully avoiding the razor-sharp edges. With his other hand he pulled Haldis from inside his coat. His forearms trembled as he lowered the blunt end of the blade toward the opening in the hilt. There was no sound as the objects met, but when the blade would travel no farther into the hilt, a ripple of light traveled from where Shay's palm gripped the base of the sword to the tip of the blade.

With no warning, the ripple exploded from the tip like a solar flare, sweeping through the room, knocking everyone but Shay to the ground. The earth beneath me moaned, and the mountain shuddered.

Then there was silence.

Silas grunted and rolled to his hands and feet. "I hope that didn't cause an avalanche. We might have just been buried alive."

"Nice attitude," Mason said.

"We'd have heard the avalanche," Adne said quickly.

"Not necessarily," Silas said, eyes bright with speculation. "We're pretty deep, and I don't recognize this form of rock. Who knows what sounds it can absorb or deflect?"

"You're sick," Connor replied. "Did you know that?"

"I'm merely pointing out—"

"Shut up, Silas!" Adne was shaking her head. "Even if a wall of snow is blocking the cave entrance, I can open a door in here. We're not trapped."

"Could we at least check?" Silas asked. I couldn't believe how disappointed he sounded.

"No!" Mason and Connor shouted.

I scrambled to my feet and looked at Shay. He stood quietly in the middle of the cavern, eyes closed, both hands grasping the hilt of the sword. The weapon was a study in contrasts. The warm glow of Haldis radiated from between his fingers, while the blade gleamed cool and clear, like lightning striking from the sky to the hilt. It was the depth of the earth wedded to the breadth of the heavens.

As if he felt my gaze, Shay's eyelids fluttered open and he offered me a smile of mystery. He pulled in a long slow breath.

"We have to get the other sword."

Something in his voice stopped my breath—strength, fearlessness, and longing I hadn't heard before. Part of me stood in awe of him—the Scion finding the source of his power—but a smaller, pettier voice told me I was also jealous.

Not jealous of his power, but of that stirring quality in his words. He was finding himself, his true self. Last night, I'd believed Shay when he said he wanted to stay at my side. That he would be my mate. Watching him now, the distance between us felt immense—he no longer seemed like a Guardian. He was only the Scion. What did that mean for me?

I'd never doubted Shay's love, but Silas's question no longer sounded ludicrous. What future could the Scion and a Guardian alpha have? Something cold and hollow settled in my bones that I thought might be grief. Was I losing Shay to his destiny?

"Get the other sword, huh?" Connor grinned. "Well, that *is* the plan." He jumped out of the way before Adne could kick him again.

"I have an even better plan," Mason said, putting his arm around Adne's shoulders.

She lifted her eyebrows at him. "What's that?"

"You open one of those pretty doors and get us the hell out of here."

EIGHT

THE CACOPHONY OF sound that flooded my ears when I stepped through the portal made me bristle. Was it panic? Fear?

I'd been caught up in the events of the ice cavern, lost in thoughts about Tordis, the sword, Shay—so that I'd almost forgotten that another team had been on a different mission.

How many had we lost so that Shay could retrieve the blade?

My growing fear splintered when it became clear that the loudest sounds of the din were raucous hoots and unchecked laughter. The celebratory noise died down as the rest of my party emerged through Adne's portal. When Shay appeared, the room suddenly drowned in silence.

Anika stepped forward. Shay didn't speak. He simply lifted the sword; its blade came to life and I heard a wind, like the rush of wings, bringing hope—that brightness was balanced by the subtle glow of Haldis, with the solid warmth of the earth itself.

The room erupted again. This time the cheers were deafening. Only Anika remained silent, her lashes wet with unshed tears.

Searchers swarmed Shay, gazing at the sword but careful not to touch it. Watching his newly formed entourage bask in the near-tangible power of the sword, I once again felt the tightness of loss, grief like an invisible hand around my neck.

I'm going to lose him. I started to inch away from them, hoping the sensation would pass.

Connor pushed his way into the crowd and began recounting our journey; from the snatches I caught, he seemed to be embellishing our exploits a bit. My suspicions were confirmed when Silas shoved Connor aside, waving his notebook as he began his version of the tale. Connor took up a strategic position just behind the Scribe and made faces and crude imitations of Silas at appropriate—or rather, inappropriate—intervals.

"Wanna check on our boys?" Mason caught my arm, jerking his chin in the direction of Nev and Ren, who were talking with Pascal.

I met Mason's teasing gaze, wondering what he meant by our boys. Nev was his partner, but did he expect that Ren would be mine? The thought made me bristle and I barely stopped myself from growling at him.

"Sure."

I glanced back, expecting Sabine to join us. But she was standing apart, beside Ethan. Their heads were close, bodies turned toward each other, lips moving in swift whispers. The din of the room didn't touch them, as if they were the only two people standing in Tactical.

Nev and Ren were grinning. The alpha leaned against the massive wooden table, looking as pleased with himself as ever. Nev was perched on a chair, sitting on its frame with his feet resting on its seat. I looked back and forth between them, puzzled, but it was Mason who asked first.

"What?"

Nev's eyes sparkled. "Dude. Bears!"

Mason frowned. "You're happy about bears?"

Ren flexed his shoulders. "They make for a good fight."

"Oui." Pascal laughed, slapping Ren on the back. "Les loups ont été trop pour les ours."

"Mais oui!" Nev grabbed Mason's hands, pulling him into a hug. "Wolves kick bear butt. How did things go for you guys?"

Mason leaned his cheek against Nev's. "No losses. Got the sword. I'd call it a win. You?"

Ren smiled; his canines were sharp. "Like he said before. Dude. Bears!" He turned to Pascal. "Besides, we had a kick-ass team backing us."

"*Merci.*" Pascal folded his arms across his chest, gazing at Ren assessingly. "But you made our job . . . less difficult than is usual."

"Happy to oblige," Nev said.

Pascal inclined his head. "I am sorry to say I had my doubt. *Les loups* have so long been numbered among our enemies. But you make *les bon guerre*. Better even than *les ours.*"

"I didn't follow that," Mason said.

Nev elbowed him. "No wonder you always copied my French homework. He said we make good war, better than those Swiss bears."

"The Keepers flubbed," Ren said, still speaking to Pascal. "Bears aren't good warriors. They're too solitary. We could keep them off balance because they're too eager to argue with each other instead of working as a team."

"Go, pack!" Nev bumped Ren's fist.

"I think you are right." Pascal stroked his chin. "We often find *les ours* alone. Rarely do they seek out one another's company."

"Let's hope the Keepers have other screwups for us to exploit down the road," Mason said. "Right, Cal?"

I nodded, but my mind had drifted. I'd been watching Pascal closely. Watching the way he was watching Ren. That assessing gaze carried a fierce admiration in it. When Ren spoke, Pascal listened. I didn't know whether to be surprised or not. Winning people over was one of Ren's strongest attributes. He was a natural leader and had so much charisma you could drown in it. A painful twinge caught my chest, stealing my breath for an instant. Gazing at Ren, I saw the alpha mate who would have been mine, and in seeing him, I glimpsed what our future might have looked like. What a great leader he would have made for the Haldis pack, the strength we would have shared as alphas. Had I ripped that away from him? Or could our pack come together again—was our future lingering, waiting to be reclaimed? The sharp pinching in my chest was overtaken by the pounding of my heart. As if he sensed my stare, Ren's eyes met mine and I couldn't look away, couldn't breathe.

It was Anika's voice that finally broke the spell. I turned to see her standing beside Shay.

"The Scion!" She took Shay's hand, lifting it high. Shay raised the sword in his other hand. It flashed, sparks of lightning alive in the blade. My racing pulse went cold as I listened to the Searchers' roaring approval for their new champion.

Did he belong to them now? Was I a fool to think it possible that the Scion could be the mate of a Guardian?

I glanced back at Ren, wondering what he thought of Shay's rapid ascension.

But Ren wasn't looking at Shay or the sword. His eyes were still on me. I held his gaze, waiting, wondering what he was thinking, feeling. Suddenly he gave me that half-cocked smile and my knees caved a bit. Then he shifted.

Still watching me with dark eyes, the charcoal gray wolf lifted his head and howled. The sound filled the room, joyful, exhilarating. My heart leapt—this howl was the opposite of the last I'd heard from Ren. The night I left him in the woods. The night I ran beside Shay, abandoning my union with Ren. That night he'd howled and I'd thought the grief in that sound would tear me in two. In this moment, in this howl there was no hint of grief or doubt. There was only an alpha, reveling in his triumph.

Instinct took over and I shifted, raising my own muzzle to match his cry. Our voices united, singing out victory. Nev and Mason joined us. Sabine hesitated, watching. She didn't change, though her eyes gleamed at the sound of our chorus.

Out of the corner of my eye I caught a glimpse of Shay. He continued to hold the sword aloft, but the lightning in its blade carried a charge of fury. A roiling storm cloud ready to explode. Like Sabine, he hadn't shifted but had gone very still. His gaze moved between me and Ren, his eyes narrowing.

As I shifted back, a wave of exhaustion slammed into me, leeching strength from my limbs. The adrenaline from our mission had run out. Shay was coming toward me, and without looking, I knew Ren was already shifting to stand beside me. Two alphas once again jockeying for position. Both wanting me. Each hating the other. I couldn't take it.

Before either of them could speak or reach for me, I whipped around and dashed from the room. The burden of keeping the peace between them had rubbed my nerves raw. Today I'd witnessed my two would-be mates staking out their places in this strange new world we'd found. Ren would still be an alpha even among his former enemies. He would lead and they would follow. Shay was the Scion, who the Searchers had spent their lives, and shed their blood, seeking. They both knew where they belonged and what they wanted. I'd escaped the life laid out for me by the Keepers, but even here I was trapped, unable to choose my own fate.

I ran through the halls, feet pounding on the marble floor, wishing I was in wolf form so I could run faster, but I thought there were enough Searchers not used to having Guardians roaming their halls that wouldn't appreciate a white wolf running full speed through the Academy. I ran as fast as I could on two feet instead of four, needing to find the two people I trusted the most and hoping they might have some answers for me.

I followed their scent until I discovered them in a hidden corner of the courtyard. Tess was kneeling in the soil, up to her elbows in dirt. Ansel crouched beside her. I didn't see Bryn until I was almost on top of them.

"Hey, Calla!" She grinned as she swung down from the branch of the apple tree she'd been lounging in.

"You auditioning for the role of Cheshire cat?" I asked, returning her embrace.

"Cat?" She wrinkled her nose. "Ugh! Never."

"Good to know you still have standards."

"So you're here," she said, stepping back to look me up and down. "Looking healthy. I take it that means the mission was a success."

I nodded. "No casualties on either end."

"None?" Tess looked up at us. "That's impressive."

"Bears are no match for wolves."

Bryn snorted, placing her hands on her hips. "Of course they aren't. Any of us would take a bear without breaking a nail."

I grinned at her.

"And Shay?" Tess asked. "He has the sword."

"Yes." I wished I wouldn't shiver when I thought about it. "He's got it. We're halfway to a fully operational Scion."

Tess's face was solemn. She nodded and then turned back to her planting. Ansel scrambled to his feet, brushing dirt from his hands. He still managed to smudge dark soil across his forehead when he pushed his hair back.

"Hey, sis." He leaned forward, giving me a quick hug before shoving his hands back in his pockets and looking away.

"Hi, An." A lump formed in my throat immediately. "What are you up to?"

I tried to keep my tone easy, knowing he wouldn't take sappiness as anything but pity. And pity was the last thing he needed.

"Learning about herbs," he said, pointing at a basket. Plants boasting diverse shapes of leaves in myriad shades of green were carefully sorted and tied into bunches, filling the woven containers.

"Herbs?"

"For the Elixirs," he replied. When I frowned, he continued, "Those are the healers who work in Eydis Sanctuary."

"We also gather herbs for the Alchemists in Pyralis Apothecary," Tess added. She was wielding a pair of pruning shears and I cringed, remembering the hack job I'd done on my hair with them. "But that will take a few lessons. Those herbs are tricky and a little dangerous."

Ansel flashed a smile at Tess, and I was thrilled to see genuine enthusiasm warm his features. "I'll take whatever you throw at me. Just say the word."

"One step at a time." Tess returned his smile before standing up, taking a full basket in each hand. "Why don't you take a break while I run these to Eydis? You probably would like to hear Calla's story."

"We can help you carry them, Tess," Bryn said. "There are more baskets."

"Don't worry about it," she replied. "I'll bring us back some lemonade. The lemons were just harvested this morning, so it will be amazing."

"Sounds great!" Ansel grinned, plopping down into the dirt. Bryn nestled beside him, snuggling into his embrace. He didn't flinch or try to pull away. My throat started to close up again and I had to look away, focusing on the ripening cherries that hung from the branches of a nearby tree. The tightness of my throat gave way to my mouth's sudden watering.

"So what are you doing hanging out with the civilians, Cal?" Bryn asked as I sprawled on a bench across the path from where they sat. "Shouldn't you be plotting the overthrow of the Keepers?"

"I guess." I lay back, letting the Mediterranean sun drench my skin.

"You guess?" Something in her voice made me look at her. Bryn's blue eyes were narrowed, searching. "What's going on?"

I ground my teeth. "Well . . . it's just . . . I . . ."

"Spit it out," she said.

"I wanted to try something. I need to . . ." *God, this is so hard.*

"You need to what?" Ansel was gazing at me; worry furrowed his brow.

"I need to talk about my feelings," I finally blurted out, and instantly felt blood rushing into my cheeks. I was sure my face mirrored the crushed velvet red of the nearby roses.

Ansel and Bryn both burst out laughing.

"Thanks," I growled. "Your support is duly noted."

"Sorry, Cal," Bryn said, grinning and wiping a tear from her cheek. "It's just . . . you're adorable."

"Adorable?!" I showed her my fangs. "I need help!"

"We'll help." Ansel was still laughing. "But it's hilarious to watch you squirm just because you want to talk to us. Talking to their friends is what people do, Calla."

"It's not what I do," I snarled. "I like to handle things on my own."

"We know." Bryn stopped smiling. "That means something's really gotten to you."

"Sure does," Ansel said. "What's up?"

Heat flooded my cheeks again. I stared at the path's paving stones.

"Oh . . . oh," Bryn said. I glanced up to see her and Ansel share a meaningful look.

"Oh God." I buried my face in my hands.

Bryn kissed Ansel on the cheek and came over to me. "Scoot. I need to sit here."

I made a place for her on the bench.

"Do you want this to just be girl talk or can your brother stay?" she asked.

"He stays," I said quickly. "I need to hear what both of you think."

"About your love life?" Ansel teased.

"You know I'm not above biting you—" I started, and instantly regretted my words.

His eyes clouded for a minute, but he forced a smile. "I'll just muzzle you if you start acting like a rabid animal."

"Enough," Bryn interrupted. "Time for serious. What's on your mind?"

Who's on my mind is the better question.

"I don't know," I said. "I just feel . . . confused."

"About what?" Bryn lowered her voice. "About sleeping with Shay? Do you think it was a mistake?"

I blushed, glancing at Ansel. He was grinning like a fool again.

"No," I said. "I'm not sorry. But I don't know that it really changed anything."

Ansel's grin faded. "You're saying you want to be with Ren?"

"Did you ever want to be with Ren?" Bryn peered at me like I was a specimen under a microscope. My skin felt hot, uncomfortable, and I didn't think it was the warmth of the sun causing it.

"I never gave it much thought," I said, edging away from her, trying to give myself room to breathe. "I just always assumed I'd be with him."

"But Shay—" Bryn said slowly.

"You said you loved him." Ansel's words sounded almost like an accusation.

"I do." I met his gaze, knowing the price he'd paid for that love. "I didn't lie about that, An. I love Shay. I want to be with him."

"So what's the problem?"

I curled my fingers around the side of the stone bench. "I don't know if he belongs with me." When I said it out loud, my heart gave an unpleasant thud, like a stone dropping against my rib cage.

"I don't understand," Bryn said. "He loves you. It's obvious."

"I know," I said. "But he's the Scion. I think . . . I think it might be changing him."

Bryn tilted her head. "He was different? After he got the sword?"

I nodded. An awkward silence settled on us, broken only by the sound of birds chirping above our heads and the rustle of leaves in the breeze.

"I never thought about that," Ansel said finally.

Bryn couldn't meet my gaze. "Me neither."

I bit my lip, taking a long, slow breath. "So what do I do?"

"Do you still want Ren?"

I listened to my own heartbeat for a minute before answering. "Yes."

"That's one hot mess, Cal." Ansel smiled at me. I almost snapped at him before I realized he was trying to lighten the mood.

"You sound like Mason," I said, making a weak attempt at laughter.

"Well, he *is* my best friend," Ansel said.

Bryn took my hand. "Calla, Ren's an alpha, but so is Shay. It makes sense that you'd be drawn to both of them. You and Ren have a lot of history, which has to make this even harder."

"Is there an answer somewhere in there?" I forced myself to laugh, squeezing her fingers.

"She's telling you there isn't an answer," Ansel said, smiling when Bryn blew him a kiss.

"There isn't an answer?" I couldn't figure out why they looked so happy. This was what they considered helping me? Then I remembered: they were still basking in puppy love. Why couldn't I have puppy love? I only seemed to have "I can't decide if I want to rip your throat out or kiss you" love. Ugh.

"There isn't an answer yet," Ansel continued. "Ren and Shay both love you. They both could be your mate."

"That doesn't mean they both will be your mate." Bryn giggled. "I don't think they're that kinky . . . but you might be able to talk them into it."

"Bryn!" I shoved her off the bench.

"Nice one." Ansel doubled over laughing.

"I hate you guys," I said, still mortified. "No wonder I don't talk about my feelings."

"You don't hate us." Bryn smiled. "You love us. And we love you."

"We always will, Calla," Ansel said. "We can't tell you the answer because you're the only one who can figure this out. You have to choose."

"Though I'd try to hold off until this war sorts itself out," Bryn said. "If Ren is fitting in with the Searchers, we can't afford to lose him. And Shay—well, if he leaves, the war is over before it starts."

"I know," I said. I guessed I was stuck in the same place as I'd been since Shay first appeared in my life, caught between two loves, two destinies. And it didn't look like I'd be getting out of this fix for a while.

"But we'll be here for you," Bryn continued. "We love you no matter what you decide."

"Thanks," I said.

"Those guys can duke it out forever," Ansel said. "But you're our one and only, Cal. You're the alpha."

This time I couldn't stop it. Tears snuck out of the corner of my eyes.

"Hey, look." Ansel smiled. "She really does have feelings!"

"Shut up." I laughed, brushing the streaks of salt water off my cheeks. "And thanks."

"No problem." He stood up. He was still smiling, but his gaze had a hard edge. I was still puzzling over his expression when I heard Tess shout.

"Who's thirsty?" She waved, beckoning to us and pointing toward a wrought-iron gazebo.

"That doesn't look like lemonade," Bryn said. "That looks like a picnic."

"Tess rocks." Ansel ran toward the promise of lunch, forsaking us for the good of his stomach.

Bryn put her arm around my waist. "He's really getting better. I think it's going to be okay."

"Good," I said, leaning my head on her shoulder.

For the first time in a long, long while my heart unclenched, my muscles relaxed. I didn't know where love would lead me, but my pack would always be at my side. More than anything else, that was what mattered.

WATER

PART II

NINE

PLANS FOR RETRIEVING Eydis—the water hilt—
were already in motion. The Roving Academy's halls were buzzing
with excitement. Even the threads in the walls seemed to sparkle a
bit brighter, as if lit with hope after our successful retrieval of the first
sword.

"Eydis is in the Yucatán." Ren was walking beside me after dinner. "They're setting up our staging ground with the Eydis Guide—
her name is Inez. The hideout is in Tulúm. Anika thinks we all need
a good night's sleep before making the next strike. So we're leaving
tomorrow afternoon."

"Not the morning?" I asked.

He shook his head. "She said something about the tides not
being right. I didn't quite follow."

"So I guess you've become the Guardian point person for the
Searchers," I said. "Nice work, alpha."

"Thanks." He smiled, but caught me with a sidelong glance.
"That okay with you?"

"It's who you are," I said, trying to keep my voice neutral. "And
the more Searchers that trust us, the better."

"Agreed."

In the space of hours we'd been back, I'd already noticed the
change rippling through the Academy. Prior to the strike on Tordis

most Searchers had eyed me with curiosity at best, outrage at worst. Now that outrage had become curiosity while the curiosity had grown into outright admiration. A few Searchers had even stopped me in the hall to thank me for joining them. I was a little thrown by all of it.

Ren stopped walking; I frowned at him and then realized we were standing in front of my door.

"This is you," he said in a tight voice. I wondered how he knew where my room was. Had he just noted my lingering scent at this spot, or had he taken the time to find out where I was staying?

"Sleep, huh?" I avoided his gaze. "Well, I'm exhausted, so I'll be happy to follow Anika's orders."

"Calla, I have to ask you something."

My heart started to climb up my throat. I forced myself to look at him. "Yeah?"

He fixed me with a hard stare. "Let me come."

"What?" I managed to choke out only that word. Come where? In the room? To sleep with me? My hands began to shake.

"Tomorrow," he said. "Anika's mission only has one team and she told me you're leading it because you're the one Shay trusts."

"Oh!" I laughed as my stomach stopped flipping. "I guess . . ."

"What?" He looked puzzled when I hesitated.

It was my turn to stare him down. "I need to know if I can trust you."

He leaned against my door. I couldn't tell if he was hurt or angry. Or both.

"You don't trust me."

"With Shay," I finished.

His jaw clenched, but he didn't speak.

"Shay is the Scion." I kept my voice steady. "He's the central part of the mission. If he gets in trouble, I need to be sure . . ."

He pushed himself off the door, glaring at me. "You think I would intentionally let Shay get hurt? Or that I might hurt him myself?"

"You've threatened him before." I could barely stop myself from shouting. When it came to Shay, all my defensive instincts kicked in with a fury. "More times than I can count!"

"That's different, Calla." His voice was growing louder too, gaining a few glances from Searchers passing in the hall. "That's here. That's about us. War has different rules. I would never—"

He stopped speaking, fists clenched, and took a deep breath. "I would never risk someone as important as the Scion in the field." He spit the words. "I understand what's at stake."

I forced my temper down, swallowing its bitterness. I knew he was speaking the truth. "Fine. I believe you. You can come."

Ren's fists were still balled up; the veins in his forearms throbbed. I reached out, but he pulled away.

"Don't." He didn't meet my eyes.

It felt like he'd punched me in the gut, and part of me wished he had. I'd rather fight with Ren than see this loss written on his face.

"Ren," I whispered. "I'm glad you want to come. I need you tomorrow."

He turned to look at me, and I caught a sudden flare in the darkness of his eyes. "Only tomorrow?"

I swallowed hard, not able to break from his gaze but not able to speak either.

One corner of his mouth twitched into a crooked smile. He reached up, placing his fingers under my jaw so lightly I could barely feel the touch.

"Thanks, Lily." His fingers moved up over my chin to rest on my lips. His other hand took mine; it wasn't until he was gazing at my fingers that I realized his thumb was circling the sapphire of the ring I wore. The ring he'd given me. "Good night."

He turned and walked down the hall. I watched until he was out of sight, wondering where his room was and pretending I wasn't wondering about where his room was. I leaned against my door, turning the knob, and let myself fall rather than walk into the room. These missions, this work of remaking the world, made for a weariness like nothing I'd felt before. It wasn't just the physical strain, it was the weight of emotion that we shouldered on this path. And Shay shouldered the most weight of all. As I collapsed onto my bed, I wondered if he was okay. He'd been shuttered with Anika and Silas most of the day, reviewing the lore of the Elemental Cross. After that, he'd gone with Ethan, Connor, and Adne for more combat practice. He had one of the swords now, and they'd wasted no time getting him used to the new weapon.

Had he finished? Was he in his own room now, like me, staring up at a night sky so clouded that you couldn't see any stars or even a hint of moonlight? A part of me wanted to go to him, to find him in his room like I had last night. Sleeping with his body curled next to mine offered a sense of comfort unlike any other, and lying in bed without him provoked an ache deep within me. I rolled out of bed, taking a few steps toward the door before growling my frustration and flinging myself back on the mattress. Twisting blankets around me like a cocoon, I dug my fingers into the coverlet. I couldn't go to Shay now, no matter how magnetic his pull seemed. And he hadn't come looking for me, which stung more than I wanted to admit.

My heart and mind were constantly chasing conflicting impulses. I didn't want to seek out one or the other of the two alphas only to slink away from his bed the next morning. Last night with Shay had been selfish, and I couldn't indulge those tendencies any longer. Especially since Ren had proven his value to the Searchers today. I hadn't been lying to him—I needed him tomorrow. Beyond that . . . I couldn't go there. Not yet.

I didn't remember falling asleep, but I woke in a tangle of sheets that showed me how restless the night had been. Bleary-eyed and more than a little cranky, I decided the best solution was a long shower.

The added possibility of an omelet overfilled with the abundance of the Searchers' garden managed to perk me up a little.

Despite the trudge to the baths, the facilities were impressive. I stood under a wide spout that drenched me in warm water, the pressure not unlike a waterfall. Using the salt scrub I'd picked out—one of many washes and oils lined up in etched-crystal containers on slender teak shelves outside the showers—I scoured myself, trying to wash away lingering sleep. The scent of lavender and mint that infused the scrub helped; there were a variety of scents among the jars. All of which carried the freshness of flowers and herbs. Clearly the Academy gardens provided more than just food and medicinal creations for the Searchers. Bryn must have been overjoyed by this bounty—I was surprised she wasn't in the baths all day.

Stepping out of the shower, I wrapped a towel around my body and headed back toward the room where I'd stowed my clothes. When I stepped out of the thick steam into the open space between the baths and the changing rooms, I froze. For a moment I wondered if I was dreaming, but the water dripping from my hair onto my shoulders and collarbone told me I wasn't.

"Hey." My heart leapt into my throat. Ren was standing in front of me, his chest bare. He finished securing a towel low around his hips, and a pile of clothes lay folded on a chair next to him. He glanced back at the door to the baths. "Did I . . . uh . . . is this a girls' bathroom? I was here yesterday and I didn't see . . . uh . . . "

"There are separate dressing rooms over there." I laughed despite the awkwardness. "I think the Searchers just share the showers."

"How progressive of them." Ren grinned. His eyes slid over my water-slick limbs. "You look squeaky clean, Lily."

"Yeah." I inched toward the dressing room door. Unfortunately that meant getting closer to Ren. I could smell the warmth of his skin, the spicy scent of his sweat mixing with the lavender-tinged oil that lingered on my skin. "I'll get out of your way."

"You could stay." He caught my arm, turning me toward him.

His smile curved wickedly. "Wash my back."

I was having a hard enough time not staring at Ren's front. Meeting his eyes didn't make it any easier. "You know I can't."

"Do I?" he said, pulling me closer. "Because I'm pretty sure I don't know that."

"Stop." I didn't trust myself. There was far too much steam rising from the thermal pools and far too little fabric covering our bodies.

He released me with a sigh. The devilish smile vanished, leaving his features drawn.

"I don't blame you for doing it," he said, though he dropped his head back to lean against the wall, staring at the ceiling instead of looking at me. "I deserve it. After what I did to you."

"What are you talking about?" I asked.

"For choosing him . . . I don't blame you."

"I didn't choose him," I said, backing toward the dressing room door. "I told you both, I'm not making a choice while we're at war."

He looked straight at me, and it was like an arrow in my chest. "That's not what I meant."

Despite the heat of the room, my skin prickled with goose bumps. "What do you mean?"

"I don't blame you for choosing him to be your first." He sounded more sad than angry.

My limbs were trembling. I didn't speak, but he pulled a question out of my gaze.

"Sabine told me."

"She didn't have the right—"

"You shouldn't be mad at her," he said, laughing darkly. "She chewed me out. Told me I'd lost you. That I was basically an arrogant moron and I deserved whatever I got. And that didn't include you."

I tore my gaze from him. "That's not really about you. She's been upset ever since—"

"Cosette," he said. "I know. After she was done yelling at me, we ended up talking. She's broken up about it. I can't blame her. I wish Dax and Fey were here."

"If it weren't sad, it would be funny," I said, leaning on the wall next to him.

"How's that?"

"Fey and Dax were our strongest warriors," I said. "But in the end they were too afraid to fight for themselves."

Ren nodded.

"I didn't sleep with Shay to get back at you." I spoke so quietly I didn't know if Ren had heard me. "I . . . he . . ."

When he didn't answer for another minute, I was sure he hadn't. But then he cleared his throat.

"I know you have feelings for him. That's obvious," he said. "But are you serious about not making a choice until the war ends?"

"I . . . yes." I had to be. If I chose either Ren or Shay to be the alpha at my side, the other wolf would leave. It was the way of alphas. Once one of them won their place, the other would be exiled, unable to tolerate a subordinate position within the pack. I couldn't afford for that to happen. It also chilled my blood to even think about either of them leaving.

"Then I need you to know something." He suddenly turned to face me. His forearms rested against the wall on either side of my shoulders, boxing me in.

"Don't." I didn't trust myself to be this close to him. I'd already slipped up with Shay, letting myself give in when I'd promised that I'd keep my distance. If I did the same with Ren, I wouldn't be able to live with myself. And part of me knew I wanted Ren to touch me now because I'd spent last night alone in a fitful half slumber, hoping Shay would knock softly at my door. But he never had. The further Shay was drawn into the Searchers' world, the more he slipped away from me.

"Just listen, Calla." His eyes wouldn't let me go. "Do you remember when we were at Eden?"

I nodded, too uneasy to speak. I didn't know if I'd even be able to hear my own words over the pounding of my heart. That night at Eden felt like a lifetime ago; I couldn't imagine why Ren would bring it up now.

"You asked if I was afraid of anything," he said.

"I remember." I pulled my lower lip between my teeth as the memory caught in my mind. "You said one thing."

"One thing." He leaned down to whisper in my ear. "Only one thing that I'd always been afraid of. I still am."

My body was frozen against the wall, locked in place by his words. "What?"

His voice quaked. "That you could never love me. Not really."

"Ren—" My hands were shaking.

"I couldn't miss the whispers," he said. "The way some of the Banes looked at me. The way my father . . . I mean, Emile . . . talked about my mother. She was dead, but it was like he still hated her. It was obvious, even to me, that when they were together he ruled her, but there wasn't any love."

My breath became shallow. I didn't know if I could bear to hear this, but I couldn't bring myself to stop him.

His lips were brushing my ear. "The first time I saw you, when we were promised to each other, I swore I wouldn't force you to love me, but I would find a way to win you."

Something inside me snapped. "If you wanted to win me, why did you spend all of high school dating other girls?"

There was more spite in my question than I'd anticipated. All that waiting, not being able to follow my own passions while I watched Ren chasing his. I resented it. It made his confession seem unfair and maybe even untrue.

He leaned his forehead against my temple. "I thought if you saw other girls wanting me, but knew that I only really wanted you, it would make a difference."

A soft growl rose in my throat. "Sabine's right. You are a moron."

"Would it help if I agreed with you?" He smiled, but his eyes were hard.

I turned my face away from him, anger, hope, desire all battling within me. "You could have told me how you felt."

"I was going to," he said. "I wanted to tell you when I gave you the ring . . . but I choked."

I looked at him, saw he was blushing, and knew everything he'd said was true.

"I . . ." Words wouldn't come. What could I even say?

"All I'm asking for is a fair shot. Or maybe a fresh start, but I needed you to know where I'm coming from," he said. "I know the odds are against me. Shay swooped in and changed your life. He saved you."

"I saved him. And myself."

"I just meant that he's been the hero all along. Of course you'd want him. But the history we have, our past. Not all of it was bad."

"I know that."

"You can't tell me that when we were at the house, alone, a part of you didn't want to stay."

I gripped the towel tighter so I wouldn't drop it. He was right. At least partly. I was still drawn to him—the one who was so obviously my counterpart. The mate I'd thought I would spend my life with. I was afraid to let go of the past that kept us bound together. That road was familiar. I knew what life with Ren would be, where I fit into that picture, and that I cared deeply for him. The temptation to keep him close nipped at me relentlessly.

"We were always meant for each other, Calla," he said, and I shivered, feeling as if he'd read my mind. "Let me show you what it could be like." His lips barely touched mine. I couldn't resist any longer and let my fingers trace the contours of his chest. He growled softly, twisting his hands in my damp hair as he kissed me. My fingers slid down, skimming his abdomen, finding the edge of the towel wrapped around his hips. He kissed me harder, urging me on.

The bathroom door swung open and Connor swaggered in, shirtless and wearing pajama pants, with a towel slung over one shoulder. He stopped whistling when he caught sight of Ren's bare back and me pressed up against the wall.

"Oh gods! My eyes!" Connor covered his face. "My innocence!"

"Shut up, Connor," I said, both relieved and disappointed by the interruption. I squirmed out from under Ren, pretty much leapt across the open area to the dressing room door, and flung myself inside. Pulling on my clothes in a rush before fleeing from the bathroom, I was mortified. As I hurried down the hall, past more sleepy-eyed Searchers heading for a hot shower, I tried to tell myself I couldn't still hear Connor laughing.

TEN

MY STOMACH WAS RUMBLING, but I was still on edge from my chance encounter with Ren in the baths. I couldn't risk running into Shay when my feelings were so scattered . . . and when it was likely Ren's scent was clinging to my skin.

Damn it, Calla. Why can't you stay away from him? From either of them?

I'd learned how powerful desire was, and love even more so, but it still frustrated me that I could lose control when my blood ran hot.

Since I'd nixed the idea of joining the Haldis team for breakfast, I headed into the courtyard in search of fresh fruit. Considering how early it was, I was surprised to find Ansel picking oranges from a small grove.

"Morning." He smiled at me.

"Any chance I could get one of those?" I said, pointing at his half-full basket.

"Sure." He tossed me one.

"You're up early." I began to peel the orange.

His shoulders tensed. "Sleeping isn't easy."

I chewed on a segment of the fruit, enjoying the bright burst of citrus on my tongue. The orange was juicy, perfect.

Ansel stayed quiet, pulling oranges off the branches.

"You seem better," I said slowly.

"Do I?"

I coughed, choking a little on the orange juice. Ansel's voice had that tinny quality that had made my bones ache when we'd first learned how the Keepers had punished him.

"You're not . . . feeling okay?" I asked.

He turned to face me. While his eyes weren't hollow, the way they'd been in Denver, they were hopeless.

"I'll never be okay, Calla," he said, turning an orange in his hands. "Not really."

"But . . ." I stared at him, wishing he wouldn't say things like that. Wanting to believe this was some sort of self-pity . . . but I knew it wasn't. "But Bryn."

"I love Bryn," he said. "And I can't stand seeing her in pain."

I watched his face. He looked older than the little brother I knew. Older and angrier.

"You're pretending to be okay so you don't hurt her."

He nodded. "She seems to think she still loves me. I tried to break it off, but she wouldn't listen."

"Don't you want to be with her?" I asked.

"I'll always love her," Ansel said. "But I'm not a good match for her. She deserves more."

"How can you say that?" I wanted to scream at him but with a lot of effort forced an even tone. "You're the same person."

"I'm not." Ansel squeezed the orange, his fingernails digging into its peel. "Believe me. I'm not."

"Yes, you are," I said. "And Bryn loves you."

"I'm not her equal, not anymore. You can't have a match without a true partnership. You of all people should understand that."

"Of course I do." I frowned. "But you're wrong about this. I already told you, Searchers and Guardians have been together in the past. They've had families."

"I know." Ansel's smile was spiteful. "I've heard. From you. From

Tess. Searchers and Guardians. Monroe and Corrine. Him and her, her and him."

"So what's the problem?" I'd crushed the rest of the orange segments in my fist. Juice leaked out between my knuckles. "It works. That was real love, real partnerships. People died for them."

"It's not the same," he said, lowering his gaze.

"Why?"

"Because I wasn't born a Searcher. I don't have their power." He looked at me again, gray eyes furious like a storm. "All I am is less than what I was. And I can't ever be more. Eventually Bryn will realize that. And she'll leave. It will be for the best."

"What if she doesn't?" I stared at the pulped mess of orange lying in my palm and felt like I could be staring at Ansel's ravaged heart. "What if she wants to be with you and have a family?"

"Where I'd play dad to a pack of wolf pups?"

"That's how it works," I said.

"I know," he said. "Tess explained that whole essence-of-the-mother thing. But the biology or magic or whatever it is doesn't matter. It's not whether Bryn and I are able to be together or make a family. It's about whether we should be."

"Just give it time, Ansel." I didn't know what else to say. I hated the desperation in his voice, the finality.

"I promise I'll never hurt Bryn," he said. "I won't tell her how I really feel. I'll be with her when she needs me, and when she wants to, I'll let her go."

We stood there, staring at each other. There was nothing else to say.

Ansel smiled, all emptiness, handing me another orange. "You still need to eat your breakfast. You murdered the first orange."

"Thanks." I managed to push the word past the thickness of my throat.

"There you are!" Bryn's voice turned me around. She was

skipping up the path, beaming. "Sorry—I took an extra-long shower. All-natural heaven! The Searchers really should find a way to market that stuff. I'm going to talk to Tess about it. Smell my skin—I'm roses and thyme!"

He turned to her and I saw it happen. The mask went up, transforming my broken brother into the Ansel we'd always known.

I couldn't be there, not in that moment. I didn't want my face to give anything away to Bryn. Making an excuse about having to meet with Anika, I hurried away from them, trying to distract myself by scarfing down my orange. But I'd only made it halfway across the garden when I ran into another reminder of how unsettled everything in my life had become.

Connor lounged on a stone bench next to the path. His shirt was unbuttoned. His chest, carved hard muscle, was crisscrossed by scars. Scars that I recognized.

I thought about turning around but realized I needed to clear the air or at least my own conscience with him.

"So how many Guardians do you think you've killed?"

"I've been trying to cut back," he answered without opening his eyes. "But they've all been kind enough to leave me souvenirs, as you can see." He brushed his hand across the scarred flesh.

I crouched on the bench next to him, letting sunlight warm my neck and shoulders. My pulse had set off at a gallop, but I forced myself to follow through on what I wanted to say.

"About what you saw this morning . . ." The gentle warmth I'd felt became a prickling heat as blood rushed into my neck and cheeks.

"Hey, no judgment," Connor said. He folded his arms behind his head, tilting his face up so he could peer at me. "Though if we lose the Scion because you can't keep your pants on, there'll be hell to pay. Literally."

When I snarled, he laughed.

"I wasn't ever going to ask you about your steamy rendezvous, sweet cheeks," he said. "You're the one who brought it up."

I wrapped my arms around my shins, resting my chin on my knees. "I just wanted you to understand."

He sat up, one corner of his mouth crinkling. "Understand what, exactly?"

"That Shay, Ren, and I are in a complicated situation."

"Complicated, eh?" His smile widened. "I thought it was all pretty clear. Two guys get you hot. You're going to have to choose one."

"That's not all—"

Connor cut me off with a wave of his hand. "Sure, there's always the nitty-gritty details, but it boils down to the basics. One of you, two of them. Love's a bitch."

"Nice." I wished I could call him a liar, but his reduction of my life story was a little too logical.

"Look, sweetheart, I can't cast any stones. Just callin' it like I see it." He pushed his chestnut hair out of his face. It was still damp from the shower. He'd already begun to tan after a few days under the Mediterranean sun. The bronze of his skin made the white zags of scar tissue appear to leap off his chest.

"You mean all your awesome pickup lines are just talk?" I grinned. "Who'd have guessed?"

He threw a sidelong glance at me but didn't answer.

"You know what I think?"

One of his eyebrows went up.

I leaned toward him. "I think all that off-color chatter of yours is just a way to distract you from the fact that there's only one person you're interested in."

"You really think I'm a one-woman kinda guy?" Connor smiled, but his eyes were hard.

I held his gaze. "I think you're in love with Adne."

He was the first to look away, staring at a nearby bubbling fountain.

"I made a mistake with Adne," he said quietly, withdrawing into his own thoughts. "About a year ago."

"A mistake?" I frowned. "Oh . . . you mean you slept with her."

His answering laugh was cold. "No."

"You didn't sleep with her?" I couldn't understand the mocking tilt of his smile.

"I definitely did not," he said. "And I think that was the mistake."

"You lost me."

He swung his legs over the side of the bench, resting his arms on his thighs. "Adne was just a kid when I met her. I was sixteen. Cocky as hell."

"Yeah, you've totally transformed since then."

He smiled, but not at me. "She was having a rough time."

"She told me," I said, remembering Adne's description of how Connor had been the friend she needed after her mother had died.

Connor was watching me, alarm rising in his eyes. "What did she tell you?"

I frowned as I saw the color drain from his cheeks. "Just that you joked around with her after she lost her mom."

"Oh . . . right." Connor returned to his casual pose.

"But you'd better be about to tell me what you thought she said."

He shook his head, but spoke quietly. "She's sixteen."

"I know that."

He glanced at me. "Last year she was fifteen . . . and I was twenty. We always get together around the winter solstice. Ethan, Kyle, Stuart, and I came in from the Denver outpost. Adne had a break from her classes."

I nodded. So far none of this seemed extraordinary.

"After the celebration—big feast, lots of drinking and dancing—I was headed to my room to crash. Adne asked if she could hang out with me for a while."

My pulse picked up speed. I could see where this was going, and I was nervous for both of them.

Connor rubbed the back of his neck. "She didn't exactly have talking in mind. And she made a pretty strong case for what she did have in mind."

"She tried to reel you in?" It wasn't hard to see Adne going after what she wanted.

"Yeah. Pretty much."

"And you said no?" That was the part I was having a hard time believing.

"She was fifteen," he said.

"I guess." Fifteen was young, but Adne was an old soul. I didn't exactly think Connor would have been taking advantage. I also couldn't see Adne being easily deterred when she decided she wanted something.

"And Monroe's daughter."

"Oh." That made sense.

"When I tried to explain why I thought 'us' would be a bad idea, she didn't take it well."

"I can imagine." I was actually imagining flying objects, breaking glass, and possibly Connor with a black eye. "So was this before or after the bet with Silas?"

He drew a quick breath. "She told you about the bet."

"She said nothing came of it."

"The bet was first, but only by a few hours," he said. "What came of it was that Adne and I couldn't dance around each other anymore. The moment I kissed her, I couldn't . . ."

"You couldn't pretend you weren't in love with her."

He tossed an unfriendly glance my way.

"It's pretty obvious," I said.

"I couldn't pretend to myself," he said. "But I thought it was best to keep pretending to her."

"I think you're wrong." My own mind had wandered back to Ren's confession. If I'd known how he'd really felt about me, would our lives have been different? Thoughts of Shay chased after that question. Did I want the past to be different? I couldn't imagine Shay's absence. My heart ached at the thought of never having fallen in love with him.

"Maybe." Connor stood up and stretched. "It certainly hasn't gone the way I'd hoped."

"What did you hope for?" I asked. "Do you want to see Adne with someone else?"

The sudden stab of his glare told me that was the last thing he wanted.

I held my ground. "Then you'd better do something about it."

"I'll make you a deal." He smiled slowly. "I'll sort out me and Adne when you pick your boy."

"That's not fair." I was on my feet, matching his steady gaze.

"All's fair in love and war," Connor replied, turning to walk up the path. I guess that meant our conversation was over.

"So what?" I called after him. "You're doing nothing?"

"I'm following your lead, alpha." He turned, walking backward and grinning at me.

"What does that mean?" My hands were on my hips.

"It means I'm going to win this war." He saluted. "Romance will have to wait."

I stared after him, frustrated by the conversation. But at least I had a little more insight into Connor and Adne's history.

"Calla!" I turned to see Bryn waving to me with Ansel hovering at her heels, his basket of oranges full to brimming. Mason was with them.

"What is it?" I asked when I reached them.

"We've got to head down to the stockade," she said.

"The stockade?" I asked. "Why?"

Mason looked at me and sighed. "Logan wants a meeting."

ELEVEN

LOGAN'S QUARTERS bore a much closer resemblance to an actual cell than Ansel's room had. I took more than a little pleasure at that observation, though I still bristled as we entered the small space. We'd all been quiet on the walk from the garden to the stockade. These rooms, used for prisoners, were located on the ground level of the Academy—set apart from the livelier sections of the Searchers' institution. While Mason had assured me that Anika would be present, this meeting didn't sit well with me. It was too familiar. Logan had something to tell his pack. We'd been summoned, just as if he were still our master. From the stiff way Mason moved down the halls, I could tell he wasn't happy about this development either. I couldn't blame him.

What had surprised me a little was that Ansel had insisted on coming with us.

"For moral support," he'd said, with a glance at Mason, when I asked him why. If there was anyone who would have more reason to hate Logan—or any of the Keepers—than Mason, it was my brother.

Shay was waiting for us outside the doorway. When the four of us entered, Logan looked far too comfortable even as he lounged on a twin mattress that featured a single pillow and undyed wool blanket, propping himself up on one elbow while smoking a clove cigarette.

Ren, Sabine, and Nev were already in the room. Anika and Ethan stood just behind the three wolves, Ethan watching Logan suspiciously while Anika's expression was more curious.

"Wonderful." Logan smiled at us, tapping ash into an empty glass on the floor.

"Bite me," I snarled. Logan might expect business as usual, but I wouldn't let him. He wasn't our master any longer and I was going to make sure he knew that.

Bryn drew a quick breath, but Mason smiled. Logan's eyes widened momentarily, but then he recomposed his face into a placid mask.

"Calla, I don't expect your affection, but we certainly can still be civil."

"You're a prisoner," I said. "Civility is off the table. What's this meeting for?"

He cleared his throat. "Two reasons. And thank you for coming."

"Calla's right," Ren said. "Drop the show, Logan. Just talk."

"Isn't everyone in a temper." Logan put out the cigarette and sighed. "My last one."

"Good," Mason said.

Logan glanced at him and my heart skipped a beat.

"Don't look at him." Nev crossed the room, shielding Mason from Logan's view. "Don't ever look at him again or I'll claw your eyes out."

"I'm fine," Mason whispered, but he'd gone pale. Ansel shoved his hands in his pockets, staring at the floor.

For the first time, Logan's voice lost its clear, imperious tone. "Well, that gets us to the first thing. . . . I want to offer an apology."

No one spoke, but everyone stared at the Keeper.

It was Shay who finally broke the silence. "An apology?"

"Despite my imprisonment, I've come to respect the strength, loyalty, and most of all resilience of your pack bonds. I tried to take advantage of your loyalty to the Keepers, and I'm sorry I let my inheritance go to my head."

"Go to your head?" Nev growled, the air around him swirling, growing hot. "You think that's all it takes to make up for what you were going to do?"

I took a step toward him. As much as we hated Logan, attacking him when he was the Searchers' prisoner wasn't an option.

"Of course not," Logan continued. He threw a pleading look at Anika, who moved between the Keeper and Nev.

"Please remain calm." She rested her hand on the sword hilt at her waist.

"You have no idea . . ." Nev glared at her.

"Leave it." Mason grabbed Nev's shoulder, drawing him back. "He's not worth it."

"And what about me?" I turned in surprise. Ansel was walking toward Logan slowly, his hands still hidden in his pockets. "Do I get an apology?"

Logan tilted his head, frowning. "I suppose. . . ."

"You suppose?" Ansel began to laugh. A thin, horrible sound. "You killed my mother. You might as well have killed me for all that you left alive."

"You look quite well to me," Logan said. "And as for your mother, that wasn't my—"

His words became a shriek as Ansel lunged, pulling pruning shears from his pocket and swinging his arm down with all the force he could muster. Ansel was fast, but Anika's reflexes were even faster. She dove forward, wrapping her arms around Ansel's waist. Thrown off balance, Ansel's blow left a long gash along Logan's shoulder. Unchecked, it would have pierced his throat.

"Ethan!" Anika jerked Ansel around and shoved him into Ethan's waiting arms. "Get him out of here. Find Tess. We'll deal with this later."

Ethan hauled Ansel out the door. Sabine didn't even bother to make an excuse. She simply followed Ethan without another word.

I started to go after them, but Bryn caught my arm. "I'll help. You need to be here—something's going on. I'm not sure what, but Logan has a bigger issue on his mind. I'll stay with Ansel."

Part of me wanted to argue. Ansel was a live wire, dangerous and unpredictable. I wanted to talk him down. But I also knew that Tess and Bryn were probably the better ones to soothe my brother. He still viewed me as part of the reason he was no longer a Guardian.

"I'm going too," Mason said, taking Bryn's hand. "I just can't be here."

"You want me to come?" Nev asked.

Mason shook his head. "I'll be okay. Fill me in later."

"Is someone going to help me?" Logan's hand was pressed against his shoulder. "I'm bleeding!"

"It looks good on you," Ren said.

"I'm sure Ethan will send an Elixir," Anika said calmly. "You won't bleed out in the meantime."

Logan's eyes bulged.

"What else do you have to tell us, Logan?" I asked. "Because an apology is pretty much a waste of our time. Your words don't hold much stock with us."

"Fine." Logan straightened as much as he could while still cradling his injured shoulder. "I want to help you."

"Help us how?" Shay asked.

"I'm more interested in the why than the how," Ren said.

Logan smiled, regaining some of his confidence. "Like I said before, I've come to respect your skills, and I've learned quite a bit about the Searchers."

"Have you?" Anika folded her arms across her chest.

"Only by accident," Logan said. "The entire building has been buzzing with news of your last mission."

He looked at Shay, his eyes wandering up to the sword strapped across Shay's back. "Congratulations."

Shay shifted on his feet, regarding Logan warily.

"This turn of events has forced me to consider my own position," Logan continued. "I'm a betting man, and I'd wager that your side will win this war."

Though I didn't want to, I gasped. That was the last thing I'd expected Logan to say.

"You're hardly a man," Nev spat, unaffected by the gravity of Logan's statement. "You're a spoiled, arrogant boy and now you're afraid. That's all."

"That's true," Logan said. "Well—the part about being afraid. I'm going to ignore the rest of what you said . . . for civility's sake."

"You're afraid?" I asked, not quite able to keep the smile off my face. A Keeper afraid of Guardians. That might have been the best thing I'd ever heard.

"Of course I am." Logan met my eyes and I knew he wasn't lying. "The writing is on the wall. It probably was the moment you stopped Shay's sacrifice at Samhain. He has one of the swords. He'll soon wield the Elemental Cross."

"And the Keepers will be no more," Anika said.

Logan shrugged. "The odds seem to be stacking in your favor."

"You don't seem too upset at your impending doom." Ren's laughter was cold.

"That's because I'm hoping to alter my own fate," Logan said.

"And how would you do that?" Shay asked. "Your legacy isn't working for you."

"Actually . . ." Logan smiled slowly. "I believe it will."

Anika was standing directly over Logan, staring down at him. "What are you offering?"

"In the final battle when you face Bosque," Logan said. "It needs to be at the Rift's current location. Correct?"

Anika nodded.

"I know where it is."

"We can simply force you to tell us that," Anika said.

"But you know that's not enough." Logan was smiling now. "Don't you?"

Anika didn't reply, but her eyes narrowed.

"The location you could probably figure out for yourself. Even if it took longer than you'd like," Logan continued. "It's at Rowan Estate, after all."

"We suspected it might be," Anika said, but the Guardians were exchanging puzzled glances.

"What is the Rift?" Ren asked.

"The gateway by which the Harbinger and his minions entered this world," Anika replied. "It was opened at the turn of the fifteenth century, but the beast moved it at his pleasure, so we were never certain where its current location might be."

"And the gateway has to be closed," Shay said slowly. "That's how you win the war."

Anika smiled at him grimly. "That is part of how we win."

"It's also how you get your parents back," Logan added.

"What?" Shay whirled, staring at him.

"The Rift can only remain open by way of a ritual sacrifice," Logan said. "That sacrifice, for the time being, was your parents."

Shay's jaw clenched. "You said my parents were alive."

"They are." Logan glanced at Anika. "I don't suppose you could get me some more cigarettes?"

"That depends on what else you have to say," Anika said. She put a hand on Shay's shoulder, pulling him back from Logan. "How are Tristan and Sarah Doran alive if they were sacrificed to open the Rift?"

"Bosque Mar is very creative when it comes to torment," Logan said. Shay winced and I wanted to go to him, but now was neither the place nor the time.

"We're aware of that," Anika said.

Logan paused, lifting his hand to check his wound. The gash was no longer bleeding. He gingerly leaned back against the pillow. "He wanted Tristan to suffer for his betrayal, so he concocted a punishment that would force Tristan to perpetually suffer while watching that which he'd risked everything for be destroyed."

"You mean his child." Anika turned away from the bed to pace across the room.

Shay frowned. "How could he see anything that was happening to me?"

My mind was racing as the temperature of my blood plunged. "Shay . . . I think I—"

Logan cut me off. "Where is the only place you've seen your parents?"

"Seen them?" Shay gazed at him. "I don't know . . . my dreams. Memories."

"Think harder." Logan was on the verge of laughter.

"Stop." I leapt forward, landing on the bed and crouching in front of Logan with my fist balled up. "Don't you dare play with him."

"Calla!" Anika was coming toward me when Shay stopped her with a sharp glance. He slowly turned to stare at Logan.

"The portrait," he said. He moved his eyes from Logan to me. "The portrait in the library."

I nodded, sliding off the bed to stand close to him. I didn't dare touch him. The moment was live with raw emotion that I couldn't risk provoking.

"Does that mean . . . ," Shay whispered. "They're alive, but . . . are they those . . . things?"

"What things?" Logan asked.

"He means the Fallen," Anika said. "Is he right? Are Tristan and Sarah Fallen?"

"No," Logan said. "They are not Fallen. The Fallen are carrion, little more than animated corpses. Bosque wanted Tristan and Sarah sentient. They're being held in stasis, imprisoned in that painting."

"How is that different than the other paintings?" Shay asked.

"The Fallen are prisoners we use to feed the wraiths," Logan replied, cringing when Ren snarled. "The paintings are a liminal space—a holding cell of sorts. Bosque enjoys observing what he calls his own 'art of war.' He can see through the dimensional wall to watch the wraiths feeding. The prisoners remain there until they have nothing left to offer the wraiths. Then they are discarded."

"But my parents haven't been given to the wraiths?" Shay asked. "You're sure?"

"You've seen it with your own eyes, Shay," Logan said. "When you looked at their portrait, how did they appear?"

"Sad," Shay murmured.

"But unharmed," Logan said. Shay nodded.

"When you close the Rift, it will free Tristan and Sarah," Logan said. "They'll have aged, just as any human being would. But they will otherwise be as you knew them."

"I never knew them," Shay said.

"I did," Anika said quietly. "Many of us did. We counted your parents as friends."

Shay looked at her, surprised. She didn't meet his gaze, lost in her own thoughts. "We failed them. We should have kept them safe, kept you hidden, but we couldn't."

The room fell quiet until Logan cleared his throat.

"I trust that information is worth something to you."

"Perhaps," Anika said.

"I'll do whatever I can to prove myself of value," Logan said. "I can help you win."

Anika nodded, but she was looking at a woman who had appeared in the doorway.

"Ethan said you needed a healer." The woman glanced around the room, eyes searching for her patient.

"Nothing serious," Anika said. "The prisoner has a cut that needs tending. Disinfection, but I don't think stitches will be necessary."

The healer nodded and went to the bed.

"We'll have more to discuss," Anika said to Logan.

"Of course." He winced when the healer peeled his shirt back. "If you won't get me cigarettes, could I have something for the pain?"

Anika smiled. "I think you can bear it."

TWELVE

"CAN WE TRUST HIM?" I watched Adne move, gleaming threads spiraling out from her skeans as she wove the door that would lead us to Eydis's resting place in Tulúm. *The writing is on the wall,* Logan had said. Was he right? We had one sword; we were about to take the first step in getting the second.

Nev shrugged. "As much as I hate to say it, yeah. Logan would stab *himself* in the back if he thought it would get him something he wanted."

"It doesn't matter." Mason had rejoined us in Haldis Tactical but couldn't seem to shake his somber mood. "None of it matters."

"Would you stop?" Nev bared teeth at him. "It's okay to be angry. You should be angry."

Mason looked away. "If he can help us win, that's what matters."

"Look." Nev's features softened. He rested his forehead against Mason's. "We'll win, then we'll kill him. Deal?"

Mason tried to pull back, but Nev gripped his shoulders. He began to laugh. "Okay, deal."

I regarded Nev thoughtfully. "Why didn't you?"

"What?" he asked, keeping Mason wrapped in his arms.

"Kill Logan," I said. "When he came through the portal with us. You stayed human. You were strangling him. Why didn't you shift and rip his throat out?"

It was an appealing idea—and one I was certain had crossed Nev's mind more than once.

He offered me a thin smile. "I wanted him to know it was me who killed him. The Keepers have never been good at knowing who we are when we're wolves."

I nodded. "Fair enough."

"It's time." Anika gestured to the now-open portal. All I could see through the shimmering door were jewel tones. Sapphire blue. Emerald green. Colors so vivid, they were both alluring and ominous.

Shay fell in step beside me. "Tell me again why he's here?"

I didn't need to ask who Shay meant by "he." "You know why. The pack needs him. And the Searchers trust him."

Ren was already moving through the portal, in wolf form, trotting beside Sabine and Ethan.

"Fine," Shay said. I was a little surprised when he also shifted, bounding past Adne and into the gem-like hues of the door.

Mason laughed. "He's a wolf, all right."

"And he doesn't want Ren to forget it," Nev finished. Grinning at each other, they both shifted and took off after Shay.

I heard Connor laughing behind me.

"Your mess," he said when I glared at him.

"Don't forget that I know about your housekeeping issues too, Searcher." I flashed fangs at him before shifting. That wiped the smile off his face. I barked my satisfaction before chasing the others.

The colors were so bright it took me a minute to realize I'd reached our destination. The environment around me was full, too full. Thick leaves bent down, surrounding us, the jade nets of the forest canopy only occasionally pierced by spears of sunlight. It was the mixture of odors that gave me a sense of place . . . and change. While the air of Cinque Terre whispered of sea salt and lemons, it was crisp and dry. This air was heavy, rain-drenched. It poured into my lungs almost like water. I caught the scent of ocean salt and knew it was nearby. But even the sea smell had changed, gained a dark, rich scent of kelp and brine that invoked the vastness of waves and endless shorelines.

"All accounted for?" Silas straightened his vest and pulled out his omnipresent pen and notepad.

I really wish he wasn't coming with us. Mason's voice sounded in my head.

You won't get any argument here, Shay replied, wagging his tail.

"Oh, wait, I forgot my sunscreen," Connor said. "Silas, be a dear and run back to the Academy to get some. We'll just wait. Right, guys?"

"Shut up," Silas said, but he patted his vest and I knew he was double checking to make sure he'd brought *his* sunscreen.

"Come on." Ethan waved for us to follow him down a game trail I could barely make out in the dense foliage. "They'll be waiting for us."

We walked a quarter mile. With each step a crashing sound grew louder. Ethan turned a sharp corner on the trail; when I reached the same spot, I stopped in my tracks.

It was as if someone had suddenly drawn the shades in a dark room. Blinding sun washed over us as the jungle dropped away, revealing miles and miles of beach with sand so white it resembled snow. The thunder of rolling surf stirred my blood, its sound both an invitation and a warning. I didn't want to admit it, but the ocean was unsettling. Wolves didn't belong in the water. Still, the mystery and beauty of endless waves tugged at something inside me. Maybe its very strangeness gave it an inexplicable appeal.

"You going for a swim, Calla?" Connor nudged me with his elbow. I'd been staring at the ocean so long I'd fallen behind. The others were heading for a ramshackle house that looked like it was on the verge of tumbling from the forest line onto the beach in a heap of wood planks and shingles. A long dock stretched from the deck of the house out into the ocean, where three boats bobbed up and down, moored to the rickety structure. I could make out the shape of a man in one of the boats. He didn't look up at us, too busy with his own tasks to note our arrival.

A woman with long, dark hair stood on the deck, waving to us. When Ethan reached her, he wrapped her in a fierce embrace. She grinned at him but quickly turned her eyes on the gathering wolves. Shay paused in front of her, returning to his human form.

"It's good to see you again, Scion." She smiled, and I realized she'd been one of the Guides who had been meeting with Shay and Anika without the rest of us. Her eyes moved to the sword on his back. "And very good to see that.

"*Bienvenido, lobos,*" she said, gazing at me and my packmates. "I am the Eydis Guide, Inez. Please tell me you don't bite."

Ren shifted forms. "Since you asked so nicely, we'll make an exception."

The rest of the pack followed Ren's lead. I wanted to laugh as I watched my friends attempt to look nice instead of menacing as we introduced ourselves.

"Guardians have a sense of humor. Who could have guessed?" She laughed, a belly-deep, genuine sound that made me smile.

"They're full of surprises," Ethan said, but went red in the ears when Sabine arched an eyebrow at him.

"Indeed." Inez threw Sabine a surprised glance. "Come inside. We've prepared you some food. We'll go over the mission parameters while you eat."

"I love Eydis," Connor said, throwing his arm around the woman. "Inez never disappoints."

"We make the most of what we have." She smiled at him and gazed inquiringly at Silas. "Anika informed me you'd be coming. It's rare to have a Scribe among us."

"I merely do what history requires," Silas said.

Connor shoved Silas toward the door to the house. "Please get to the table so you can eat instead of talk."

Like the Haldis outpost in Denver, this hideout was built for function—though that function caught me off guard.

"Is this a dive shop?" Shay turned in a circle to look at the masks, fins, and tanks that lined the walls.

"We don't get a lot of business, but it's a good cover." A young man with curly black hair and sparkling eyes answered. "Look at that sword! You must be him."

"Nothing gets past you, does it, Miguel?" Connor, laughing, hugged the new arrival. "Good to see you, friend."

"And you, *amigo*," Miguel answered before greeting Ethan. "How's Grumpy?"

"I've been worse." Ethan grinned.

"Can we cut the class reunion short?" Adne's hands were on her hips. "I'm starving and the clock's ticking."

"Class reunion?" I asked.

Adne gestured to three men, who were huddled together, whispering and laughing. "The Three Amigos over there were in the same Academy class. They had quite the reputation."

"Had?" Connor looked up. "When did our reputation become past tense?"

Adne rolled her eyes, but Inez put an arm around the girl's shoulders and led her into the next room, beckoning us to follow.

After our Italian meals I expected all future food to be a disappointment. I couldn't have been more wrong. A feast of *sopas, panuchos,* and delicately seasoned, unbelievably fresh fish was spread before us. Every bite was heaven. I wanted to gorge myself on the food—which was unlike anything I'd ever tasted—but my mind quickly fixed on the battle ahead. Inez, seated at the head of the table, spoke to us as we ate.

"Once you've finished, we'll head out," she said. "Gabriel is making preparations now."

"What kind of resistance are we expecting?" I asked. "More Guardians?"

"There are Guardians here," Miguel said. *"Yaguares."*

"Yaguares?" Nev asked. "You mean like panthers?"

Inez nodded. Ren and Nev exchanged a glance.

"I was kind of hoping for more bears," Nev said. "Cats are gonna suck."

"We're fighting cats?" Mason's face squished up. "Yuck. They taste terrible."

"You ate a cat?" Shay asked. My stomach twisted. I could imagine little more disgusting than cat meat.

"Not ate," Mason said. "Bit . . . and killed."

We all stared at him.

"Hey—" He held his hands up defensively. "It attacked me. Crazy feline."

"If all goes well, you will not face *las sombras*," Inez said. "Our plan is to avoid them. It is never easy to fight in the jungle, and it is where *las sombras* are deadliest."

"*Las sombras* favor the trees," Miguel said. "They drop from above."

"How many?" Ren asked.

"Like the bears, they prefer solitude," he replied. "But still, they are deadly."

"So what do we do?" I asked. "Same as Tordis? You lure the kitties away while we head into the cave?"

Miguel shook his head. "It is no cave. *Es un cenoté.*"

"Oh, man." Shay shuddered. "Seriously?"

Miguel nodded.

"What's a si-note-ay?" Mason fumbled with the word.

Shay had gone slightly green. "It's where the Mayans made sacrifices to their gods—deep sinkholes that run for miles beneath the surface. Sometimes they lead into networks of underwater caves. They're all over this region, right?"

"*Sí.*" Miguel's face was grim.

"The Spanish called them *sagrados*," Silas said. "Wells of sacrifice."

"Wells of sacrifice?" Sabine's eyes widened.

"They threw people in," Shay said.

"And Eydis is inside one of these sacrifice wells?" I asked.

"Yes," Silas said.

"Does that mean we have to climb down into a sinkhole?" Sabine asked. "'Cause that doesn't sound like fun."

"*Las sombras* watch from the branches," Miguel said. "We would not have time to rappel into the cave before they attacked."

"What about that thingy Adne can do?" Mason asked. "Can't she open a portal down inside the cave? Like in Eden?"

"Sorry. No can do." Adne shook her head. "We don't have any idea what's down there. We'd be in serious trouble if I ended up accidentally opening a portal underwater. Or on the wrong side of a sheer drop. We don't have any descriptions to go on. In Eden, I had Ansel's experience working for me. I used his story to open the door."

"Then what's the plan?" Shay asked.

"Gabriel found another entrance," Ethan said, though he didn't look too happy about it.

Inez's mouth had an equally grim set. "He's been scouting it for the past three days. It is our best option."

"Another entrance?" Mason asked. "But won't the panthers be guarding that one too?"

"No," Miguel replied, meeting Ethan's stony gaze.

"They won't?" Shay frowned.

"No." Connor rolled his shoulders back. "Because cats hate water."

My skin prickled at Connor's words. Wolves didn't exactly hate water, but we weren't dolphins either.

He winked at me. "That's right, sweetheart. We're all going for a nice, long swim."

"How long?" Shay asked.

"We're going in at low tide," Ethan said. "Hopefully we won't need the scuba gear for long, but you're all getting a crash course in it. Just in case."

"Awesome." Shay grinned. The rest of the wolves glared at him. "What?" He glanced around the pack, giving us wide, too-innocent eyes. "I like trying new things."

"Chosen One shows an aptitude for adventure and risk taking," Silas murmured as he wrote. He hadn't touched a thing on his plate.

"Can't you stay here?" Connor asked him. "You can't write underwater."

Silas drew himself up. "I shall commit each event to memory and transfer it to paper upon our return."

"Of course you will," Connor said, pushing himself away from the table. He looked at Inez. "We're not swimming for at least an hour, right? 'Cause I don't want to get a cramp."

THIRTEEN

GABRIEL, IT TURNED OUT, had been the man working in the boat. The boat we were all now boarding. He smiled, despite having to coax six reluctant wolves off dry land. With a mess of sun-streaked hair, Gabriel looked more like a surf god than a Searcher. From the way he tossed around scuba gear—tanks, regulators, buoyancy vests, lead weights, masks, fins, wet suits, and flashlights—with efficient care, I guessed that he'd been assigned the task of instructing us in the ways of water too.

As I scrambled toward a seat, the boat lurched over a wave and I wondered if eating all those *sopas* had been such a great idea after all.

The outboard gurgled to life and Miguel navigated us away from the docks while Inez waved her farewell.

"The Eydis Strikers, except Miguel, are keeping an eye on the *cenoté* topside," Gabriel shouted over the roar of the outboard engine. He watched us, his grin widening as we flopped around the floor of the boat like fish out of water, struggling into our wet suits.

"I thought we weren't attacking the Guardians," Shay said.

"No attack, just watching in case we have any surprises," Gabriel said. He picked up a tank. "Listen up—we only get one shot here, so pay attention."

It was hard to pay attention when it felt like championship Ping-Pong was taking place in your stomach, but drowning didn't hold any appeal either, so I clenched my teeth and did my best to focus. The wet suit didn't help matters, as it fit like a tight, thick second skin that I desperately wanted to claw off.

"We can make it almost all the way to the *cenoté* without being submerged," Gabriel said. "But the last ten yards are a tunnel and we will have to swim it."

"We're going into an underwater tunnel?" Mason already looked green, and this news made him clutch his stomach.

Gabriel nodded. "And the tunnel narrows just before you can access the *cenoté*. When you hit that gap, you'll have to take off your vest and tank and push them through."

Nev laughed. "You've got to be kidding."

Gabriel's expression wasn't a kidding one.

Mason leaned over the side of the boat and retched.

"You can't fit through the opening wearing your tank," Gabriel said. "But it will only take you a minute to push the tank and then yourself through. Don't overthink it."

"You're assuming it's just us down there," I said. "What if we have to fight our way in? Did anyone tell you about the spider?"

"No spiders down there, *preciosa*," Gabriel said. "I swam the tunnel twice already—it's a clear passage. The Keepers are only watching the top."

His smile was warm and reassuring, but I felt uneasy.

"Listen," he continued. "I'm serious about not overthinking this dive. Below the surface, the mixture of nitrogen and oxygen in the tanks can play tricks on your mind. At worst, hallucinations, panic attacks—and if you start to freak, it will be hard to turn it off. *Comprende?*"

Mason wiped his mouth and nodded.

"Besides," Adne added, "it's a one-way trip. No use getting all worked up."

"Thanks for the vote of confidence." Ren gave her a weary smile.

She punched him on the arm. "Not that kind of one way. I just mean once Shay has Eydis, I'll weave a door and we'll be back to Inez in time for dinner."

"Fish tacos?" Connor brightened.

Gabriel shrugged. "Likely."

The trip along the coast took an hour, during which we skirted a dark and unfriendly limestone coastline. The jungle hung over the water, its vines appearing to writhe just above the swells. By the time Miguel lowered the anchor, everyone but the Searchers and Shay had been sick at least once. Apparently wolves can't find their sea legs.

I rinsed my mouth out with salt water as Gabriel gave final instructions on scuba safety procedures. "Remember, if you get into trouble, the person with a functioning tank is in charge. That's how buddy breathing works. Got it?"

We all gave him a thumbs-up.

Gabriel pointed to the tangle of jade leaves and thick branches. "That's where we're headed."

I peered at the shore and could just make out a sliver of darkness cutting through the glistening green.

"I will wait here for an hour," Miguel said as he settled into one of the seats. "In case any of the *lobos* can't handle the dive. None of you seem to have sea legs."

Mason threw him an unfriendly smile, taking a deep breath before he and Nev put on their masks and fins, placed their regulators in their mouths, and jumped into the water.

"You okay?" Shay held my tank while I slipped my arms into my buoyancy vest and secured the safety belts.

I nodded. Bile was sloshing in my stomach again. I didn't think talking would help.

"You'll do fine," Ren added, handing me a mask.

"I've got this," Shay said. "Get your own equipment on."

"I can help her too," Ren growled. "Back off."

"Don't start," I said, swallowing hard. "And I don't need help from either of you. Just get in the water."

They were both still glaring at each other, so I jabbed them away with my elbows, closed my eyes, and did a back roll into the sea.

Other than the way my blood roared in my ears as I sank beneath the surface, my world had gone quiet. Nearly silent.

Slowly, I adjusted to my surroundings. I wasn't quite floating, but I wasn't sinking either. The air in the vest kept me buoyant while I gently kicked my fins. I equalized the pressure in my ears by holding my nose and applying a bit of pressure until they popped and cleared, just as Gabriel had promised. The fins propelled me forward much more quickly than I'd expected. An adrenaline spike sent shivers through my limbs. I twisted in the water, graceful, unencumbered by weight. Maybe wolves were dolphins in another life.

Mason and Nev had also gotten comfortable breathing underwater and were now chasing a sea turtle, circling it the way they would a rabbit. I giggled and bubbles spouted up around me.

Four booms, like miniature explosions, came from above. I looked up to see that Shay, Ren, Adne, and Connor had entered the water. One final boom signaled Gabriel's arrival. He immediately took off toward the shoreline, moving through the water lithe as a sea lion, with only a quick wave to indicate that we should follow.

Having just gotten comfortable with my new underwater surroundings, I didn't feel ready to leave the open sea for the confinement of the cave, but I didn't have a choice.

The tunnel loomed ahead, an absolute darkness in contrast to the aquamarine sea we were leaving behind. As we approached the black maw carved in the shoreline, the surge of excitement I'd felt earlier gave way to gnawing anxiety.

Gabriel surfaced just inside the mouth of the cave and pulled off his mask. I looked past him, trying to judge the distance between the water's surface and the cave's ceiling. Four feet, maybe five, but my flashlight's beam showed that the ceiling sloped down farther into an ever-narrowing tunnel.

"I've already placed a guideline in the corridor where we'll be submerged," Gabriel said. "If you start to lose your sense of direction, just focus on the line. And remember, don't overthink it. Just breathe, clear your ears as you descend, and everything will be fine."

"Is this really the best plan?" Silas asked. For the first time, his arrogance was overridden by fear. "Cave diving requires special certification. Perhaps—"

"I teach that certification," Gabriel cut him off. "I know what I'm doing. We wouldn't be doing this if there was any other option."

He shook his head. My heart had begun to pound as I wondered about the degree of danger we were on the verge of confronting.

"It's the only way." Gabriel turned on the light at his wrist. "And we're wasting time discussing it."

Silas had begun to tremble, and I didn't think it was from anger at Gabriel. I felt a little sorry for the Scribe.

He might be an ass, but he doesn't have to be here. He only came because he believes in what he's doing.

I swam over to him, keeping my voice low. "I'll watch out for you."

His eyes widened, but he managed a nod. I gestured for him to swim in our single-file line just behind Shay and before me. If he needed help, it was my guess that other than Gabriel, Shay and I would be his best shot. Shay seemed to take to any new hobby that caught his fancy—and I was just too stubborn to suck at anything I considered a challenge.

Gabriel led us forward at a slow and steady swim. The farther we moved into the cavern, the narrower the passage became. I tried to keep my breaths slow, but I couldn't do anything about my amped-up pulse. The tunnel was closing around us, becoming ever tighter. The sunlight, which had pierced the cave's mouth, now faded, leaving us only with the lights strapped to our wrists to guide us.

Gabriel stopped. He didn't turn around, but his voice bounced over the surface of the water and the tunnel walls.

"We're going under now," he said. "Follow the diver in front of you and the guideline. It will take about five minutes before we hit the gap where you'll have to take off your vest and tank. I'll be on the other side; you'll push them through the opening and I'll light the way with my flashlight."

One by one we submerged. Unlike the glittering vastness of the open ocean, diving in the tunnel plunged us into a choking darkness. As we swam forward, the passage became less of a channel and more of a craggy, cave-like enclosure with sharp ridges in its walls and stalactites through which we had to weave our way.

Five minutes. Five minutes. Five minutes.

So little time. But the swim seemed to be taking so much longer. We passed other tunnels, offshoots of the path we followed. The current kept shifting around me, pushing and pulling me away from the line of divers. Blood thrummed in my head. I was starting to feel dizzy. Words floated through my mind, a mesmerizing but deadly chant.

Drown. Crush. Lost.

Silas stopped moving forward and the voices in my head began to shriek.

Lost! Lost! Lost!

Why weren't we moving? What was wrong?

Blood screamed through my veins. I started to turn around. If I could just swim back—get out of this cave. Find my way out, out, out. It was too tight. Too dark.

Silas began to move again. His slow, easy kicks broke through my panic. After a few feet, he paused again. I remained still, watching him, trying to remember what I should be doing.

Behind me, Ren gently tugged the tip of one of my fins. I craned my neck to stare at him. He tilted his head, giving me a puzzled look, motioning for me to go forward, and I understood.

The gap. We'd reached the gap. Of course we'd stop while waiting for each diver to pass through.

My heart was still slamming inside my chest, but my head had cleared enough to stop me short of a full-on freak-out.

But it didn't do anything to make the wait less agonizing. As our group moved forward, one by one, I couldn't stop the fearful images that played in my mind's eye. Getting stuck. Being crushed. Drowning in this darkness.

I gripped the regulator hose with one hand. Right now, it felt like the only connection I had to the outside world—to the light, and earth, and air where I belonged.

Silas was unbuckling his buoyancy vest, wriggling out of it one arm at a time and pushing it and the tank through an opening that I could barely make out. A gap that looked impossibly narrow. Next, the Scribe kicked his fins and slid into the dark hole, his body blocking the flashlight's beam as it disappeared in the tunnel's walls. When the tips of his fins were no longer visible, I thought my heart would stop.

A hand reached through the hole and Gabriel's face appeared. He was waiting, beckoning to me. My mind screamed at me as I separated myself from my vest and tank and guided them into Gabriel's hands. He'd been right—any type of thinking would work against me, fueling the fear that could kill me.

I forced my mind to go blank, willing my legs to kick slowly, mechanically. Stretching my body, I propelled myself through the narrow gap like a torpedo shot out of its tube.

I didn't know that I'd made it to the other side until Gabriel gripped my arm tight, helping me through.

He was shaking his head, forcing me to slow to a stop. He held up my vest as I slipped it on. The crinkling around his eyes told me he was smiling. Shay was beside him, waiting for me and smiling as well.

When my vest and tank were in place and the buckles secured, Shay took my hand and we swam to the surface. I ripped off my mask, gulping air and shuddering. Shay pulled off his mask and spit out his mouthpiece, grinning at me.

"What?" I asked.

"You were supposed to go through the gap slowly, Calla," he said. "You caught Gabriel so off guard you almost knocked the regulator out of his mouth."

"I just wanted to get it over with," I said, feeling defensive. That swim ranked high on my list of things I never wanted to do again. When Adne surfaced, I wanted to kiss her. *Thank God it's a one-way trip.*

Shay splashed me, still laughing.

Ren surfaced beside us. "Man, it's good to be able to see again."

With drowning no longer a threat, I gazed around the cavern. Ren was right. The light was dim, but we didn't need our flashlights.

"That must be the opening of the *cenoté*," Shay said, pointing at the ceiling.

Far, far above us—at least a hundred feet up—was an opening in the cave through which jungle-filtered sunlight spilled into the darkness, flickering only with occasional movement near the opening, a fluttering of birds that nested inside the cavern.

"You guys like swimming that much?" Mason called. He and Nev were sitting a few feet away with Ethan and Sabine. "Dry—okay, not dry, but damp, solid land right here."

"I knew there was a reason I liked you." Ren laughed as we swam to the spot where slippery stones of the *cenoté* floor were lapped by salt water.

I hauled myself out of the water. Only a sense of dignity kept me from sprawling on the stone, pressing my cheek lovingly to the earth.

The air was still too heavy, thick with brine and decaying fish, but at least it was real air.

"Everyone okay?" Gabriel asked.

"I'm a little dizzy," Adne said, squeezing water out of her hair.

"That's normal," he replied. "But tell me if it gets any worse."

"Thanks," she said drily.

"You all did great," Gabriel said. "Let's get what we came for."

"Where are we headed?" Shay asked.

"An alcove." Gabriel started walking. "You can see it from here."

"The light," Shay murmured.

I followed his gaze. One corner of the *cenoté* gleamed with the marbled sapphire and emerald tones of the sea that contrasted with the sheer sunlight in the rest of the cave.

Our group began to head after Gabriel, except Silas, who was squinting at the ceiling.

Nev glanced at him. "Yeah, I think our arrival made the birdies unhappy."

Looking up, I saw what he meant. The flutter of wings above had increased; shadows darted back and forth across the cave's opening. A tittering sound swelled, echoing in the chamber.

"I don't think those are birds," Silas said.

"What?" Nev frowned.

The noise grew louder; sunlight from above winked in and out, at times fully blocked off by the movement above us.

"What is that?" I asked.

Silas whispered something, but I couldn't quite hear him. The *cenoté* amplified sound, transforming the fluttering of wings into a rush of wind.

It was too late when I understood he'd said, "Get back in the water. Now!"

FOURTEEN

THE CEILING WAS MOVING, every inch of it.

"Cave-in!" Mason shouted, running for cover.

Gabriel had already leapt from shore, donned his gear, and submerged.

How would getting in the water protect us from falling stone?

Mason hesitated, looking up like the rest of us. The movement above wasn't a deadly shower of rock; it was swooping, swirling mobs of shadow. For a moment I thought it was wraiths, but wraiths didn't have wings. And they made no sound.

"Move it!" Ethan shoved me as Sabine dove into the pool. I stumbled backward, falling into the water without my mask on or the first stage of my regulator in my mouth. I came up coughing, struggling to see and to breathe.

Connor and Adne were in the water, like me struggling with their gear.

Gabriel surfaced, ripped his regulator out of his mouth, and shouted, "What the hell are you waiting for!"

Mason, Nev, and Silas were still onshore.

"What's that?" Nev and Mason both stared at the dark, living cloud—moving slowly toward the water.

"Gabriel's right—get underwater!" Silas waved at them frantically, even as he fumbled to pull on his own vest and tank. "You can't stay there!"

His furious movements caught the attention of the swarm above. Suddenly, the cloud of beating wings with its shrill, chirping chorus plunged down. Silas cried out, falling to his knees as it surrounded him.

I could no longer see him, only make out the shape of a body beneath the pulsing mob of tiny furred bodies, leathery wings, and enormous ears that dwarfed their heads.

"Oh God." Mason grabbed Nev's hand, dragging him toward the water.

"We have to help him." I started to swim toward shore, but Gabriel, who was much faster in the water, cut me off.

"He's already dead."

"No, he's not." I fought Gabriel off only to find both Shay and Ren in my way.

I snarled at them. "What are you doing?"

"Look," Ren said, jerking his head toward shore.

The cloud had lifted from Silas's body, which wasn't moving. The skin I could see was ghastly pale, the rest of it covered with tiny red incisions. Even his wet suit had been cut to ribbons.

"There's nothing we can do," Ren said.

"I said I'd watch out for him." My voice shook. "I said . . ."

"There wasn't any way for you to know." Shay glanced at the swarm, which now hovered above us.

I was shivering in the water. It felt as though my bones rattled beneath my skin.

"They'll dive at us, even out here." Gabriel watched the swooping mass of fur and wings. "We'll need to submerge and resurface. That will throw them off."

I didn't want to go underwater again. Breathing was already hard enough, and what had happened to Silas had been so sudden, and so horrible.

After we dove down, I heard hundreds of pings on the surface like it had begun to rain. Gabriel led us to the far edge of the cavern.

He kept us close, huddled together, arms linked as we waited. At his signal we surfaced.

"Keep your voices low," he whispered. "And don't make any loud splashes or sudden movements. The water keeps them at bay, but they'll still hunt us."

He gestured to the area from which we'd come. Small winged carcasses floated on the surface. Bats that had tried to get to us, become sodden, and, unable to fly again, eventually drowned.

"Bats?" Mason asked. "Bats can do that?"

"Vampire bats," Gabriel said.

"But vampire bats don't kill people," Nev said. "Right? That's just a myth."

"Vampire bats don't hunt in swarms either." Gabriel gazed up at the ceiling. "These have been changed. They're like piranhas."

"More Keeper tricks," Shay said.

Connor was gazing at the shore where Silas's body lay. "Damn it. I knew he shouldn't have come."

Guilt tightened my chest again. Why hadn't I helped him? I could have grabbed him and pulled him in the water.

"What now?" Adne asked.

Ethan looked at the shoreline. "We need to buy Shay time."

Connor laughed. "You mean draw fire?"

"Exactly." Ethan smiled grimly.

"Buy me time for what?" Shay asked. "I won't leave you to fight without me."

"It's only temporary, kid," Connor said. "I don't find this cave any cozier than you do. I'm itching to say adios to this place. But you need that hilt and you can't get it without us."

Shay nodded slowly. "So you'll distract the bats . . ."

"And you run for that alcove," Ethan finished. "It's set far enough in the corner that if the bats are already distracted, they won't notice you heading there."

"You need to let us lure the bats," Sabine said.

"I don't think so." Ethan glared at her.

"I'm a big girl." She bared her teeth. "And wolves are faster than Searchers. We can jump in and out of the water. And the group of us running around will confuse them."

"She's right," Ren said. "Let the pack handle this."

"Yes," I said, knowing I'd snatch a few bats out of the air in the process. There was no way I was going to let that happen to Silas and not get a little payback.

Connor shrugged. "As long as you've all had your rabies shots."

"I'm going to pretend you didn't say that," Sabine growled. "But only because Ethan likes you."

"Jumping in and out of the water, huh?" Mason smiled. "I hope you're prepared to accept how bad wet fur smells."

"We'll manage," Adne said. I noticed she was shivering too and there were streaks of water on her cheeks that I didn't think were from the dive. "Can we just do this? I can't look at Silas lying there anymore."

Connor nodded. "Okay, Scion, you run back here as soon as you have Eydis so Adne can weave a door and get us out."

Shay shrugged off his tank, pushing it toward Gabriel. "I'll be faster without it."

"Ready?" Ren was looking at me. As alphas we'd lead this strike.

"As ever," I snarled, drawing on my anger to push away any fear.

I'm sorry, Silas. I'll try to make it up to you.

One by one our pack submerged, swimming away from Shay and the others. We stayed beneath the surface as long as we could. When the water was too shallow, Ren and I shifted forms in sync, two wolves bursting from the water. The ceiling came to life. Mason was running at my flank, while Nev and Sabine stayed close to Ren. The swarm of bats dove; I could feel the wind stirred up by hundreds of tiny wings brushing across my fur.

Now. I sent the thought to the pack.

We scattered.

A horrible shrieking echoed in the cavern. I leapt up at intervals, snapping at the air. Sometimes my jaws ripped apart a wing or crushed a small body. At others I bit nothing, the swarm having moved on to pursue one of my packmates.

A yelp jerked me around and I saw a dozen or more bats clinging to Nev's shoulders. His muscles bunched and he jumped off the shoreline, crashing into the water, sending some of the bats careening through the air while others were sucked beneath the surface when Nev shifted forms and fully submerged again.

It was working. The bats couldn't track so many of us, moving so quickly. And when the swarm did fix its hunt on one of our number, we were fast enough to get into the water before they could do too much damage.

Another splash echoed through the cavern. Sabine was in the water, taking bats with her—a lot more of the creatures clung to her than had to Nev. They were getting better at focusing on one of us at a time. I felt the rush of wind again. I didn't have to look over my shoulder to know the swarm had targeted me. The first bat landed on my spine; its teeth cutting across my back was light as a pinprick, but the feeling of its tiny tongue lapping up my blood almost made me stumble. Another bat clung to me. Then another.

Calla! Ren's shout filled my head. *There are too many on you; get in the water now!*

I didn't want to know how many was too many. But I could feel their weight on my back and my blood leaking from dozens of minuscule cuts. I wheeled and flung myself into the water. The force of my leap slammed my chest hard into the surface, knocking the breath from my lungs. The bats struggled to free themselves from my fur and take flight before the water captured them. I shifted forms, trying to put in my mouthpiece and get air. My heart was pounding, but I forced myself to be still, drinking in the silence of submersion.

Beneath the surface everything was dark, though my eyes were open. I felt as if I were floating in empty space rather than underwater. I was desperate to get back into the fight, but I had to be steady first. When I was sure I had my breath back, I swam to the shore, shifting, and burst back into the fray.

But there was no fray. The rest of my pack stood still, ears flicking back and forth, watching the ceiling.

The bats had vanished.

What happened? I padded to Ren's side.

They left. He pawed the ground in agitation. *The cavern shook and they all flew out of the opening to the cave.*

The cavern shook? I hadn't felt anything underwater.

Just a little. Sabine was licking a cut on Nev's shoulder.

Mason and I exchanged a look. His tongue lolled out in a wolf grin. *He's got it. Shay found Eydis.*

How do you know? Ren's ears flicked back and forth when he turned toward Mason.

The cave shook in Switzerland. I nipped at Mason's shoulder playfully. *Go, Shay!*

Right. Ren remained tense. *But why would that make the bats leave?*

I bristled. *Let's get back to the others.*

We had started toward the alcove when the cavern rumbled again. The earth rolled under my paws, throwing me onto my side. The water's surface began to stir, spilling over the edge of the shore. Soon it looked like a boiling cauldron.

What's happening? Mason called to us.

I could hear the Searchers shouting, but I couldn't make out their words over the roar of water pouring into the cavern. Scrambling to my feet, I started to run toward their voices. My paws were splashing through ankle-deep water. It should have been impossible. Water coming through that tiny cleft in the rock we'd had to worm through couldn't be this forceful. But somehow it was. Water that had been at my knees was already at my waist and rising, forcing me to swim. The cave shuddered again. Slabs of stone dropped from the ceiling.

I could see Connor waving to us. Adne was beside him, fumbling with her scuba gear while Gabriel tried to help her. Ethan began swimming toward us.

Where was Shay? I couldn't spot him among them.

"We have to get out of here!" Connor shouted.

The water was at my neck, but I'd almost reached them. A deafening roar filled the cave and then the ocean was crashing around us, roiling, hitting us with the force of a tidal wave. We were thrown apart.

I slammed into the cavern wall. My instincts screamed at me to swim up and find a way to surface, but whatever rational cells were left in my body stopped me. There wasn't a way to surface, not anymore. The cavern was flooding with a speed that could only be credited to magic. Was it a final trap left by the Keepers or just a result of Shay claiming the water hilt? Whatever the cause, I knew my salvation lay in working with the water, not against it.

I shifted forms and shoved my mouthpiece in, knowing that I had to find Shay. He'd left his tank behind when he went after Eydis. He'd drown without an air source. I struggled against the new currents that swirled through the water, grabbing a single fin before it could float past me. Even the help of one fin would be better than trying to swim without them.

I worked my way toward the gleaming tones of the alcove, which wavered now that they were submerged. A flicker above me drew my gaze. I saw kicking feet. Shay was pushing himself toward the surface. Without a tank he had no other options. My fin gave me extra speed as I went after him.

When I grabbed his ankle, he jerked around, ready to strike at me. I pulled him down, taking my mouthpiece out and pushing it onto his lips. I held his shoulders, trying to remember Gabriel's instructions. I had the tank, so I was in charge of the breaths. Keeping my eyes on Shay's lungs, I counted: one breath, two breaths. He nodded at me. I took the mouthpiece from him and took my two breaths. We began to swim slowly toward the spot where I'd last seen the Searchers.

Shay pointed ahead. A light shimmered in the water—golden against the turquoise currents—a tall, narrow slab of light.

Adne's door. She'd opened a door underwater. Shay squeezed my arm and we swam faster. Adne was hovering near the portal. She had her tank and mask on, and when she caught sight of us, she began waving frantically. But she wasn't waving at us, she was pointing to something behind us. I flipped around and though I didn't have a mouthpiece in, or air to waste, I screamed.

Gabriel was swimming toward us and the portal, but he wasn't alone. He was dragging something with him. The limp body of a wolf.

Nev wasn't struggling to swim or free himself from Gabriel's arms. He wasn't moving at all.

Shay shoved the mouthpiece between my lips with a shake of his head. Gabriel swam past us, dragging Nev with him into the portal. We swam after him, pushing through the shimmering passage and landing in a muddy puddle on the jungle floor.

"No!" Mason was kneeling over Nev. "Please, Nev!"

"Get out of the way!" Gabriel pushed Mason aside.

Mason snarled. He shifted forms, ready to lunge at Gabriel. Connor jumped between them.

"Wait!" Connor shouted. "Give him a minute. He's a dive instructor, remember? He's certified in CPR."

Mason stalked back and forth whining as Gabriel pushed on Nev's chest and breathed into his muzzle.

Breathe, Nev. Breathe.

Someone took my hand. I leaned into Ren, beyond grateful that he was here and alive. But when I looked up at him, I saw how pale he was as he watched Gabriel trying to bring Nev back to us.

Adne fell onto the ground beside me. "Tell me we saved him," she gasped.

Even as she spoke, Nev's jaws opened and water spewed out of his mouth. He coughed and shook his head, rolling onto his stomach with a whimper.

Mason yelped, scrambling close to Nev and covering his face and muzzle with licks. They both shifted to human form, clinging to each other fiercely.

Sabine sobbed while Ethan held her. Ren squeezed my hand before going to Nev and hugging him.

"Thank God," Connor murmured. "Nice work, Gabriel."

"A wolf." Gabriel grinned. "CPR on a wolf. That's a first for me."

"All I can taste is fish." Nev groaned, coughing up yet more water. "I will never eat fish for as long as I live."

"Shut up," Mason said. "Just shut up." And he kissed Nev again.

FIFTEEN

WE TRUDGED THROUGH the jungle, sodden and dripping. The joy of saving Nev and retrieving Eydis were muted by losing Silas. As we came around the bend in the trail where the forest dropped down toward the sea, the dive shop peeked out through the cover of branches.

"There's Inez waiting on the deck," Gabriel said. "She's got those mother-hen instincts big-time."

Inez's back was to us; she was lounging on a deck chair. Miguel was sitting in the shadow cast by the dive shop's eaves. Two more chairs were pulled up between Miguel and Inez. A woman in a bikini stretched languidly in one. Next to her, a man in an open linen shirt and khaki shorts laughed, threading his fingers through hers.

"Who are they?" I asked.

"I don't know," Gabriel said. "I didn't think we had any dive groups scheduled for today."

He picked up his pace, not running, but taking swift strides toward the figures on the deck. The woman in the bikini saw him and began to wave. Her companion stood up, pushing back his sunglasses.

Ren's nose crinkled up. "Hang on. . . . Do you smell that?"

"Yeah . . . shit," Nev snarled, glancing at the thick jungle that surrounded us.

"You smell shit?" Ethan asked. "Thanks for sharing."

"No," Nev said. "We smell cats."

I sniffed the air. They were right. It was subtle but definitely there. An acrid scent like burning silk and dried sage. A growl rose in my throat.

Gabriel's eyes widened. "*Las sombras . . . no!*"

"Gabriel, wait!" Ethan shouted. But the other man was bolting toward the hideout, yelling.

"Inez! Miguel!" Neither of the Searchers on the deck moved.

It happened in the space of a blink. Gabriel had just reached the deck and it dropped onto him—a shape descending like an ebony cloak. The panther screamed as it leapt from its hiding place on the other side of the roof. Then it was on Gabriel, who was screaming when the cat's claws sank into his shoulders. His cry cut off abruptly when its jaws locked around his neck and twisted sharply, breaking the bones.

"Damn it!" Ethan glared as the panther darted off the deck and into the jungle's shadows.

I waited for the woman on the deck to scream. But she rolled over, laughing. Her oiled, golden skin blurred into a sleek coat. The man beside her took two huge bounds and leapt, hitting the roof in cat form. They vanished into the dark vines just as the other panther had. Hisses and wicked purring filled the branches above us, drowning the air with their menacing sounds.

How many are up there?

The Guardians had all shifted form. Our pack huddled up, glancing into the forest canopy. But the cats seemed to be invisible, slinking among the branches, remaining out of sight.

"We've got to get out from under them," Connor said. "Stay close. Head for the house. We need a defensible position we can hold while Adne weaves a door."

Ethan took point, Sabine and Nev beside him, while Mason, Shay, and Ren stayed closed to Adne. I hung back with Connor, watching the trees as our group slowly moved forward.

We were ready when the next panther leapt. Its scream became a grunt when Ethan hurled his tank at it, catching the beast fully in the chest. It hit the ground, struggling to catch its breath. Mason and Ren took advantage of its momentary disorientation, charging the cat. It lashed out at them with its claws, but Mason held its attention while Ren tore at its flank with his teeth. When it finally turned to scream at Ren, Mason went for the kill, lunging at the cat's throat and crushing its windpipe.

The trees came alive with rage-filled screams, and *las sombras* rained down on us in a torrent of sleek midnight fur and razor-sharp claws.

"Run!" Connor shouted.

Ethan took off toward the house with wolves at his heels. Connor cried out as a panther sprang on him, knocking him to his knees. I snarled and threw myself at the cat, forcing it to release Connor for the sake of fighting me. The force of my blow sent us rolling onto the beach. Our bodies were twisted around each other as we wrestled in the sand. I yelped when the panther's claws sank into my back but answered immediately with my own ferocious bites into its chest. The cat screamed, rolling away from me. I scrambled to my feet, squaring off against it as I tried to brace myself in the soft sand. It hissed at me, bright green eyes filled with rage . . . and intelligence.

My heart skipped a beat. A Guardian—the cats were like us, slaves to the Keepers. For a moment I wanted to reach out, to see if I could somehow make a connection to this unwanted enemy. But such a thought belonged only to me. The cat bunched up and leapt at me. I went flat, rolling over on my back so the panther sailed past me. I kept tumbling until I was right-side up and without hesitation lunged at the cat's unprotected back, tearing into its flesh. The cat screamed and bucked, trying to get away from my ripping teeth. But I was unrelenting; its blood—invisible against its black coat—stained the beach sand crimson. Desperate, the cat reared up and tipped over backward. I leapt off before it could crash down on top of me. Free of attack, the panther didn't turn to face me again. Instead it bolted for the cover of the jungle.

"Calla!" Connor was waving at me. The others had made it to the deck. I shook sand from my coat and ran for the hideout.

You okay? Ren came to meet me. *You're bleeding.*

The cuts aren't deep. I nipped at his flank. *We'll deal with it once we're out of here.*

Ethan was at the door, flinging it open. Sabine and Nev bolted inside. I looked over my shoulder as I ran toward the house. The jungle had become still. No cats pursued us.

They aren't giving chase. Ren snarled, sharing my anxiety.

I know. I bared my teeth at him. *That can't be good.*

Connor swore as we passed the still forms of Inez and Miguel on the deck. They'd been propped up, throats torn out, and they stared at us with unseeing eyes.

"I swear I'm getting payback for this," Connor said, slamming the door behind us. The Guardians stalked around the Searchers, bristling and snarling. Something was very, very wrong.

"Start weaving, Adne," Connor said quietly. "As fast as you can."

She nodded, moving toward the entrance to the kitchen to give herself more space. She had just pulled out her skeans when I caught the scent. It wasn't *las sombras* but another, even more acrid odor. Like that of the panthers, it was burning and too sharp, but the cats had smelled unusual, new. This scent was old. One I knew all too well. A raw scent of boiling pitch and singed hair.

I was already moving when I saw the inky, formless creature looming behind Adne.

Calla! Shay's cry of alarm sounded in my mind, but I had no choice. I couldn't think or Adne would die. If she died, everyone died.

"Adne, run!" I'd shifted forms, barreling toward her with all the speed I had.

She turned to face me, startled. Confusion locked her in place.

"Connor! Ethan!" I kept running. "Get everyone away from here. Run now!"

I stretched out my arms, grabbing Adne at the waist. As I pivoted around, I threw her across the room, hoping Connor would be ready to catch her.

"No!" I heard Shay's desperate yell at the same moment Ren howled.

I closed my eyes and let the wraith engulf me.

Pain.

As the darkness rolled over my skin, it felt like a thousand small, white-hot hooks had lodged in my flesh. They slowly began to pull, tearing skin from muscle. I was screaming, but I couldn't hear anything. Not even the sound of my own agony. I was being torn apart. I was on fire.

And then there was nothing.

FIRE

PART III

I WOKE WITH A START, gasping for breath.

Outside the window a blizzard raged. Sleet and snow, sharp as darts, careened from clouds to earth. My eyelids drooped as I tried to sort through my dim memories. Warm breeze. The smell of salt air kissed by lemons.

Now I was surrounded by familiar scents. The must of dog-eared paperbacks, the dull bite of sharpened pencils, and the crispness of denim. I sat up, looking around.

I was in bed. In my room.

Goose bumps crawled up my arms.

I was in Vail. A scream got caught trying to explode from my lungs, as if it had been choked off by an invisible hand.

I'm home. What do I have to be afraid of?

"Good morning, sleepyhead."

My mother was sitting in a chair near my dresser. My father stood at her shoulders, looking oddly stiff.

"Mom?" My voice cracked. I tried to move again, but my limbs tingled. They felt so heavy.

"Of course it's me," she said, while I stared at her.

Something inside me was sobbing. *Why does seeing my mom make me sad?*

"We thought you might sleep all day." Her teeth were very bright when she smiled. "Didn't we, Stephen?"

My father nodded. Something in his eyes made fear curl at the base of my spine. He was too alert. The Nightshade alpha was bristling, ready to attack.

Distant voices echoed in the recesses of my mind.

"There is no Nightshade alpha."

"Ansel?" I murmured.

A flash of pain tried to split open my skull. I bent forward, cradling my head in my hands.

"Your brother is patrolling with Mason," my mother said. "He'll be back soon. Don't worry."

I nodded. That made sense. Why did my head hurt so much?

My father's brow furrowed. "Are you in pain?"

"Stephen." My mother's eyes rolled up at her mate; a warning flashed within them. "Don't coddle her. She is an alpha, after all."

"Of course, m—Naomi," he said. His hands gripped the back of her chair.

"I think I might be sick," I said. "My head hurts."

"We'll get you some aspirin in a second, sweetie," my mother said. "But you drifted off before you finished telling us about your adventure."

"My adventure?" I peered at her.

"Yes," she said. "You were just telling us about all the places you've been. You were traveling with friends. Remember how that was your gift from the Keepers after the Union? All the places you've seen?"

She smiled. A wave of ease washed over me, making my limbs heavier, but bliss coursed through my veins. "All the places I've seen."

"That's right." Her pearl white teeth gleamed. "We want to hear all about it. What were the places you visited like?"

She adjusted her weight. When she moved, her body blurred and for a moment, her face contorted and I saw—

I cried out when my head throbbed.

"Calla!" My father stepped toward me.

My mother's hand shot out and he froze. She stood up, taking very slow steps toward me.

Why was she moving so slowly?

With each step her figure blurred again. The pounding in my head forced me to keep closing my eyes. I couldn't focus on her as she approached.

The mattress squeaked when she settled next to me. She placed her hands on my temples and the pain gave way to another surge of ecstasy.

"There," she cooed. "Isn't that better?"

I nodded, but I still wanted to cry. There was something I wanted to tell her, something so important that my mother needed to know.

I leaned my head against her shoulder. "I'm sorry."

But I didn't know what I was apologizing for.

She stroked my hair. Her scent wafted into my nostrils—a stiff scent of parchment and red wine. I pulled away, staring at her.

"Feeling better?"

I inhaled, letting the scent linger. A scent that was not Naomi Tor's scent. My mother always smelled of gardenia and ferns.

These scents, old, rich smells blending into a heady perfume, were familiar and they belonged to someone else.

"Lumine," I whispered.

The moment I spoke my mistress's name, her spell shattered.

The air around me crackled, splintering before my eyes. My mother had vanished. Only Lumine Nightshade sat before me. My father stood silently on the other side of the room. His eyes were bright with fear.

Shock welded me to the bed as the illusions drifted away. I began to shake and sob.

Lumine sighed, straightening the dark jacket of her Chanel suit. "That's not very becoming, Calla."

"You bitch." I snarled, my teeth sharpened. I was about to lunge when my father shouted.

"Calla, no!" The command of the Nightshade alpha was still enough to pull me up short.

My eyes met his for a moment before I followed his gaze to my closet. The door was ajar and something was moving inside it. Shadows, thick as tar, undulating in the darkness. A wraith.

My stomach knotted up at the memory of the wraith taking me. A wave of pain crashed through my limbs, nearly sending me back into unconsciousness.

Lumine smiled. "Really, Calla. Did you think I would just bare my throat for your fangs?" She patted my hand. "You should know better."

I snatched my fingers out from under hers. While I couldn't attack her, I wasn't about to play nice.

"Get away from me."

"Restrain yourself, child," she said. "You've had quite a journey, and it takes a while to fully recover from a wraith's embrace."

She laughed softly when I shuddered.

"I just have a few questions for you," she said. "Then you can rest."

"I have nothing to say to you."

"Oh." Her smile became chilly. "I think you do."

I swallowed hard, glancing at the wraith in the closet before shaking my head.

"Yes." Her gaze followed mine. "That's one way it could be. Efron has been pleading with me to hand you over to him and Emile."

Forcing my eyes off her, I stared at the window, watching snow buffeted by wind. My body felt that way: bruised and battered. The sun and sea of Italy seemed like a distant dream. And Lumine wasn't the only one with questions. I was desperate to know what had happened after the wraith took me. Had the others escaped from the Eydis hideout? Were they prisoners too?

"But I've explained to him that I don't think you're likely to break," she continued. "No matter how much pressure is applied."

I offered her a thin smile. "You're right."

"Of course I am," she said. "But we're not without options. Are we, Stephen?"

"No, mistress." His face was blank, but his muscles twitched with nervous energy. My father was unhappy; I could smell his grief, his outrage from across the room.

"Why would I do anything for you?" I glared at her. "You killed my mother. You destroyed my brother."

"You've seen Ansel?" My father took two steps toward me. "How—"

Lumine didn't speak, but she stiffened. My father checked himself, falling silent.

"What happened with your mother was unfortunate," she said, folding her hands on her lap. "But necessary under the circumstances."

"It was necessary for you to murder her?" My eyes were burning, but I blinked away tears as quickly as I could. There was no way in hell I would let Lumine see me cry.

She clucked her tongue with a soft laugh, and it was all I could do not to throw myself on her in a fury of claws and teeth. "Murder? Hardly, Calla. And I'm quite certain you wouldn't see it that way if your mind hadn't been so horribly corrupted by . . . outside influences."

I dug my fingernails into the coverlet.

"You once believed in duty. In loyalty," she continued. "Your mother failed in her most important role. And she paid the price."

I glanced at my father, but he was still frozen. Neither looking at me nor Lumine, instead his gray eyes were lost in some unknown, distant place.

Lumine was still speaking. "Your brother's punishment was a warning."

"A warning," I said quietly, a growl curling around my words.

"To the rest of your pack," she said. "Treachery must be met by swift retribution."

"He did nothing wrong." I bared my teeth at her and she smiled.

"Didn't he?" she asked. "Can you show me those deadly fangs and believe that your brother, who has always adored you, had no suspicions that you wanted someone other than your intended?"

Blood climbed from my neck into my cheeks as my heart began beating too quickly.

"Don't you think he guessed you would risk your own life, and the well-being of your family and friends, all for a teenage girl's infatuation?"

"Infatuation!" I shrieked. "I fell in love with Shay and found out you were going to sacrifice him! You wanted Ren and me to kill him!"

Despite my outburst, Lumine's smile became more serene. The heat in my cheeks gave way to a creeping cold.

Damn it. She'd been provoking me and I'd just given her information. I didn't want to give her anything. Except maybe some ugly scars.

Lumine appeared to interpret my sudden silence as submission rather than frustration.

"I can't give you all the time I'd like, Calla." Her voice wrapped around me like a python about to constrict. "But I've discussed this matter in depth with your father. Listen to him. Listen to us and everything can be all right. Even for your brother. And your pack."

I met her eyes, searching for deception, but only found a confident, hard gaze.

"You'll help Ansel?"

She nodded. "Everything can be as it was."

As it was. My broken past made whole again.

"If you'll help us," she said.

I didn't answer her. I couldn't have spoken if I'd wanted to. My limbs were shaking, my head still throbbing, and my throat was parched.

"Stephen." Lumine extended her hand to my father. He approached the bed warily. "Emile and Efron will arrive within the hour. Use this time wisely. As we've agreed."

"Of course, mistress." My father inclined his head as Lumine rose. She left the room with the wraith trailing behind her.

The moment the shadow creature was out of sight, I shuddered and slumped against my pillows.

"Here." My father picked up a glass sitting on the nightstand. "Drink this."

I eyed the glass and shook my head.

He smiled wryly. "It's just water, Calla. I poured it myself."

"Thanks," I said hoarsely, taking the glass. I looked at the clear liquid for a moment, wondering if I could trust my father. Wondering if it even mattered. The water eased the pain of my dry throat as I drank.

"How long have I been here?"

"They brought you in the night before last," he said. "You've been in and out of consciousness because they let the wraith continue to feed on you." He growled, glancing toward the door. "So you'd be weak for questioning, open to suggestion."

"What do they want?" I asked, handing the glass back to him.

"They want you to tell them where Shay is," he said without missing a beat.

I crumpled a bit as relief blanketed my limbs. Shay wasn't here. He was safe. That at least was something.

"I won't," I said, meeting his steady gaze. "I would never betray him."

"I didn't think you would."

He was watching me closely, but I couldn't read the emotions on his face. Confusion, maybe? Worry?

"Your brother . . . ," he said carefully. "Is he—?"

"He's safe," I said.

"Is he well?"

I began to shake my head and something burst inside me. I cried out, burying my face in my hands. My body shuddered as I sobbed, the recent losses finally overtaking me. My mother, my brother, Lydia, Silas, Mr. Selby . . . and maybe others that had been killed after I'd blacked out. What had any of it been for? After everything I was back where I'd started in Vail, subject to the whims of my mistress. Maybe there wasn't any way to escape destiny.

My father's arms were around me. I was too distraught to react, though I knew I should be startled. I couldn't remember the last time he'd hugged me. He'd often tussle affectionately with Ansel and me when we were wolves, but that served as a fighting exercise as much as a form of bonding. When we were human, my father was always reserved. Now his shoulders were shaking and he was weeping as openly as I was.

We stayed that way, leaning on each other, both lost in grief, until I pulled away. Rubbing my bleary eyes, I turned back to the window. Though my room was on the second floor, it wasn't a far drop to the ground. Maybe this was my only chance. Maybe my father would come with me.

"No, Calla," he said, resting his hand on my shoulder. "There are

Banes all around the perimeter of our compound. You might be able to fight off two or three of them, but eventually they'd overwhelm you."

I turned to face him, unsurprised that he'd read my thoughts so easily. After all, he'd raised me to think and act like a warrior, always seeking a way to gain the upper hand.

"Can we talk?" I whispered, searching his eyes for any sign of his true feelings about all that was happening around us. My father loved order, control. His world had devolved into chaos. And from the way he'd just held me and wept with me, I knew something inside him had been ripped apart by what the Keepers had done to our family.

He glanced at the door, nodding. "They'll have a wraith posted outside. But the room is ours."

My heart was racing. How much time did we have? What were the most important things for me to know?

"Did they take anyone else?" I asked. "When they brought me here, were there other prisoners?"

"Not that I'm aware of," he said. "But I'm not exactly their confidant these days."

I bit my lip, realizing this was the moment. Maybe the very thing the Searchers needed.

"Dad," I began, trying to keep my voice from shaking. "What if I could help you?"

He turned sharp eyes on me, and my heart skipped a beat. Did my own father consider me a traitor? After all that had happened, was loyalty to the Keepers still important to him?

"Help me how?"

I felt breathless, but forced myself to go on. "I saved Shay because the Keepers were going to kill him."

He didn't respond, but watched me closely as I spoke.

"He's the Scion," I said. "A descendent of the Keepers themselves who can destroy them."

"If he's one of them, why would he turn against them?" My father's brow creased.

"He's not exactly one of them," I said, words rushing out. "His mother was human."

"I don't think that's possible—"

"It is." I took his hands. "Everything we've been told about the Keepers and Searchers. About the war. Even about who we are. It was all lies."

His hands gripped mine, so tight it was painful, but I kept speaking.

"The Keepers twisted us, this world, so they could rule it. The Searchers are trying to change that. They only fight to make things right again. Shay is the key to all of that."

"How can you be sure?" he whispered, eyes wild.

I racked my mind. He hadn't seen what I'd seen. The Academy—the beauty and grace of the Searchers' magic, so contrary to the cruel manipulations of the Keepers' spellwork. He hadn't fought alongside my new allies, didn't have reason to trust them as I did. What could convince him? I knew I had to bring him around. His help could change everything for me . . . for all of us.

"Calla." He sounded as desperate as I felt. "What do you know? We don't have much time. Emile—"

He couldn't say the Bane alpha's name without growling. My mind crackled as realization hit me like a flash of lightning.

"Corrine," I said.

"What?" He frowned.

"Corrine Laroche." I squeezed his hands. "She wasn't killed by a Searcher ambush."

My father stiffened, but I hurried on. "The Searchers were coming to fight with her. She was leading a revolt against the Keepers."

Meeting his gaze, I expected to find disbelief, but it wasn't there.

"But the plot was uncovered and they killed her and all the other

Banes who'd sided with her," I said. "And when the Searchers arrived, the Keepers were waiting for them."

My father pulled his hands from mine as his fists clenched. "You were only one. Just an infant when that happened."

"I know," I said. "It happened on Ren's and my first birthday."

"I always thought . . ." He paused, a growl rumbling in his chest. "That something wasn't right. When the Keepers summoned us to fight, we went after the Searchers—tore into them at the Bane compound, chased them all the way to Boulder. But there weren't any bodies."

"What do you mean?"

"The Banes," he said. "The Keepers called us to battle because the Banes had been ambushed by Searchers. But when we reached their compound, no Bane wolves were there, injured or dead. There were no casualties. The Searchers are hard fighters; they leave wounded and dead in their wake."

"But wraiths don't," I whispered.

His eyes met mine, glinting like steel. He nodded. "The Searchers told you this?"

Though his own memories were offering bits of truth, I could still hear his reluctance to trust his longtime enemies.

"The Searchers filled in some blanks," I said. "But I read about Corrine's death and the trap."

"Where?" he asked, startled.

"In Bosque Mar's library," I replied with a shiver. "At Rowan Estate. There was an account in the *Haldis Annals*."

"Corrine was a good wolf," he said quietly. "She didn't deserve the life handed to her."

"I know," I said.

"I suppose it's a blessing in disguise that her boy never knew."

My breath caught at his mention of Ren. "He knows now."

"You know where he is?" My father's eyes went wide. "The

Keepers told us he'd run off. Couldn't take the shame of losing his pack. Like Logan."

A smile tugged at my lips. "I know where Logan is too."

One of his eyebrows rose. "Really?"

"They're both with the Searchers," I said. "Ren because Adne wanted to save him . . . and I did too."

"Who's Adne?"

"Monroe's—one of the Searchers—daughter. And she's . . ." I realized just how much I'd learned and how little my father still knew. "She's Ren's sister."

He gave me a long look, finally sighing. "Corrine and the Searcher Monroe?"

"You don't sound surprised," I said.

"You said before that Shay had a human mother," he said. "So it follows that pairings between humans and our kind would have happened too." Drawing a slow, deep breath, he said, "And no one takes the kind of risk Corrine did without something enormous at stake. Something like love."

I blinked away the new tears that gathered in my eyes. "I know."

The smile he gave me was kind. "You love that boy . . . the Scion?"

I nodded, drawing my knees up to my chest.

He watched me, frowning slightly. "But you also came back for Ren?"

My cheeks burned, as suddenly I was a daughter caught in an awkward conversation with her father. "It's complicated."

"I suppose it is." He laughed. "And I understand now why Renier is nothing like his father."

"His father . . . his real father . . ." I had to clear my throat to finish. "Was a good man. A warrior like us."

"It's good to know Corrine found at least a bit of happiness in her life," he said quietly. "Even if only briefly."

"I guess," I said, thinking about the cost for Corrine, Monroe, Ren, and Adne. Adne was an orphan now, but she'd saved her brother. Did that balance things out? I didn't know.

"Love," my father said softly. "Real love, even in moments, is worth more than any of us can say."

I stared at him, the clear gaze in his eyes forcing truth into mine.

"Who are you and what have you done with my father?" I cracked a smile.

He chuckled. "There are times for war—many times. But sometimes it's necessary to risk speaking the truth of our own vulnerabilities."

Watching him, my chest pinched with sadness. "Did you . . . did you love Mom?"

"Yes." His smile faded. "Even more after you and Ansel were born."

I wanted to believe him, but I couldn't stop my next question. "But you seemed so different?"

"We were very different," he said. "But we were both always trying to be the alphas we thought we had to be. To protect the pack. To keep you and your brother safe."

My nails dug into my hands. She'd been trying to protect me and my rebellion had killed her.

"I'm sorry," I whispered.

"No," he said, tucking my hair behind my ear. "She never blamed you for any of this."

I nodded, wishing his words would take away the guilt that twisted like a knife in my gut.

"And your mother had a wild side," he said. "No one could out-hunt her. When we were free in the forest, running together—those were our happiest times."

I smiled at him, remembering the boundless joy of hunting with Shay. "I'm glad."

"These Searchers." He stood up, rounding the foot of the bed to stand near the window. "Do you think there's any chance they could win?"

"Logan thinks so," I said. "That's why he's giving them information."

My father glanced at me. "He's turned on his father?"

"I don't think he'd put it that way," I said, smiling grimly. "I think he's just trying to keep his own hide intact."

"That sounds about right."

"Shay has a weapon," I said. "Or most of it. The Elemental Cross."

"A cross is a weapon?"

"It's two swords," I said. "Once he has them both, he can defeat the Keepers. He'll be able to kill wraiths."

"Nothing can kill wraiths." He spoke the words to the swirling snow outside rather than to me.

"The Scion can."

"How will they attack?"

I cringed, wondering if I should say anything more. What if my father was still hoping he could regain his status among the Keepers?

His fingers were twitching. Knowledge and hope bubbled up inside me. He didn't want anything to do with the Keepers. My father was a warrior. He wanted to fight.

"I don't know how the attack will happen." That much was true. We'd been focused on retrieving the pieces of the cross. Who knew what the future held after that? "But we'll need an army to back up Shay."

My father turned to face me, tilting his head thoughtfully. "An army?"

I nodded.

"The Searchers aren't enough?"

"No," I said. "They'll fight to the end, but they need help. That's where we come in."

"We?"

"Guardians."

He laughed. "You expect to lead a wolf army against the Keepers?"

"It's happened before," I said. "It's part of our history. The Harrowing was a Guardian revolt."

"More secrets in the library?"

"Yes," I said. "But I can only lead my pack . . . and there are only seven of us. Hardly an army."

He'd gone very still.

"I'm a young alpha," I said slowly. "We need a veteran. A leader who the other wolves will follow."

"Calla—" There was a warning note in his voice, edged with pain.

"You're still the Nightshade alpha."

His shoulders were tight with fury. "I've been stripped of that role."

"No one can take your pack from you," I said, rolling onto my knees. "Are the Nightshades happy that the Keepers are calling Emile their alpha?"

He grimaced.

"I didn't think so," I said. "You can lead them. You have to lead them."

"When?" His question was hardly more than a whisper.

"Soon." I slid off the bed and took his hand. "I wish I knew more."

"If the Searchers win, what happens to the wolves?"

I opened my mouth to answer before I realized I didn't have one. What would happen to us if we managed to win this war? Where did Guardians belong?

The door to my bedroom swung open. Emile Laroche swaggered in, glanced at our clasped hands, and grinned.

"A Tor family reunion." He smirked. "Isn't this touching?"

I glared at him and he ran his tongue over his sharpening canines.

"Too bad it can't last."

SEVENTEEN

MY FATHER DROPPED to the ground, a gray-brown wolf blocking Emile's path to me. Emile shifted forms, bristling and snarling. He began to stalk toward us. My father gave a warning bark, muscles bunching as he prepared to attack.

"Now, now." Efron Bane strolled into the room with Lumine at his side. "We don't have time to let you boys tussle."

The two alphas were still facing off, fangs bared and hackles raised.

"Enough." Lumine's command snapped through the room. "Shift back at once."

Both wolves reluctantly obeyed, their snarls giving way to angry glares when they returned to human form. My father still stood in front of me, his body shielding mine.

"Have you had any success, Stephen?" Lumine asked.

He shook his head. "A terribly stubborn girl, mistress. I can't bring her around."

"Give me five minutes." Emile snorted. "I'll bring her around."

My father's fist balled up, but Efron put a hand on Emile's shoulder. "Now, now. World's turning, rapidly shifting circumstances, remember? We won't be able to spare you a round of fun with the girl."

Emile shrugged Efron's hand off. "This is a mistake. The little bitch is a traitor and should die."

I watched their exchange, increasingly perplexed. What was happening?

Lumine crossed the room, assessing me with her gaze. "Apparently you've earned some friends among the Searchers, Calla."

"And they have something we want," Efron added.

"Your son was a fool to let himself be captured," Emile spat. "You should leave him to rot in a Searcher hole."

Emile rocked back on his heels when Efron cuffed him. "Remember yourself, wolf. The son of your master deserves your respect."

Emile glared at him, but bowed his head in submission.

My mind reeled. Logan? Logan was claiming he'd been kidnapped. What the hell was going on?

"Come with me, Calla." Lumine beckoned. "We don't want to be late."

I glanced at my father before walking to her side. She reached up, fingering tendrils of my shorn blond locks.

"It's such a pity about your hair," Lumine said. "What were you thinking?"

I didn't answer her.

"Stephen, wait for me to return," she said, pursing her lips as she watched my father. "You and I still have things to discuss."

"Of course, mistress." He bowed his head.

As I followed Lumine out of the room, I resisted the urge to look back at him. Right now I was supposed to be a headstrong, rebellious daughter who had no respect for her father. I couldn't let the Keepers know that only two out of those three things were true.

I couldn't see out of the dark tinted windows of the limo, but we drove for about an hour. My mind was still back in Vail. I wished there were some way to talk with my father. He would help us. He would fight the Keepers. But how could we possibly link his pack with the Searchers?

My body was exhausted. My mind in a frenzy. I still had no idea where I was being taken or what would happen when we arrived at our destination. No matter how confident I wanted to appear, curiosity won out when the car pulled to a stop.

"Where are we?"

"A terribly inconvenient location insisted upon by your friends." Efron set down the glass of brandy he'd been sipping during the ride. "We should be commended for our cooperation."

Emile growled quietly. He'd been staring at me for the entire trip. I knew he wanted to intimidate me, but it only made me hate him more. When he climbed past me, following Efron out of the limo, I whispered, "Someday I will watch you die."

He smiled at me. All fangs. "Too afraid to try and kill me yourself?"

I slid a hard smile back at him without flinching. Fear had no part in it, but there were a number of people on the list of Emile's enemies who deserved revenge more than I did. Including my father. Including Ren.

"Move along, Calla," Lumine said, flicking me with her long nails.

I climbed out of the car. Emile stayed at my side, playing the role of prison guard, while the Keepers spent time smoothing the lines of their respective Chanel and Gucci suits. The driver and another man exited the car. I recognized both as elder Banes. They took up flanking positions beside the Keepers.

I looked around, trying to figure out where we were. We stood at the edge of a small meadow that broke up the pine forest. In the distance I could see the outlines of mountain peaks where snow-laden clouds curled around jagged rock. The air was too fresh to put us near any city, but we weren't in the territory around Vail either.

We'd driven out of the storm as well. Here the occasional icy flake drifted past, but there was almost no sign of wind and the snow only reached our ankles in depth.

I caught the sign of movement in the trees across the open space. Figures emerged from the forest, coming toward us.

When I recognized the tumble of chestnut hair and long duster, I almost called out. Connor was alive. Just seeing him gave me hope that maybe the mission in Eydis hadn't ended in disaster. Without thinking, I stepped toward him. Emile grabbed my arm, his fingers digging into my flesh hard enough to bruise. I ignored the pain as my eyes moved over the rest of the party, but I didn't find who I was looking for. The two people I'd expect to lead an effort to rescue me, Shay and Ren, were nowhere to be seen. Neither were Bryn or Mason or Nev.

Connor was leading a slumped figure, who stumbled through the snow. Logan looked in much worse shape than the last time I'd seen him. When he got close, I saw his swollen, split lip and black eye.

"Father!" Logan cried out. Connor shoved an elbow into his ribs and Logan doubled over coughing.

"How dare you lay a hand on my son!" Efron shouted, eyes blazing. I saw power rolling over his shoulders like lightning and hoped Connor knew what he was doing. Even if an exchange had been agreed upon, if a wraith was in the mix, I didn't have a lot of faith in our chances of getting out of this alive.

Anika glanced at Connor, shaking her head. "Enough."

Connor continued to hold Logan's gaze and dragged a finger across his throat. The young Keeper cowered and threw a pleading gaze at his father.

Quite the show they're putting on for the Keepers. Please let it work.

Even though I wasn't in on the plan, I trusted it was a good one.

A proud, stiff figure whose wrists were cuffed with steel kept pace with Anika. Sabine's eyes were bloodshot, limbs trembling in the cold.

Sabine? What is she doing here? And why does she have metal restraints on her wrists?

Two more Searchers, armed with crossbows, took up the rear of the small party. They kept their weapons trained on Emile and the other two Banes. The small party came to a halt when they were about five feet away from us.

"I'd offer you refreshments, but you turned down my offer of hospitality," Efron said to Anika, though he was watching Sabine. He looked as puzzled as I was by her appearance. His gaze was hard, shifting from fury to curiosity as she kept her own eyes downcast.

"Your offices hardly make a hospitable meeting place to us, Efron," Anika said with a cold smile.

Efron shrugged. "Shall we do business, then?"

"As we've agreed," Anika said. "The wolf for your son?"

Efron nodded.

Sabine stumbled forward suddenly, throwing herself at Efron's feet. "Wait! You promised I could speak!"

The Banes sprang forward, shifting into wolf form. They stalked around Sabine.

Efron's lips curled back in a sneer as he looked at the trembling girl on her knees in front of him.

I stared at her. What the hell was she doing?

"Please," she said. "Please."

"What is this?" Efron spat.

"That girl is useless to us," Anika said stiffly. "But unlike you, we aren't monsters. We don't execute prisoners for no reason and we can't risk her seeing our operations. She's a liability."

Sabine was sobbing and trying to tear out her hair through her bonds. "I didn't know. I'm so sorry. I made a terrible mistake."

"How pathetic," Lumine said. "What a joy that we don't share your burden of conscience." She looked at the Banes and raised her hand. I couldn't breathe, knowing she was about to give the order for them to rip Sabine apart.

"No." Efron threw her a sharp glance. "This is for me to deal with."

Lumine sighed, letting her hand fall. "As you wish."

"Please forgive me, master." Sabine stared up at him, her face wet with tears. "Show me your favor. Take me back."

I felt sick, knowing this wasn't real but unable to understand how it could be part of the Searchers' plan. Why would Sabine come back to Efron? What good would come of that?

A smile slowly curved Efron's mouth. "Dear Sabine, why would I open my arms to you? Betrayal cuts like the sharpest knife. Surely you know that."

"I know," she pleaded. "I didn't understand. But I don't belong with them. I belong with you." She turned to glare at Anika. "They are fools," she hissed. "I want to live. Let me come back to the Banes."

Efron nodded. "You always were a survivor."

She nodded.

"Dax and Fey would certainly welcome your return," he continued, lazily trailing his hand through his golden hair. "Particularly since the third in your party proved a poor replacement for you."

My blood felt colder than the air around us. *Oh no.*

Lumine smiled cruelly. "I told you she wouldn't last."

Efron shrugged.

Sabine wasn't moving. She kept her eyes on Efron but didn't speak.

My voice broke the silence. "Cosette?"

The question earned me a knock on the head from Emile that made my ears ring as I hit the snow on all fours.

"Keep your mouth shut, bitch."

"Such a frail girl. Not much of a wolf either." Efron shook his head slowly in mock regret. "One day after you'd left, we found her hanging from a tree outside the Bane compound. Only one day."

His gaze slid over Sabine, his smile razor sharp. She didn't flinch; instead she murmured, "Cosette was always weak."

"Indeed." Efron stretched his hand to Sabine. She took his fingers, letting him pull her up. "Welcome home, my dear."

"Thank you." She bowed her head.

"Can we move this along?" Connor suddenly bellowed, shoving Logan to his knees. "This one smells like his own piss."

Efron glared at him. "If you've harmed my son . . ."

"No permanent damage has been done," Anika said. "I assure you."

"Give him to us," Efron said, though he kept his hold on Sabine. "Now."

"Not before we have the wolf," Anika replied.

"Emile." Efron jerked his chin toward Connor.

With a sweep of his arm, Emile lifted me onto my feet and had me stumbling toward the Searchers. At the same time, Connor kicked Logan, who began to scramble through the snow, Connor behind him. We stopped less than a foot apart.

Emile grinned at Connor. "Well, well. I haven't seen you since a minute before I made meat out of your leader."

"I won't forget to show my thanks for that," Connor said.

"I look forward to it," Emile said.

Connor grabbed Logan by the shoulders, thrusting the Keeper out in front of him. "Let's just do this."

"Happily," Emile snarled, tightening his grip on my waist. "Sorry we didn't have more time to chat, Calla."

I glared at him. "Go to hell."

Despite my outrage, my heart was pounding as I glanced over my shoulder at Sabine. We couldn't leave her here. We just couldn't. Then I was being shoved forward and I saw Logan tumbling past me. I threw Connor a pleading look as Emile let me go.

Connor shouted before I could catch my breath, and in the next moment I was in the Searcher's arms and we were running through the snow toward the other side of the meadow. Light blazed ahead of us as a portal opened and I heard voices calling my name.

The Banes were already lunging after us, but the Searchers had anticipated Keeper treachery. Crossbows twanged as Connor pulled me into the shimmering doorway with Anika at our side, calling orders even as we ran from the snow-filled meadow. I twisted in his arms, looking for Sabine. Just as the portal's light poured over me, I met her gaze and thought I saw her smile.

EIGHTEEN

"WE HAVE TO GO BACK!" I shrieked at Connor, who struggled to hold me as Adne closed the door.

"What did they do to you? Have you lost your mind?" Connor shouted as I thrashed against him. "Why the hell would we go back there? And by the way, that's some thanks for the rescue!"

"You left Sabine!" Tears were running down my cheeks and I couldn't stop them. I was too angry and too afraid for what would happen to her.

Connor rolled his eyes. "We didn't leave her." He shoved me away with a grunt.

"It's part of the plan, Calla," Adne said gently.

"Thanks for the vote of confidence." Connor glared at me.

"The plan?" I forced myself to take a breath, shuddering out my wild emotions.

"Like I said." Connor laughed. "No confidence in us at all."

"We needed someone who could watch the Keepers and communicate with the Guardians," Adne said.

"And Sabine was your best choice?" I couldn't quite keep the anger out of my voice. "Do you know what she's been through?"

"It was Sabine's idea," Anika answered, giving me a measured gaze.

I opened and closed my mouth again, unable to reply. Sabine came up with this plan?

"And it was a good plan," Anika said. "We need her help. She's the best link between Keepers and Guardians we have."

"You didn't worry that Efron wouldn't take the bait?" I asked, feeling a bit unsteady in the current of this information.

"Logan was sure he would," Connor said. "Something about pride being his father's greatest weakness, Sabine as an Achilles' heel, blah, blah, more metaphors."

"Fine." I bared my fangs at Connor. "But how does Ethan feel about all of this?"

"He only agreed if we let him go too."

I felt like I'd been punched in the gut. "Ethan is in Vail?"

"Yep," Connor said. "He insisted."

"But they'll kill him."

"God, Connor." Adne glared at him. "Don't say it like that."

Connor grinned. "But it's so much more fun when she looks like she's going to throw up."

She ignored him, turning to me. "Calla, Ethan isn't with the Keepers. He and Nev are with Tom Shaw."

"At the Burnout?" I asked.

"He built what's pretty much a bunker under that bar," Connor said. "We've used it as a safe house from time to time. Nev and Ethan are staying there, coordinating intelligence coming in from the Guardians through Sabine and Logan. Logan's keeping tabs on his father and the other Keepers. Sabine is lining up allies among the Banes and hopefully getting your father to do the same with the Nightshades. We're using them to set up the final offensive on Rowan Estate."

I swallowed the hard lump that formed in my throat. "When is the attack?"

"If we pick up this last piece," Adne said quietly, "we attack at midnight."

"That soon?" I asked.

"Well, considering we've jumped a few times zones, it's actually already in the past." Connor wiggled his eyebrows at me.

"I have no idea what you're talking about."

I'd assumed Connor had dragged me through a portal back to the Academy. But we weren't in the Searchers' building. It had been afternoon when we'd left the mountain meadow. Now we were outside and it was dark, but not night. The air was full of the promise of dawn. Hushed pink light crept upward into deep gray sky.

"We're in New Zealand," Adne said. "Where it's already tomorrow morning."

"But when we get back to Vail for the attack, it will still be midnight yesterday," Connor said.

"You're giving me a headache," I said.

"It's what he does best." Adne grinned.

"Let's be on our way." Anika started walking. "The others are waiting."

"Where are they?" I asked as my mind began to settle.

"They're at the boat," Adne said.

"Another boat?" I groaned.

"Different sort of trip this time," Connor said. "No swim at the end."

He led us into the brightening morning, pushing through a forest unlike any I'd seen. The ground beneath my feet was rough, broken rocks that seemed to be halfway to becoming sand. Trees with spiky limbs and thick leaves stretched over us, complemented by dense brush, tightly packed along the forest floor.

When the path opened up, the trees thinning to slope down onto a wide beach, I heard two familiar voices shout at once.

"Calla!"

Ren and Shay were both staring at me. They were sitting back to back. And they were tied up.

I stared at them. "What the—"

Mason, who'd been circling the captive boys as a wolf, shifted forms.

"Thank God!" He ran to me, catching me in a tight embrace. "It is so good to see you."

"You too." I hugged him and then pointed to Ren and Shay, who were now squirming against their restraints. "What's going on?"

"We had to tie them up," Adne said.

"And I had to guard them," Mason said. "Even after creating the most intricate knots known to mankind. I even bit Shay once."

"I wasn't being that difficult," Shay said.

"Yes, you were."

"Why did you have to tie them up?" I asked, watching as Connor drew a knife and began to saw through the ropes holding Shay and Ren together.

"You didn't have to tie us up!" Shay shrugged the frayed ropes off.

"Yes, we did!" Adne's hands were on her hips. "You would have torn right through that portal to get to her. You were both acting like morons."

"She's right," Ren said. "They probably did have to tie us up."

Shay grinned.

"Shut up!" Adne glared at Ren. "You're still on my list of people I'm angry with. Don't think you'll get off it by agreeing with me."

Ren gave Connor a sidelong glance. "She keeps a list, huh?"

"Don't worry," Connor said. "I've been on it for years."

"I heard that." Adne's voice jumped up a couple of octaves.

"I'm sure you did, gorgeous." Connor jumped back, having cut through the rope, as Shay and Ren both leapt up and rushed at me.

I took a few steps back, anticipating a tackle. But they both pulled up just short, breathing hard, glancing from each other to me.

"Hey," I said, unsure what to do. I wished they would both just hug me, but it didn't look like that was going to happen.

"Hey," Ren said, folding his arms over his chest. "Sorry we

couldn't come save you ourselves." I could see his pulse jumping at his throat.

Shay looked just as uncomfortable, giving Ren an uneasy smile. "Not that we didn't want to. Hence the being tied up." He raked a hand through his windblown hair. "Are you okay?"

"Yeah." I shoved my hands in my pockets. "The wraith was awful. But it was over pretty quickly. At least from my perspective. After I passed out, I don't remember much. I woke up in my room. Lumine was there."

"What happened?" Ren asked.

"They asked questions I didn't answer," I said. "Then came the trade. I wasn't there long."

"But you were back in Vail?" Shay asked.

"Yes." I shivered at the memory of my room, of Lumine pretending to be my mother. "I saw my dad, though. I think he could help us."

"That's the point of having Ethan and Sabine working in Vail," Connor said. "Let's hope they can make that connection."

"We'll send a dispatch to Ethan and Tom," Anika said. "It's good that you could speak with your father, Calla."

I nodded, wondering if my father really could bring the Nightshades over to our side.

"Open a door, Adne," Anika continued. "It's time for me to update the Guides and set the stage for tonight."

"Tell them to cross their fingers and toes," Connor said.

Adne began to weave, the threads from her skean mirroring the light of dawn that spilled from the shoreline up into the forest where we stood. Ren stood close to his sister, entranced by her work.

"So Pyralis is here?" I asked Connor, drawing him away from the others.

"It's out there." He pointed to the silhouette of an island in the distance. "That's Whakaari."

"And we're going there now?" I glanced at my companions. Our group had shrunk. Ethan, Sabine, and Nev were in Vail. Silas was gone. "Just us? We don't get reinforcements?"

"We don't know what's out there." Connor's jaw clenched. "We wanted to risk as few as possible."

"That's reassuring." I tried to laugh, but it came out like my voice cracking.

"We'll manage." Shay rested his fingers lightly on my arm. The gentle touch warmed my cold skin.

"We'd better," Connor said. "This is it. Last stop on the big ride."

"You know where it is on the island?" I asked.

"We know where the entrance to the chamber is," Connor replied. "Our best guess is that the blade is somewhere inside the volcano."

"Wait . . . volcano?" I could feel my eyes bulge.

Shay nodded. "There are lots of active volcanoes in New Zealand. Look." He pointed at the sky above the island. A plume of ash rose steadily into the clouds.

Mason came up beside me and slid his arm around my shoulders. "I didn't believe it when they first told me either."

"We're going into a volcano," I said, shoulders slumping. "That's . . . that's just fantastic."

There is no way in hell we'll pull this off.

"What's a volcano compared to a mutant spider? Or piranha vampire bats?" Shay grinned at us. "Come on, it's an adventure. Besides, tourists go out there all the time. The volcano can't be that dangerous."

"I'm guessing the tourists aren't trying to steal a forbidden object out from under the noses of evil witches."

"Not unless they've paid for the deluxe package," Shay replied solemnly.

I stared at him for a moment before I began to laugh.

"You're crazy, man," Mason said, but he was laughing too.

"What did I miss?" Adne asked as she and Ren joined us. I turned to see the portal was gone, along with Anika.

"Only Shay's twisted sense of humor," Connor replied. "Let's get to the boat."

Mason, Adne, Connor, and I clambered into the boat while Shay and Ren shoved it off the beach into the water. Connor gunned the motor, sending us bouncing over the waves toward Whakaari.

"So where does Logan fit in to this plan?" I shouted over the roar of the motor and crash of waves.

"We need Logan on the inside." Adne shielded her eyes as the sun crested the horizon. "He'll be pivotal when Shay gets to the Rift."

"Why?" I asked.

"A Keeper and only a Keeper can summon Bosque and force him to reveal his true form. Shay won't be able to banish him unless that happens."

"How can a Keeper force Bosque to do anything?" I asked. "He's the one who controls them."

"It has to do with the oath Keepers make in order to get their power—a test of loyalty," she said. "Their allegiance to the Harbinger can only be sealed when he isn't masked by a glamour. They have to commit to the real thing—and from what I understand, it isn't pretty."

"Warts and all," Connor said.

"I think it's a lot worse than warts," Adne said.

"With luck we'll see that for ourselves," he said.

"Some luck," Mason said.

Connor threw him a thin smile. "When Logan completes the invocation, Bosque will be in his true form. It's a means of subjugating the Keepers to the Nether, but in our case it creates the opening in the veil we need to banish the Harbinger."

I hated the thought that we were relying so much on someone with loyalties as slippery as Logan's. "Do we really trust Logan to keep his end of the bargain?"

"Of course not!" Connor laughed. "But we don't have a choice."

"But what if he changes his mind?" I shouted. "Or he decides the writing on the wall actually says the Keepers are going to win?"

"It might happen." Connor shrugged. "Not much we can do about it."

"But he knows where the Academy is!"

Adne shook her head. "Doesn't matter. We took care of that."

"How?" I wiped water off my face as a wave splashed over the side of the boat.

"Sorry!" Connor yelled. "I'll try to find a smoother route."

"We put a hex on him," Adne said. "If he so much as mentions Italy or the Academy or even tries to point it out on a map, he'll choke to death on his own vomit."

"Like what happened to Mr. Selby in Big Ideas," Shay said. "Anika said that hexes are something all witches can pull off pretty easily, whether they're amateurs or the professionals, like these guys."

"Of course, the Keepers could always figure out a way to break our hex," Connor said.

"We don't need your commentary, Connor." Adne slapped him on the back. "Just drive the boat!"

"Are you okay?" Shay was leaning over Mason, whose eyes were closed as his fingers, white-knuckled, gripped the edge of the boat.

Mason didn't open his eyes but grimaced when Connor hit another wave, soaking us.

"Sorry!" Connor shouted, though he whooped as we bounced up and down.

"Just promise me that if we win, I'll never have to get in another boat," Mason said. "That's all I want. No more boats."

"Deal." Shay put his arm around Mason. "No more boats."

Ren climbed over to sit next to me. "How are you doing?" He leaned close and slipped his hand over mine.

"I'll be okay," I said, licking salt spray from my lips. "Though I think Mason's whole 'no more boats' plan is a good one."

"Yeah." He smiled. "Wolves and the ocean. Just not natural."

"No kidding," I said.

He bent down, murmuring in my ear. "Did they hurt you, Calla? I was worried . . . Efron . . . or my . . . Emile . . ."

I shook my head. "Just the wraith."

He squeezed my fingers tight and I looked up at him. "I'm really fine, Ren. But Sabine—"

My throat closed. No matter how good a plan it was, I hated the thought of her being at Efron's mercy.

Still clasping my fingers tight, he growled, staring at the island that loomed before us. "I didn't want her to go. None of us did. We argued for a long time."

I nodded. At least I wasn't the only one who wasn't comfortable with this strategy. The price seemed too high.

"I thought Ethan would kill someone," Ren was saying. "He went crazy."

"I'm sure," I said.

Ren smiled at me. "Kind of like Shay and I did when they took you."

"What happened?" I asked, blushing at the warmth in his eyes. "After the wraith attacked me."

"There was another wraith." His smile vanished. "Two Keepers were waiting for us in the dive shop. Connor got Adne out onto the deck. She wove as fast as she could."

"But the wraith?" I shivered, hating the memory of its stench in my nostrils, burning through my lungs. The way it had felt like I was being flayed.

"It came at us." Ren stiffened. "I thought at least a few of us would be dead before anyone could get out."

His eyes moved over to Shay, who was chatting amiably with Mason. He'd managed to get the seasick wolf laughing, which was impressive.

"Connor was shouting at everyone to stay back, but Shay jumped in front of him," Ren said. "And he pulled out that sword."

I could see the hilt peeking out over Shay's shoulder. "The sword stopped the wraith."

Ren nodded. "It didn't destroy the thing, but when Shay hit the wraith, it screamed. I've never heard a sound like that. I thought my ears would explode. It couldn't get past him and he held it off until Adne had the door open and we escaped."

He growled. "But we couldn't do anything about you. You were gone."

"I'm here now," I said, pulling my hand from his grasp.

"I know." He frowned, but leaned forward and kissed my cheek, swift and soft, despite my warning growl. "If we lost you . . . I can't think about it. But you're here and that's all that matters."

I glanced over at Shay. His eyes were on us, and while he didn't look happy, he wasn't lunging at Ren either, which struck me as odd. He nodded once and I realized he and Ren were gazing at each other, their faces calm and mutually respectful. What the hell?

Something had changed while I was gone. I knew I should be happy they weren't fighting, but instead my skin prickled. What was going on with them?

"Almost there!" Connor shouted, bringing the boat's speed down.

"Hallelujah!" Mason lifted his arms to the sky.

Shay laughed. "You realize you're cheering our arrival at an active volcano."

"I'll take dry land over the sea any day," Mason said. "Even dry land that could blow up under my feet."

As we closed in on Whakaari, the ocean swells calmed in the shelter of the island resting on the edge of New Zealand's Bay of Plenty. The engine purred as Connor navigated the coast, beaching us on a narrow strip of sand amid bleak volcanic rock that sprawled across the landscape. The only signs of life were the birds that swooped in the air above us. As I jumped onto the sand, I was struck by the strange mixture of colors that painted the island. Dark gray and brown stones contrasted with the slices of lime green and yellow crystals that grew among them. At intervals rivers of rust-colored rocks appeared, as if Whakaari had wounds that bled freely.

Steam rose from crevices in the island, filling the air with noxious gas.

"I take it back," Mason said, covering his nose. "The water is better than this smell. Why do we keep doing things that make me want to throw up?"

"Almost forgot." Connor tossed gas masks to each of us. "In case the fumes get too strong."

"Where are we headed?" Shay asked.

"Just east of here." Connor climbed out of the boat and began fumbling inside his jacket for something. "It's a little ways up the slope. Not far, though."

"And we don't know what's waiting for us?" Ren asked.

Adne shook her head. "Anyone who's been sent here hasn't come back."

"Do you guys ever have good news?" Mason said. "Or have you heard of the power of positive thinking?"

"I'm too honest to be positive." Adne threw him a wicked smile.

"What are you doing?" Shay peered at Connor, whose back was turned to us. "What is that?"

Shay grabbed Connor's arm, turning him around to reveal a small notebook tucked in his palm.

"Hey!" Connor shouted. "I was in the middle of a sentence."

"Are you . . . taking notes?" Shay asked.

Connor cleared his throat, rubbing the back of his neck uneasily. "It's just . . . I thought that . . . you know . . . Silas."

Adne walked over to Connor, stretched up on her tiptoes, and placed a chaste kiss on his lips. "You're a good man after all."

She smiled sadly, beginning to turn away, but Connor slid his arms around her waist, lifting her off her feet. The kiss he crushed onto her mouth was anything but chaste and lasted so long that soon we all turned away, blushing.

When he finally set her down, his voice was thick. "I give up. I love you, Adne. I am goddamned crazy in love with you."

Adne threaded her fingers through Connor's, squeezing his hand. "Just don't die in there. Okay? We have lots to talk about after all this is over."

"I'll do my best." Connor almost fell over when she threw herself at him, kissing him again. Mason whistled and started clapping.

We all gazed at each other—our silly grins momentarily washing away the tension of an impending fight. Only Ren wasn't smiling. He was eyeing Connor suspiciously.

"What?" Connor asked, frowning at the alpha.

"That's my sister," Ren growled.

Connor stared at him. "I know. And I love her."

"Great," Ren said. "But what are your intentions?"

"My intentions?" Connor looked from Ren to Adne, frowning.

Ren grinned, showing Connor his sharp canines. "When all this is over, you and I have a lot to talk about too."

NINETEEN

CONNOR LED THE WAY as we scrambled over rough rock that cut into my paws. It wasn't a long climb, but it was tiring. We had to avoid deep punctures in the earth where bursts of steam or poisonous gas could spew up without notice. Unlike the vibrant forest of the coast, Whakaari was devoid of life, an utterly alien environment. Though breathtaking, the landscape was far too ominous to be beautiful, its very appearance serving to warn away intruders.

"It's here!" Connor called, waving us forward. We'd reached a point where the slope pitched up suddenly. Straight ahead was a gash in the rock face. Tendrils of steam slipped from the crack, dancing like silk ribbons carried off by the wind.

Drawing closer to the opening, I could see the way the steam caught light flickering within the cavern. Its colors moved from silver to crimson to gold as it fled darkness to dissipate in the air above our heads.

Mason trotted up to the entrance, sniffed, and pawed the ground anxiously. Connor raised his eyebrows and Mason shifted forms.

"You want us to go in there—seriously?" He stared at the cave. "It smells like death. Horrible, farty death."

"Is there any other kind?" Connor asked.

"He's right." Adne covered her mouth and nose. "It smells nasty."

"Are we all going to make nosegays or just get this over with?" Connor pointed to the cavern.

"Do you really know what a nosegay is?" Adne laughed. "I'm impressed."

"That is impressive," Mason said. "Very nineteenth century of you. Not very manly, though . . . nosegays."

Adne put her hands on Connor's chest. "Don't listen to him, sweetie. I still find you very manly."

Connor swore and ducked into the cavern while Adne laughed.

"You're not going to ease up on him after what he said to you?" I asked her.

"Explain to me how that would be fun," she said, grinning at me.

"You'd better keep him on his toes," Ren said as he followed Connor. "I'd be disappointed if you didn't."

"And I wouldn't want to let my big brother down."

"Good girl." He flashed her a smile and disappeared into the cavern.

I squeezed my way into the cave. The air was hot, close, and smelled awful. I began to sweat immediately. Noxious gases seeped into each breath, unpleasant but not harmful enough to merit donning our masks. The tunnel was narrow but not too cramped; we could move along without stooping. Subtle, flickering hues that mimicked firelight illuminated our path. The gentle slope of the earth told me we were slowly making our way into the belly of the volcano.

Connor suddenly stopped, dropping to his stomach and squirming forward. As I got closer, I saw why. The tunnel had opened up, revealing a broad ledge. Connor had crawled to the edge, peering over it. One by one we bellied up alongside him. My breath caught at the sheer drop off the side. The path continued beyond the ledge, where it cut down sharply, transforming from a straight line into a tight, steep spiral.

More than a hundred feet below, I could see an open space, carved in a broad circle out of the volcanic rock. Its smooth surface was broken only by the occasional crevice, belching out steam. A raised stone slab—an unpleasant reminder of the sacrificial dais in the Keepers' Chamber below Eden—lay at the center of the space. Hovering above the altar was the shimmering figure of a woman. Diaphanous robes of crimson and gold floated around her body, lending her a quality of substance that I knew wasn't actually there.

"Cian," Shay breathed.

Connor issued a slow string of curses. "She's not alone."

I followed Connor's stony gaze to three bonfires posted like sentinels alongside Cian's gleaming form.

"Wait a second." Mason frowned. "How can the fires move?"

The flames' positions were shifting, traveling around the dais in a slow circle. I peered down at them, realizing they weren't shapeless. The dancing gold and crimson of each bonfire had a form.

"Oh my God," I whispered. "That isn't possible."

Ren glanced at me and nodded. "I know."

"Yes, it is." Adne's mouth set in a grim line. "Those are wolves."

"I thought they were myths," Connor said, rubbing his temples. "No wonder nobody ever comes back."

"What are they?" Mason whispered, staring at the fiery creatures that circled Cian far below us.

"Lyulf," Adne said. "Fire wolves."

"Those aren't wolves," I hissed, hating the scent of sulfur and burning coal that surrounded us.

"Not the furry kind," Connor said. "But they're wolves, all right. Lyulf are the Harbinger's favorite pets by repute. He used them in the first battle between Keepers and Searchers. Only he can summon them and—"

He broke off as Adne threw him a warning glare.

"And what?" I asked.

"It doesn't matter," Adne said.

"Just tell us." Shay shifted the sword on his back, angling for a better view of the three Lyulf.

Connor grimaced. "By rumor they inspired the Keepers to create Guardians."

"Not exactly a great copy." Mason laughed. "I for one cannot become the human torch . . . or a wolf torch, for that matter."

"It doesn't matter what they inspired or when they fought," Shay said. "How do we kill them?"

"We can't." Connor rolled onto his back, staring up at the cavern ceiling. "That's the problem. Lyulf are powerful Nether beings, like wraiths. Worse than wraiths, actually."

"I have a hard time believing anything is worse than a wraith," I said.

"I support that lack of belief," Ren said.

"Have you ever burned your tongue?" Connor asked. "Did you enjoy it?"

I frowned at him. "What are you talking about?"

"How do you plan to bite something that is made of fire?" He glared at me. "You'd scorch your lungs and be dead within a minute. We can't fight them. I don't know what we're going to do."

"I drove off that wraith," Shay said. "I'll do the same here."

"You can't draw three of them at once," Connor said. "And we need you to get the blade."

"Interference," Ren said. "Like with the bats. That's what we have to do."

Connor met his gaze and then looked away. "We won't all make it."

"We don't have a choice," Ren said. "Besides, isn't that why it's just us? Because we knew we wouldn't all make it."

Connor swore softly, his swords hissing out of their sheaths. "Anybody remember to bring a squirt gun? That could make all the difference."

"So how will this work?" Shay asked, ignoring him.

"We'll draw the Lyulf's attack," Ren said. "If we can keep them on the chase, we can buy you time and maybe avoid serious injury. You get the blade. Connor keeps Adne safe so we can get out of here as soon as you're packing."

Connor didn't turn to face him, but he nodded.

"Let's go." Ren crouched and shifted forms. He glanced at me. I nodded, meeting Mason's eyes as we both slid into our wolf forms. The three of us stalked down the spiraling path, into the belly of the volcano where the fire wolves circled Cian, eternally hunting any who dared trespass. I glanced back to see Shay, Connor, and Adne following behind us at a creeping pace.

The fumes grew stronger while we descended, turning my stomach. I shook my muzzle as my nostrils twitched with discomfort.

This would be so much better if we didn't have to breathe, Mason complained.

Ren's thought traveled back to us. *Stay focused.*

Mason dropped his muzzle low in compliance. I kept close to Ren's flank. We were close enough to hear them now. Steady low snarls emerged from the Lyulf as they stalked their constant unchanging path, their muscles flexing, living flame, their movement like a ring of fire around Pyralis.

Ren paused in the shadows of a rock outcrop. The last place left to remain out of sight before the steep trail ended, leaving only the broad chamber in front of us. Another few steps and we'd be in the open, facing off with the Lyulf.

Try to keep them separated and moving. Don't get cornered.

He raised his muzzle and howled. The Lyulf stopped their circling, turning in the direction of the sound, which now filled the entire cavern. The fire wolves lifted their heads in an answering cry. Smoke billowed from their mouths.

Ren leapt from his hiding place with Mason and me at his heels. The Lyulf stood their ground, snarling, watching us approach. As we closed in, I could see their eyes, smoldering coals set in the flames of their bodies. Empty save for hate and lust for the kill.

Ren bounded for them. The first of the Lyulf crouched and sprang at him. At the last possible moment Ren threw himself to the side, rolling away, and the Lyulf sailed past him. Ren was on his feet again. He barked, wagging his tail. Taunting the wolf.

Split. I shouted my thought at Mason and Ren. *Hold their attention. We need to give Shay time.*

I wheeled away from Ren, snarling at the second wolf while Mason snapped his jaws at the third. The heat pouring off the Lyulf was like a furnace. As I dashed past it, drawing its attack, I could smell my fur singe. I headed for the far side of the chamber, hoping to keep the fire wolves away from the path that Shay would need to take. I didn't need to look back to know the Lyulf was at my heels. With every burst of speed I could feel its heat, flames licking my tail.

I heard Mason yelp and pivoted around, searching for him. He was still running ahead of the other Lyulf, but his flank was smoking.

Just keep running, Mason. I scrambled away from my own attacker. *Hang on!*

Darting, changing direction, doing everything I could to stay out of reach. My only choice was to run. Fighting wasn't an option. Out of the corner of my eye I saw a blur of motion. A golden brown wolf sped across the room, reaching the dais where Cian hovered. He shifted forms, throwing himself at her outstretched arms. A flare of heat brushed across my heels and I leapt into the air. And froze.

The room went black. I was suspended in the air, hanging in empty space. No light. No sound. I could still breathe, but I didn't want to. All our hopes were held in this moment.

Then I was falling. I hit the ground hard, my body slamming into rock.

The Lyulf was still behind me. It shook its muzzle, smoke boiling out of its nostrils. When its eyes focused on me, it snarled and lunged.

I rolled onto my back, smelling burnt fur again but managing to avoid its attack.

Shay was shouting. "Adne, open the door!"

In the far corner of the room I saw twinkling lights as Adne began to weave. The Lyulf saw it too. Turning away from me, the fire wolf howled, drawing the attention of the wolf chasing Mason. The other wolf gave its own howl and the two burning beasts plunged in Adne's direction.

We have to stop them, I called to Mason. Even as we chased the Lyulf, I searched the cavern for any sign of Ren. When my eyes found him, my hackles rose. He was limping, holding one paw up as he tried to dodge the fire wolf's attack. But it was closing in on him, backing him up against a steaming fissure in the rock.

I didn't know what to do. The other two Lyulf were racing toward Adne. I couldn't block their attack and help Ren.

Calla? Mason saw the fire wolf stalking Ren too.

Before I could reply, I heard Connor shout, "Calla! Get your ass over here!"

Ahead I saw Connor holding his swords low, his expression bleak as the wolves approached. My heart felt like it was being torn in two. I knew what I had to do.

Ren stands a better chance against the Lyulf than Connor. I sent a shaky thought to Mason. *Adne is our only way out of here.*

I know, Mason answered, putting on another burst of speed.

Keep moving, Ren, I called to him, not daring to look in his direction again. *We'll be there as soon as we can.*

Just keep her safe. His answering thought came almost immediately. *Don't worry about me.*

Shut up, I snarled. *And stay alive.*

We'd almost caught the wolves. I threw all my strength into the leap as I hurled myself over the flaming bodies, landing in front of them and skidding to a stop in front of Connor. I wheeled around, snarling. My appearance startled the Lyulf, which gnashed its white-hot fangs. I dashed forward, teasing it by putting myself nearly within its reach and then sliding just out of range of its teeth. Out of the corner of my eye I saw Mason mimicking my actions.

It seemed to be working. Fury at their inability to reach us drew the wolves' attention off Adne and Connor.

Let's try drawing them toward Ren.

I was about to make a dash for the alpha, but when I turned, I was shocked to see Ren barreling straight for us. I could see the pain in each movement as he hit the ground with his injured paw. The Lyulf was right behind him and it was faster now that Ren was hurt.

I barked a warning as the fire wolf leapt, but there was nothing I could do. The flaming creature rose into the air, about to come down on Ren's back.

Roll! I shouted a warning, hoping Ren would hear me in time. *Roll to the side!*

Ren threw his body away from the descending wolf. But in the same moment another wolf took Ren's place beneath the attacking Lyulf. And then it wasn't another wolf but instead it was Shay, a sword in each hand.

The twin swords sliced through the wolf. It screamed, belching smoke. And then there was nothing but ash falling like gentle snow on Shay's shoulders. He whirled, meeting my eyes as I bounded past him. Shay wielded the blades so swiftly I could barely follow their movement. A second scream signaled the demise of my own Lyulf attacker.

Connor whooped. "Scion!"

The celebratory cry was a terrible mistake. The Lyulf that had been focused on Mason spun around, its burning-pitch eyes narrowing as it stalked toward the Searcher. Mason howled, trying to draw its attack, but the Lyulf ignored him.

Connor lifted his swords as the fire wolf leapt. "Adne, stay back!"

I was running, all too aware I couldn't get there in time. Shay was at my side, in his wolf form, his toenails clattering on the rocky floor as we ran.

Adne's scream cut through the chamber. "No!" And then she was there, shoving Connor aside.

Her sudden appearance startled the wolf, throwing its attack slightly off. She threw her arm up and the Lyulf's jaws locked around her biceps. She shrieked as it took her to the ground.

Connor rolled to his feet. "Adne!"

He threw himself at the wolf, but I reached him first, knocking him aside. Shay shifted, running the Lyulf through even as it stood above Adne. The wolf shuddered and crumbled, blanketing Adne in ash.

"Get off me!" Connor shoved me away from him, struggling to his feet. He rushed to Adne's side.

"Connor." Shay was kneeling beside her. "Just wait."

"Let me see her!" He knocked Shay over, cradling Adne against him. Her eyes were glassy and she wasn't moving.

Connor began to sob. I shifted into human form, crouching beside him. My breath caught when I saw what he was staring at. Adne's arm from fingertips to shoulder was unrecognizable. Her skin was charred to black, and I glimpsed the white of bone where the wolf's jaws had torn through her flesh. Her shirt had been partially burned away, revealing blistering red on her neck and chest.

Ren limped up beside us, whining. He shifted forms, kneeling behind her head.

"Is she breathing?" he asked.

"I don't know," Connor choked. "I can't tell."

"Let me have her," Ren said.

Mason pulled Connor back and Ren stretched out beside his sister, laying his head on her sternum. After a moment he blew out a long breath.

"It's faint, but it's there," Ren said. "I need to give her blood."

"She's in shock," Shay said. "I don't know if she'll be able to swallow."

"All we can do is give it a shot."

When Ren bit his arm, I saw that his own hand was badly burned, the skin broken and blistering.

"Lift her head," he instructed Shay. When Shay had her chin tilted up, her head resting in his hands, Ren carefully opened her mouth, letting blood slowly drip in. It began to fill her mouth, red liquid trickling down her chin.

"Come on, Adne," I murmured. "You're a fighter."

"Please." Connor twisted out of Mason's grasp, dropping on his knees beside her. "Please come back to me."

Her throat began to move. She swallowed.

"More," I said. Ren pressed his arm to her mouth. She swallowed again. And again. Her other arm came up, fingers curling around Ren's wrist as she drank. Slowly, her body began to remake itself. The redness and blisters faded from her chest and neck. New flesh flowed over her arm, the charred remnants of her muscles falling away as Ren's blood healed her. After another minute, all signs of the Lyulf's attack were gone. She sat up, wiping her mouth.

"That was incredible." She looked down at her healed arm, flexing her fingers.

Connor swooped her into his arms. "Damn it, girl." He kissed her, curling his body around hers. "What kind of crazy stunt was that? Don't ever try to save me again."

"You were about to sacrifice yourself to protect me." She smiled up at him. "There was no way I was going to let you get out of our relationship that easily."

TWENTY

WAVES LAPPED THE SHORELINE a few yards from where we lounged on the rocks. We'd been staring at the Elemental Cross for several minutes, catching our breath, trying to believe we'd succeeded in our impossible task.

"I'm itching to make a clever remark like 'I thought they would be shinier,'" Mason said, clamping his hand over the wound on his arm that he'd opened to give Ren blood. "But I have to admit they seem to be the perfect shininess."

Shay laughed, flipping the blades in the air and catching them effortlessly. I didn't know if it was indeed the shininess, but something about the two swords was perfect, complete.

It was the first time I'd seen Eydis, having been taken out of the fight in Mexico ahead of schedule. Of all the pieces of the cross, I thought it might be the most beautiful. The hilt of Shay's second sword was the same size and shape as Haldis, but where the earth hilt gleamed with the rust of clay and depth of fertile soil, the water hilt boasted shimmering azure and sea green. The colors shifted constantly on its surface, giving it the appearance of containing moving waters within.

The blade rising out of Eydis made me shudder. Its surface leapt with flames that seemed alive, like the burning flesh of the Lyulf. Shay swore that he couldn't feel the heat of the flames, but whenever any of the rest of us came near Pyralis, its intense fire prevented close inspection.

While we rested, taking in the enormity of what happened, Shay practiced using the blades in concert. Though I'd already watched him fight with the Elemental Cross against the Lyulf, its power still mesmerized me. When Shay moved, the swords became extensions of his body. He flowed with the sweep of blades. And the sound. The sound was unlike anything I'd heard before. With each strike, each movement, came the rush of wind, the crash of waves, the roar of fire—all balanced by the stillness of the earth. The power running up and down the blades, grounding in the strength of each hilt, was palpable, making my skin tingle. But it wasn't just the swords, it was Shay himself. Grace, strength, and unwavering focus came from him, working in concert with the Elemental Cross. Wielding the swords, he was beautiful . . . and terrible.

I shivered as I watched him, a part of me wondering if he could be this thing—this force that was the Scion—and still be the boy I loved.

I glanced at Ren, who sat between Mason and me. His eyes followed Shay's every movement, narrowed in concentration. He looked pensive as he tracked the Scion. He gaze struck me as odd. I could have sworn his dark eyes were sad, almost regretful.

"We should get back," Adne said. "Anika needs us."

"You're right," Connor said. He was stretched lazily across the ground with Adne leaning against him. His pose was deceptively casual, but I'd been watching the way he had one arm curved around her, holding her close to his body as though he never intended to let her go, while his other hand stroked her hair. "We took our victory lap. Time to return to battle."

Adne kissed the underside of Connor's jaw before hopping to her feet.

A bittersweet sensation climbed up my spine as she wove the door that would return us to the Academy. We'd accomplished our goal, but this brief celebration meant the stakes had just been raised. In a matter of hours we'd be making a full assault on the Keepers. Everything about my world had been turned inside out. The masters I'd once served had become my enemies, and I was about to go into battle in the hopes of destroying them.

"You ready for this?" Ren asked. When I met his eyes, I knew his thoughts were similar to mine.

I flexed my fingers and stood up. "I have to be. We all do."

"History awaits you," Connor said to Shay as he gestured to the shimmering portal.

"Just because you're trying to keep notes for Silas doesn't mean you have to sound like him," Adne said.

Connor grimaced. "Point taken."

On the other side of the portal we were greeted by a roar from the assembled Searchers. Haldis Tactical had never been intended to hold all the Searchers at once. They'd crowded into the room, pushing up against the walls and spilling out the doorway into the hall.

When Shay appeared, the crowded hushed, waiting. When he lifted the Elemental Cross, the room erupted into cheers. Anika strode up to Shay and bowed. When she raised her face, her cheeks glistened with tears.

She lifted her arms and the noise settled into a low buzz.

"We only have a few hours. You know your assignments. Be prepared to move at six a.m."

The room emptied in a few minutes. A handful of Searchers lingered, gazing at the swords and murmuring their thanks to Shay, but soon only our group plus Anika remained.

"You're all well?" the Arrow asked. "No need of the Elixirs?"

Connor slid his arm around Adne. "A close call, but we have ready-made healers in our wolf friends."

Anika glanced at Connor's tight grip on Adne. A smile flickered across her mouth and then vanished.

"Yes," she said, turning her gaze on the wolves. "We're grateful for that gift."

"What time is it anyway?" Mason yawned.

"Four o'clock," Anika said.

"Two hours," Ren said.

"I'm afraid I need to make it only one," Anika said. "The teams are fully debriefed, but I need to get you up to speed. Take a bit of rest and meet me back here."

"Any word from Vail?" I asked. Our mission had been vital, but it wasn't the only one in play. The stakes were high on all fronts.

"Nothing," she said. "Though we'll see if that's changed when we alert them that we've retrieved the Cross."

I bit my lip, wondering if Sabine had been able to find my father. What had Nev and Ethan been doing? Was Nev risking himself by trying to find other wolves on patrol? Could he bring them over to our side?

So much depended on each piece falling into its place. With only one missing, we'd fail.

Connor had leaned over to whisper to Adne. She nodded and he cleared his throat, speaking to the rest of us.

"If you'll excuse us, we'll be taking that rest. See you in an hour."

As they left, I heard a quiet growl and turned to see Ren starting after them.

I grabbed his arm. "Don't you dare."

"He's taking advantage." Ren was bristling, ready to attack.

"No, he isn't." I tugged Ren backward. "Trust me."

He shot me a suspicious look but stopped trying to pull away from me.

"What are you going to do?" he asked. "Rest?"

"There's no way," I said, feeling the rush of my own heartbeat. "But I am going to change. I've been in these clothes for two days. Maybe a shower—"

He grinned and my cheeks flamed.

"Never mind." I let go of his arms, backing up a few steps as images of Ren clad only in a towel flashed in my mind.

He laughed softly. "I'll see you in an hour, Lily."

I hated that I was still blushing, so I settled for growling at him. It only made him laugh harder.

"Am I the only one who's hungry?" Mason rubbed his belly.

"You'll find your friends Bryn and Ansel in the kitchen," Anika said. "Tess should be with them."

"In the kitchen?" Shay frowned. "Why?"

"After that incident with Logan we thought it best to keep him in one place."

"So kitchen duty?" I asked.

"Washing dishes is punishment enough for someone who has been through what your brother has," Anika said with a sad smile. "He can't behave that way and be free here. But any one of us might have felt justified in such an attack if we'd been in his place."

"I'm glad you see it that way."

"The kitchen should keep him out of mischief," Anika said.

"That's where I'll be, then," Mason said. When he passed me, he leaned in, whispering, "Doesn't she realize how many knives An could steal from the kitchen?"

I glanced over my shoulder to see Anika engrossed in conversation with Shay as he held out the blades for her inspection.

"I'll walk out with you," I said, taking Mason's arm. I managed to keep myself from meeting Ren's eyes again. I didn't know what I'd find there and I wasn't sure I was in any state of mind to handle it. Too many thoughts about our chances, the risks, and all the losses that had already happened were racing through my mind. The sort of thoughts that led to impulsive, irrational decisions. I needed to be steadier than that before this battle.

"You wanna come see Ansel and Bryn?" Mason asked, pausing by the staircase.

"I'll be there soon," I said. "But I really do need to get out of these clothes."

"Yeah, you do." Mason nodded. "I was just too polite to bring it up."

"Thanks." I punched him on the arm.

"See ya!" He pecked me on the cheek and bounded down the steps.

Weariness settled deep in my bones as I slipped into my room, letting the door close quietly behind me. I forced myself to change first, though the bed was calling my name. If I lay down, I might not get up before it was time to go. I used my shirt to rub as much grime and soot from my skin as I could. A shower would have been ideal, but I was too worried about time and a possible Ren ambush to return to the baths.

I'd just finished buckling my belt when a quiet knock sounded at the door.

"Who is it?" I called.

"Shay."

A knot formed low in my belly. I'd been worried about Ren, but the sound of Shay's voice drove all other thoughts away. His life was so focused on the fight to come. He was the key. He was the Scion. And now he had the Elemental Cross.

But he was knocking on my door, and he was still the boy I loved . . . wasn't he?

"Come in."

He came into the room, keeping his distance. "Can we talk?"

The knot in my stomach petrified, becoming a painful lump, heavy in my gut.

I nodded.

"I don't mean to go all emo on you," he said, "but I want you to know that you're going to be okay. No matter what happens tonight."

The rock-like sensation dissolved into surprise. "What?"

"You won't be alone." He walked toward me.

I stared at him, utterly perplexed. "I won't be alone?"

"No." He took my hands in his. "Ren and I . . ."

I snatched my hands away with a hiss. "Ren and you?"

"Uh . . . we—"

"You what?" I snarled.

"Well . . ." He swallowed, backing off as he saw my teeth sharpen. "We had a chance to talk."

"Talk about what?"

"You. . . . We thought that—"

"When were you and Ren talking about me?"

"They had us tied up together for a while." He grabbed an armchair, shoving it between us like a fortification. "Mason took a nap . . . that was after he bit me."

I strolled toward him, kneeling on the chair cushion while my fingers wrapped around its frame. "I'm listening."

"After we stopped trying to get out of the rope, we argued for a while."

"That's a shocker."

"Arguing about you led to talking." He took another step back when my fingers pierced the chair's upholstery.

"Go on."

His eyes were wild. "Maybe I should just go—"

"Tell me, Shay." It was more of a growl than a sentence.

"Listen, don't be mad," he said. "I hate to say it, but I think I may have been wrong about Ren."

"Wrong how?"

He raked his fingers through his hair. "I still don't like him, but I didn't get how he felt about you."

The fire of my rage was in danger of being outpaced by the fear that drove my pulse. How much had they talked about? What right did they have to talk about me at all?

"He's been in love with you for . . . well, pretty much forever."

"You believe he means that?" I lowered my gaze, blood thundering in my ears. I knew it was true, but for Shay to believe it *and* for him to be talking about it . . . I couldn't understand where this was leading.

"I wish I didn't," he said quietly. "But yeah. He's for real."

We didn't speak. Silence hovered around us thick as fog. Finally he sighed. "But I'm willing to accept that it's a good thing for all of us."

I looked at him sharply. "Why would you say that?"

"Because when I'm gone"—he took a deep breath—"I know he'll be here to take care of you. He promised me that."

"When you're gone?!" I glared at him. "What are you talking about?"

"Calm down, Calla," he said. "This is probably our last chance to talk. I don't want to fight with you."

"Oh, we're going to fight." I sprang out of the chair, shifting mid-air and slamming him. As we slid across the floor, he shifted forms, leaving two snarling wolves to crash into the wall.

What the hell? He growled, rolling onto his feet.

I barked, crouching to leap again. *I will show you how much I need to be taken care of.*

His nails scraped against the floor as he backed away. *Stop.*

There was no way in hell I was stopping. I couldn't remember a time when fury had shrieked through my veins like this. Without hesitation I lunged at him. We rolled across the floor, teeth snapping as we each struggled to gain an advantage. He almost had me pinned, but I squared a solid kick with my hind legs into his belly, which sent him careening across the room. Scrambling up, I chased him around the bed.

I do not need to be protected. I threw my shout at him as I ran. *And if I choose to be alone, I will be.*

That wasn't what I meant. He jumped away from my bite and onto the bed. *I just want you to be happy.*

Then don't make decisions for me. Ever.

He bent down, grabbed the coverlet in his jaws, and leapt off the bed. A net of opaque cotton captured me.

Hey! I struggled, blinded by the blankets that covered me. *Not fair.*

Innovation isn't fair?

We were evenly matched, neither of us giving ground nor gaining a lasting advantage. I had years of fighting as a wolf on my side, but Shay was less inhibited by his wolf instincts. He made choices in the fight that never would have occurred to me.

I was ready for him when he tackled me. I bucked up immediately, tossing, keeping him off balance. Frustration won out and I simply shredded the blanket rather than trying to find my way out of it.

Shay was snarling, circling behind me. I whirled around, bracing myself for his attack.

He pawed the ground, agitated.

Come on. I threw the challenge at him as I growled. I was about to throw myself on him again when he shifted forms, holding his hands up.

"Wait, Cal. Not that this isn't fun, but I'm not here to fight you. I was just trying to make a point."

I snarled as I shifted forms. "A point about giving up?"

"I'm not giving up. I'm being realistic," Shay said. "How likely is it that I'll come out of this battle alive?"

"As likely as any of the rest of us," I said. Though admittedly that wasn't too likely either.

"No," he said. "Not considering what I have to do."

"What?" I said. "So you're the hero, which automatically means you die in the end?"

"Probably. And that's why I made Ren promise to take care of you," he said. "Even Harry Potter died. Well, for a few minutes."

I ignored his joke, baring my teeth at him. "Why would you bring Ren into this? You hate him."

"I hate him because he's your mate. . . . You two are the perfect match." He broke his gaze from mine with a shrug. Suddenly he laughed, shaking his head. "If I thought things would turn out differently, I swear I'd fight him until we were both ripped to shreds. I'd fight for you forever, Calla. I don't give a damn how much he loves you. But like I said, we talked and I can live with what we decided."

"If you both are making decisions for me, why isn't he here too?" I asked, still throwing knives at him with my eyes. "Now that you've become such good friends."

"I wouldn't go that far. It's more of an understanding," Shay said. "I think he feels a little bad for me."

The hairs on the back of my neck stood up. "Why?"

"After we all heard what I have to do to finish this, I think he's pretty sure I'm dead too."

"You mean facing Bosque?" I asked.

He nodded. "I have to kill the only relative I've ever known. Plus he's an über-demon and all."

"He's not your blood kin. Not really," I said. "You know that. And if this works, you'll have your parents."

"I guess." He sighed.

I took his face in my hands, holding his gaze. "You're not going to die."

"You sound pretty sure." He smiled, but his moss green eyes were sad—like he'd already lost me.

My hands dropped to my sides. "You're not going to die, because I will always save you," I said. "That's what I do."

"Not this time," he said. "This is different. This is the end. I know it."

I growled and then I slapped him.

"Hey!" His hand pressed to his cheek.

"You always say that when I slap you," I said.

"I think it's a problem that you know what I say when you slap me," he said. "That's not the kind of intimacy I'm looking for."

"You're not looking for intimacy at all!" My hands balled into fists so tight the blood drained from my knuckles. "You're running away from it! You're running away from me!"

"I have no idea what you're talking about," he said, rubbing his reddened skin. "I was just trying to be honest."

"Honest about giving me up?!" I refused to cry, so I kept shouting. "Honest about not loving me?!"

I stumbled away from him, muscles quivering with rage and shame. I'd seen this coming. He wasn't mine. Now that he was the Scion, his destiny was all that mattered. Didn't he understand that I'd abandoned mine for his sake? Betrayal stung up and down my chest like the fury of a dozen wasps, making it hard to breathe.

"Calla." He was behind me, turning me gently to face him.

"How dare you?!" I beat my fist against his chest. "How dare you try to push me away?!"

"I could never . . ."

"You just did." My teeth were sharp and I was ready to attack him all over again.

He put his hands on my shoulders. "Just listen to me. I'm not trying to push you away. I'm trying to give you what you deserve. Ren loves you."

"Stop saying that," I snarled. I didn't want to hear any more about Ren loving me. I wanted Shay to take away my growing fear that he didn't want me . . . that maybe he'd never loved me.

"And you love him," Shay said. I fell silent, surprised not only by his words but by the way he held my gaze. I watched pain flare in his eyes. "I didn't want to face it, but it's true. You love him, Calla."

It took me a moment to catch my breath. I threaded my fingers through his, finally understanding what Shay was trying to do. He was giving me a choice. He was setting me free. "You're right. I love him."

He sighed, but I tightened my grip on his hand.

"But not the way I love you," I said.

I leaned forward, pressing my lips against his, waiting until he responded to the kiss. He pulled me closer, the soft kiss building in heat and strength as it lingered between us.

"It doesn't matter that Ren and I have a past," I whispered against his mouth. "You're my future. You're the path I chose from the moment I saved you on the mountain."

He didn't speak, but rested his forehead against mine.

"You will make it through this fight, Shay," I said. "You have to. I will not lose you."

He laughed quietly and kissed me. "I'll do my best. I'd hate to disappoint my alpha."

"And I can't afford to lose my alpha," I said.

His smile remained, but light flared in his eyes. "You mean me?"

"You know I do. You've always known who you are to me—to the pack. Even before I did. You were a lone wolf. Then you found us."

"I didn't know who I was or where I belonged until I met you," he said, leaning down to brush his lips across my cheek.

"So, alpha . . ." I took his hand. "You ready to go get the bad guys?"

"If you insist," he said, placing one last gentle kiss on my lips. He paused just before we reached the door. "Calla, I'm sorry . . . I just wanted—"

"I know what you wanted, Shay," I said, lifting his fingers to my mouth and gently kissing them. "And that's why I love you."

TWENTY-ONE

WE LEFT THE ROOM. Shay shifted into wolf form in the hallway, as did I. Searchers passing by occasionally exchanged hushed murmurs or gave us startled looks. But the most common reactions were nods of respect or knowing smiles.

Shay wagged his tail. *Nice to be part of the team.*

Still a little odd. I nipped his shoulder. *But yeah. It's nice.*

I watched Shay's ears flicking back and forth, his eyes alert as we moved. He'd adjusted to his wolf self so naturally. Sometimes I felt like he truly had been a lone wolf when I'd met him—he just hadn't found his wolf half yet. As much as his "talk" with Ren made me want to bite both of them hard, their negotiations over my status were so classically alpha male behavior it was almost funny. Almost.

We trotted down the hall toward Haldis Tactical, our toenails clicking on marble. Anika was sitting at the large round table with Bryn, Mason, Ansel, and Tess. Mason chomped on the largest sandwich I'd ever seen.

Catching sight of us, he pulled it close to his chest. "You didn't come to the kitchen. I'm not sharing."

I shifted forms and laughed. "I don't think I could eat right now."

"Good." He grinned, still baring his fangs. "I'm starved and this sandwich is my own masterpiece."

Ansel coughed.

"With Ansel's assistance, of course." Mason nodded at my brother.

"You sitting in on this?" I asked him.

"He's going," Mason said around a mouthful of sandwich.

I glared at the Arrow. "What's this?"

Tess jumped in before Anika could answer. "He's staying with me, Calla."

"I'm helping the Elixirs clear casualties," Ansel said. I winced at the accusatory look he shot me. "The Weavers will be bringing wounded off the field as fast as they can. They need helpers who won't be in the battle."

"That's great, An," I said. He dropped his eyes as his anger gave way to humiliation.

Great, Calla. Nice move. I wished I hadn't hurt his feelings, but the truth was, I didn't want Ansel anywhere near this fight. Without his wolf he'd be much too vulnerable. And it wasn't only that I was worried he couldn't fight as a human. With everything Ansel had been through—and how I knew he was still feeling—I worried he'd purposely try to get himself killed.

Anika pushed a chair out and I sat down beside her. Bryn, in the next chair over, leaned in to hug me.

"Glad I'm not missing all the heroics this round," she whispered. "You okay?"

"Surviving," I said.

She squeezed my shoulders. "That's what we do best."

I gripped her fingers, giving her as much of a smile as I could manage.

"Everybody's already here?" Connor came into the room with Adne at his side. "Does that mean we're late?"

They were both flushed, but had done a pretty good job of making themselves presentable . . . or at least appearing only slightly rumpled after a "nap." Mason snickered anyway. Connor rubbed the back of his neck uneasily, but a mischievous smile hovered on Adne's lips.

"You're actually right on time," Anika said, gesturing for them to sit. I thought I heard the hint of laughter in her voice, though her expression remained solemn.

"Glad to hear it." Ren smiled as he entered the room. His hair was damp. I guessed he had decided to make a trip to the baths.

He was about to take a seat beside me when he stopped. His nose wrinkled. He stared at me and then at Shay, who was watching him from the other side of the table, arms folded across his chest.

A growl rumbled out of Ren's throat. "What the hell . . ."

I stood up. "Ren, don't. Not now."

"Why is your scent all over her?" He ignored me, glaring at Shay. "You two were together? What were you doing? I thought we had an agreement."

"So did I," Shay said. "But someone convinced me that it was stupid and I was very, very wrong."

Ren leaned on the table, snarling. "It's time for me to teach you a lesson that's long overdue."

Shay didn't move, but he smiled. "You're welcome to try."

"Stop!" I shoved Ren as hard as I could, sending him several steps back from the table.

"Stay out of this, Lily!" He only glanced at me for a second before returning his outraged stare to Shay.

"The hell I will!" I put myself between him and Shay, forcing Ren to look at me. "Is this the kind of love you want from me? Love that's chosen for me instead of being my own?"

He stopped growling. "Calla . . ."

"I know that's all you've ever been taught to do," I said. "But that is not how I want to live. Do you understand?"

"So . . . it's him, then." He dropped his gaze.

"Stop talking about him," I said. "This is about me. My life. My choice. And if you really stopped to think about it, you wouldn't want me any other way. If you have a problem with that, I'll kick your ass. Right here. Right now."

He looked at me then. "You're something else, Lily."

"Don't forget it," I said, relieved that he'd begun to smile.

Connor coughed. "So, uh . . . about the end of the world."

Ren laughed, heading for the table. When he passed me, he bent his head, voice low. "This isn't over."

I didn't answer. But for me it was over. I knew what I felt, who I wanted, but sharing that with Ren had to wait until after the fight.

When we had all settled around the table, Anika unrolled a large map. I stared at it, my breath catching at the sight of Rowan Estate's grounds laid starkly before me.

When I looked up, I met Anika's hard gaze.

"If we're going to succeed," she said. "This is what has to happen."

Anika fell silent, the battle strategy still ringing in our ears. Ren's hands were folded on the table in front of him. If I didn't know him better, I would have thought he was meditating. Shay paced alongside Anika. The Elemental Cross hung in two sheaths at his back. I could sense their power even from where I sat, but Shay moved casually, as if he barely noticed the swords' presence.

Bryn was holding Ansel's hand. Tess had her arm around his shoulders.

I was wondering if I could do what I would need to do. Kill who I would have to kill.

"We are all gonna die." Mason leaned back in his chair. "That's for sure."

I swallowed a growl when Shay met my eyes.

"Shut up, Mason," I said.

"Just trying to keep things in perspective." Mason grinned. "It'll be a good fight, though. I'm okay going out like this."

"Mason," Bryn snarled at him. "Like Calla said, shut up."

"Our chances are slim," Anika said. "But this is the only way."

Ren leaned forward. "This plan rides on Nev and Ethan."

Anika nodded.

"Have you heard anything from them?" he asked.

"No," she said. "But we don't have time to wait. We must attack tonight before the Keepers have time to amass forces when they realize we have the cross. Without catching the Keepers off guard, we'll never be able to pin the Harbinger down."

"You're also relying on Logan," I said. It was the part of the plan that left a bad taste in my mouth. "And he isn't reliable."

Mason snarled. "He shouldn't be part of this."

"We don't have a choice," Anika said. "His blood oath enables him to summon the Harbinger. Without that ritual, the Scion will fail."

"If Logan hadn't turned up," Mason said, "how were you going to get this ritual done?"

"We'd intended to capture a Keeper and force them to do it," Anika said. "And we can still force Logan to act for us if he has indeed turned traitor."

"And you really think the five of us will be enough?" I asked, glancing at my companions.

"You retrieved Pyralis," Anika answered. "And the rest of us will be engaged on the main front while you enter the estate. We'll shield you from attack."

"Except from Bosque," Shay muttered.

"Which raises one last issue," Anika said.

"There's another issue besides Shay's demon uncle?" Mason asked. "Wonderful."

"Once Bosque has been summoned, he'll likely call the Fallen to his aid."

"Those zombie things?" Shay said. "Well, at least they aren't fast."

"They aren't zombies," Connor said.

Anika nodded. "They may be slow moving, but they are the husks left of people driven insane by torment. And their attack is just as deadly as a physical assault."

"Their attack?" My skin crawled, remembering their shuffling gait and Ethan's cry of grief when he'd recognized his own brother among the Fallen.

"Their touch brings instant madness," Anika said. "You must not let them touch you."

"Can they be killed?" Ren asked.

"They'll go down if you cut their heads off," Connor said. "But if you bite them, you'll regret it. And we'll probably have to kill you."

Ren growled at him. "You'll have to what?"

"One of the reasons the Harrowing was so costly for us"— Anika's face paled—"was the arrival of the Fallen. Our friends and family reduced to that horror, and when our Guardian allies tried to fight them—"

"The Guardians attacked the Fallen?" I folded my arms across my chest so I wouldn't shudder.

"Yes. And their minds were overtaken by their worst nightmares," Anika said quietly. "They turned on each other, on us. We didn't understand what was happening until it was too late."

"So the moral of the story is: wolfies leave the Fallen to us," Connor said, patting his sword hilt.

"Gladly," Mason said, shoving away the last bites of his sandwich.

More Searchers arrived in small groups, their mood somber as they gathered in Haldis Tactical. One by one Weavers began to open doors, and I knew this deployment was happening all over the Academy as the Searcher army moved into position outside Rowan Estate. Anika rose from her chair.

"We'll fight with all we have to buy you time," she said, and then turned to Shay. "All our hopes are with you."

He gave her a thin smile. "Thanks."

As we stood up, Tess came over and took my hand.

"We'll be working from the Eydis Sanctuary," she said. "That's where they want us to bring the wounded."

A lump rose in my throat and I nodded. "Be safe."

"Thanks for lending me your brother, Calla," she said. "The Elixirs are grateful too. He's been a great help to us."

"Take care of him," I said.

"Of course." She squeezed my hand.

Ansel tried to sneak behind Tess, but I grabbed his arm.

"Don't say good-bye," he mumbled, not looking at me. "I don't want to hear it."

"I'm not saying good-bye." I dug my fingers into his arm and he stared at me in surprise. "This is a warning, Ansel. You stay with Tess. Any running off, any stupid heroics and I will hunt you down myself no matter what's happening on the battlefield. You are still my baby brother and I am still your alpha. I'm not going to let you get hurt out there."

He nodded, still wide-eyed. I wrapped my arms around him, knowing I'd be too far from him to track his movements during the attack. But I hoped he'd at least listen to me and that some of his instincts to obey his alpha might still be lingering.

I turned, sensing someone behind me.

"He'll be fine," Ren said, searching my eyes with his own. "Tess won't let anything happen to him."

"I know," I said, forcing a smile.

"So the plan really pissed you off, huh," Ren said as we walked toward Adne, who'd begun to weave the door our party would take to Vail.

"Did you expect me to be happy when I found out?"

"I didn't bet on Shay telling you about it," Ren said. "He overshares."

"I appreciate honesty," I said. "It's a winning trait."

"I honestly will play dirty to win this fight," he said. "Is that a winning trait?"

"Drop it."

Shay and Connor were standing near Adne, watching the shimmering portal take shape.

I glanced at Shay. Ren waved at him and Shay made a rude gesture at Ren, but then gave me a sad smile that made my chest tighten. Did he really believe he wouldn't survive this fight?

The tightness in my chest became so painful I had to close my eyes to push it away. My mind had to be in this fight, no matter what else might be tugging at my heart. I couldn't afford to think about what this war would ultimately cost me.

Mason came up to us, grinning. "You guys ready to roll?"

"You look awfully happy." I eyed him warily. "Considering."

"I miss Nev." He shrugged. "Sure, it's a war and all, but at least he'll be there. I'll take what I can get."

Ren slapped him on the back. "I love you, man."

"Of course you do." Mason smoothed his hair back. "I'm irresistible."

Bryn tossed her curls. "I think this fight is going to be fun."

"I hope you're right," I said.

"All right, hellhounds." Connor was waving at us. "Get your butts through that door."

"We are not hellhounds," I growled. "We are wolves."

"Really?" Connor gave me a crestfallen look. "You didn't like my new nickname for your pack? I thought it was inspired or maybe awe inspiring. You know, like Hell's Angels."

"We're not a motorcycle gang either, dude," Ren said, then he shifted into wolf form and bounded through the portal.

"Are his jokes always this bad?" Bryn asked.

"Usually." I smiled at Connor. "But don't tell him that. I'd hate to hurt his feelings."

Connor shook his head. "Alas, I will always be unsung."

"Yep." Shay smiled. "I'd say you're right."

"Thank God for that." I flashed a grin at him, shifted, and leapt after Ren.

My paws crunched into snow that reached the middle of my legs. The moon hung high above us, offering considerable light despite the late hour. Adne's portal opened onto a crest at the edge of the forest. The grounds of Rowan Estate stretched out below us. The garden with its curving paths and sculpted hedges lay cloaked in shadow. Caught in early winter's grasp, the fountains were dry and the flower beds empty, devoid of the life that made gardens so inviting.

At intervals along the forest ridge and at points closer to the gardens other winking lights appeared. Shadows moved under the night sky. The Searchers were arriving, our forces gathering. As our numbers amassed, the strike teams began to move forward into the garden, making their way toward the manor house. Rowan Estate's windows were black. The stately home stood silent, giving every indication that it was empty.

I pawed the ground anxiously as we waited. With our separate mission in play, we were among the last of the teams to move out. I lifted my muzzle, testing the air for any signs of danger. Or allies.

Where were the Nightshade and Bane packs?

As much as this was a quasi-surprise attack, the Keepers would be anticipating our arrival. Anika and all the Searchers knew that. Our enemies were waiting for us, but where?

Would my father be running with Emile's wolves, ready to turn on his adversary when the right moment came? Were they on their way here now?

"It's time." Adne closed the portal, sheathed her skeans, and pulled out that wicked steel whip she'd used in the practice match with Shay while we were in Denver.

"You should stay here." Connor frowned. "I don't like risking you."

Adne laughed. "Sorry, Connor. All the Weavers are in this fight. Including me. Anika's orders, remember?"

He shook his head but trudged down the slope with Adne grinning as she kept pace with him.

Ren, Mason, Bryn, and I formed a protective ring around Shay and the two Searchers. I took point, while Bryn and Mason trotted beside them. Ren stayed at our rear. As we entered the garden, I snarled at the marble incubi and succubi that were arranged like sentinels all around us.

"Don't worry, Calla," Shay said. "We're keeping an eye on them."

"Yes, we are," Connor said. "And if they break open those shells, we'll know that Bosque is already here."

I sniffed the air, still bristling.

Is that supposed to reassure us somehow? Mason barked at him, baring his teeth at Connor.

We'd made it a few yards into the estate grounds when the first shouts rose from the teams ahead of us.

"Looks like we've got incoming," Connor said.

Shay drew his swords, squinting into the distance.

I waited to hear the ringing of steel and snarls of wolves, assuming that our allies would encounter Guardian resistance as they closed in on Rowan Estate. But the Searchers' shouts weren't battle cries. They were confused yells, filled with fear.

"What's happening?" Adne and Connor were standing back-to-back as they scanned the gardens around us.

I snarled, wanting to run into whatever conflict was taking place ahead. But our directive was to keep out of the fray.

"Look!" Shay pointed the tip of one sword at the tall hedges that lined the garden's paths. The hedges were moving. Not moving, growing.

Connor swore, bolting forward as the thick knotted branches

swarmed over the path, breaking through the paved walkways and twisting in wild patterns around us. The hedge climbed before our eyes, rising at an impossible speed.

"Connor!" Adne shouted as a new hedge burst up between us, blocking our way to him.

I heard him yell but couldn't see through the wall of branches that separated us.

Adne was running along the hedge, shouting Connor's name. A yelp sounded behind me. I wheeled around to see Mason being thrown backward as new branches, fast and hard as whiplashes, slammed into his body. Bryn barked, leaping after him, snapping at the attacking vines. I howled in frustration as Bryn, Mason, Ren, and Shay disappeared from sight.

I turned back around, racing after Adne, who was still running and shouting. She changed direction as a new hedge appeared, blocking her path forward. I threw myself into the air, crashing into her. She struggled as I pinned her down.

I was still snarling when I shifted forms. "Stop it! Adne, stop!"

She was breathing hard, but she pulled her fists back so she was no longer beating at my chest and shoulders. "We have to find him!"

"It's not just him." I stood up, pulling her to her feet. "We lost the others too."

"What?" Her eyes widened as she wheeled around to see the labyrinth that had exploded from the earth to surround us.

"We're cut off." I pressed my hands against the hedge and thorns pierced my skin.

A howl broke through the night.

Adne looked at me, her eyebrow raised. "Friends?"

"No," I said quietly.

Another howl sounded, and another. The wolves' cries rose one by one, filling the air with their battle song. I turned in a slow circle, listening, tracking their calls.

"We're surrounded."

Adne swore under her breath. "They're separating us. Keeping the teams apart."

I nodded. "They were waiting for us."

She strode along the labyrinth walls, turning corners, finding dead ends. "What do you want to bet that the Keepers' side has a map that solves this maze?"

"That does seem likely." I looked up at the hedge. It was too high to jump.

"We're sitting ducks in here," Adne said. "The wolves will hunt us, take each group one by one, and none of us will see them coming."

"We have to find a way out," I said. "Keep going."

The howls were close now. Hundreds of wolves were running. I could smell them, hear their paws crunching in the snow as they descended on the garden from all sides. The other Searcher teams were still panicked, shouting as they tried to escape the maze. Men and women were calling out for one another, trying to find their allies.

Then the screams began.

Adne closed her eyes. "It's started."

TWENTY-TWO

THE SOUNDS OF BATTLE filled my ears and I wished I could shut them out. The buzz of crossbow bolts whizzed in the air; growls and snarls rose toward the sky. If I were in the midst of the fight, it wouldn't have bothered me. But this unseen war—violence and death that might be lurking around any corner—sent fear scurrying up and down my spine. We hadn't run into any wolves yet, but it was only a matter of time. Adne and I could fight off three or four, but I had a feeling we wouldn't be facing anywhere near that few.

And there were other sounds too, building my anxiety. Screams of a pain beyond the kind any Guardian could cause.

"There's a wraith in the maze," I whispered. "Maybe more than one."

Having hit another dead end, Adne and I crouched low, desperate to come up with a plan. The maze wasn't only cutting us off, it constantly changed shape. Hedges sprang up only to sink back into the earth. Thorny branches shot out in the middle of the path, tripping us as we'd run.

"Are you sure?" she asked.

I nodded, wishing I wasn't. "We have to find Shay."

I shifted into wolf form, prepared to attack any enemy Guardians we encountered, and we started to run again. I hoped we were heading in the direction of where we'd first been separated.

"Look!" Adne turned toward a new opening in the labyrinth. "Let's go."

I caught the scent just before we turned the corner. Grabbing Adne's shirt as I shifted forms, I screamed, "Stop!"

I was dragging her backward when it came into view. The wraith slithered from behind the curved hedges, moving slowly toward us.

"Come on." Adne gripped my hand and we bolted back in the direction we'd come from.

The maze had shifted again, presenting yet another path.

"Damn it," I said as we pulled up in front of a dead end.

I turned around only to see the opening in the hedge through which we'd just passed closing up.

"Well, at least the wraith is on the other side," Adne said. The words had only left her lips when the wraith emerged through the hedge, its form oozing from between the branches like tar.

"Oh, no fair!" Adne shouted.

The wraith was closing in. There wasn't anywhere to go.

"Shay!" I screamed, not knowing what else to do. "Shay! Help us!"

We backed against the wall; my eyes were locked on the swirling shadows of the wraith's body. Its scent filled my nostrils, making me want to retch. Memories of the pain it could cause sent shuddering tremors through my limbs.

"Adne, you have to get out of here. Weave a door!"

"A door to where? Do you want to run back to the Academy? If I weave into the battlefield, I could put us right on top of a wraith! There's no out that way." Her voice shook. "I don't know what to do. Unless . . ."

"Unless what?"

She'd turned around, facing the hedge behind us.

"Shay!" I screamed again.

"Calla!" His voice was right behind. "Where are you?"

I whirled around, ignoring the pain as thorns tore my skin when I pressed my hands against the hedge. "I'm here! With Adne!"

"I can't get to you," he shouted. He was right on the other side of the maze wall. "Bryn, Mason, Ren! Get over here! They're behind this hedge."

I could smell his scent, just out of reach.

"Calla!" Ren shouted. "Are you okay?"

"There's a wraith." My voice was raw. "We're trapped."

I heard Mason's whining and his paws scratching at the dirt, trying to get to us. Bryn's nose poked beneath the branches, but she yelped when a thorny vine lashed her muzzle like a whip.

"I'm going to try to cut through the hedge," he yelled. "Stand back."

"No, wait!" Adne cried.

"What do you mean, wait?" I glanced over my shoulder at the wraith.

Adne ignored me. She'd dropped her whip and held her skeans in her hands. With a sudden cry she plunged the slender spikes into the earth.

I shoved my hands over my ears as a horrible sound pierced the air all around me. The shriek was full of pain and outrage. And it was coming from the hedge.

"That's right, bitch," Adne hissed. "Get off this earth and go back to hell where you belong."

The branches of the hedge were shaking. Its leaves began to wither, shriveling up and crumbling. The shuddering of the limbs became more violent. Thorn-covered branches splintered into brittle pieces. The living walls of the hedge spilled down in a wave of dried bits and ash that had been leaves. The maze vanished, leaving only shallow piles of debris marking its pattern on the white snow. Shay stood in front of me, swords still raised high. "What the—"

Adne groaned and slumped onto her side.

I began to turn toward her, but Shay shouted, "Calla, get down now!"

He leapt over me as I shifted, flattening my body against the snow. I rolled along the ground, scrambling to my feet. As I pivoted, I saw the wraith bearing down on Adne and Shay hurtling through the air toward the creature.

I barked in alarm, starting after him, but Ren jumped in front of me, snarling.

No.

Get out of my way. I bared my fangs at him.

But the growl died in my throat.

Shay flung himself at the wraith. The Elemental Cross spun in his hands at blinding speed. The blades sliced into the dark mass of the creature's body faster than whirling helicopter blades.

The wraith screamed.

I'd never heard a wraith scream before. I'd never heard them emit any sort of sound. But there was no doubt that it was shrieking in agony.

The wraith's inky tendrils crackled as if full of electricity. It screamed again and then its body spewed upward, like black steam exploding from a geyser, and it was gone.

Shay landed on the other side of where the wraith had been. He wheeled around, blades ready to strike again. When he realized the wraith was gone, he straightened and threw me a sheepish smile.

I barked at him, wagging my tail.

"Adne!" Connor was running toward us through the snow and the remnants of the maze.

Adne pulled herself into a crouch, leaning back on the heels of her hands. "I'll be okay . . . I think."

Connor helped her to her feet and grinned at Shay. "Nice work. I didn't know you could do that."

"Do what?" Shay frowned. "You knew I could kill wraiths. Because of these." He held up the swords.

"Not the wraith," Connor said. "Though that was good too. I meant the maze. If you hadn't gotten rid of it, this party would have been over before it started."

Connor turned, gesturing in the direction of the manor. "The teams will be able to regroup their attacks now."

"I didn't do anything to the maze," Shay said. "The hedges fell apart and the next thing I knew, I was looking at Calla. Then I saw the wraith going for Adne."

Connor stared at him, his brow furrowing. Adne brushed snow from her clothes, avoiding eye contact with any of us. I shifted forms, watching her closely.

"She did it." I pointed at her. "She . . . killed the labyrinth." I didn't have any other word to describe what Adne had done. Somehow she had attacked the Keepers' living hedge as it trapped us. And she'd defeated it.

Connor gripped Adne's arms, fixing a hard gaze on her. "How? How did you do that?"

"I don't know," she said. "I knew it wasn't natural—that it didn't belong. So I asked her for a favor."

"Asked who?" Shay paced around our huddled groups, scanning our surroundings for signs of danger. From what I could tell, the Banes' attack had been concentrated on the teams ahead of us.

Even in the moonlight I could see Adne blush. "The earth."

"You can call in a favor from the earth?" Connor asked. "That's on your resume?"

She smiled. "That's what all Weavers do. I just took it a step further."

"No one has ever done that, Adne," Connor said slowly. "No one."

"I know," she murmured.

Their eyes met and something important, but unspoken, passed between them. I couldn't be sure what it was.

With the wall of tangled branches gone, I could see the storm of battle that raged ahead of us. Wolves crashed into the Searchers with the force of a tidal wave. Sharp teeth tore into human flesh, cutting off screams of pain as quickly as they began. The unending wails that rose horribly into the sky told me wolves weren't the only enemy waiting in the darkness. Wraiths slid through the shadows, engulfing Searchers at will.

My eyes scanned the edge of the garden. It didn't take long to find them. A line of twenty Keepers—our masters and some of their children, whom I recognized from school—had taken up positions at the edge of the dry reflecting pool. All were elegantly dressed, as if they were about to be seated for a formal dinner, not observe a battle. But they stood overlooking the carnage, like generals directing their infantry. With casual grace, the Keepers' arms began to twist in the air, their fingers dancing in intricate movement.

Screeches filled the air and the sky above us came alive with dark, writhing shapes. Succubi and incubi appeared, summoned by their masters, to enter the fray. Searchers cried out warnings and crossbow bolts shot past the Nether creatures' javelins. Some of the winged attackers dropped to the earth. Others dove at the Searchers, snatching them from the field of battle, rising to impossible heights to drop the human fighters to their deaths. A few Searchers, snagged in incubi talons, managed to get in a fatal blow with a dagger or sword as they were borne into the sky, taking the Keepers' minions along with them into death's veil.

I watched bodies fall and writhe beneath fur and claws, leathery wings and talons, or simply disappear into the darkness of a wraith's smoke-like body. Wolves went down too, bright blood scattering across the pristine snow, pooling beneath the still bodies of Bane Guardians. But the number of Searchers lying on the ground, unmoving, was quickly outnumbering that of wolves. The Banes were stalking, circling the strike teams. They moved in unison, their pack instincts guiding the hunt, allowing them to coordinate their attacks in ways the Searchers could never hope for.

I watched the wolves take down warrior after warrior. If I'd watched this no more than a month earlier, I would have howled with pride. This was how Guardians waged war. It's why we always won. Why the Searchers were losing now.

The heavy weight of growing despair settled beneath my ribs. We couldn't win. Even if we got inside, if Shay somehow defeated Bosque, the battle outside was lost. How many Searchers would die today?

Connor cleared his throat, his gaze, like mine, locked on the brutal scene ahead of us. "We need to keep moving. The fighting seems to be concentrated to the east. That's good; we'll head for the north side of the garden and to the house from there."

He didn't mention that it looked like our side was losing. Badly.

"There are other wraiths," Shay said. "I should go after them."

Connor shook his head. "Not part of the plan. We need you inside."

"I'm the only one who can kill them," Shay growled.

"We knew that there would be wraiths in this battle," Connor said. "There always are. But you can't be caught up at the front. We don't have time."

Shay stiffened but turned to the north. "Let's go, then."

I shifted back into wolf form, sticking close to Shay's side as we skirted the edge of the battle. Adrenaline had my pulse racing. I could smell the Banes and taste blood on the air.

A low growl rumbled in my chest.

I know. Ren's voice entered my mind. *I want to be in that fight too.*

Wish granted. Mason came to a halt, bristling.

We'd reached the northern edge of the garden, and part of the battle had spilled out in front of us. Wolves and Searchers danced around each other in a blur of deadly movements. Steel flashed as blades caught the moonlight. The wolves' muscles rippled beneath their fur as they slammed into the Searchers' bodies. Shouts and snarls blended into a terrible roar as they fought. And they were blocking our path to the house.

Backup plan? Bryn asked.

I'll tell you if I come up with one. I braced myself. If we were going down, it wouldn't be without a fight.

"Damn it," Connor said. "So much for containment."

"Do we make a run for it?" Adne asked.

"Yep."

My eyes scanned the fighters, searching for any sign of Night-shades or my father. But I could only see Searchers and Banes.

"You should change forms, Shay," Connor said. "The last thing we want is for those Guardians to mark the Scion. If they spot you, you're the only one they'll be hunting."

"Good call," Shay said, sliding into his other form. The golden brown wolf shook his ruff. *That's much better.*

Ren looked at him. *Really?*

Of course. Shay lifted his muzzle, taking in the cool night air. *Don't you think so?*

Well, yeah. Ren pawed at the snow. *But—never mind.*

"Calla, you take point," Connor said, oblivious to our conversation. "I'll be right behind you. Ren and Shay, stay close to Adne. Mason, Bryn, guard our flank."

He took our steady gazes as assent.

"Okay." Connor peered at the tangle of bodies in our way. "On my mark. . . . Now!"

My muscles bunched and I hurtled out of the garden into the open. Keeping my focus on the long shadows cast by the building, I steered us away from the center of the fighting. If we could just reach the house, we'd have cover again.

A sharp bark drew my attention. Several Banes had broken from the battle and were barreling toward us.

Keep running, Calla! Ren's howl rose in the air behind me. *Mason and I will draw them off.*

I snarled, frustrated to be running when my packmates were heading for a fight.

Another howl sounded, close but coming from the west.

Is that— Ren wheeled around, heading in the opposite direction of the battle.

Hell, yeah! Mason dashed after him.

Bryn dropped to her haunches and howled joyfully. Answering howls rose from the wolves barreling toward us. The sound made hope spark in my veins . . . but I wasn't ready to let my guard down yet.

"Holy . . . !" Connor shouted. "Incoming!"

"There are too many!" Adne yelled. "We won't be able to get past them."

"Calla! What the hell are you doing?!" Connor screamed as I pulled to a halt, staring in amazement at the massive horde of fur and fangs charging us.

I couldn't believe it.

"Calla!" Connor threw me an exasperated look before grabbing Adne and shoving her behind him.

The wall of wolves hit us, abruptly splitting and flowing around us like a river.

"What the—" Connor gaped as dozens of wolves streaked past us, with more following in their wake. The Banes barked and yelped in alarm as Nightshades swarmed among them. The newly arrived wolves pulled the Banes off of Searchers, wrestling them to the ground in a chaos of claws and teeth. Soon the hiss of steel was overwhelmed by growls and snarls loud as thunder as the two Guardian packs tore into each other. Years of animosity fueled their rage as they spilled each other's blood in the gleaming snow.

A huge brown and silver wolf, bearing an unusual black mark on his forehead, slowed as he approached us, stopping in front of me.

It's good to see you, Calla. His tongue lolled out in a wolf grin. *I hope we haven't kept you waiting.*

Your timing is perfect, Dad. I pushed my muzzle into his chest. *And you definitely know how to make an entrance.*

TWENTY-THREE

"STOP SQUIRMING!" Connor shouted. "I'm trying to protect you."

"Just let me go, Connor!" Adne tried to wrestle out of his grip. "They obviously aren't here to attack us."

You have some interesting friends, my father remarked, watching them struggle.

It helps if you spend more time with them. I barked, catching Adne and Connor's attention. When I bared my teeth, they stopped arguing. I looked back at my father. *The man is Connor and the woman is Adne. I swear they really are good in a fight.*

He sniffed Connor's hand while the Searcher's eyes bulged at the massive wolf's inspection. *If you say so.*

Bryn flattened against the earth, wagging her tail at my father. *Hi, Mr. Tor.*

You look well, Bryn. My father nipped her ear. *Ready for the fight?*

She hopped up. *Always.*

Shay trotted up to us, lowering his muzzle as a sign of respect. My dad tilted his head in curiosity, though he quietly snarled a warning. *I don't know you.*

Dad, this is Shay. I lowered my muzzle as well, but my tail was wagging ecstatically. *Shay, this is my father, Stephen Tor.*

The Nightshade alpha. Shay kept his head low. *I'm honored to meet you. Thank you for coming to our aid.*

My heart skipped a beat when my father put his head below Shay's muzzle, lifting his head. *The honor is mine, Scion. You make an impressive wolf.*

Shay yipped his delight and I snarled at him in frustration.

Still a bit of a puppy, though, I see. My father's laugh traveled with his thought.

Shay put his paw over his nose. *I'm working on it.*

So am I. I snapped at his ear.

We should move away from the fight. My father nudged my shoulder. *Get me updated before we make our next move.*

I barked at Connor, tugging at the sleeve of his leather duster so he would follow me.

"I guess we're going this way," Connor said, casting a nervous glance at Adne as I pulled him toward the long shadows cast by the manor.

My father stopped when we were cloaked by darkness, though even if we'd been spotted, the battle raged at a fever pitch that would probably keep anyone from trying to reach us.

Connor was still eyeing my father warily when I shifted form, gesturing for the other two wolves to follow my lead.

I'd forgotten how intimidating a full-fledged alpha could be. Having spent my whole life as the daughter of one and growing into the role myself, I'd taken his regal bearing and stern gaze as a matter of course. Everything from his towering stature to his steel gray eyes commanded respect. Connor didn't look any more at ease even after my father returned to his human form. Even Adne slid back to peer over Connor's shoulder rather than get too close to the alpha.

"Connor, Adne," I said. "This is my father, Stephen Tor."

"The Nightshade alpha?" Adne asked, her eyes widening. "You came!"

"For the win!" Connor shouted, pumping his fist in the air.

My father's mouth curved up in a quizzical smile. Connor dropped his hand, looking embarrassed.

"Uh, sorry about that," he said. "It's just really, really good that you're here."

"It's my pleasure." My father extended his hand so Connor could shake it.

Adne smiled shyly when the alpha greeted her, her gaze flicking over to me. "I can see the resemblance."

I laughed, but my father flashed me a proud smile that made my heart sing. Bryn giggled, squeezing my hand.

Three more wolves trotted up to join us. When Ren, Mason, and Nev changed forms, they were all grinning.

"The more the merrier, eh?" Mason laughed.

Connor punched Nev on the arm. "You could have given us some warning that you're on our team. I thought we were dead for a second there."

"Poor Connor," Adne said. "Such a delicate soul."

He threw her a reproachful look.

"We did give you warning," Nev said. "Just look."

He shifted forms, bowing his head to reveal a black symbol painted on his forehead.

"Hey!" Shay smiled. "That's my tattoo."

"The mark of the Scion," my father said. "We thought it best to identify ourselves. All the wolves who joined us were marked by Ethan. It was his idea."

"Yeah." Nev was back in human form. "So no one shoots us. Particularly Ethan."

"He's always had an itchy trigger finger." Connor laughed. "Is he with you?"

"He came in on the southern attack," my father said. "I imagine he'll be looking for us soon, though."

"You mean there are more of you?" Adne asked.

"We split into three strike teams," my father said. "Mine was the largest. We outflanked the Bane ambush and came in behind them."

"That many wolves?" Ren's eyebrows went up. "You brought over some Banes too."

"Your father was not a kind alpha, Renier." My father watched Ren with wary eyes. "He drove his own son away, as well as many others. Such is the price for cruelty."

"Emile Laroche is not my father," Ren said, unflinching. "I owe him no allegiance."

"True enough," my father said. "I would seek peace with you, alpha."

"And I you." Ren inclined his head, sliding a glance at me. "Your daughter is the bravest wolf I've ever known. She's the true alpha."

"Indeed." My father smiled at Ren and then at me.

Bryn leaned over to me. "I think Ren's trying to score points with your dad."

"Shhhhhh." I stomped on her toes.

Shay shifted his weight uncomfortably at the exchange. My father's gaze slid over to him; his smile became knowing. "It must be a challenge having so many leaders in one small party."

"Finally, someone had the courage to say it!" Mason grinned. Nev cuffed him on the back of the head.

"I'm glad you convinced Banes to join us," Connor said to my father, ignoring Mason and Nev's impromptu shoving match. "We didn't know if anyone would."

My father nodded. "I was glad too. It's Neville who deserves most of the credit for swaying them."

"Thanks, Stephen," Nev said; he'd gotten Mason into a headlock. "But I had help. Sabine and Caleb—the Bane you guys met at Eden who played with me at Burnout—were vital. Tom supplied a safe place for us to meet while we gathered allies. Definitely a team effort."

Mason flipped Nev onto his back. "Gotcha!"

"Would you two behave?" I said, exasperated. "We are at war."

"We're always at war, Cal," Mason said even as he kept Nev pinned to the ground.

Nev laughed, kicking Mason off. "That's why we make our own fun in between kicking ass."

"Can't argue with that logic," Bryn said. She shifted into wolf form, pinning Mason and dousing his face in long, slobbering licks.

"Ack!" Mason shouted. "You win! You win!"

"Hey!" Ethan ran up to us, breathless and bleeding from a deep scratch on his cheek. "There you are!"

Connor clasped his arm. "Good to see you."

"Likewise," Ethan said, giving Adne a one-armed hug. He turned to Nev. "She's not fighting. I couldn't find her."

"I was worried about that," Nev said.

"Who?" Adne asked.

"Sabine," Ethan said, his face bleak. "She's not among the Banes here."

Mason and Bryn stopped wrestling. Bryn shifted forms, giving me a somber glance at the mention of Sabine's absence.

"Neither is Emile," Stephen said. "I can smell him a mile away. They must be inside."

I glanced at the dark manor, unable to make out any sign of light within. "In Rowan Estate?"

Ren tested the air. "Efron and Lumine are nearby."

"And they don't take part in the real fighting," Mason said. "Ever."

"The information we received said you'd be sending a small group in with the Scion to finish this," my father said.

Connor nodded. "That would be us."

"With your permission I'd like to join you."

"You don't want to oversee your pack?" Connor asked.

"They're in good hands." My father gestured to Nev. "He and

Ethan planned this strike. He's the one who should continue to lead it."

Nev shifted forms and barked his approval.

"I'll stick with Nev," Mason said, looking at me. "If that's all right."

"Go with him." I nodded. "And keep an eye out for Ansel and Tess."

"You know I will," Mason said with a wink. In the next moment the two wolves howled and dashed to join the fight.

My father looked at me sharply. "Your brother is here?"

"Not fighting," I said. "He's helping Searchers tend the wounded. He'll be safe enough." *I hope.*

"I wouldn't have left him." Bryn threw my father a guilty look. "But I thought we needed all the fighters we could spare."

"Of course," he said. "You belong with your pack."

My father shot an inquiring look at Connor. "Well?"

"You don't need to ask," Connor said. "Another alpha would be a great help."

"Good. I owe Emile a personal visit," my father said. "One that's been a long time coming."

"Those are the best kind of visits," Ethan said. "I have one in mind myself."

Connor grunted. "Then let's not keep anyone waiting."

My father, Ren, Bryn, and I slid into our wolf forms, taking up positions like sentinels around the three Searchers and Shay as we stalked along the north wall of the manor.

"The side door will bring us into the kitchen," Shay said. "We'll be on the back side of the house. We can make our way to the library from there."

My skin crawled beneath my fur. That meant we'd be slinking through the halls of Rowan Estate, passing all of those horrible paintings and ghastly statues. Any of which could come alive should Bosque Mar already be waiting for us.

I could still hear the battle raging at our backs, but as we approached the far end of Rowan Estate, the sounds of war seemed to be swallowed up by the walls of the manor. The immense building cut us off from the conflict, separating us from enemy and ally alike. Though I'd known it had always been the plan, I felt a sense of dread wash over me as I realized our small party would face the horrors on our own.

"There's the door." Shay strode forward and I saw the dark shape bloom within the shadows.

I barked at the same moment Connor shouted, "Shay! On your right!"

Shay had his swords ready as the wraith attacked. But it wasn't only the wraith that was moving. From around the back of the manor four wolves appeared, bearing down on us in a storm of fangs and furious howls.

The first wolf leapt, knocking Connor down. Adne pivoted, her steel whip flying out. The wolf squealed as sharpened steel tips lodged in its body. It yelped again when Ethan's crossbow bolts thunked into its flank. The wolf twisted, trying to pull the bolts out. Its final cry died in a gurgle as Connor plunged his dagger into its chest.

My father had thrown himself into the second wolf. They were tumbling across the ground, snarling and tearing at each other. A few feet away Ren was facing off with the other two wolves. None of the three had attacked, but instead they all stared at each other, bristling, filling the air with low, threatening growls. Bryn and I stalked up to flank Ren.

My pulse buzzed through my veins as I realized why he'd hesitated. Dax and Fey glared at their former alpha. Their muzzles twisted in frustrated, furious snarls.

Don't do this. Ren's mind opened to all of us. *We shouldn't fight.*

I ran to his side. *Listen to Ren. Please.*

Why? Dax ignored me, barking at Ren. *So we can bow down to your bitch too?*

Don't ever talk about her that way. Ren took a menacing step forward. *You know nothing about what's going on here.*

Really? Fey sniffed the air disdainfully. *I think you're just afraid to be the alpha you should be. You're weak.*

You're an idiot, Fey. Bryn snarled.

At least I don't let Calla think for me. Fey glanced at Ren and Bryn. *You're both weak.* Her muscles quivered.

Fey, don't! I braced myself. But she was already lunging.

I was ready when she slammed into me, but the force of her leap sent us sprawling through the snow. Bryn rushed after us, sinking her teeth into Fey's side. Snapping jaws and savage growls told me that Ren and Dax were fighting alongside us.

Our best fighters. I remembered what Ren had said about Dax and Fey. Like attracts like. But now their skill in combat was working against us. We were their alphas, but would we be able to best them?

I rolled to my feet. Fey was faster. She landed on my back, sinking her teeth into my shoulder. Ignoring the pain, I bucked hard, flipping us over so she slammed into the ground beneath my weight. Bryn leapt at her, crushing Fey into the snow. Fey twisted and kicked up, sending Bryn flying.

I scrambled up, knowing what I should do. Fey was still on her back. The soft flesh of her belly was exposed. Two bites to open up her gut would be fatal. But I had to do it now.

My breath caught in my chest. Fey squirmed on the ground, about to roll over. I couldn't wait any longer.

Something buzzed past my ear. Fey's bark of pain became a yelp as a second and then third crossbow bolt entered her abdomen. She rolled over, snarling but trying to limp away. A trail of blood soaked the snow beneath her as she tried to flee.

Ethan was beside me, raising his crossbow. "I've got this." He jerked his chin to my right. "Help him."

I pushed away regret as Ethan took aim, turning to see Ren and

Dax circling each other a few feet away. They were both panting. Blood darkened their fur, dripping onto the snow. I rushed at them, throwing myself into the air and locking my jaws around the back of Dax's neck. Even with the force of my attack, he was too big to take down. I bit down harder, struggling to hang on.

He snarled, spinning in a circle as I clung to him. Finally he reared up. I knew he would come down on me just as I'd landed on top of Fey. I couldn't afford to be knocked down. I released him, twisting in the air as he fell backward.

Feeling my weight vanish, Dax spun in the air and landed on his feet again. He pivoted around, snarling at me.

God, you're a pest. His eyes were full of hate. *Time to squash you for good.*

I'm waiting. I dug my paws into the snow, bracing myself for his attack.

He snarled but then barked, twisting his head around as Ren's teeth tore through his hamstring.

Now, Calla. Ren's shout filled my head.

I knew what he meant. Forcing any doubt from my mind and moving on pure instinct, I lunged. My jaws locked on Dax's throat. I bit down hard, ripping through muscles and finally crushing his windpipe. His blood poured into my mouth as his body stiffened and then went slack. I dropped his deadweight, backing away from the hulking wolf's unmoving form. My muscles were shaking.

Ren limped up beside me. *It had to be done.*

I whined, leaning my muzzle against his shoulder. I knew he was right, but I felt sick.

You're hurt. He pushed against me. *Take some blood.*

You first. I turned my shoulder to his muzzle. His teeth pierced my skin. I stood still as he lapped up blood.

I'm good. He licked my muzzle. *Go ahead.*

I bit into his chest. The smoky sweet, wild taste of his blood slipped over my tongue. The sparkling warmth of healing poured over me.

Thanks. I lifted my muzzle to press my nose against his cheek.

Looks like we're clear. My father padded over to us. His muzzle was bright with blood, but I could see no sign of injury on him. Behind him the corpse of an elder Bane lay sprawled on the ground.

He looked at Dax's body and then at Ren. *Your packmate?*

Ren lowered his head. *My second.*

I'm sorry. My father rested his muzzle on Ren's shoulder.

Ren whimpered softly, leaning into my father.

I dropped to the ground, grief heavy in my bones, and stared up at the night sky. Bryn, covered in snow, snuggled in beside me with a low whine. I rested my head on her back, catching the scent of Fey's blood in her fur. The moon was gone now, covered by thick bands of clouds. As tiny silver flakes drifted down to settle on our bodies—both the living and the dead—I thought perhaps the moon had hidden her face from us, as full of sorrow as we were. But she couldn't stop her tears from spilling out in the form of silent snow.

TWENTY-FOUR

CONNOR STOOD BEFORE THE DOOR, reaching in his pocket for lock-picking tools. Ethan shook his head.

"Logan was supposed to leave it unlocked."

Connor shrugged and tried the door. It swung open.

"That's a good sign," he said. "Right?"

"It's a sign that Logan is at least pretending to be on our team," Ethan said. "Let's not read anything else into it."

"Agreed." Connor had his swords drawn and moved slowly into the kitchen.

We followed him into the cavernous room. In the darkness I could make out pots and pans hanging from the ceiling. A long prep table stretched nearly the length of the room, and a huge brick oven took up most of one wall.

"You could cook for all of Vail in here," Adne said. "How many big parties does your uncle host? Like one a week?"

"None," Shay said. "At least not that I've seen."

"Does anyone even use this kitchen?" Connor asked.

"I came down here for snacks," Shay said. "They keep the fridge stocked." He pointed to a walk-in refrigeration unit beside an equally huge pantry.

"You ever find bodies in there?" Ethan muttered.

Shay didn't answer, but he shuddered. I was sure he hadn't ever considered that possibility before he learned the truth about his uncle. I wondered if coming back to Rowan Estate was as frightening for Shay as it was for me. The more I thought about it, the more I became convinced it was probably much worse for him. He'd lived here, called this place home without knowing what lived in the walls, the tortured prisoners trapped in paintings. He'd laughed at statues of incubi that he now knew could come to life and attack. He must have felt as if the very ground was constantly rolling under his feet.

I trotted to his side and licked his fingers, hoping I could lend him some comfort. He smiled down at me.

"Home sweet home," he said, but the haunted quality of his gaze let me know I'd been right about his feelings.

This has to be the creepiest house of all time. Bryn stayed closed to my heels.

I glanced over my shoulder. *It's definitely in the top ten.*

Did you guys really make out here? 'Cause I think I'd be too freaked out to focus.

I bared my teeth at her. *Speaking of focus, now is not the time to be asking about my love life.*

When we were about to exit the kitchen, Shay paused. "Do yourselves a favor and don't look at any of the paintings."

Connor nodded, moving quietly into the hallway.

The corridor was dark. Connor led us at a cautious pace. I knew it was wise, but creeping forward set my teeth on edge. A stifled gasp hit my ears. Ethan's head was bowed. Adne laid her hand on his arm, leaning in to him to whisper in a calm voice. When he lifted his face, I saw his jaw clench and the veins in his neck throb.

Shay glanced at him. "I told you not to look."

"Just keep walking, Scion," Ethan snarled, but his voice shook. "He wasn't your brother, he was mine."

I made the mistake of glancing over my shoulder at the painting Ethan had just passed. A man in tattered clothes lay stretched out on a table, agony etched on his face, his mouth open in an eternal cry of pain. Dark shapes loomed in the shadows at the edge of the painting, watching him. I wished I didn't recognize the man, but I knew Ethan's brother, Kyle, the moment I looked at the painting and I felt sick. It was my fault he was trapped forever, his torture feeding the wraiths. I'd thought I was doing my duty, protecting Shay, when I'd killed his partner, Stuart, and handed Kyle over to the Keepers for questioning. How many other choices had I made while serving the Keepers that had destroyed the lives of people I now called allies and friends?

A hand brushed my fur. I turned to find Shay watching me, his eyes bright with concern.

He offered me a thin smile. "I'm not trying to pet you. I just want to say that the past is the past. You didn't know. Neither of us did."

I pushed my nose against his palm as I tried to erase the horror of the painting from my mind.

We had turned the corner to enter the manor's central corridor when Connor gave a shout. His blades flashed out, hitting something solid and then clanging off as the blow was deflected.

He spewed curses, stomping his feet and kicking the wall. "Statues! For the love—" He began to swear again.

"Connor, you're making me blush," Adne said, stepping forward to inspect the marble succubus.

I barked at Shay, wagging my tail. He flashed a grin at me, sharing the memory of my first visit to Rowan Estate. I couldn't blame Connor for his reaction. The statues were just too realistic.

"You'll have to watch out for that," Shay said. "The statues are all over."

"A ready-made army," Connor said. He glared at the statue. "Just waiting."

"An army that we fought during our last visit," Ethan said. "Remember? How come these aren't outside playing with their friends?"

"Rowan Estate's creatures are still dormant." Shay rapped his knuckles on the succubus's stone forehead. "The minions outside must be the Keepers' pets from Eden. That means Bosque isn't here. He hasn't summoned them."

"Or he wants us to think he isn't here," Connor said.

Shay frowned. "I don't think so. Only the wolves are fighting. Bosque had all his creatures in the mix in the last fight. He's not here. Not yet."

"Only one way to know for sure." Connor made a rude gesture at the statue and then continued down the corridor.

My heart seemed to be stuck in my throat, beating hard as we stepped into the grand foyer of the manor. Suits of armor and more hideous creatures cast in marble circled the room, standing like guards before the immense staircase.

The Searchers' footsteps and the clatter of our wolf nails echoed in the enormous space, bouncing off the walls all the way to the immense crystal chandelier hanging above our heads.

"Up the stairs," Shay murmured.

Connor nodded and we began to ascend. With each step my body felt colder.

Ren brushed up against me. *Did you really spend time here?*

Yeah. I glanced around. *Quite a bit, actually.*

Ugh. He shuddered. *You've got a stronger stomach than me.*

It's better when you don't know the whole place wants to come alive and kill you. I flashed my teeth at him.

Oh, I'm sure it is. He nipped my shoulder.

When we reached the top of the stairs, Connor drew a long breath. Then he reached for the library door. The handle turned and I heard a soft click.

"Open," he murmured. "I don't think I can take this one as a good sign."

"It's not," Shay said. "But I didn't expect this to go well. Did you?"

"Go on," Ethan said, jerking his chin at Connor. "No rest for the wicked."

"Is that our slogan?" Connor asked as he pushed the door open. "Or theirs?"

"Take your pick." Ethan lifted his crossbow.

A soft glow filled the library; the subtle light of lamps ensconced among the shelves made the room feel warm and inviting. If I hadn't known any better, I'd have thought it a peaceful place to curl up with a favorite book.

My father stiffened as a growl rumbled in his chest. His nose crinkled up.

Emile.

Bryn began to snarl, her hackles rising.

Familiar scents drew my attention too. The Bane alpha was here, but he wasn't alone.

"Welcome." Lumine stood alongside the bookcase that contained the *Haldis Annals.* She extended her hand to us.

"We've been expecting you." Efron smiled. He was sitting beside her in a high-backed leather chair. Two wolves lay at his feet, their eyes fixed on us. Sabine's gaze was steady, while Emile's gleamed with malice. Logan stood behind his father, his face fixed in a mask of indifference.

"That's disappointing," Connor said. "Now we can't yell 'surprise!'"

"Glib. How charming." Lumine offered him a condescending smile and arched an eyebrow. "We can make you this offer. Leave the Scion alone with us and your lives will be spared."

I snarled and Ethan lifted his crossbow. "That's an offer?" His eyes were on Sabine, and he was gripping his weapon so tightly the blood had left his knuckles. She returned his gaze calmly, remaining so still she could have been one of the statues in the hallway.

"Not very tempting, is it?" Adne's whip hissed along the floor.

"Fine." Lumine's ruby red lips parted, her smile revealing gleaming teeth. She raised her hand and began to draw a flaming symbol in the air.

"Here comes the wraith," Connor muttered.

"I've got this." Shay stepped forward as the fiery symbol exploded into a writhing, dark creature.

"Kill them," Lumine said, waving her hand lazily in our direction.

The wraith slithered across the floor. Shay took two bounds and launched himself in the air, flipping across the room to land in front of the wraith.

"Now he's just showing off," Connor said.

The Elemental Cross sliced through its shadowy form. The wraith shrieked, its body boiling away into smoke.

Lumine didn't flinch, but I saw her throat move as she swallowed. "How interesting."

"Let's try that again," Efron said. "But make it sporting, shall we? Emile! Sabine!"

The two wolves leapt to their feet. Emile bolted toward Shay, but Sabine whirled on Efron. She lunged at the hand he was using to summon the wraith, crushing his fingers in her jaws. He shrieked, falling to his knees in front of the chair. His eyes bulged in disbelief as Sabine dropped his bloodied hand only to knock him onto his back.

Efron's blood-choked screams pulled Emile around. He howled his fury and barreled down on her. Sabine's focus didn't waver. She had Efron pinned. Still snarling, she struck again and again, tearing his throat apart. When he stopped clawing at her fur, she shifted into human form and spat on him.

"Weren't expecting that, were you." She gazed at his body. "Bastard." She spat again.

Logan ran to his father's side, but the elder Keeper was already dead. Efron's throat had been so ravaged that his head was nearly severed from his body. Logan fell back, drawing his knees to his chest and hiding his face. Sabine turned on him, snarling as he cowered beside Efron's corpse.

"Sabine!" Ethan shouted. His crossbow bolt whizzed past Emile, who slammed into her. She was sent spiraling through the air, crashing in a heap against the stones of the fireplace. My father howled and hurtled across the room. Ren and Bryn chased after him with Ethan firing bolts as they rushed to her aid. Emile spun around, ignoring the bolts that hit his shoulder and flank. His eyes were locked on my father.

Ethan jumped over Emile's crouching, snarling wolf form, throwing himself protectively over Sabine's limp body. While the Searcher kept watch over Sabine, my father and Emile stalked toward each other, ignoring the chaos around them.

Lumine gasped, her hands going to her neck. She began to tremble, but she quickly drew another flaming symbol. A wraith bloomed before her.

"Protect me!" she shrieked at it.

The wraith swirled around her like a cloak as she scrambled for the door.

I snarled, wanting to fight, but Shay was the only one who could fight off wraiths.

"Shay!" Adne screamed as wraith-draped Lumine approached us, forcing us away from the door.

"Stay with me!" Lumine hissed at her slithering bodyguard as she ran from the library. "Don't let them near me!" The wraith oozed away from us, taking Lumine out of the room as it moved.

Shay ran to us, gazing after her retreat, but Connor grabbed his arm. "Let her go. Our fight is here."

Shay nodded, though his jaw twitched in frustration.

"We have to be sure Logan doesn't make a run for it," Connor said to Shay. "You need to watch him while we help the others."

Shay glanced at Logan, who was rocking back and forth where he sat, his head still hidden behind his knees. "I don't think he's going anywhere."

"I would say the same thing if he were unconscious," Connor said. "We need to keep him here."

"I'll stick with Shay," Adne said, grabbing his arm and pulling him toward Logan. "You help the others."

Bryn! I called to her. *Get to Adne and Shay. You need to protect them.*

She wheeled around, rushing to act as a sentinel for the Scion and our Weaver. *On it!*

I ran with Connor across the room to where Ethan was cradling Sabine against his body. She wasn't moving, and we weren't close enough for me to know if she was even alive. I needed to help her if I could.

But my eyes kept moving to the other side of the library. Emile and my father squared off, now only a few feet apart, snarling at each other while Ren stood bristling at my father's flank. But the younger wolf could have been invisible for all the attention the other two wolves gave him. Their gazes were locked, full of hate.

My father lifted his muzzle and howled a challenge. Emile responded with an answering cry, his bulky muscles rippling as he pawed the ground, fury building. The fight they'd both been waiting for as long as they'd been rival alphas was about to begin.

TWENTY-FIVE

MY FATHER SNARLED, dropping his muzzle low as he stalked sideways, watching Emile.

The Bane alpha shook spittle from his jaws, giving a final howl.

They both leapt, throwing their bodies at each other with such force that I thought their bones would shatter.

"Calla!" Connor's shout pulled my gaze off the battling wolves. "Help us!"

Ethan repositioned Sabine against his chest, propping her up. "She's breathing, but I think she's hurt."

Sabine stirred in his arms, groaning softly.

"Better safe than sorry," Connor said, locking my gaze.

I nodded, shifting forms to bite my wrist. Taking Sabine's chin in my hand, I opened her mouth, pressing my bleeding arm to her lips. She swallowed immediately.

"If she's hurt, it's not bad," I said as she drank. "Maybe a broken bone or two."

"That's not bad?" Ethan asked, stroking her hair.

"Not for us," I said.

Sabine's eyelids snapped open. She pushed my arm away, wiping off her mouth.

"Thanks."

"No problem." I braceleted the wound on my wrist to stop the blood flow and let the punctures close.

Her gaze moved to Ethan. His Adam's apple moved up and down as he swallowed hard, running his finger over her cheek.

"Ethan," she whispered.

He drew her shaking body into his arms. "It's over now."

He was partly right. With Efron dead, one nightmare had ended for Sabine. But that was a single battle and we were still in the middle of a war.

Connor went to join Adne and Shay as they watched over Logan. The Keeper was still huddled in a ball. Bryn stalked around him, snarling.

I shifted forms, moving as silently as I could toward my father and Emile. They were both bloodied, despite the short time they'd been fighting. Gashes marred my father's right side, while a flap of torn flesh hung from Emile's chest.

I slid behind Emile, ready to spring. But my father's voice was suddenly in my mind.

Stay out of this, Calla. That's an order.

But— I snarled, drawing Emile's attention. He barked a warning at me.

Relying on your whelp, Stephen?

Like I said, Calla. My father growled. *Stay away. This isn't your fight.*

I backed off, but not far. My instincts still compelled me to submit to my father's will, but my blood was singing, screaming that I should attack.

Ren was still behind my father, also keeping his distance as the two wolves circled each other, watching for any opening, waiting for any sign of weakness. Ren paced back and forth, as agitated as I was. I could only guess that my father had ordered him out of the fight as well.

Emile lunged, but my father dodged the attack. He wheeled around and struck Emile's flank, tearing out another chunk of flesh. Emile howled in pain as blood spurted from his body. My father struck again, but this time Emile was ready for him, kicking his back legs high. He caught my father in the face. The blow sent my father crashing back. He landed with a loud crack half onto a table, his body folding around the wood. The table's edge splintered with the force of the impact.

Dad! I screamed a warning.

My father shook his head in an attempt to clear his jarred senses as he scrambled to his feet. While he wasn't out of the fight, the blow had dazed him.

Emile didn't hesitate. He thundered toward my father, never slowing as he hit the other alpha. He used my father's body to break through the already-stressed wood. The table split in two when Emile drove my father into the wall on the other side of the library.

They slammed into the bookshelves and were thrown apart. Emile landed on his feet, muscles quivering in anticipation of the next attack. My father was lying on the ground, his head hanging low.

That's when I saw it: a sharp piece of wood had pierced deep into his back. The blunt end of the wooden spear protruded from his fur. He struggled to his feet, twisting his neck to grip the impaled wood in his jaws. But in doing so he exposed his throat to Emile.

Without hesitation the Bane alpha lunged at my father.

I was already running, hoping to block his attack, no longer caring whose fight this was supposed to be. Emile Laroche would not kill my father. I couldn't watch that happen and do nothing.

But Ren was closer still. I was a few feet short of my father when Ren hit Emile in a flying leap, sending both of them tumbling away from me and my father. They scrambled to their feet, turning and lunging again. Within moments they were wrestling on the ground, tearing at each other without mercy.

Beside me, my father snarled. He'd pulled the huge splinter from his chest. Blood gushed from the wound and he faltered.

Take my blood. I turned my shoulder to his muzzle. *Hurry!*

He bit into my flesh as I wrenched my neck to see what was happening behind us.

Emile's attention remained focused on Ren. The elder Bane's muzzle was bloodied, but I didn't know if it was only my father's blood or if Emile had wounded Ren as well.

That's enough, Calla. My father pushed me away gently. *Thank you.*

He turned his attention to Ren and I heard his command. *Renier, do not attack Emile.*

Ren didn't move, didn't even glance in my father's direction. He was shouting, his mind open to us.

My whole life was a lie. Ren's muscles were shaking with rage. *My mother died because of you. I swear I will kill you.*

Emile's laugh sounded in my mind. *Is that any way to speak to your dear old dad, boy?* His thought finished with a menacing snarl.

You are not my father. Ren growled. *My father died when you broke his neck.*

One of the best days of my life. Emile crouched low. *Just like today will be when I finish this.*

Ren howled and lunged at Emile.

Renier, no! My father threw himself toward the other two wolves as Ren attacked. *Stop!*

I saw Ren's mistake even as he made it. In his anger he'd jumped too high, giving Emile time to change position beneath him. Emile leapt, angling his body to meet Ren in the air.

Emile's shout rang in my mind. *I should have done this the day you were born.* His jaws closed around Ren's neck.

Ren! I screamed his name as they fell to the ground, their bodies locked together.

Emile gave a sudden jerk of his head. I thought I was splitting in two when a horrible crack stopped Ren's steady growl.

When they hit the ground, my father slammed into Emile, shoving him away from Ren, who lay horribly still on the library floor. I howled, skidding to a stop beside him. Dropping my muzzle, I pressed my nose against him.

A squeal across the room tore my gaze off Ren.

Emile was on his back, pinned under my father. The Bane alpha writhed beneath my father's weight, kicking and struggling. My father ignored Emile's desperate attempts to free himself. His jaws were around Emile's neck and they were slowly closing. Emile cried out, a half howl, half shriek that became a gurgle as my father crushed his throat.

Emile stopped struggling. My father lifted Emile's limp body in his jaws and with one swing of his head tossed the Bane's carcass aside.

My father came toward us, shifting forms as he walked.

Ren. Ren. I nipped his muzzle gently. *Please get up. You have to get up.*

I breathed into his charcoal gray fur. His scent was the same as always, sandalwood and fire wrapped in leather.

Ren. I whined, pawing at him. *Answer me. I can heal you, but you need to wake up so I can give you blood.*

Someone dropped to the ground next to me. Adne was on her knees, staring at me with wide, brimming eyes. Bryn was beside her, whining softly.

"Why?" Adne said. "Why did you have to leave too?" She began to reach for him, but I snarled, knocking her back. I didn't want anyone else near him. They couldn't help him. She stared at me, limbs trembling as the color drained from her face.

"Hey!" Connor was still standing over Logan, but he pointed the tip of his sword at me. "Back off, wolfie."

Shay glanced from Connor to me. "Stay here." He returned the Elemental Cross to its sheaths and then shifted forms.

Calla. He approached slowly, keeping his head low.

I bristled, a steady menacing growl rising from my throat. *Stay away.*

Let me help you. His voice was soothing and he dropped to his belly, still inching toward me. *I only want to help.*

I snarled again, showing him my fangs when he reached me. He lifted his muzzle and gently licked mine. It was soothing; his scent— fresh and hopeful, like rain that rinsed away the sludge of fear muddying my senses—reassured me. I stopped growling. He stood up, resting his muzzle against mine.

We can help him. But not like this.

He shifted to human form and I understood. Ren was a wolf; he couldn't drink when he was unconscious. We'd need to bring him back, just like Gabriel had helped Nev breathe again. I shifted forms.

Bryn dropped to the ground, remaining a wolf. A quiet steady whine continued to rise from her muzzle.

"Help me," I said to Shay. But he hesitated, not moving any closer to Ren. Something was flickering in his eyes, something he didn't want me to see.

"Help me," I said again.

Shay gazed at Ren's still form. He stretched a hand toward me. His fingers were shaking. I turned my back on him with a growl.

"Fine." I crawled closer to Ren. "I'll do this without your help."

When my father reached my side, there was no triumph in his eyes. Only loss.

"We need to wake him so he can drink," I said. *My father can fix this. He's always led us. He'll know what to do.*

My father gave me a long look before he crouched beside Ren, resting his hand on the deep gray wolf's neck. He bent down, laying his head against Ren's chest. He let out a slow, regretful breath.

"What should we do?" I asked.

My father slowly turned his face to gaze at me. I couldn't accept what I found in his eyes.

"There isn't . . . ," Shay murmured from behind me; I felt his fingers encircling my upper arm. "Calla—" His voice was thick and he couldn't manage any more words.

I wouldn't look at him, asking my father again, "What should we do?"

"Emile broke his neck." My father lifted his head, rocking back on his heels with a heavy sigh. "His heart isn't beating,"

I'd already sunk my canines into my forearm. When I stretched my bleeding flesh toward Ren's muzzle, Shay caught my shoulders, pulling me back.

He didn't say anything when I snarled, craning my neck to glare at him. "Let me go."

He shook his head.

"Calla," my father said quietly. "Renier's heart isn't beating."

"No."

"You can't save him. It's too late."

"No."

Adne had begun to sob. She stood up, stumbling away from us and into Connor's arms.

My limbs had gone numb. I let myself melt into the floor, stretched beside Ren's body. My fingers twisted in the thick charcoal fur.

He can't be dead. He can't be.

I shifted into wolf form with the only will I could muster, settling my muzzle on top of Ren's.

Shay didn't try to approach me, but I glanced at him when I heard his shaky breath.

"I'm sorry, Calla," he said. "I didn't want it to end this way."

I whimpered and turned my face away from him. Closing my eyes, I sent a final plea out, trying to touch Ren's mind.

I love you.

But he was gone.

TWENTY-SIX

"LEAVE HER." My father stepped between Shay and me. I was still curled against Ren's body. I could hear my blood pounding through my veins, but I couldn't feel anything.

"But—" Shay gazed at me, his features hardening with resolve. "We still have to face Bosque. We need her." Adne was wrapped in Connor's arms, crying quietly.

"Losing another alpha is like losing part of yourself." Stephen bared sharp canines at Shay.

"I understand that." A challenge flashed in Shay's eyes, but he withdrew to stand beside Adne and Connor. "It doesn't change what's at stake. We can't stop. This isn't over. We still have to summon Bosque."

Sabine approached us slowly. Ethan trailed close behind her, but kept a respectful distance as she knelt beside Ren.

I didn't move, watching her stretch her hand to touch him. She bent forward, placing a kiss on the top of his head.

She turned her eyes to me for a moment, and I saw my sorrow reflected there.

I understood now why Shay had come to me in wolf form. Why he'd coaxed me to shift. He'd already known there was no hope for Ren, but he knew I wasn't able to face that loss. That I would have attacked any intruders—just as I'd almost attacked Adne—that had come too close to Ren's body.

But that time had passed, leaving me numb, exhausted. I wouldn't attack anyone now. I wouldn't do anything. The battle might not be over for Shay. But it was over for me. Doubt and regret stole my will to fight.

Sabine bowed her head and stood up, letting Ethan fold her into his arms.

"Come on," Connor said, beckoning to Shay. "It's time to end this."

Shay nodded. "Get Logan up." He turned to me. "Calla?"

I snapped at his fingers, unwilling to move from Ren's side. So what if this battle was the last? We'd lost Ren. I didn't want to fight. I couldn't look at Shay.

I couldn't stop thinking about Ren's voice, his words warm against my skin. *We were always meant to be together, Calla.*

He'd loved me, but I'd found my mate in another wolf, another alpha. Had I been reckless because of my choice? Could I have done more to save Ren? I'd been fighting other Guardians, tasting wolves' blood that flowed between my fangs, killing my own packmates. And now this. What could be worth losing Ren?

A warning growl slid through the space between me and the Scion. All I wanted was to be left alone. Shay gritted his teeth but turned away from me, following Connor to Logan's side.

Bryn stayed in place, watching me, but she didn't try to move any closer.

Connor kicked the Keeper, not too hard but enough that Logan finally lifted his face. "Is it over?"

"It's about to begin," Connor said. "And you're the opening act."

Logan didn't move. He scanned the room, taking in Emile's corpse and Ren's. He swallowed hard and began trembling as he stared up at Connor.

"If I do this," he whispered, "do you promise to let me live?"

His gaze slid onto me. I bared my teeth at him, snarling.

"Give me your word!" He rolled his eyes up at Shay.

"If you keep your promise, we'll keep ours," Shay said. "You won't be harmed."

"Now get on your feet," Connor said. "Our friends are still dying out there."

Logan scrambled up, stumbling forward as if he were barely able to force his muscles to work. He shook as he dropped to one knee in front of the fireplace. He unbuttoned his shirt, shrugging the crisp fabric from his body. Sabine hissed and my breath faltered. Logan's back was covered in scars.

"Blood oath," Connor muttered, gazing at Logan's ravaged skin. "It's a bitch."

Logan began chanting, his voice low and feverish.

"Oh God." Shay stepped back as one by one the scars on Logan's back opened.

Fresh blood began to seep from the wounds. Then it was flowing, spilling down his back and dripping onto the varnished wood floor.

The fireplace, which had been empty and silent, stirred. It began like a gentle breeze. As if a breath of wind had been caught in the tall chimney, so that the sound barely reached us. The murmur of sound grew louder. Within the darkness a shape began to form. The angry noise buzzed like a swarm of insects.

My father snarled, pacing restlessly in the space between me and the fireplace.

The flowing mass began to congeal, stretching into the shape of a man. A putrid green aura surrounded the moving body that stood tall in the shadows.

Connor swore, shielding Adne as the sickly light grew brighter. Behind the dark figure shadows flickered in and out of the gleaming green, creatures that remained just out of sight.

"There it is," Ethan murmured. "The Rift."

Sabine shifted into wolf form, hackles raised. Shay moved forward so he stood directly behind the chanting Keeper.

Logan's voice rose to a shout and then he collapsed.

Bosque Mar laughed as he stepped from the fireplace. Bryn snarled, scrambling to her feet and placing herself in front of me, as if she feared I wouldn't be able to fight for myself.

"Logan, Logan." Bosque's smile glinted like the edge of a blade. "Whatever are you up to?"

"Master," Logan breathed, though he scuttled backward like a crab, only stopping when he ran up against a bookcase.

Bosque scanned the room; his eyes settled on Efron's body. "How tragic."

"Hardly," Shay said.

"Welcome back, my nephew." Bosque's voice almost sounded warm. He turned a stony gaze on Logan. "Did your actions lead to your father's untimely demise?"

Logan stammered something, but all I could hear was the chattering of his teeth.

"I think you'll find the price of treachery to be quite high," Bosque murmured. Logan moaned, pressing his body tight against the wall.

Shay moved sideways, blocking Bosque's view of the Keeper. He slowly withdrew the Elemental Cross. The power of the blades reacted instantly to the aura of the Rift, making the air around Shay crackle as if it were alive with electricity. The sight stirred something inside me. I forced myself to my feet, keeping my gaze fixed on Shay.

Calla? Bryn's ears flicked as she watched me uneasily.

I'm fine. I bared my teeth. *Get ready to fight.*

I crept toward Shay, keeping my body low. Positioning myself behind him, I crouched, ready to leap at any hideous creatures that Bosque might conjure.

Bosque's gaze flitted over Shay's swords. "What a pretty toy you've brought me."

"The better to kill you with," Connor said. Beside him, Ethan raised his crossbow and Sabine growled.

Bosque glanced at the two Searchers. "Oh my, toy soldiers as well." He flicked his wrist and the men went flying. They crashed into the far wall, books tumbling down around them. Sabine yelped and tore across the room.

Go! I didn't want to leave Shay, but Bryn could help the others. Without hesitation, Bryn bounded after Sabine.

"No!" Adne shouted, running toward the mess of wood, pages, and limbs where Sabine had already begun digging in an attempt to reach the bodies of Ethan and Connor.

"What a lovely young thing." Bosque watched Adne move, running his tongue over his lips as if tasting the air. "And with such power. You've been playing with my garden, dear. Without permission."

He twisted his fingers and Adne stumbled. "Please stay awhile. I think you could be quite useful to me."

She rolled over, clawing at the rug beneath her feet, which had begun to unravel. Its loose threads wound together into thick ropes that wrapped around her ankles and continued to snake their way up her body.

"Logan, do it!" she screamed. "Do it now! Finish the ritual!"

Logan cowered, his eyes rolling up at Bosque, full of fear. My father ran to Adne's side. More ropes appeared to bind her even as he chewed through the first cords that had sprung out of the rug.

He stared at me and then at Bosque, who was laughing as my father struggled to free her.

"Let her go!" Shay advanced on Bosque. The blades of the Cross moved with such speed I couldn't make out either weapon. It appeared as though Shay was walking with a fiery tornado clearing his path.

Bosque laughed. "You can't touch me, boy. Put those down before you hurt yourself."

"Stop talking," Shay snarled. "I don't want to hear anything you have to say."

"Whyever not?" Bosque said. "I still have room in my heart to forgive you."

Shay shook his head, lunging at him. Bosque raised his hand. Shay wasn't thrown backward as Connor and Ethan had been, but the swords were blocked as if Bosque had thrown up a shield.

Shay snarled and swung the swords again, but he couldn't pierce whatever force Bosque held up against the attack. Bosque's human shell was protecting him. We had to strip it from him.

I heard groans and was relieved to see Ethan and Connor struggling out from under the rubble as Sabine and Bryn clawed through broken shelves and mounds of books.

"You coward!" Shay gritted his teeth, holding the swords low. "Fight me!"

"But the fight isn't happening here, is it?" Bosque closed his eyes and smiled. "It seems we have quite the gathering happening just outside." He lifted his arms. "I believe I'll invite a few more guests."

The sound sent chills up and down my limbs. I barked a warning to Connor and Ethan as a hundred tormented sighs swelled in the air around us.

"It's the Fallen!" Ethan shouted.

The sighs became moans, but more noises layered on top of the Fallen's cries. Shrieks and hisses followed the cracking of stone. Rowan Estate's statues were coming to life.

"Not just the Fallen," Connor yelled. "Here they come!"

"Block the door!" Adne shouted, still futilely twisting against the ropes around her. She shook her head at my father. "Go help them. You can't get me out of these!"

Bosque was laughing. The sound made my chest tighten, stirring me out of regret and self-pity, making the tension in the room crackle like electricity in my fur. The joyful gleam in his inhuman silver eyes set my blood boiling. I'd already lost too much today. I would not lose anything more.

Snarling, I bolted across the room to the spot where Logan crouched. He rolled his eyes up at me.

"Just leave me alone," he whimpered. "Run for your life, Calla. Get out of here."

I barked at him, baring my teeth close to his neck so he could feel my breath. He jerked back at the sight of my fangs but shook his head. "I won't do it. He'll kill me."

Shifting forms, I laced my fingers around his throat.

"It's too late," he said hoarsely.

"It is never too late," I said. "The ritual. Now."

The groan of heavy furniture scraping along the wood floor filled the room as Connor, Ethan, and my father barricaded the library door. I could already hear bodies slamming against the wood, claws tearing into the barrier.

I tightened my grip. Logan's eyes widened and he croaked, "Stop, please. I'll do it."

"Now," I hissed.

Logan reached around his back, smearing his hand in the blood that still leaked from the whiplashes. Using the blood as ink, he drew a symbol on the floor and began murmuring in a voice so low I could barely hear.

Bosque's laughter died instantly. Apparently it didn't matter how quietly Logan chanted; the Harbinger could sense that the ritual had begun. The stream of Logan's whispers faltered.

"Don't you dare stop." I bared my teeth at him. "Stop and I'll kill you."

He continued his fevered whispers, but his eyes were wild as they moved back and forth from me to Bosque.

"This isn't wise, Logan." Bosque took a step toward us. But Shay was there, holding the Elemental Cross at the Harbinger's eye level. Bosque scowled, but he stopped moving.

My heart jumped. The shield worked both ways. Shay couldn't attack Bosque, but Bosque couldn't move past the swords either.

Realizing that Bosque's attempt to reach him had been thwarted, Logan stopped shaking. His voice grew steadier and louder.

The scratching at the library doors had become banging. Slow, heavy thuds signaled that the Fallen had arrived.

"Hurry!" Ethan shouted. "We can't hold them."

"No." Bosque whirled away from Shay. "You can't."

He swept his hand through the air and Ethan, Connor, Sabine, and my father were tossed aside. Bosque struck out with his fist and the doors blew open.

"Don't touch the Fallen." Connor drew his swords, shouting at Sabine and my father. "Ethan and I will fight them. You take care of the rest."

The rest appeared as succubi and incubi flew into the room, their shrieks piercing my ears. Ethan took down two with his cross-bow before drawing his own swords and advancing on the moaning Fallen. The Searchers began to mow through the slowly advancing mass, which fortunately had formed a bottleneck in the doorway. Thuds began to offset the high-pitched shrieks as Connor and Ethan parted the Fallen's heads from their bodies. My father, Bryn, and Sabine were dodging the winged creatures' spears, taunting them to the ground before the wolves wheeled to attack.

Logan was on his feet, shouting. He thrust his hands at Bosque, fingers outstretched. *"Aperio!"*

Bosque screamed. His eyes flashed like lightning as he glared at Logan. "You will pay for—"

His words stopped as he screamed again, doubling over and clutching his stomach. When he lifted his face, his silver eyes were widening into disks shaped like footballs and just as large. His pupils gleamed red as they morphed into reptilian slits. His features went slack, then slowly puffed out as if someone were pumping air in the space between his muscle and skin. He continued to expand, his skin ballooning until it began to tear, beginning at the top of his head and following a line down the center of his body.

Bosque's human shell cracked open like a husk. A gelatinous yellow substance oozed from the crack. An awful scent filled the air, decaying flesh and ammonia that burned my eyes and nose. I fell to my knees, certain I would be sick.

Shay made a retching sound and stumbled backward, trying to stay on his feet.

An appendage covered in bristling spikes emerged from what had been Bosque's body. Then another. And another. Six segmented limbs pushed skin and gore aside as it struggled to free itself. The thing that shrugged off its human guise stretched to its full height, towering over all of us. Its large silver eyes were set in a quasi-human face that featured Bosque's aquiline nose and full mouth. A set of pincers sprouted from his cheeks, clicking together as he opened and closed his lips with a hiss. His slicked-back hair had transformed into hard, sharply raised ridges that rippled along the surface of his skull and continued down his spine.

The skin covering its body was a mottled gray and black, dripping with slime. Wings, iridescent like those of a dragonfly and covered in the same thick yellow slime as the rest of his body, protruded from his back. They fluttered at intervals, trying to rid themselves of the sticky liquid.

Bosque's torso still resembled a man's, except that the thick carved muscles of his chest sloped down not to a human abdomen, but instead swelled to curving mass where skin transformed into a shiny black exoskeleton. His lower body ended in a needle-sharp, curving spine that glistened, making me suspect its sting was venomous.

The beast stretched its four upper limbs toward the ceiling, shaking its body as if it had just woken from a long slumber. Slime splattered on us and I coughed up bile as I scraped the yellow ooze from my skin. Four of its limbs lashed wildly, clawing at the air in fury. It screamed and the Nether creatures' shrieks grew louder. They abandoned their attacks on the wolves and Searchers, streaking toward the fireplace to hover above the creature's head.

"Oh my God." Connor, tracking the sudden flight of Bosque's minions, dropped one of his swords when he saw what was standing in front of the Rift.

Ethan shoved him aside, swinging his blade as one of the Fallen groped for Connor. Its head went flying.

"Come on." Ethan dragged Connor to the center of the room, where Adne was still bound to the floor. Sabine, Bryn, and my father chased after them. They huddled in a tight group around Adne.

The Fallen didn't pursue them but stayed close to the library doors. Their empty eyes gazed toward the Rift, mouths agape, as they swayed mindlessly, holding their position.

Logan fell backward, gazing up at the creature that had taken Bosque Mar's place. "Behold, the Harbinger. Master of the Nether and Lord of the Keepers."

TWENTY-SEVEN

"I WILL HEAR YOU SCREAM for this treachery, Logan Bane," Bosque rasped.

The sound of his voice startled me. It was the same as it had been when the Harbinger had been cloaked in a human body. The only change was the repetitive clicking of his pincers meeting each other in front of his lips.

He clawed the air with one of his upper limbs and Logan dropped to the floor, gasping in pain. Blood poured from four deep, symmetrical gashes in his chest.

"No!" Shay rolled to the balls of his feet.

"The Rift!" Adne shouted. "You have to drive him into the Rift with the Cross!"

Bosque shrieked his rage at her, raising his spiny limb once more.

Shay was already moving. The blades of the Elemental Cross whirred through the air, sparks of its power leaping from the swords. I could no longer distinguish his body from the whirlwind of light and sound that built up around him. The column of the elements that enveloped his form was ever changing, sliding from the roar of a firestorm to the crash of a waterfall only to morph again into the scream of a hurricane followed by the shuddering strength of an earthquake.

I knew Shay was there, wielding the blades, only because the limb Bosque had pointed at Logan suddenly went flying. It twitched on the library floor where it landed.

Bosque screamed as black blood leaked from the stump on his torso.

"Defend me, children!"

In a rain of leather wings and sharp talons, the throng of succubi and incubi descended on Shay. The moment they touched the edges of the sphere that surrounded the Scion their bodies dissolved, pouring to the ground in harmless piles of sand.

"No!" Bosque screamed, and there was real fear in his cry. His bulbous silver eyes searched the room in desperation. His frantic gaze settled on me. Laughing wildly, he grinned at Shay, revealing rows of sharp fangs behind his pincers.

"Very well, Scion," he said. "You've claimed your legacy. But continue on this path and you shall lose that which you love the most."

He stretched his arm out, shrieking an unintelligible order to the surviving Nether creatures. One of the incubi swooped low, dropping its spear. Bosque gripped the weapon, using the spines on his upper left limb like fingers. He turned that terrible smile on me and hurled the spear. I bolted, but not quickly enough.

Bosque's aim had been true. It was only my scrambling aside that left me with a spear impaling my shoulder and not my heart. Bosque was strong. Very strong. Not only was the spear lodged deep inside me, but it had pierced all the way through my body to lodge in the wall behind me. I was pinned there.

"Calla!" Shay's voice broke through the torrent of power shielding his body. I knew his advance faltered when the storm of elements surrounding him flickered, its light beginning to fade.

"No, Shay!" I screamed, struggling to break the spear or at least pull it free of the wall. "Forget about me. Kill him!"

Bosque shouted, "Take her. Tear her apart!"

The swarming Nether beings shrieked in unison and flew toward me. I thought about shifting, but a wolf pinned on its back was even more helpless than a human.

"Kill him, Shay!" I threw my arm up over my face as I waited for talons to rip into my flesh.

The screams of the flying horde grew louder, but the attack I'd been expecting never came. Snarls that were even closer than the furious shrieks made me look up. Bryn was almost on top of me, bristling at the Nether creatures. My father and Sabine stood just beyond her. One dead incubus already lay at their feet. Others dove but were met by the wolves' teeth tearing through their wings, taking them to the ground and making sure they didn't get up again.

"Move it, Scion!" Ethan shouted from the center of room, where he and Connor still stood guard over Adne. "Your lover girl is safe enough."

Shay raised the swords again, striding forward. The sound in the room became deafening and the house began to shake. The flying Nether creatures stopped their attack and began to swarm above the fireplace like wasps panicking in their rattled nest. Near the door the Fallen's moans became frantic. Their shuffling turned to chaos as they started to move, bumping into one another, swinging wildly at bookshelves and tables as if they'd lost any sense of purpose.

Bosque was backed up against the fireplace. He stretched out the three remaining limbs of his upper body, clawing at the stone frame.

"I will not be conquered," he screamed. "I am your master. I gave you everything. You are nothing without me."

"The Scion has no master." Shay's voice boomed over the chaos of noise in the library. It was his voice, but somehow different than the voice of the boy I knew. It was a deeper, older voice that echoed in my flesh and bone.

Bosque's grip on the stones faltered. He slid a foot backward into the fireplace.

The storm of the Cross pursued him, the voice from within booming through the library. "The earth will no longer bear your corruption."

"I will not yield," Bosque spat.

The torrent of earth, wind, water, and fire around Shay flared brighter. "Begone, fiend."

Bosque winced as the light of the Elemental Cross touched him. "No!"

"Begone!" the voice that wasn't quite Shay's cried out.

Bosque screamed as the sickly green aura of the Rift expanded, curling around him like arms drawing him into an unwelcome embrace. He screamed again as the thick tendrils wrapped around his body.

Then I could see Shay moving in the firestorm. He leapt forward, spinning as he hurtled toward Bosque. He brought the swords down in two lightning-fast strokes. Bosque howled in agony as three limbs were shorn from his torso. The green aura in the fireplace flared into immense spires of flame, consuming Bosque. I could hear him shrieking even though I couldn't see him.

The roar of the Elemental Cross became deafening and the storm surrounding Shay thickened, making it impossible to find him amid its chaos of sound and motion.

"Take cover!" Connor shouted, throwing himself over Adne.

My father shifted forms, grabbing Sabine and hauling her to my side. He pushed her tight against me and Bryn while he shielded us beneath his body.

Rowan Estate was shaking. Bookshelves groaned and cracked, sending volumes tumbling to the floor in a cascade. The sound continued to grow until the air swam with it, as if the very stones of the building were screaming.

An explosion rocked the library. I buried my face in my father's chest, biting my lip as the violent movements of the earth made the pain in my shoulder—where the spear still pinned me to the wall—almost unbearable. Sabine shifted forms and gripped my other arm, distracting me from the throbbing wound. I looked at her, grateful for the strength I found burning in her gaze. She leaned her forehead against mine and I laced my fingers through hers.

Crashes echoed all around us. I thought I heard Connor shouting. My father, Sabine, and I clung to each other. Bryn's fur pressed into our bodies and she whimpered. Though Sabine's hair whipped around my face, I caught snatches of the chaos just beyond our huddled trio. Clouds had poured into the room, swirling in the sickly green shades of the Rift itself, mirroring the sky just before a tornado. The winds that raged around us made me wonder if a funnel cloud had indeed touched down nearby. Shapes were hurling past us. Succubi and incubi screamed as they were sucked into the Rift, clawing at the air as they were dragged from the earth. Some had horrified Keepers locked in a fatal embrace, pulling their masters shrieking into oblivion. A few husk-like bodies sailed past, skin so parched that I could hardly believe they didn't crumble as they were battered by the storm. Though lifeless, the dusty figures weren't the Fallen. I couldn't tell what they were, but at least a dozen sailed past us, falling into the Rift alongside the other Nether creatures.

The screaming wind built into a final sudden gust, followed by a low rumble. The sound built, finally rolling through the library like the loudest thunderclap I'd ever heard.

It was followed by silence.

The wind was still there, but the violent blast had become a steady, gentle pour of cold winter air.

My father slowly unfurled himself from the protective ball he'd been curled into around Bryn, Sabine, and me. I winced, straining against the spear that impaled my shoulder, as I searched for any sign of Shay, but my gaze was caught by the shocking source of the icy wind. The wall of the library had been obliterated. The room opened up to the snow-covered ground outside. Only the stone frame of the fireplace remained, standing tall in a stark outline against the winter night.

"You all right?" Connor shouted to us. He was helping Adne to her feet. The ropes that had been holding her fell away as she stood. Only frayed threads remained. Ethan was hopping over piles of books and splintered wood in an attempt to reach us. Sabine squeezed my hand before running to meet him. He pulled her against him, drawing her into a long kiss. She wrapped her arms around his neck, clinging to him as he buried his fingers in her hair.

"Brace yourself, Calla." My father had taken hold of the spear still lodged in my shoulder. Bryn, now in human form, took my hand. I gritted my teeth, managing only a brief cry as he dislodged the spear from the wall and jerked it out of my body.

"Here." He already had his bleeding wrist pressing against my lips. I tried not to think about the pain in my throbbing shoulder, focusing instead on the soothing warmth that poured over me as I took my father's blood.

I leaned back against the wall, drawing a slow, shuddering breath. "I'm good."

He smiled at me. I took his hand, letting him pull me to my feet.

"They've all gone." Ethan came toward us, hand in hand with Sabine. "No more Nether freaks."

"Where did they go?" I asked, scanning the room. There was no sign of the creatures that had assailed us.

"No idea," he said. "I pretty much went for duck and cover once the building started coming down."

"That's not all that's gone," Connor said. "I think Logan made a run for it."

A drying pool of blood marked the spot where Logan had fallen, clutching the gashes Bosque had carved in his chest. The pool lengthened, stretching into a line and then becoming splotches as the trail headed toward the door.

"Good riddance," Adne said.

"I'd rather have him where we can keep an eye on him," Ethan muttered.

A shiver raced up my spine. Logan was gone. But where? Had he gone after Lumine? Would he come back, seeking revenge?

"It doesn't matter now," Connor said. "We'll have to track him down eventually. But he's not a threat with Bosque gone. He has no power to draw from."

"If the Nether creatures are all gone, why are the Fallen still here?" Sabine said, looking over her shoulder.

"They aren't Fallen anymore," Connor answered. Adne was beside him, rubbing the rope burns on her arms.

Ethan nodded. "Those are just bodies."

I peered past the Searchers. The shambling horrors that I'd come to know as the Fallen were strewn across the floor. They were now corpses in varying states of decay. Some looked as if they'd been dead only weeks, while all that remained of others were skeletons.

Our enemies had vanished. Did that mean we'd won? Was the war over?

I looked at the fireplace. All signs of the Rift were gone. No putrid green glow filled its depths. The gaping maw was empty and silent.

Shay had done it. I expected to see him striding toward us, a wide smile lighting his face. But he wasn't there. My eyes swept around the fireplace, searching for any sign of him and finding none.

Where was he? My heart skipped a beat.

"Shay!" I ran toward the austere stone frame.

A frenzy of terrible questions hammered against my skull.

What if the Rift had pulled him in too? What if the power of the Cross was too great, consuming Shay even as it destroyed Bosque?

"I'm here." Shay stepped out from behind the other side of the remaining structure. The storm created by the Elemental Cross had vanished. The swords were sheathed at his back. The power that had changed his voice was gone. Shay was wholly himself again.

But he wasn't alone.

A tall man with golden brown hair was resting his hand on Shay's shoulder. A woman with dark hair and pale green eyes had one of Shay's hands clasped in both of hers.

"Calla." Shay smiled at me. "I'd like you to meet my parents: Tristan and Sarah Doran."

TWENTY-EIGHT

THE LIBRARY WAS IN SHAMBLES. Snow

was already drifting from outside. And that wasn't all.

Wolves had gathered outside the building, gazing at the rubble and the ruins of the library.

"Nev!" Sabine shouted, waving at two wolves who bounded past the others.

Nev and Mason skidded to a stop near our huddled group. The appearance of Shay's long-lost parents had thrown us into a stunned silence. No one had worked up the courage yet to ask how Tristan and Sarah had gotten out of the portrait to stand among us.

I didn't know if we were afraid of offending them or too shocked to muster any questions. Only Shay seemed unruffled, his smile child-like in its exuberance.

Mason shrugged off his wolf form, shaking a fist at Connor. "What the hell were you thinking?"

"Huh?" Connor frowned at him.

"You had a bomb and you didn't tell us?" Mason shouted. "We had no warning. Do you have any idea how far that blast went? Part of the wall crushed the Bane I was fighting. It almost killed me!"

"It wasn't a bomb, Mason," I said.

"Then what the hell was it?" he asked, still glaring at Connor.

"And why am I getting blamed for a bomb?" Connor began to laugh. "What the hell would I know about bombs?"

Nev shrugged. "We discussed it and decided that if anyone had snuck in a bomb, it would have been you."

Connor look at Adne. "What do you think? Is that the sort of thing I should say 'thank you' for or do I just slug them?"

"Shut up, Connor," I said. "Mason, the wall blew out when Shay closed the Rift."

"Dude." Nev turned his gaze to Shay and grinned. "Nice."

Mason was still frowning. "So the Elemental Cross was actually a bomb?"

"Mason!" I snarled. "There was no bomb!"

"Just magic." Adne smiled at him.

"A magic bomb," Mason grumbled, and ducked when I swung at him. "Hey! You didn't almost get pancaked by half a house falling on you."

"Believe me," Ethan said. "We had more than our share of trouble in here."

"But you did it." Nev was still looking at Shay. "This means we won, right?"

"I guess." Shay's smile faded. "I don't know what happens now."

"Speaking of winning, what about the Banes?" I asked. "I mean, the ones that didn't come to our side."

"When the house blew up . . ." Nev threw me an apologetic glance as Mason mouthed "bomb" again. "They panicked. I guess seeing the Keeper fortress crumbling made them panic."

"We were winning anyway." Mason grinned.

Nev shrugged. "Yeah. We probably were."

He frowned, looking around our group. His eyes rested on Shay's parents for a moment, but then returned to me. He drew a long breath.

"Where's Ren?"

I looked away. Bryn slipped her arm around my waist. I hadn't forgotten Ren. But I'd had to push his death out of my mind to make it through the fight. Now a pit of emptiness gnawed at my belly as the truth crashed over me. I swayed on my feet. Bryn leaned her head on my shoulder.

My father answered, "He fell in battle."

Nev's fists balled up. "How?"

"Emile killed him," my father said.

Mason snarled. "Is Emile dead?"

"Yes," I said.

"We saw Dax and Fey's bodies outside," Nev said quietly. "Did you?"

"We had to fight them to get in the house," I said, nodding.

We fell silent, the weight of so many deaths settling on us.

I shivered, glancing at my packmates. "Follow me."

Shifting into wolf form, I led my packmates to the place where Ren's body lay. To my relief he hadn't been buried in rubble. Debris encircled him in a ring of destruction without encroaching on him, as if the wild fury of the Elemental Cross had shielded his body from its chaos.

We spread out around him, forming a circle. I paused, letting myself gaze at the wolf I'd known from childhood, who I always had expected to be at my side leading our pack.

My father was standing beside me. I looked at him, waiting.

No, Calla. His quiet words entered my mind. *This is* your *pack.*

I turned back to Ren, dropping my head low to honor the fallen alpha. The circled wolves did the same. I lifted my muzzle first, my howl singing out the pain of Ren's death, mourning him. One by one my packmates joined the song. Our howls filled the library, spilling out into the winter night. The death song grew as the wolves still outside raised their voices to honor the lost young warrior. The chorus of wolf cries, full of heartache, swelled in the night, carrying Ren's memory to the very stars.

I shifted back into human form. Listening as the song continued, even as the howls began to quiet, the chorus echoed on the wind.

A hand encircled my wrist. Adne gazed at me. "Can I?" She gestured to Ren.

I nodded. She slid to her knees beside him, stretching the length of her body against the huge gray wolf. She wrapped her arms around him, burying her face in his fur.

She hid her grief from us, but I watched her shoulders trembling, wishing I could give her back the brother with whom she'd been granted so little time.

Shay was standing apart from us. Tristan had an arm around his son's shoulders, while Sarah was still clasping Shay's hand. I met Shay's gaze, finding his own sorrow there. And a question.

It was a question flickering in my own heart as well.

Had Ren's death changed what I felt for Shay?

Meeting his moss green eyes, I had my answer.

Love wasn't forged by circumstance or changed by sorrow. It simply was. Fierce and free as the wolf within me.

My love for Ren had been real. We shared a bond, a history. Losing him would leave scars on my heart forever. But I was a warrior, and love's scars weren't so different from battle scars.

At so many junctures I'd been given a choice: to follow my heart or leave Shay behind, forsaking my passion for the life I thought I was destined for. Every decision had drawn me closer to him and pulled me away from the world I'd known.

Those choices had led us here. I stood in the rubble of my well-ordered life, gazing at the boy who had changed everything.

And knew that I loved him still.

As Adne knelt beside my packmates near Ren's body, I went to Shay. He held out his arms to me and I stepped into them, lifting my hands to touch his face.

"You didn't die." I forced a smile. "I told you so."

"I know," he said. "What happens now?"

"We live." I pulled his face to mine, letting my lips touch his gently.

His fingers traced the tear tracks on my cheeks. "I love you, Calla."

"Sarah!"

I looked up to see Anika running toward us, or rather toward Shay's mother. The Arrow threw her arms around Sarah Doran. The two women clung to each other, laughing and crying. When they finally parted, Tristan grinned at Anika—he had the same mischievous, curving grin as Shay.

"I missed you too, Anika," he said. She hugged him, and when he stepped back, he glanced at the iron compass rose hanging from her neck. "I see you've been promoted."

Anika laughed, turning to Shay. "How did you reach them?"

"I don't know," Shay said. "When I pushed Bosque into the Rift, he was gone and I was standing in front of my parents."

"Standing where?" I asked.

Shay glanced at his parents. "To me it just looked like a dark, empty room."

"You stepped into the oblivion. Betwixt and between," Sarah said. "You broke open our prison."

Anika nodded, her face solemn as she spoke to Shay. "You crossed over."

He frowned. "What does that mean?"

"Bosque imprisoned us in the emptiness between the earth and the Nether," Tristan said. "We *were* the gate between the worlds. When you banished him, you were able to reach us and lead us out."

Shay went very still. I took his hand, twining my fingers with his.

"Are you in pain?" Anika asked, her eyes moving over Tristan and Sarah.

"No," Sarah said. "Our torment wasn't physical. It was separation from the people we loved. Seeing them and knowing we couldn't do anything to protect them. Especially our son."

"You could see me?" Shay asked. "Was the painting like a two-sided mirror?"

"No." Sarah smiled at him sadly. "More like a waking dream."

"The passing of time wasn't clear," Tristan said. "And we couldn't know if what we saw was the truth or a form of torture Bosque had devised for us."

"Calla! Bryn!" Ansel was running toward us, waving. Bryn shrieked her joy, opening her arms. But a huge brown and silver wolf was streaking toward him from the side. My father shifted forms, lifting Ansel off his feet as he ran and clutching my brother against his chest.

"Dad!" Ansel threw his arms around our father.

Bryn and I ran to meet them. My father pulled us into their hug. The four of us stood together, holding on to each other as we shook with tears and laughter.

Ansel broke free when Shay approached us. "Hey! You did it!"

But Shay was frowning.

"What's wrong?" I asked.

His shoulders tightened. "Anika says it's not over yet."

TWENTY-NINE

AS NEWS OF THE BATTLE'S END spread, Searchers began gathering around us. Some stood in groups, speaking quietly and gazing around the destroyed library in awe. Others moved quickly into the practical work of recovery, gathering up the piles of books that were strewn across the floor and carting them away. Still others had assigned themselves to burial duty, solemnly carrying out the remains of the Fallen, now returned to their natural state.

"What do you mean it's not over?" My skin prickled.

Anika strode past us. "Come with me."

We followed her to all that remained of the library wall. The stone fireplace, solitary and austere, appeared untouched by the force that had destroyed so much of the estate.

I leaned over to Bryn and whispered, "Get the others." Growing anxiety snaked through my veins.

"I don't understand," Shay said. "Bosque is gone. He's banished. So are his monsters." He gestured at the quiet darkness of the empty fireplace. "The Rift is gone."

"Not gone," Anika said. "Closed."

"As in, it could be opened again?" I asked.

She nodded at me but spoke to Shay. "That's why you have to seal it."

His eyes narrowed. "How?"

"The Rift can't be destroyed, but the Elemental Cross serves as a lock, sealing it off from our world."

I relaxed a little when Bryn rejoined us, bringing my packmates as well as Connor, Adne, and Ethan with her. Anika glanced at the Guardians and then turned a sharp look on the Searchers. Ethan dropped his gaze, fidgeting, and Connor raked a nervous hand through his hair.

What was going on?

Adne met my questioning gaze without flinching, but there was a sadness in her eyes—a new sadness that had nothing to do with her brother's death—that raised my hackles.

"What if someone opens it?" Shay asked.

"You're the only one who can retrieve the swords." Anika traced the crossed swords emblazoned on her necklace. "No one else will be able to open it."

"So don't go to the dark side," Connor said. " 'Kay?"

Adne dug her elbow into his ribs. He shot her a warning look. Now I had no doubt they were hiding something.

I leveled my gaze on Anika, putting strength into my voice. "And that's all?"

She could only match my steadiness for a moment before she pulled her eyes away.

Shay caught it too. "What?"

Tension rippled through the room. My packmates threw nervous glances at me. My nails dug into my palms. Beside me my father growled.

"Is this a betrayal?" He glared at Anika.

"No!" She drew herself up, assuming an authoritative air. "It is simply what must be."

"What the hell are you talking about?" Shay took a step toward her.

Anika's lips thinned. Connor moved between the Scion and the Arrow.

"We have to tell them, Anika," he said. "We owe them that. We owe them a lot more than that."

Ethan paled, the veins in his neck throbbing. Sabine's face was turned up toward his, puzzled. He couldn't seem to look at her.

Anika turned to face the empty fireplace, but she raised her voice so we could all hear her. "When you banished the Harbinger, you sent him into the Nether along with his minions. But his corruption lingers here, living on through the ways the Keepers have manipulated the earth."

My heart hardened like a stone. I remembered Silas eyeing me like a specimen, calling me and my kind an abomination.

I flashed fangs at Anika's back. "You're talking about us."

"Partly," she said without turning around. "Guardians are one of many alterations the Keepers created in the centuries they've walked the earth. Their own lengthened lives are another."

"Anika," Shay said. "What will sealing the Rift do to the Guardians?"

She turned slowly. "When the Elemental Cross locks the Rift, it will restore the balance of nature, returning all creatures to their true essence."

Shay frowned. "What does that mean?"

I stared at Anika, stunned as the truth settled into my bones. "It means we'll be wolves."

She nodded, folding her arms over her chest.

Shay's brow furrowed. "But you're wolves now."

"No," I said slowly. "We will only be wolves. Not human."

I glanced at Anika. "Am I right?"

"Yes," Anika said. "Guardians were made from the beasts that rule their souls, forced to share a human body so they would be servants to the Keepers."

"We won't be able to shift anymore?" Mason asked.

"You will be returned to your true selves," Anika said.

Sabine glared at Ethan. "Did you know about this?"

The muscles in his jaw worked as he forced himself to meet her furious eyes. "Yes."

She shoved him backward. "You didn't say anything!"

He grabbed her arms, holding her tight. "I'm sorry."

"Why?" She was shaking, still glaring at him in fury.

"I didn't think we'd live to see this happen." He smiled sadly as he pulled her into his chest. "I hate this too, Sabine. I don't want to let go of you."

A deep ache was building inside me, but Sabine and Ethan weren't the only lovers I was worried about. I searched for Ansel, finding him shaking and pale. Bryn stood beside him, eyes wide with disbelief.

Shay followed my gaze. He pivoted around, shaking his fist at Anika.

"No," he said. "There is no way in hell."

"You must."

"You can't do this to them!"

Shay's shouts drew the attention of the Searchers in the library. They moved slowly. Some of the warriors encircled us, while others gathered to flank Anika, their hands casually resting near their weapons.

"Shit." Connor rubbed his temples. "Anika, we can't fight these Guardians. They're our friends. They risked their lives for us."

"We don't have a choice." Anika's eyes were flinty. "The Rift must be sealed."

"No!" Ansel pushed past Bryn. Only Tess grabbed him, stopping him from reaching Anika. "This is my family! I'll be alone."

Tess leaned down. "You'll stay with us, Ansel. We'll take care of you."

Ansel began to weep. My father pulled him out of Tess's arms.

"Ansel," he murmured. "Find your strength. You can endure this."

I stared at my father, not believing what I was hearing. "You want this to happen?"

"It's not a matter of wanting, Calla," he said slowly. "Only necessity. The evil the Keepers brought to this world cannot be allowed to return."

Mason's voice startled me. "He's right, Calla."

Beside him Nev was nodding. "We are wolves. That's what we've always been."

Ansel wiped his face, looking at Mason, who came to his side and pulled him into a fierce hug. "I'm sorry, man."

"Don't be," Ansel said, smiling weakly. "My father is right. I'll survive and this has to happen."

"Ansel." My voice broke.

"It's okay, sis." Ansel's smile remained brittle. His eyes slid over to Bryn, full of regret. I felt cold, remembering his words in the Academy courtyard.

"All I am is less than what I was. And I can't ever be more. Eventually Bryn will realize that. And she'll leave. It will be for the best."

My limbs trembled as I grasped for any other options. My father's steady gaze weighed on me. A part of me knew he was right, as was Anika. The Keepers twisted everything in their world. The earth should be rid of any traces of their influence. It wasn't the thought of forever living as a wolf that I feared. That possibility felt strange, but somehow exhilarating. The wildness of that life called to the deepest parts of my soul. And I knew my father, Mason, and Nev were already yielding to that call.

But another part of me was breaking, defeated. Had we come this far only to lose so much? I couldn't imagine a life without Ansel running at my side. He was my packmate, my brother. He belonged with us. And with Bryn.

She was crying, reaching for Ansel even as he moved away from her, shaking his head.

"Wait." Sabine broke out of Ethan's embrace, striding toward Anika. The Searchers behind her drew their swords and blocked her path. Ethan swore and aimed his crossbow at them.

"Oh, please." Sabine rolled her eyes. "I'm not going to attack you. I just want to ask a question."

Anika raised her eyebrows.

"When Ansel told us how Guardians were made, he said you wouldn't do that for him."

"That's right," Anika said. "It violates our code. We won't destroy a wolf to make a Guardian."

Sabine took a deep breath. "What if you weren't destroying a wolf?"

Ethan slowly lowered his crossbow. "Sabine, no."

She ignored him, her gaze moving to Ansel. "What if it was given freely?"

I stared at her. She couldn't be offering what I thought she was. Could she?

"I don't understand," Anika said.

Ansel's eyes widened. "You would do that?"

She nodded, but looked back at Anika. "If it's possible."

Ethan shoved his way to Sabine's side. "Stop this. It's too much."

"This isn't your decision." Sabine put her hand on his chest.

He folded his hands over hers but didn't stop her when she turned to Anika.

"If you took the essence of the wolf from me," Sabine said, her voice unwavering, "could you give it to Ansel?"

"Yes." Anika gave her a long, measured look. "But only if it is of your own free will."

Ansel was trembling, his face full of hope and fear.

"Oh, Sabine," Bryn whispered.

Ethan turned Sabine to face him. "Wait."

"Are you that desperate to get rid of me?" Sabine smiled wryly.

"Hell no." His fingers dug into her upper arms, as if he were afraid to let go. "You think I'd let you get away if I had a choice?"

"Then why are you still arguing with me?" she asked.

"Because I don't want you to do this for me," he said. "I can't ask that."

"I'm not doing this for you." She stretched up to kiss him gently. "You're just a bonus."

Ethan threaded his fingers through hers. "Are you sure?"

"Going back to Vail," she said. "Pretending I belonged there. It reminded me that I will never be happy in that life."

"That life is over," I said. "The Keepers are gone now." As much as I wanted my brother's wolf restored, I needed to know Sabine could find happiness without the pack.

"I know, Calla," she said. "And I've made my choice."

Nev reached for Sabine, pulling her into an embrace. "Is this what you really want?"

She nodded, resting her head on his shoulder.

"We'll miss you," Nev said, kissing her on the cheek.

Sabine turned around, facing Anika. "It is of my own free will. Take the wolf from me and make Ansel a Guardian again."

Bryn threw herself at Sabine, hugging her and sobbing.

"Oh, stop," Sabine growled, but her eyes were glistening too. "You're making a scene."

Anika motioned to Tess. "We'll need an Elixir for this task."

Tess nodded, threading her way through Searchers and out of the library.

The Arrow scanned the assembled pack. "And if we do this, you'll agree to the sealing of the Rift?"

My father and I exchanged a look.

I opened my mouth to speak, but Shay beat me to it.

"No."

Anika and I both stared at him in shock.

"Why?" Anika asked.

Shay slowly shook his head, casting an apologetic glance in my direction. "There's something else. Something I need to know before I agree to this."

Anika stared at him, waiting.

"The Guardians will be wolves again," he said.

Anika nodded.

His gaze hardened when it locked with mine. "But what happens to me?"

My pulse jumped as Anika went pale. I began to shiver, realizing why Shay had asked. He hadn't been born a wolf; I'd turned him.

When I'd imagined spending the rest of my life as a wolf, Shay had been with me. It had never crossed my mind that when we left our human forms behind, Shay's origins might mean he couldn't follow.

But did he want to follow? Was his objection because he wouldn't choose life as a wolf?

Anika still hadn't answered him.

"I'm a wolf too," he said. "But I wasn't always."

She nodded, still uneasy.

"What will happen to me when the Rift is sealed?"

I glanced at the faces of my Searcher companions. Connor, Ethan, and Adne were all watching Anika. I couldn't find any clues about the answer in their expressions.

Anika gripped the medallion at her neck and sighed. "I'm sorry, Shay."

Shay swallowed hard. "Why?"

"Because we simply don't know."

THIRTY

"HOW CAN YOU NOT KNOW?" Shay's teeth were

clenched.

Anika held her ground, despite Shay's glare. "We had no way of anticipating that you would be turned by a Guardian alpha."

She glanced in my direction, making me wince.

"You were born human," she said. "My guess is that you will remain with us."

"Not a wolf," he whispered. "Are you sure?"

Something inside me began to scream.

"How can you say that?" Mason said. "He's a wolf. He's one of us now."

Nev nodded, gazing at Shay. "You've always been a wolf, man. The change was just a technicality."

"Is that true?" Shay asked Anika. "Could I become a wolf instead?"

"When the Rift is sealed, you'll become your true self," Anika said. "That is the only answer we can give you."

"I—" Shay's voice faltered.

"Shay." Sarah came forward, sliding her arm around his shoulders. "You know this must be done."

He looked at his mother. Her eyes were kind, full of love.

My heart thudded, a heavy weight in my chest. If Shay remained human, he would be able to stay with her. To know the parents who'd been stolen from him. He would have a new life.

But I wouldn't have the mate I longed for, hunting with me, leading our pack.

As if my thoughts drew his gaze, Shay's eyes were on me. "Calla?"

I forced myself to swallow the hard lump in my throat. "Anika is right." He flinched like my words hurt him, but he nodded.

Anika bowed her head. "Thank you."

Shay didn't answer.

"Wait a sec," Connor said. "If Sabine could choose to be human, can't all the Guardians stay human too?"

"Sabine gave her wolf essence to Ansel," Anika said. "If the others chose a human life, it would mean we would have to destroy the part of them that remains ever a wolf."

I shuddered. "Like the Keepers did to Ansel."

She nodded.

"But you'd be human," Connor said. "So—glass half full, right?"

"Dude," Nev said. "You have obviously never been a wolf."

"Sabine wanted to stay human," Connor said.

"It's different for me," Sabine said with a shudder. "Pack life didn't mean to me what it means to the others."

"You saw Ansel after his wolf was destroyed," I said. "It destroyed him, too. The wolf is who we are. There is no choice here."

Ethan frowned at Sabine. "Will it hurt you?"

"Physically, yes," she said. "I know it will be painful. But this is what I want. Ansel's wolf was taken violently from him. He's been grieving a stolen life. I'm choosing to become only human. It's different."

"And you all feel like Ansel?" Connor asked. "You'd rather be wolves?"

"We're a pack," Mason said. "We belong in the wild."

"But what about your singing?" Adne was looking at Nev.

"What do you think howling is?" Nev grinned.

"I guess I don't get it," Connor said.

"I would never expect you to," I said. "But if you could run with us, hunt with us. If the moon called you into the forest at midnight . . . then you would know how we feel."

Connor looked at me, still puzzled, but I was watching Shay. His eyes were shadowed. I walked over to him.

"But you do," I whispered. "You understand."

He nodded, threading his fingers through mine. His grip was so tight it hurt. "I remember the first night after you turned me. We hunted under the moon. We ran for miles and I never felt tired. There is nothing on this earth like it."

I stood facing him, letting memories slide over me. My mate. My alpha. I didn't want to race through the woods without him at my side. But what I wanted paled in the face of what had to happen. I'd made the choice to follow my heart, to pursue forbidden love, but neither Shay nor I had a choice now.

"I'm sorry," I said at last, leaning my head against his neck. "But we have to do this."

"I know," he said. He cupped my chin in his hand and kissed me.

"Anika?" Tess was standing beside a woman wearing a deeply cowled blue robe that shimmered like the surface of the sea when she bowed to the Arrow. A throng of curious Searchers and Guardians, some in wolf form, others human, had filled the library, pressing in on us.

Anika extended her hand to the Elixir. "Thank you for coming, Miriam."

As Sabine and Ansel made their way toward the Elixir, I slipped through the crowd until I reached Shay.

When I touched his arm, he gave me a thin smile, quickly looking back toward the activity nearby. "Quite the sacrifice Sabine's making."

"It is," I said. "I think she's right. She'll be happier this way."

"Happier," he said quietly.

"How are you?" I asked.

"I really don't know," he said. "I can't decide what to feel—maybe that's for the best."

Then he looked at me again, this time holding my gaze. "How about you?"

"I'm afraid." I took his hand. I'd never said that before. But it was the truth. I was about to lose Shay and I was terrified. "If we had any choice . . ."

"I know." He leaned in to kiss me. "I know, Calla. You don't have to apologize. I don't want you to."

He wrapped me in his arms as we watched Miriam instruct Ansel and Sabine to join hands. The Elixir rested the tips of her fingers against each of their temples. She began to murmur. A quiet but rapid river of sound flowed from her lips.

Sabine gasped. Ethan moved toward her, but Connor pushed him back.

"You have to let her do this alone," Connor said.

Ethan gritted his teeth, paling as Sabine's gasp became a scream. Ansel was breathing hard, but he didn't seem to be in pain the way Sabine was. Sabine screamed again, dropping to her knees. In the same moment Ansel cried out, but his cry became a howl. Where a boy had been standing a minute before, a young wolf now shook its muzzle.

"It is done." Miriam bowed to Anika.

"Sabine!" Ethan shoved his way past curious onlookers to reach her. She was still on her knees, her body trembling.

She put her hand up. "I'm okay. I'll be okay." But she didn't re-sist as he picked her up, cradling her in his arms.

A bronze-furred wolf bolted from among the Searchers, barrel-ing into Ansel. Bryn yipped and jumped around him, pawing at him and licking his muzzle. Two more wolves jumped through the crowd. Nev and Mason gave playful nips and barked as they circled Ansel. The huddled group soon looked only like a blur of wagging tails.

"You should go to them," Shay said. "You're their alpha."

I turned in his arms. "So are you."

"Not anymore." His smile was broken as he shook his head. "If I ever really was."

"Shay—"

"Just go." He pulled away from me, disappearing into the crowd of Searchers behind us.

Resigning myself to our suddenly diverging paths, I shifted forms and ran to join my packmates.

Ansel! I wormed in between Mason and Nev to nuzzle my brother.

I can't believe it. Ansel yipped, spinning in a circle. *I just can't believe it.*

It wouldn't have been the pack without you. I bit his ear gently. *Nobody else is as fun to boss around.*

When Nev suddenly whimpered, I pivoted and saw Sabine standing nearby. She was still leaning against Ethan, watching us.

Ansel shifted into human form and went to her.

"Feel good?" She smiled and it almost reached her eyes.

He nodded. "Are you okay?"

"I will be," she said.

Ansel shyly stretched his arms out toward her. She laughed and fell into the hug.

"Thank you." He squeezed her tight. "I owe you everything."

"Make Bryn happy," Sabine said. "I kind of like her."

Ansel smiled, but then gave a stern look at Ethan. "Speaking of that, if I ever hear you've broken her heart, I will hunt you down."

Ethan grinned. "I'll keep that in mind."

Anika appeared beside us and my joyful mood drained away. Shay stood next to her, his eyes resolved.

"It's time."

I took Shay's hand as we walked to the fireplace.

My father fell into step beside me.

"I'm taking the pack outside," he said. "I don't think we should be confined when the transformation happens."

I nodded.

"I understand if you want to stay closer." He glanced at Shay. "But don't wait too long."

"I know."

"You're going to leave before it's over?" Shay asked as my father shifted forms and loped to the crumbled wall. The other wolves began to trail after him, congregating on the snowy grounds outside Rowan Estate.

"I won't leave," I said. "But I'll have to keep my distance. Wolves who feel cornered are dangerous. If I stay inside—"

He cut me off. "I understand."

Nev, Mason, Bryn, and Ansel loped across the room, shifting into human form beside Shay.

"You should go with my father," I said. "It isn't safe for us to stay here."

"Sure," Mason said, sliding his arm around Shay. "But did you think we'd leave without saying good-bye?"

"For now," Ansel mumbled, staring at the floor. "Good-bye for now."

"We're pulling for you, man." Nev clasped Shay's hand. "Team Wolf!"

Shay managed a smile. "Thanks."

"No matter what happens, take care of yourself." Mason pulled Shay into a hug.

"I will," Shay said.

Nev gave Shay a quick nod before he and Mason shifted back into wolf form, leaving us with Bryn and Ansel.

Bryn couldn't manage to say anything. She kept looking at me and at Shay, sniffling and wiping her eyes. She tried to get words out but couldn't catch her breath between sobs. Finally she threw up her hands, grabbed Shay, and kissed him on the cheek. Then she shifted into a bronze wolf and bolted away from us.

Ansel's hands were shoved in his pockets. He kicked the floor, shaking his head.

"You deserve to be with the pack more than I do."

"Don't be an ass." Shay pulled Ansel into a hug. "You're right where you should be."

Ansel gripped Shay tight, murmuring something too low for me to hear. Shay gave him a weak smile.

"I'll see you soon," Ansel said to me. And then he was bounding away from us.

Shay was watching me closely. I raised my eyebrow at the strange expression etched on his face. He looked like he was trying not to laugh.

"What did he say to you?"

"He said I couldn't stay with the Searchers." Shay grinned. "Because I'm the only one who can keep you from picking on him."

"I do not pick on him," I said, returning his smile. "Unless he deserves it."

"Shay!" Anika called to us from in front of the fireplace.

"I guess I can't put this off any longer." Shay began to turn away.

I grasped his arm, pulling him back. I stretched my arms around his neck, molding my body against his. When I kissed him, I let everything I'd ever held back pour into my embrace. I needed Shay to know what I felt, what I wanted, why I was so afraid of letting him go. His hands slid up my back, pressing into my shoulder blades.

I let my mouth linger on his, until I had to pull away.

He traced the shape of my lips with his fingers. "Thank you for saving me."

"I didn't save you," I said. "You were the one who banished the Harbinger."

He leaned in, brushing a soft kiss against my mouth. "I wasn't talking about today."

The gazes of the assembled Searchers were fixed on Shay as we walked together to meet Anika.

"You'll need the Elemental Cross." She gestured to the swords on Shay's back.

"What do I do?" Shay asked her.

"Hold the swords aloft, so they create the mark of the Scion," she said. "And speak these words until it is finished: *obtineo porta.*"

"*Obtineo porta,*" he murmured.

A sliver of green light appeared in the depths of the fireplace, like an enormous eyelid had briefly slid open.

Shay looked at Anika. "It's still there, isn't it?"

She nodded, glancing at the stone structure, which had gone dark again. "That is why this must be done."

Shay squared his shoulders.

The Searchers in the library fell silent, watching as Shay moved toward the hidden Rift.

Shay held the swords at arm's length. The earth and air sword he held vertically, while the water and fire sword crossed the first blade horizontally. He drew a slow breath and paused, turning to look at me.

I walked up beside him, laying my hand on his back just below his neck so my fingertips brushed the cross tattoo on his skin. He shivered.

"I don't know if I can do this."

"You have to," I said, but each of my heartbeats hit slow and heavy in my chest, like a stake being pounded into the ground with a sledge.

"I can't leave you, Calla."

I closed my eyes, knowing what he felt because the same grief clawed at my heart. I'd already lost someone I loved today and in the next minute I might lose another. But what else could we do?

The world created by the Keepers had been forged from greed and cruelty. It wasn't a world we could suffer to exist, no matter what the cost.

I forced my eyes open and found Shay's winter moss irises gleaming softly. Leaning forward, I pressed my lips onto his tattoo. "I love you."

I splayed my fingers wider on his back, hoping that somehow touching him would make the universe hear my plea—to have Shay's wolf essence win out over the human one. If it didn't . . . I would be alone.

I'd have my pack, but would I stay with them? If Shay didn't come with me, I was already envisioning what would happen. I would become a lone wolf, wandering, solitary. My father would remain the alpha of my packmates, as he'd always been.

Maybe that was the way things were meant to be.

"Calla." Shay's brow was furrowed. He could see the goose bumps running up and down my arms, the way my muscles were trembling.

"I love you," I whispered one last time, slowly backing away from him toward the spill of night air and the beckoning howls of my pack. "Close the Rift."

THIRTY-ONE

I'D ALWAYS WELCOMED WAR, but when the last

battle ends, what life is left for a warrior?

Shay faced the emptiness of the fireplace. He turned the swords slowly while he chanted. And then, where there had been nothing, the darkness began to move. Shadows clung to the Elemental Cross, gripping the blades, pulling Shay forward. When the swords had marked a quarter turn, Shay froze. The darkness became solid, locking the cross in place, but within the ebony shadows glimmered a soft light, opalescent like twinkling stars.

The light streamed over the swords, touching Shay's fingers and making him shudder. Like glimmering ribbons, it twined around his arms and chest. When the light coursed over his neck and met my fingers, the sparkling tendrils began to claim my body too.

The light grew brighter until I could see nothing—not even Shay, though I still felt my fingers on his neck—nothing but the pale, shimmering air around me. Air that was alive with power.

I thought it would hurt. Ansel said having the wolf torn from him was like being ripped apart and burned.

But I didn't hurt. Not at all. There was no pain. Only a sense of lightness, giddy and dizzying, like flight—of a burden that didn't belong to me being lifted.

Suddenly I knew the truth and the lights surrounding me exploded.

I am free.

EPILOGUE

> Look not at the greatness of the evil past,
> but the greatness of the good to follow.

—Thomas Hobbes, *Leviathan*

SABINE SHIVERED, wishing she'd borrowed that sweater Ethan had offered her. Sunlight filtered through the scaffolding that ran along the edge of Rowan Estate, but the tarps hanging between the outside world and the library couldn't keep out December's cold. And the space heaters just weren't cutting it.

She sealed another box with packing tape, scrawling the words *History—17th century* in black marker across the top. Almost all the books she'd packed so far seemed to be history. Really old history. Weren't there any interesting books around here?

"Aren't you finished yet?" Ethan strolled into the library. "Why are all these books still lying around?"

"I'm going to pretend you didn't say that." She carried the box over to the growing stack that would be taken back to the Academy to be cataloged and stored. "That way I can still like you."

Ethan laughed. She walked over to him, rubbing her arms. He frowned, shrugging off his long leather jacket, and put it around her shoulders.

"You should have taken that sweater."

"Yeah, yeah," she said, snuggling into the body heat still warming the inside of his coat. "You were right. Be happy about it. Next time I'll be right."

Sabine glanced at the evidence of construction at the other side of the room. "You know it would be warmer in here a lot faster if you didn't have to ship special stones in to rebuild this place."

"We got it onto the National Register of Historic Places." He shrugged. "Special stone is obligatory."

"Great," Sabine said. "I'm freezing my ass off."

"Really?" He widened his eyes. "That'd be tragic. I'd better check it out."

She shrieked when he lunged at her. They were still chasing each other around the stack of boxes when the shimmering door opened.

"Howdy!" Connor hopped into the library.

Adne came after him, shaking her head. "Connor, don't say 'howdy.' You're not a cowboy, no matter how much you wish you were."

She closed the portal and pivoted around to face him, hands on her hips.

"Sorry if I gave offense, little lady." He pretended to tip his hat.

She scowled but dissolved into laughter when he began to tickle her.

"Stop!" she squealed. "Stop it! I take it back. You can be a cowboy!"

Connor wrangled her into a one-armed embrace, grinning at Ethan.

"So how was it?" he asked. "Did you find them?"

Sabine looked away. Connor had asked the question she hadn't been ready to voice but that had been running through her mind since Ethan returned.

Ethan cleared his throat as he watched Sabine tense. "Yeah. It wasn't hard. They're right where we thought they'd be."

"Old stomping grounds." Connor shrugged. "It makes sense."

"It's a little strange, though," Adne said. "Don't you think? Going back to Haldis after everything that happened."

"It's their territory," Sabine said, glancing at her and then staring into the distance again. "They belong on that mountain."

She hesitated and her voice grew softer. "Do they seem happy?"

"They really do." Ethan moved closer to her. His fingers gently rested on her upper arm. "You should come next time. See them."

Sabine managed to smile at the kindness in his eyes, although her heart had gone jagged. "Maybe."

"Sabine—"

She turned to face him head-on, reaching up and resting her palm against his throat. She let his pulse drum against her skin for a few seconds before speaking again. "That's the past. I'm here now. With you."

He frowned. "You don't want to see them?"

She lowered her lashes, not wanting him to see the pain in her eyes. He'd know it was there. He always did, but sometimes she wanted to keep it veiled from her new companions. She was grateful for their friendship and Ethan's love. She didn't want the past to mar the hope she had for their future. "What about the other pack?"

"They've moved to the western face," Ethan said. "Stephen's pack has taken over the Banes' former range. What was left of the Bane pack after the fight seems to have moved on."

"That's justice."

"I thought so too."

"So one alpha got her happy ending," Connor said. "But how's our boy adjusting to his new role?"

"Not that I'm an expert, but he seems fine." Ethan put his arms around Sabine, drawing her back against him.

"I feel kind of sorry for Tristan and Sarah," Adne said, hopping up on the table. She swung her legs back and forth as she mused. "They had about a ten-minute reunion. And then they lost their son again."

"They didn't lose him," Ethan said. "Not exactly."

"I don't think they'll be having family picnics in the forest, though," Connor said.

"Are you ever serious?" Sabine asked.

Connor flashed a smile at her. "Not unless it's absolutely necessary." He frowned at Adne. "Why do you feel bad? I thought you talked to Sarah and, you know, explained about Calla."

"I did," Adne said. "And I think they're trying to be happy for him, but I think they still feel like he's just gone."

"I'm just glad he ran out of the library when he became a wolf," Connor said. " 'Cause if he'd attacked Anika, and Ethan had shot the Scion right after he'd saved the world . . . Can you imagine? *Awkward*."

"You really aren't that funny," Adne said.

"Yes, I am." Connor smiled.

"Sabine?" Adne shot her a pleading look. "A little help here?"

Sabine stuck her tongue out at Connor.

"I rest my case." Adne grinned.

"Ethan gets a vote too," Connor said. "Ethan?"

"I abstain." Ethan laughed. "Wait, no. I hate to give Connor credit for any of his humor, but he has a point. All the wolves, including the Scion, ran for the hills. I count that as a good thing. If they'd attacked us, it would have been ugly."

"They were being called home, I think," Adne mused. "Back to the wilderness. They didn't have any reason to be interested in us."

"Do you think they remember?" Connor asked. "When Shay became a wolf, do you think he knew what was happening?"

"There's no way to know," Adne said.

Sabine drew Ethan's arms more tightly around her body. "It's good that he changed. Shay and Calla belong together. They always did."

Ethan bent down and kissed the crown of her hair. "I know the feeling."

"Apparently the earth thought they belonged together too," Adne said. "So are you guys ready? I'm starving and Anika is giving out new assignments in a few hours. I don't want to miss dinner."

"What exactly is your work now?" Sabine asked. "The war is over."

"I think you mean *our* work." Adne smiled at her. "You're part of the club now. And we aren't about to let you forget it."

"We've got to keep an eye on that." Connor pointed to what had been the library's fireplace.

A massive iron door filled the stone frame. The Elemental Cross was set in the center of the door, giving all appearance that the two swords had been welded to the metal barrier. "Make sure no evildoers try to mess with it."

"Like Logan?" Sabine asked.

"Logan," Adne said, "and any other Keepers who hadn't already passed their human expiration date. There won't be a lot of them, but some are still around."

"And we'll go back to doing what we did before this war broke out too," Connor said.

"You remember that far back?" Sabine asked.

"I'm pretty sure somebody wrote it down somewhere." Connor smiled.

"Before there were Keepers and Searchers, we were all one group," Adne said. "We made sure no one was abusing the mystical realm or messing with forces that shouldn't be messed with."

"We were called *Conatus*," Ethan said.

"Speaking of names," Connor said, "since we're not searching for the Scion anymore, are we gonna get a new label?"

Ethan shrugged. "Ask Anika."

"We could be Conatus again," Adne said.

"That was six hundred years ago," Connor said. "I vote no. Besides, the first Keepers were part of Conatus. Sharing a name with any Keeper would make me feel dirty."

"Fine." Adne ignored his teasing. "I just think using Latin would add dignity to our cause. Come on, we can argue about it over dinner."

She began to weave a door.

"Dignity?" Ethan pulled away from Sabine, grinning at Adne. "Nobody actually speaks Latin anymore. Explaining that word anytime we met someone would get old fast. Besides, any group Connor is part of can't actually be dignified."

"Hey!" Connor shoved him.

Sabine laughed; her smile was full of mischief. "I've got a name for us."

Ethan reached out, fingers tilting her chin up. When she looked into his sea blue eyes, the world opened up before her. Just like it always did.

"Okay, beautiful. What's our new name?" he asked.

"Guardians."

His smile softened. "That might take some getting used to. But it does have a nice ring to it."

He leaned forward, kissing her gently.

"You guys coming?" Connor asked as he backed toward the portal. "Or are we going to wait here while you make out?"

"Oh, leave them alone." Adne grabbed the front of his shirt, pulling him toward the shimmering door. "Why are you so grumpy?"

Connor patted his stomach. "I'm hungry."

"Dinner's right through there." Adne pointed at the gleaming door.

"Wait," Sabine said. "I . . . want to see them. I have to see them. Just once."

"Right now?" Connor frowned.

Adne pushed Connor aside, closing the portal with two swift strokes of her skeans. "Your stomach can wait, Connor."

"We clearly need to have a talk where you get to know my stomach better." Connor laughed.

"Are you sure?" Adne asked.

"Please." Sabine's heart pounded while Adne wove. She couldn't breathe for a moment when the familiar landscape near Haldis took form on the other side of the portal.

"You ready?" Ethan took her hand.

She nodded, but it wasn't a matter of being ready. It was what she needed—to see the pack whole, to know that the world was right again.

Connor started toward the door, but Adne grabbed his arm.

"No," she said. "Just the two of them."

"No dinner and no wolf hunt?" Connor said. "You're a cruel woman."

"You know it." Adne gestured for Ethan and Sabine to enter the door.

The now-familiar sharp tingling of passage through the portal gave way to bitter cold. The wind swirled steadily over her limbs; occasional gusts made her shudder. She pulled Ethan's coat tight around her.

"This is frostbite weather, honey," Ethan said, handing her a pair of binoculars. "I don't mean to rush you. . . ."

"I only need a few minutes," she said.

Sabine climbed along the ridge where Adne had opened the door, crouching in the shelter of a pine tree. Lifting the binoculars to her eyes, she peered toward Haldis Cavern.

It didn't take long to spot them. The wolves were celebrating a fresh kill. The pack had gathered around the large doe's carcass, frolicking as they prepared to feast.

Ansel and Bryn chased each other outside the cave entrance, kicking up clouds of snow as they ran. Mason was digging into the venison, his muzzle bloodied. Nev sat beside him, his tongue lolling out as if Mason had told a hilarious joke.

A white wolf emerged from the cavern. Calla's golden eyes surveyed her pack. A golden brown wolf bounded out of the forest, coming to greet her. Shay circled Calla, nipping at her until she barked a protest. To Sabine it sounded like laughter.

The two alphas trotted together to the kill, nuzzling and licking each other as they moved. Mason and Nev rose when they arrived, bowing their heads and wagging their tails. Calla barked again and Ansel and Bryn joined the pack. The wolves gathered together, ready to share the bounty of their hunt.

Sabine stood up, satisfied that her friends were safe and content. When she moved, Calla lifted her head. Her eyes focused in Sabine's direction. Despite the distance between them, Sabine could have sworn Calla was looking right at her.

The white wolf's ears flicked back and forth. She lifted her muzzle and howled. The sound filled Sabine with a mixture of sweetness and sorrow. The other wolves joined the song, their familiar voices blending in the winter air. Sabine watched them for another minute, then she turned and walked back to Ethan.

"Everything okay?" he asked.

She handed him the binoculars. "They're happy. So I'm happy."

"Good." Ethan started toward the portal, but Sabine hesitated as the wind lifted her hair, its cold caress beckoning her toward the wilderness. She turned, listening to the song carried on the stiff winter breeze. Nev's voice rose above the other wolves' as the chorus of howls wove through the air. Sabine wondered if somehow they knew she was here, and if they might be saying good-bye or if they were asking her to stay.

"Sabine?" Ethan waited in the light of the door, watching her.

She took his hand. The wolves' howls still sounded in the forest behind her, but she no longer needed to look back. With Ethan at her side, she stepped into the light of the portal, into her new world.

ACKNOWLEDGMENTS

A book is a journey—a series an epic journey—and a trip such as this is best completed with willing and able companions. I've been fortunate enough never to want for amazing publishing colleagues, who've become dear friends. I am always indebted to my talented, tireless team at InkWell Management. Charlie Olsen and Richard Pine offer support, guidance, and cheer in perfect sync with both my joys and my sometime neuroses. Lyndsey Blessing is a force of nature when it comes to foreign rights, and I thank her for that! At the time of this writing, the Nightshade series has found homes in twenty-four territories and counting. Thank you also, wonderful editors, translators, and sub-agents across the globe.

Nightshade's first home will always be Philomel Books. My gratitude to Michael Green is full of candy and sports goodness. I will never have the words to describe the wonderful, thoughtful, and adept editor that is Jill Santopolo. Thanks also to Julia Johnson and Tamra Tuller for all your hard work. For getting the book out to readers I thank the marvelous sales, marketing, and publicity teams at Penguin Young Readers: Emily Romero, Lisa DeGroff, Erin Dempsey, Jackie Engel, Casey McIntyre, Caroline Sun, Scottie Bowditch, RasShahn Johnson-Baker, Courtney Wood, Anna Jarzab, the rockin' sales reps, and especially to Shanta Newlin for all that she does and for rescues in a pinch. The beauty of the book is due to the skill of Suza Scalora, Linda McCarthy, Katrina Damkoehler, and Amy Wu. Thanks also to Jennifer Haller and Don Weisberg for their confidence and kindnesses.

Friends have been steadfast traveling companions as well. Thank you, Lisa Desrochers, for being such a dedicated and creative author with which I can trade critiques. I would flail without the support of writing friends and role models, especially David Levithan and Heather Brewer. Thanks also to my colleagues at Macalester College, especially Casey Jarrin, Marlon James, Lynn Hudson, and Daylanne English. Here's a big shout-out to my students, whose intelligence and enthusiasm keep me going. Thanks also to the librarians, teachers, and booksellers who've welcomed me into their world and whose love for literature renews my idealism. My book wouldn't be anywhere without the generosity of readers and bloggers. I can't thank you enough for taking this wild ride with Calla and her pack.

Though this trilogy is at an end, once there were beginnings. I am still ever grateful for the overwhelming support of my hometown, particularly the morning crowd at the Golden Glow, who keep me grounded. My brother always reminds me that the pursuit of passion is reward in itself. My husband keeps me laughing and holds me tight when I need it most. And for my parents, to whom this book is dedicated, before there were books there were dreams, which you never allowed to languish in obscurity. Thank you.